TAKE

MY

HAND

TAKE
MY
HAND

DOLEN PERKINS-VALDEZ

PHOENIX

First published in the United States by Berkley,
an imprint of Penguin Random House LLC

First published in Great Britain in 2022 by Phoenix Books,
an imprint of The Orion Publishing Group Ltd
Carmelite House, 50 Victoria Embankment
London EC4Y 0DZ

An Hachette UK Company

1 3 5 7 9 10 8 6 4 2

Copyright © Dolen Perkins-Valdez 2022

The moral right of Dolen Perkins-Valdez to be identified as
the author of this work has been asserted in accordance
with the Copyright, Designs and Patents Act of 1988.

A CIP catalogue record for this book is
available from the British Library.

ISBN (Hardback) 978 1 4746 2267 7
ISBN (Export Trade Paperback) 978 1 4746 2268 4
ISBN (eBook) 978 1 4746 2270 7
ISBN (Audio)978 1 4746 2538 8

Printed in Great Britain by Clays Ltd, Elcograf S.p.A.

www.orionbooks.co.uk
www.phoenix-books.co.uk

For Elena and Emilia

Ben, make sure you play "Take My Hand, Precious Lord"
in the meeting tonight. Play it real pretty.

—Martin Luther King Jr.'s
reported last words, April 4, 1968

PART I

ONE

———

Memphis
2016

A year never passes without me thinking of them. India. Erica. Their names are stitched inside every white coat I have ever worn. I tell this story to stitch their names inside your clothes, too. A reminder to never forget. Medicine has taught me, really taught me, to accept the things I cannot change. A difficult-to-swallow serenity prayer. I'm not trying to change the past. I'm telling it in order to lay these ghosts to rest.

You paint feverishly, like Mama. Yet you got the steadfastness of Daddy. Your talents surely defy the notion of a gene pool. I watch you now, home from college, that time after graduation when y'all young people either find your way or slide down the slope of uncertainty. You're sitting on the porch nuzzling the dog, a gray mutt of a pit bull who was once sent to die after snapping at a man's face. In the six years we've had him, he has been more skittish than fierce, as if aware that one wrong look will spell his doom. What I now know is that kind of certainty, dire as it may be, is a gift.

The dog groans as you seek the right place to scratch. I wish someone would scratch me like that. Such exhaustion in my bones. I will be sixty-seven this year, but it is time. I'm ready to work in my yard, feel the damp earth between my fingers, sit with my memories like one of those long-tailed magpies whose wings don't flap like they used to. These days, I wake up and want to roll right over and go back to sleep for another hour. Yes, it is time.

Two weeks ago, I heard the news that India is very sick. I'm not sure what ails her, but I take this as a sign that it's time to head south. I know what it looks like. No, I am not going to save her. No, I don't harbor some fanciful notion that she'll be the first and last patient of my career. I have prayed about that. Please, Lord, reveal my heart to me.

I call your name, and you look back through the screen into the kitchen. You're used to my hovering, though each year you need me less and less, and I mourn the slipping. Soon it will be just me and the dog, an old lady muttering in that rambling, crazy way owners talk to their pets when no one is around.

But before we both head into that next chapter, we need to talk. You and I always have been open with each other. As soon as you were old enough to wonder, I told you everything I knew about your birth parents. I told how you came into my life, about the gift of our family.

I told you the story of your parentage, but what I didn't reveal was the story of your lineage. How you came to be. How you came out of a long line of history that defies biology. What I am trying to say is that your story is tied up with those sisters. The story of my welcoming you into my life, of my decision not to marry or bear children, is complicated. I have tried not to burden you, but I'm beginning to believe that not telling you the whole truth, letting you walk this earth without truly understanding this history, has done you a disservice.

I reach into the pocket of my dress and pull out the paper. Without opening it, I know what it says because I have memorized the address, mapped out the directions on my cell phone, and I know the route I will take. The car is gassed up, the snacks tucked into a backpack. The last of my carefully packed wardrobe capsules are squared off in a suitcase that sits behind the door. The only thing I have not done is tell you where I am going or why. You know a little about the sisters, about the case that engulfed the country, but you don't know the whole story. And it is time for me to tell you.

"Anne?" I call your name again. This time, I wave you inside.

TWO

———

Montgomery
1973

There were eight of us. When I think back to the time I spent at the clinic, I cannot help but stumble over that number. What might have been. What could have passed. None of us will ever know. I suppose I will still be asking the same question when I'm standing over my own grave. But back then, all we knew was that we had a job to do. Ease the burdens of poverty. Stamp it with both feet. Push in the pain before it exploded. What we didn't know was that there would be skin left on the playground after it was all over and done with.

In March 1973, nine months after graduation, I landed my first job at the Montgomery Family Planning Clinic. On the day I started, two other newly hired nurses, Val and Alicia, began with me, the three of us like soldiers showing up for duty. Hair straightened. Uniforms starched. Shoes polished. Caps squared. Child, you couldn't tell us nothing.

Our supervisor was a tall woman by the name of Linda Seager. I swear that woman had three eyes. Nothing escaped her notice. Despite her stone face, a part of me couldn't help but admire her. After all, she was a white woman working in a clinic serving poor Black women. Trying to do the right thing. And doing that kind of work required a certain level of commitment.

"Congratulations. You are now official employees of the Montgomery Family Planning Clinic."

And with that, the training was over. One week. A fifty-page orientation manual, half of which concerned cleaning the rooms and the toilet, and keeping the supply closet organized. We had spent three days just going over that part. Long enough to question if we'd been hired as maids or nurses. On day four, we finally covered charting patients and protocol. When the more experienced nurses noticed our downcast expressions in the break room, they promised to help us in our first few weeks. We were in this together.

As we dispersed, Mrs. Seager pointed a finger at me. "Civil."

"Yes, Mrs. Seager?"

She pointed to my fingernails with a frown, then retreated to her office. I held up a hand. They did need a clipping. I hid my hands in my pockets.

The three of us new hires squeezed into the break room and removed our purses from the shelf. One of the nurses nudged me gently with an elbow. She'd introduced herself earlier in the week as Alicia Downs. She was about my age, born and raised in a small town up near Huntsville. I'd known girls like her at Tuskegee, pie-faced country girls whose wide-eyed innocence contrasted my more citified self.

"I don't think it's real," she said.

"What?"

She pointed to her own head. "That red helmet she call hair. It ain't moved an inch in five days."

"Look like a spaceship," I whispered. Alicia covered her mouth with a hand, and I caught a glimpse of something. She'd been putting on an act all week in front of Mrs. Seager. Alicia might have been country, but she was far from timid.

"I bet if you poked a finger in it, you'd draw back a nub," she said.

The other nurse glanced at us, and I rearranged my face. Val Brinson was older than me and Alicia by at least a decade.

"You crazy, Alicia Downs," I told her as we walked outside. "She might have heard you."

"You look at your file yet?"

I took a yellow envelope from my bag. I had been assigned one off-site case: two young girls. Nothing in the case jumped out at me other than wondering what on earth an eleven-year-old would need with birth control. According to the file, she and her sister had received their first shot three months ago and were due for the next one.

"You got anybody interesting?" she asked.

I wanted to tell her that was a dumb question. This wasn't a talent search. Alicia had been trained as a nurse at Good Samaritan in Selma. She was pretty in a plain way, and there was a ready smile beneath her features. At one point, Mrs. Seager had asked, *What do you find so funny, Miss Downs?* and Alicia had answered, *Nothing, ma'am. I just felt a sneeze coming on.* Then her face had gone dull and blank. Mrs. Seager glared at her for a moment before continuing with her instructions on how to properly clean a bathroom toilet in a medical facility.

"Not really." I didn't know how much I was allowed to reveal about my cases. Mrs. Seager hadn't said much of anything about privacy. "Two school-age girls on birth control shots."

"Well, I've got a woman with six kids."

"Six?"

"You heard right."

"Well, you better make it over there quick before it's seven."

"You got that right. Well, I'll be seeing you." Alicia waved to me and I waved back.

I'll be honest and tell you there was a time I was uppity. I'm not going to lie about that. My daddy raised me with a certain kind of pride. We lived on Centennial Hill, down the road from Alabama State, and all my life I'd been surrounded by educated people. Our arrogance was a shield against the kind of disdain that did not have the capacity to even conceive of Black intellect. We discussed Fanon and Baldwin at dinner, debated Du Bois and Washington, spoke admiringly of Angela Davis. When somebody Black like Sammy Davis Jr. came on TV, it was cause for a family gathering.

But from the very first day I met Alicia, she ignored my airs and opened up to me. As I watched her walk away, I knew we would be fast friends.

I'd parked a block and a half away on Holcombe Street to hide my car. Daddy had given me a brand-new Dodge Colt as a graduation gift, and I was shy about anyone at the clinic seeing it. Most of the nurses took the bus. Mrs. Seager had assigned me two sisters way out in the sticks because she knew I had a reliable set of wheels.

"Civil?"

Oh Lord, what did she want now? I turned to face Mrs. Seager.

"Might I have a word?"

"Yes, ma'am."

She went back inside the building and let the screen door slam shut behind her. A gust of warm air swirled around me. I could swear that woman surged fire when she spoke. There had been scary professors at Tuskegee, so she wasn't the first dragon I'd met. Professor Boyd had told us if we were so much as two minutes late, he would mark down our grades. Professor McKinney divided the class between women and men and dared us to even think about glancing over to the other side. That kind of meanness I could handle. The thing that bothered me about Mrs. Seager was that I always had the sense I could mess up without knowing how.

Inside the building, the reception desk was empty. I positioned my cap and smoothed the front of my dress before knocking on her door. She had taken the trouble to not only go back into her office but to close the door behind her.

"Come in," she called.

The clinic had formerly been a three-bedroom house. She'd converted the smallest bedroom into her office. The other two were examination rooms. The old kitchen was now a break room for staff, the living and dining spaces served as a reception and waiting area. From the back of the building we could hear the roar of the new highway behind us.

Bookshelves lined one side of Mrs. Seager's office, file cabinets the other. On the wall behind her desk hung at least a dozen community awards. Salvation Army "Others" Award. Junior League Lifetime Member. The surfaces were clutter-free. On top of the desk sat a cup of pencils, the sharpened points turned up. She cradled a file in her hands.

"Sit down."

"Yes, Mrs. Seager." I took a seat. The window was open and a sparrow was chirping insistently.

"I understand your father is a doctor in town."

I could now see that she was holding my employment file. When I tried to speak, I coughed instead.

"Are you sick?"

"No, ma'am."

"Because in our profession we have to maintain our own health in order to help other people. You must rest and eat properly at all times."

"Yes, ma'am."

"Very well. So your father is a doctor." She said this as a matter of fact.

I knew what she was about to say. The same thing my professors at Tuskegee had lectured when they discovered my father and grandfather were doctors. *Your marks are impressive. Of course, as a woman, you have other issues to consider. Starting a family, for instance. You have wisely chosen the nursing profession, Miss Townsend.* I never knew what to say when they sounded off like that. The beginnings of a compliment always ended up stinging like an insult. Usually, I mumbled something incoherent and wondered if I was just being too sensitive.

"Yes, ma'am."

"We have been sanctioned by the federal government to execute our duties. We must take our mission very seriously. A wheel cannot work without its spokes. We are the spokes of that wheel."

Alicia was right. The woman's hair didn't budge.

"What I'm saying to you, Civil, is that you are a smart girl. It's why I hired you. I have high expectations of you because I think you'll make a fine nurse someday. I don't want you to go getting ideas."

She had just paid me a compliment, but it sounded strange in my ears. "Ideas about what, ma'am?"

She frowned and, for a moment, I worried that my tone had slipped into insolence. "About your place in all this. You have to work together with your fellow nurses. Our mission is to help poor people who cannot help themselves."

"Yes, ma'am." I sat quietly, digesting her words. My daddy had made sure that I was educated not only in my books but also, as he had once described it, in the code that dictated our lives in Alabama. Knowing when to keep your mouth shut. Picking your battles. Letting them think what they wanted because you weren't going to change their minds about certain things. It was a tough lesson, but I'd heeded it well enough to get some of the things I wanted out of life. Like this job, for instance. *The woman is just trying to pay you a compliment, Civil. Show her you can gracefully accept it.*

"Yes, ma'am. I won't disappoint you, Mrs. Seager."

She nodded. "And Civil? Don't forget to clip those fingernails."

"Yes, ma'am."

I'd been called into the fold of the health profession as early as junior high school. Although my daddy wanted me to go to medical school, I'd always known nurses occupied an important space when it came to patients. Medicine was a land of hierarchy, and nurses were closer to the ground. I was going to help uplift the race, and this clinic job would be the perfect platform for it. Mrs. Seager could have been doing something else, but she had chosen to help young colored women. Her approval meant something to me. Our work would make a difference.

This was the way I figured it. There were all different kinds of ministers. Ministers of congregations. Ministers of music. To minister was to serve. This work was a ministry serving young Black women.

The wind tugged at my nurse's cap. I walked quickly, and as soon as I was in the car, I unpinned the cap and took it off. I'm telling you, in those early days I was pretty sure I'd work at that clinic for as long as they'd have me. I had a new friend. A new job. A Tuskegee degree. I was sure enough ready.

As soon as I got home I asked my mama if we could trade cars. I didn't want to call any more attention to myself than I already had, and her Pinto was much older than my Colt. I was determined that Mrs. Seager would not be disappointed in me. I was going to have that dragon eating candy out of my hand before it was over and done with.

THREE

I got to admit something to you before I go any further. Something I ain't shared before, and I pray you'll understand.

I had an abortion in the spring of 1972.

I was twenty-three years old, a nursing student two months before graduation, ready to start my life. At the time, I planned to work in a hospital, perhaps on the surgical floor. The moment I noticed the telltale signs, I told myself it couldn't be true. I was supposed to be more than a wife and mother. Even though the baby's father was Tyrell Ralsey, my best friend since childhood, I was not ready and neither was he. After the procedure, he drove to Tuskegee to see about me. We said little over bowls of cabbage soup. Then he drove home and we did not speak about it for months.

I wanted things to be different for my patients. Through the miracles of birth control, they would plan their pregnancies. I intended to decrease the uncertainty, the unwelcome surprises. If Ty and I had taken the necessary precautions, we wouldn't have found ourselves in that situation. Most of our patients at the clinic had already learned that lesson the hard way. They'd already had babies or miscarriages. And yes, in some cases, abortions. They usually showed up at the door without an appointment, looking resigned to the fact that they were going to have to share their private business in order to get the help they needed.

Then there was the outreach side. We visited some patients at home because it had been determined that if we did not go out into the community, there would be women we'd never reach. The new nurses were each assigned one off-site case in the beginning. Our load would increase once we'd worked there six months. My home case was out in the country and scared me. I had no idea how I was supposed to talk about sex and birth control in somebody's front room. On top of that, my two patients were minors. Would the mama and daddy watch while I stuck them with the needle? Just the thought of making a home visit scared the living daylights out of me.

You see, I'd believed in the mission of family planning clinics long before I applied to work in one. I knew that the rate of pregnancy in young unwed mothers in Montgomery was terrible. Earlier that year, the US Supreme Court had ruled that abortion was legal in certain circumstances, but Alabama had not yet caught up with the law. And even if safe hospital abortions had been made available, the procedure was expensive and out of reach for most poor folks. The best solution had always been a prophylactic one. Although I refused to believe there was such a thing as an unwanted child, there was such a thing as an unwanted pregnancy—and I could speak to that firsthand.

On Monday morning I set out for the clinic in my mama's car though I could have walked. It was only two miles from my house, but Daddy insisted that I drive. He said he didn't want anybody harassing me in my uniform. That may have been true, but I also think he wanted me to drive because he prided himself on it. Having a car was further evidence of our status. I rolled down the window and let the wind blow across my face.

I arrived at the clinic early that morning, but I wasn't the only one. Eager Seager was already walking around checking lightbulbs. The bulb in the waiting room lamp popped as she turned it on. She seemed satisfied at this discovery and marched off in search of a fresh one in the supply closet.

The receptionist left the appointment book open on the desk so we could see the schedule as we walked by. Usually, there weren't many names in the book. As I said, most women just walked in. After the patient signed in, the receptionist would put their file in the plastic slot holder outside the examining room door. We worked in rotations. Whoever was next would take the file and step into the room. During training, I'd raised my hand and asked a question. *Wouldn't the patients feel more comfortable if they saw the same nurse each time they came in?* Mrs. Seager had just scrunched her face at me.

I didn't see any complicated cases that first day—mostly women coming in for birth control. One woman complained of pain when she urinated. I prayed she didn't have a venereal disease. She wore a satin blouse and skirt, like a secretary might wear. A good job uniform in a city where many Black women wore aprons. The test came back positive for a urinary tract infection.

The clinic didn't serve male patients at all, and during orientation Mrs. Seager emphasized that wasn't our mission. *But doesn't family planning include men?* After getting my second shutdown, I kept my mouth closed for the rest of the training.

BY AFTERNOON IT was time for me to go see my off-site patient, but I was dreading it so I stopped by Daddy's office first. In the old days, the office had been just a few blocks over from the clinic. Holt Street had been home to a lot of Black businesses, but the interstate project cut right through the old neighborhood and he'd moved over to Mobile Road. Daddy still mumbled about the project and how it had destroyed the Holt Street businesses. As Montgomery grew and expanded its boundaries, Black folks got shoved this way and that, he complained. He wasn't incorrect, but without political representation there was little we could do in those years.

When I entered, Glenda was sitting at the front desk, eating. She was a light-skinned woman with a smile that took up her whole face. In all the years I'd known her, Glenda had never called in sick. Same bouffant hairstyle, same baggy dresses. Daddy called her good-ole-Glenda. She did it all—nurse, receptionist, office manager. Her loyalty to the practice always made me feel guilty for not going to work there as Daddy's only child.

"Late lunch?"

"Folks been in and out that door all day. I don't think your daddy has had a chance to put anything in his stomach. When he comes out that room, can you stick this sandwich in his hand?"

I took the foil-wrapped sandwich, and Glenda buzzed me through the door. At the end of the hall, the doorway to Daddy's office was cracked open. Books covered every surface. Even though Daddy loved the sciences, he was a born literary man. He especially loved poetry and had a whole shelf of collections. He was from the generation that memorized poems, and he would recite lines as a bedtime ritual when I was a little girl. We loved to talk politics in Alabama, and if you asked Daddy about the state of the country, he might reply with, "If this is peace, this dead and leaden thing / Then better far the hateful fret, the sting." Half the time, I didn't know what he was talking about, but I always loved the song of verse on his tongue.

"You come back and see me if it doesn't clear up," I could hear him saying. When he was finishing up with a patient, he always sounded the same. He'd raise his voice and add a tone of finality to it. I had probably sounded like that with my first patients that morning. I was my daddy's daughter, after all.

I settled on the couch. All the pictures on the wall were of me

"I wouldn't be so tired all the time if you went to medical school and came to work with me."

"Daddy, sexual health is health care, too. Besides, I wouldn't want to take attention away from your disciple." I poked a thumb toward the door.

"Civil, be nice."

"She spends more time with you than Mama does."

He crumpled the foil and tossed it in the trash can. "I'm proud of you, Civil. You did fine in school. Don't let that self-righteous attitude overcome you and you'll be alright."

When he opened the door, I watched his shoulders relax and straighten. It was as if another person took over his body when he went in to see patients. He was himself, but he was also someone else. Daddy was short, not a hair over five foot six, with a wide girth that gave him substance.

He closed the door behind him, and I let loose a breath. He had not noticed the missing picture, though even I could not explain why I'd hidden it. Daddy might have been the family's rock, but I was all pillow, a coward to this hurt that I could not bear to talk about with anyone. The photograph of me as a baby had left me feeling unsettled, a scraping rawness in my stomach. Would my baby have looked like me? I reached under the sofa for the picture and put it in my purse.

FOUR

Alabama. Heart of America's Bible Belt. Home at one time to nearly half a million enslaved humans. I am a born and raised Alabaman, but up until the time I met the Williams family, much of my life in Montgomery had been circumscribed by my little community on Centennial Hill. Mama was a Link. Daddy belonged to the Boulé. When I was four years old, Dexter Avenue Baptist Church hired a twenty-five-year-old pastor named Martin Luther King Jr. Not long after, he was elected to head the bus boycott, eventually leading the voting rights march right up to the steps of the state capitol in Montgomery. When Daddy took me to see Dr. King, he pointed at the gathered crowd and said, *You see these people? You got to make your place among them.*

I know you want to argue that there isn't one Black community, that we aren't a monolith. But back then, when we talked about the community, it was something real, something defined by shared experience. Course that doesn't mean we didn't have our fissures. A big one was between the educated and uneducated, the poor and the not-so-poor. Fact is, the only time I remember us going out to the country was when we were passing through on the way to someplace else, maybe a church picnic or something like that. We definitely had never been in folks' houses out there. That was something else entirely. Now when I say *the country*, I'm talking the *country* country. No running water. Outhouses. Unpaved roads. The places off Old Selma Road weren't that physically distant from my house, but they may as well have been on another planet.

When I drove up, at first I assumed that the Williams sisters lived in the neat, brick rambler with the two pickup trucks parked out front. A thick cloud of dust swirled around my mama's little car, and when it cleared, I spied two little white boys standing on the house porch. I rolled my window all the way down, hoping they'd see my uniform.

"I'm looking for the Williams family?" I was positive I had read the number on the mailbox correctly.

One of them pointed behind the house, and I understood. I wound the car around the pickups, following the scant outline of tire tracks. The Pinto pushed through the ruts, bouncing so hard I was afraid I'd hit my head on the roof. I prayed I wouldn't get stuck. The last thing I wanted was to have to walk back down to that house and ask those boys to go get their daddy. Fortunately, it hadn't rained in a while and the ground was dry.

The trees cleared and the land swelled up into a hill. At the top sat a cabin. The car sputtered, but I tapped the gas pedal and somehow made it to the top. Everything leveled out, and the tire tracks disappeared into brush. Off to my left, I could see a wide field of green stalks. I didn't know a thing about farming, but anybody with eyes could tell that was wheat growing out there. Cows grazed in a lot beside the barn. A lone chicken peeked at me as it stepped through knee-high grass. Up close, the structure was more of a wooden shanty than a cabin. And it looked tired, as though a wind had blown it askew and it hadn't had the energy to right itself. A skinny black dog scratched its back in the dirt. In the rearview mirror, I could see my lips were dry. I licked them and my cracked bottom lip scratched my tongue.

I got out of the car and stepped into a huddle of gnats. The air smelled of burning wood. Something told me these girls couldn't be in school. If they were, they didn't go every day. They should have been expecting me, but they didn't have a phone and I wasn't confident they even knew about our appointment. They had initially been assigned another nurse who had quit the clinic the month before. I was there to pick up where she left off.

A girl wearing grubby pants and an orange T-shirt shaded her eyes with a hand. The backlight of the sun darkened her face.

"How you doing? I'm Civil Townsend from the Family Planning Clinic." It didn't make sense for us to be out here in our uniforms, but Mrs. Seager insisted. It was March chilly and I had left my sweater in the car. The wind reached my neck.

I stepped up closer. Someone had tried to braid the girl's hair, but the roots were so matted with dirt that only the ends of the hair could be plaited. I clutched the file under my arm and tried to remember what I'd read. "Are you India?"

The dog rubbed against my leg, and I fought an urge to push the animal off. It sidled away. I looked down, and sure enough, it had left a brown mark on my white pantyhose.

"She don't talk."

I jumped. I hadn't seen the other girl standing inside the screen door. I remembered the contents of the file. The younger sister was mute. I had skimmed that detail, but it came back to me now.

"Oh, okay. I'm Civil Townsend. I'm the nurse sent to give y'all shots today."

"What happened to the other one?"

"I-I don't know," I stuttered. The nurse's leave-taking baffled me, too. Maybe the demands of the job had been too much. Maybe she'd found something that paid more. Being out here on this farm wasn't anybody's idea of a good time. Even so, there weren't government jobs just laying around, waiting to be picked up.

"Is your daddy home?"

"No, ma'am."

I blinked as I pieced together their story in my head. Mace Williams, father, thirty-three. Milked cows, tilled the land, did whatever the white man told him to do in exchange for this shanty and a pittance of money. Constance Williams, mother, deceased. Patricia Williams, grandmother, sixty-two. In the distance, the inky outline of grazing cows flickered in the light.

"Your grandmama here?"

"Grandma, the nurse here!"

I tried to smile, but I wasn't sure if my expression passed for polite. I didn't know whether I should ask to come inside or if I should wait for the grandmother to come out.

The older sister settled it. I remembered now that her name was Erica. "You can come in if you want."

She opened the door for me. The screen pulled away from the edge of the wooden frame, not much protection against the flies. It creaked on its hinges. I'm not sure if I said this before, but walking into that house changed my life. And yes, it changed theirs, too. I walked right up in there with my file and bag of medicine, ready to save somebody. Little old me. Five foot five inches of know-it-all.

The first thing that hit me was the odor. Urine. Body funk. Dog. All mixed with the stench of something salty stewing in a pot. A one-room house encased in rotted boards. A single window with a piece of sheet hanging over it. It was dark except for the sun streaming through the screen door and peeking through the holes in the walls. As my eyes adjusted, I saw that there were clothes piled on the bed, as if somebody had stopped by and dumped them. Pots, pans, and shoes lay strewn about on the dirt floor. Flies buzzed and circled the air. Four people lived in one room, and there wasn't enough space. A lot of people in Alabama didn't have running water, but this went beyond that. I had to fight back vomit.

In the middle of it all, their grandmother sat stirring a big pot of steaming something or other. I stepped closer to a hole in the ground in the middle of the room. A wire grating covered the hole and the pot sat on top. The heat rising from it warmed the cool air. Up close, she looked older than her sixty-two years, but she was still a good-looking woman with a bronze complexion and high cheekbones. Her eyes were hazel, but they had lost their glow; the surrounding whites were dark and yellow-tinged.

"You want something to eat? You don't look none too hungry to me."

In Alabama, comments about my size weren't usually meant to insult. Weight was a sign of prosperity. But it made me self-conscious around people I didn't know well.

She wiped her hands on her dress. Her armpits were stained. She opened her mouth and revealed the dark of missing teeth.

I stuck out my hand. "Good afternoon, Mrs. Williams. My name is Civil Townsend. I'm the new nurse assigned to India and Erica. I'm here to give their shots."

"I suppose that mean you don't want none of this here stew."

"I'd love to stop by and try some another day, ma'am. It's just that I got to get back to the clinic within a certain time. I tried to come after the girls got out of school." I was talking quickly. This was exactly the kind of thing I'd worried about. Refusing food or drink in somebody's home could be taken as an insult.

She didn't say anything, just stared curiously at me.

"They make me sign a logbook," I added.

"A log what?"

"A logbook."

She squinted her eyes, then broke into a laugh. "You stay around here?"

24

"Yes, ma'am. Well, no, ma'am. I live in town."

"And what you say your name was?"

"Civil."

"Sybil."

"Civil."

"Well, it's nice to meet you, Miss Civil." She pointed a crooked finger. "Y'all clear a space for the woman to sit now."

"Thank you. I appreciate that."

The two sisters sat down on top of the clothes. I perched on the bed beside them on top of a pair of men's shorts. My throat clenched. A deep odor that went beyond a few missed baths filled my nostrils. These girls smelled like they hadn't cleaned up in weeks. Surely there was a pump outside?

I breathed through my mouth and tried to make small talk to get them comfortable. "Did y'all go to school today?"

"No, ma'am," responded the older sister. A broad forehead covered in acne narrowed into steep cheekbones that ended in the point of a chin. When she talked, she did not show teeth, and the words came out tight-lipped and mumbled. There was something defeated about her, and it made me want to draw her out.

"Why not?"

"We don't go."

"Your daddy don't make you?"

"No, ma'am."

Parents in Alabama who did not send their children to school could get in trouble with the law. To the best of my knowledge, the days of children dropping out of school to work on the farm had ended.

It was difficult to work without a table, but I went ahead and uncapped the first needle. The older sister slid down her sleeve and exposed a meaty bicep. "You might feel a pinch," I said, but the girl just looked at me. The needle slid easily into her flesh. Erica held her younger sister by the waist after they switched places. India's skin was the same soft shade of deep brown, but her face was rounder, the lines softer. The sides of her hair were pulled too tightly into rubber bands, the edges of her hairline ridged by tiny white bumps. She did not flinch when I inserted the needle.

After we finished, they wandered outside and I accepted a cup of the grandmother's stew. I tried not to focus on the grimness of the place. The stew was good; there was no denying it.

"It's delicious, Mrs. Williams."

"I grew those carrots myself." Satisfied that she had fed me, the hazel-eyed woman stepped outside the house, and I was left alone. Shame washed over me, but I did not know if it was mine or theirs.

The girls came back inside as I was opening the bag at my feet. "Y'all need some more of these?"

"What's that?"

"Sanitary napkins."

"What's that?"

"These are the things you put in your panties during your cycle. Kotex. Wasn't your nurse dropping these off every month?"

"Oh yeah. I had some of them. But after while they stopped working."

"What do you mean stopped working?"

"Blood went through it."

"Well, did you change it?"

Erica didn't answer.

"Erica, you got to change the pad every few hours. You can't just leave it all day long. If you heavy, you change it more often. You understand what I'm saying?"

"Yes, ma'am."

"Your other nurse didn't tell you that?"

She did not respond.

"Don't worry about it. Take these and I'll bring you some more, okay?"

"Yes, ma'am."

I wanted to ask her how they washed up, if there was a pump or a creek on the property. But I held my tongue. There would be time enough to figure all these things out. I gathered my things. When I was almost at my car, I turned to see Erica had followed me outside.

"Miss Townsend?"

"Call me Civil."

"I don't think I got enough of them napkins."

"Don't worry. I'll bring y'all some more my next visit."

"But see . . . truth is . . . I bleed all the time."

"What do you mean all the time?"

"I mean. Near about every day."

"You bleed every day? Are you bleeding now?"

"Yes, ma'am."

No wonder she smelled like that. I told her I'd be back soon with extra supplies for her and her sister.

"My sister don't bleed yet."

"What do you mean she don't bleed yet? You mean to say India hasn't started her cycle ever?"

She shook her head. Before she walked into the house, she turned back and watched me. I sat in the car with my hands wrapped around the steering wheel. I was shaking so bad I had to hold that wheel tight. They had that young girl on the shot and she wasn't even bleeding. Even worse, I had just stuck a needle in her. I focused my eyes on the smooth backs of my hands, trying to take it all in. In the funk the girls had left in my nose, I could barely breathe.

FIVE

Summer
2016

I have driven this Volvo since I bought it new fifteen years ago. I
live just a few miles from the hospital so it only has a little over
fifty thousand miles on it. You suggested I rent a car with all the
latest technology for this trip. I refused. *Wait until you get in those
little country towns with weak radio stations,* you said. *I prefer the silence,*
I replied. *How will you charge your phone? In the cigarette lighter, the way
I always have. Did you change the oil? Girl, be quiet.*

The route from Memphis to Montgomery could take me
through Olive Branch and get me there in as little as five hours, but
I got things to do before I reach my hometown. Business to take
care of. Visits. I have called and texted to let folks know. I don't
like surprises, never have. So I am careful not to do it to others.

I gas up the car and wipe my hands with sanitizer. As I settle
behind the wheel, my phone rings. It's Dr. James, my relief at the
hospital. He has a question about a patient. I gently inform him
that I completed all my charting before I left. I offer to log in to the
portal when I reach my hotel, but he is chastened enough. *Enjoy
your trip,* he says. *Where are you vacationing, anyway?* I pause. *Home,* I
say. *Montgomery.* As I utter the word, it weighs on me that I have
not been back in a decade. Since Daddy passed and Mama moved

to Memphis, there is little reason to visit. And to call it vacationing is a stretch. The road in front of me does not promise a respite.

I pull back onto the highway and push the Volvo a little faster. I think of my old Dodge Colt, the gift from Daddy, how much I loved that car and mourned when I sold it. I considered buying you a car for graduation, then stopped myself. I have tried not to over-compensate for adopting you as a single mother. Such folly. It is a burden to stubbornly remain single even when you know it is the right decision for you. I hope I have rightly modeled these modern choices. Mama says, *You're warping that girl with your guilt, Civil.* When she says this, I'm silent. There are a lot of things a mother can say to hurt her child, even long after the child is an adult.

Three more hours to Jackson. And to Alicia. Despite our sporadic communication over the years, she may be the one person who understands the path I have chosen. When it becomes clear that a woman of a certain age has not married or had children, folks like to think there's something wrong with her. As if we can't find love or tragically let the childbearing clock run out. I always expected this perception from strangers. The myth of old maids is a powerful one. But when you began to ask, Anne, it unsettled me.

I want you to know something. Of course I had opportunities at love. They didn't work out, but I have not been entirely loveless. And yes, I took prophylactic precautions with a dedication that was more powerful than any maternal urge. These were my decisions. There is no greater right for a woman than having a choice, Anne. And I exercised that right. Fully and consciously.

I'm glad I'll see Alicia first. Her evenness should calm my mind. I wonder how she'll look. It's my fault we haven't kept in better touch. When we have talked, she has always been the one to reach out. It's true I haven't joined social media like some of my generation. Maybe that would have made a difference. The last time I saw Alicia, I was about to graduate medical school and was home visiting my parents. She stopped over at the house and I asked for an update on the Williamses. They have been the glue between us over the years, me asking for news and Alicia providing it. Who would have thought she would be the one to keep in touch with all of us? I guess she was always good at being the go-between. I plan to thank her. I'm even hoping she might come with me. Alicia, the only one who really knows what happened back then, might be able to make sense of it all.

The car hums along steadily as I roll past an eighteen-wheeler and watch the numbers slowly tick up on my odometer. The faster I drive, the longer the miles.

SIX

——

Montgomery
1973

A nd then she said, *We have to maintain our health if we want to help other people. You got to rest and eat properly at all times.*"

Both of us burst out laughing. Alicia snorted when she laughed. For a moment, I thought she was going to spit out her coffee.

"Girl, Mrs. Seager is so strict," she said. Alicia spooned a chunk of pancake in her mouth. She had ordered a double stack. "But she seem like her heart in the right place. I saw my first patient yesterday and the lady ain't never even seen a blood pressure cuff. Can you believe that?"

I shook my head and sipped my coffee. "So tell me something, Alicia. How'd you end up in this job?"

We were sitting near the window at the Regent Cafe. Regent had been on Jackson Street for as long as I could remember, but Alicia had never been there. When we sat down, I told her how it had been the place where King and his minister friends had gathered to discuss strategy. I recognized half the people in there, mostly friends of my parents.

Alicia put down her fork. "I was raised in the church."

"Okay, everybody in Alabama was raised in somebody's church. What does that have to do with nursing?"

I had invited Alicia to breakfast because I wanted to talk to her about the Williams girls, but once we were seated in a booth across from each other, our conversation veered left and then right. It was so easy to talk with her.

"No, I mean *in* the church. In it, like several days a week in it. The church was practically family. But when I was sixteen I found out Mama was messing around with him."

I set down my coffee cup. "With who?"

"The pastor."

"How did you find out?"

"I walked in on them."

"Girl, no you didn't."

She shook her head, as if the memory were still fresh. "I threatened to tell my daddy, but Mama begged me not to. She said Daddy might murder the man. And the only reason I didn't tell was because I believed her. I didn't want my daddy going to jail. But it was an awful secret."

"I bet it was."

"Y'all want something else?" Irene, our waitress, had gone to high school with me. Back then, you couldn't spit in that part of Montgomery and not hit somebody you knew. I caught her watching Alicia. The neighborhood was small enough for new faces to be a curiosity.

"We're fine. Thanks, Irene."

"I'll take some more syrup," Alicia said through a mouthful of pancake.

After Irene walked away, we continued. "So then what happened?"

"After that, I decided to put that church and town behind me. I came here to strike out on my own because I can't stand carrying that secret."

"Alicia, you know that's not your burden to bear."

"Turns out the old liar's sermons are hard to shake. I want to do right by people. I'm still a believer, but it's up to me and my choices to prove that God is real." She lifted her chin. Alicia's eyebrows were penciled in, and they rose in a half-moon shape around her eyes. She looked away from me, and I studied her round face, the cut of shadow across her cheek. She had not told her father, and now she carried the wound that would have been his.

"So you decided to become a nurse to turn the world right-side-up again," I said. She wiped at a tear on her cheek and I put my hand over hers. "It's okay. I get it. But why the Montgomery Family Planning Clinic?"

"Oh, now that's an easier question." She smiled broadly and her face cleared. "I took this job because the last time I checked, the man wasn't standing on the corner handing out jobs to the first person who walked by!"

If Alicia didn't want to return home, that meant she was out here doing this all by herself. Things were different for me. If things didn't work out, I could always go work for my daddy, though having that fallback cushion didn't comfort me. I had never considered working for him to be a real job.

I took another sip of coffee. "Alicia, I want to ask your opinion."

"Okay, shoot."

"I got this family, these patients. Remember the file we talked about? The home visit? I went out to visit them this week, and one of the girls ain't even on her cycle yet."

"What you mean?"

"Alicia, I gave that girl the shot and she ain't even bleeding."

"Then why on earth did you give her the shot?"

"I didn't know she wasn't bleeding until afterward. That's what I'm trying to tell you." I lowered my voice. "It's not in the chart."

"You got to tell Mrs. Seager. Some nurse has messed up."

It was as if the previous nurse had assumed it. Poor, inexcusable health care from somebody who didn't know her ass from her elbow.

"The girl is only eleven years old," I said. "Even if Mrs. Seager doesn't know about the mistake, don't you think it's messed up that an eleven-year-old is on birth control in the first place?"

"I don't know, Civil. Some of these young girls are fast. They are starting earlier and earlier these days. Especially . . ."

"Especially what? Poor girls?"

"That's not what I'm saying."

"What are you saying, then?"

Behind her, I saw the door swing open. Ty must have seen us through the window because he made a beeline for our table.

"What's up, y'all?" He swung his big body into the booth and next to mine.

"What are you doing here?" My tone was unintentionally sharp.

"You going to introduce me to your friend?"

"No, I hadn't planned on it."

"How you doing? I'm Ty."

"Alicia."

The way she smiled at him, I could tell she thought he was cute. I turned away. I had not seen him since I moved back months ago, and here we were both acting like nothing had happened between us. I'd known Ty since kindergarten. His parents were my parents' good friends. When we graduated high school, Ty stayed home and enrolled in Alabama State up the road. He'd run track, sprints, and hurdles for the college, but when he came to visit me at Tuskegee I had still been surprised at how much he'd developed. A boy in a man's body, I told myself. Until he kissed me and I understood that he was a man in a man's body. One visit turned into three turned into more. Before I knew it, we were going steady.

34

"What y'all doing in this new job? Do you really need a clinic to give out rubbers?"

My face grew hot. He had some nerve talking like that. Alicia began to spout statistics about teenage pregnancy. "Sixty-five percent of unmarried mothers in Alabama are Black. We've got to get that number down. So we give them this shot," she said, "called Depo-Provera. They don't have to worry about remembering to take a pill."

"Well, ain't that something."

How easily the word *rubbers* skipped off his tongue when he had not used one. The truth of the matter was that I had allowed it. My trust of our long friendship had blinded me. He was not some stranger. He was Ty, my best friend. My first boyfriend. It had not occurred to me that giving in to my feelings would change my life.

"What you doing here anyway?" I asked.

He pointed to my plate. "I came to get me some breakfast." He grabbed a piece of my sausage before I could stop him, and started talking with his mouth full. "Them girls shouldn't be messing with boys, anyway. Y'all ever heard of a chastity belt?"

Alicia laughed loudly, but I didn't even crack a smile. The day I called him and told him about the pregnancy, he had calmly offered to marry me; I thought he was joking. When I realized he wasn't, I said, *Are you crazy?* and hung up the phone. Now I could feel him watching me behind his smile. He raised his hand for Irene and asked her to bring our check.

"That's awful nice of you to pay for our breakfast," said Alicia.

"I'm not a knucklehead like she thinks," he said.

"Shut up, Ty." I rolled my eyes.

Alicia looked between us. "Oh, I see. You two like each other."

He shook his head. "Civil need an attitude adjustment."

After he paid the check, we made our way outside. Two boys

rode by on bikes. They waved at Ty. "Hey, y'all better stay out of trouble," he yelled at them. A truck rolled past and kicked up dust. I sneezed and drew my sweater around my shoulders.

"Bless you. Hey, y'all want to come to my house tomorrow night? My mama is cooking Sunday dinner, and I'm sure she'll want to hear all about the clinic," Ty said, watching me.

"I can't. I got something to do," I said.

"You haven't come to dinner in almost a year, Civil. You hurting my mama's feelings."

"I said I got something to do."

"You want to come, Alicia?"

"Go," I said before she could refuse. "You need to meet some folks in town, and Ty's mama knows everybody."

"Alright, then. Where you live?"

As Alicia reached in her purse for something to write on, I waved at them and crossed to the other side of the street, where my car was parked. I did not glance back because I could not look at him without revealing more to Alicia than I already had.

THE MONTGOMERY PLANNING Agency was sandwiched between a laundromat and a donut shop, an unlikely place for a federal agency, but it did make it easy to find. I'd already been there once before when I was in the process of applying for the clinic job. The agency oversaw our clinic and I'd had an interview there.

The desks were arranged in rows. The only person with his own closed office was the man who ran the agency. I remembered him from before. He constantly talked about his grandchildren. Only three of the six desks were occupied. Two women typed and the third was on the phone. The woman on the phone, the one with the bushy eyebrows that joined in the middle, placed the receiver to her chest. The brows gave her an intent look, and by the way she asked if she could help me, I figured I'd interrupted her from something important.

"Hi, um, yes, ma'am, my name is Civil Townsend." I talked quickly. I hadn't had a chance to run my idea past Alicia, so I figured I should just go on and do it before I changed my mind. "I'm a nurse over at the Family Planning Clinic. I'd like to ask about public housing for one of my patients, a family that lives out on Old Selma Road."

"Are they already on public assistance?"

"Yes, ma'am," I said. Technically, the clinic's services were public assistance. Whatever else they were getting was a mystery to me. The Williamses barely owned a pot to piss in, as Daddy would say. If anybody was a candidate for public assistance, they were.

"Have a seat, dear." She put the receiver back to her ear. I sat down in one of two plastic chairs across from her desk and waited.

When she finished with her call, she turned to a low file cabinet beside her desk. "Does the family have a social worker assigned to them?"

I hadn't thought about that. I'd just charged in there with my plan to get the Williamses into a real apartment, but it made sense that if they were on public assistance, they probably also had a social worker.

"Yes, ma'am, I believe they do."

"Well, the social worker will have to fill out the paperwork. Do you know her name?"

"No, ma'am."

She looked down at the paper on her desk as if her mind were already elsewhere. "Tell the social worker to come here, and we can get the process started."

"If you give me the paperwork, I can get it done. I think I'll see her next week." Well, now I was flat-out lying. The public assistance question had been an educated guess. Meeting up with the social worker was a whole nother level of lie.

"How many people are in the family, dear?"

"Four."

"So you're looking for a two-bedroom?"

"Actually, no, I need a three-bedroom. The grandmother lives with them."

She frowned at me. "We don't have a lot of apartments that size. They're in high demand, and some of the families are a lot bigger than yours."

"Yes, ma'am, of course."

"Honey, we got families of five in two-bedroom apartments. That's how stretched we are. Now, there will be some more apartment units built in the next few years. Maybe if we put your family on a wait list—"

"No," I said. The clicking of the typewriter at the back of the room ceased, and I lowered my voice. "I mean . . . You see . . . These people are living in squalor, Mrs."—I read the nameplate on her desk—"Livingston. They living in a shanty out on the back of a farm." My gumption surprised my own self. I was being pushy like Diahann Carroll in that episode of *Julia* when she convinces Dr. Chegley to allow this family to work off their son's medical bill.

"I understand. But we even got some homeless families, Miss—"

"Townsend." I shifted one leg over the other. "These folks might as well be homeless. That house ain't barely shelter. It's riddled with holes. You ought to see it. And the grandmother, I don't even know how she can stand it, what with the weather coming all through the walls."

Yes, I could have been an actress except it was all true. Everything except the part about meeting up with the social worker. The lady reached over to her cabinet again.

"Take this and have the social worker fill it out and get the family to sign it."

I took it from her. "Yes, ma'am. Thank you. I will do that. Thank you very much."

As I walked back out to my car, I held the papers out in front of me so that I wouldn't wrinkle them. I'd taken the first step to helping the family, and it felt good. Maybe getting them this new apartment would erase the wrong I'd done by injecting that little girl with birth control. This was why I'd taken the job at the clinic. I wanted to be like Alicia: doing right by people, proving God was real.

SEVEN

Getting the social worker's name turned out to be harder than I'd thought. When I searched the Williamses' medical file, there was no mention of one. Aside from outright asking the agency to give me a name, there seemed to be only one way to find out: ask the grandmother, Pat Williams. If I did that, she might ask what I was up to, and I didn't want to mention my plan until I was sure it would happen. I needed to figure something out.

That week, while we were cleaning the clinic, I asked Val if she had any ideas on how to find the social worker. She suggested I try St. Jude, a hospital that ran some social service programs in Montgomery.

"I got another question for you." I stopped sweeping. We were standing in examination room number two. Val sprayed the bed with a bleach solution and ran a rag over the vinyl while I talked. "Why you think Mrs. Seager hired all Black nurses? Ain't no white nurses in Alabama?"

"Hush, child. You saying you don't want this job?"

Val had gone to nursing school after her children grew up and moved out. When her husband died and left her some insurance money, she used it to go back to school. She actually believed her late husband's spirit had guided her on this path. As far as I could tell, Val hated when anybody criticized anything. The woman was beyond grateful.

"Just asking," I said.

"I'm sorry, Civil. I don't aim to sound mean. I just think they figure it's easier for us to deal with these families. But it ain't so easy, huh? This one patient I saw yesterday fought me like a wildcat right there on her living room couch. The girl ain't but twenty-two and got three kids."

"Fought you? Why?"

"Didn't want the shot, but her mama was making her."

I stared at her for a moment, then opened the drawers to make sure they were organized properly. On the left: syringes, glass vials, bandages, alcohol wipes, latex gloves. On the right: condoms, speculum, retractor, curette, plastic pill wheels.

"My two home patients are so young," I said. "Just eleven and thirteen years old. I knew I would be visiting people out in the country, but I'm telling you, they living in terrible conditions. Nobody should live like that."

"Yeah, a lot of these folks live out back on the white man's land. Now, baby, tell me you knew about that, didn't you?"

"Yes," I lied. Daddy had done me such a disservice by sheltering me on Centennial Hill, telling me we were never better than our people while at the same time keeping those people away from me.

"Oh, alright. I thought you might not have known that still happened around here. The man probably don't pay them hardly nothing. Just like sharecropping, if you ask me."

"I can't stand the thought of them living like that. You should have smelled them. It was a crying shame. I got to get them out of there." I waited to see how she would respond.

She did not visibly react, but I was pretty sure she'd heard me. She stooped over and wrung the mop out. "Tell me something. How that man going to keep his job if he move off the land?"

I hadn't thought my idea through that far.

"Listen, child, the best thing you can do is make sure the girls don't get pregnant. Think of how they live, and try to keep them from bringing a baby into that."

"Don't you think I know that? But surely we can do more. I can't just walk in there and pretend like I don't see folks suffering."

"Civil," she said, "people got to reckon with the hand God dealt them."

We finished up the room. We were the only two left so we began turning out the lights and closing down the clinic. I waited for Val at the door with my purse on my shoulder. As she came out she handed me a file.

"Take a look at this one."

I opened it. *Gertie Sims. Age: 14. Three-month old baby. Father: Unknown. Mother: Daisy Sims, 37. Full hysterectomy 11 years ago. Possible alcohol abuse. Siblings: Carolyn Sims, 17, three children, ages 18 months, 3, 4.*

"We doing important work, hear? You might not be able to change folks' house of cards. Only God can do that. But what you can do is make sure babies don't have babies. You understand me?"

She was right. I was focused on the wrong thing. I tried to picture an infant in that one-room shanty with all of those folks, and the thought made my head hurt. Erica wouldn't know what to do with a child, and their grandmother already had more than she could handle. My job was to give the shot and that was all.

I TRIED TO take Val's advice and shake off my idea of moving the family. Since my last visit, I'd learned that frequent bleeding while on the shot was common. It surprised me that no one had talked to Erica about this. Or to me. One day I dropped by the Williamses' house without an appointment. When I drove up, the girls were outside playing in the dirt.

"Hey, what y'all doing?"

"Nothing."

I squatted down and showed Erica the inside of a brown paper sack. "I brought you some more Kotex. You been using the other ones I brought you?"

She nodded.

"Your grandmama home?"

She pointed to the house with a stick. I hooked my purse over my shoulder and walked up to the door. I tried to be respectful enough not to peer inside without permission, but I could see the dog lying in the middle of the floor and a man beside it stroking its back. He waved me in. For a minute, I was speechless. I had never seen a prettier face on a man in my life. The screen had blurred his features, but I could see now he took after his mother—same complexion, same bone structure. Thick, black eyebrows framed heavy lids. The light shone just enough to reveal the glint of green in his eyes.

"Which place you from?" he asked.

"I'm a nurse from the clinic."

"A nurse." He continued rubbing the dog.

"I apologize for barging in on you. I came to bring the girls some supplies and ask if I could take them out for a few hours." I looked through the window for a sign of Mrs. Williams, the grandmother. I needed to ask her for the social worker's name.

He slowly stood up as if it pained him. When he walked over to me I could make out the semblance of a limp. I stepped back and bumped against the door. It was like a wall against my back.

"Civil Townsend." I stuck my hand out, and he took it for a brief second.

"You a new one."

"A new what?"

"A new government lady."

43

I didn't have an answer for that. I didn't think of myself as a government lady even though my clinic was funded by the federals. I thought of all the people who must have entered that front door asking questions about their habits, diet, physical maladies, all the information that would justify the state to step into their lives and deliver a handout. Yes, I knew what he meant when he called me a *government lady*, but it bothered me.

"You're Mr. Williams, right?"

He laughed. His voice sounded like his mother's—deep and throaty. The only thing that kept me from getting caught up in looking at his face was that, like the girls, he smelled bad. I didn't understand it. Maybe the house was just too funky for a body to get clean.

"So can I take the girls or not?"

"You taking them for shots?"

"No, sir. I'm taking them for . . . well, the truth is I wanted to take them shopping."

"I thought you said you was a nurse?"

"I am."

"Shopping for what?"

"Necessities."

"Don't you want to sit down first?"

The house was no cleaner than it had been on my previous visit. There were only two chairs, and they were both covered in stuff. He must've seen my expression because he hastily picked clothes off a chair. It creaked when I sat in it. A spring poked into my underside.

"I'm sorry about this place," he said as he rummaged around until he found a glass jar. He wiped it with a T-shirt. "Mr. Adair ain't no kind of boss. And Mama ain't no match for the weather stick." He pointed to the straw stuffed in the holes in the wall. He went outside with the glass, and when he came back it was filled with water. So there was a spigot close by.

"Thank you."

I didn't want to drink from that jar, but he was watching me. I closed my eyes and took a long swallow. It tasted like iron, but it cooled my throat. I awkwardly crossed my legs at the ankle. I had on my uniform, but I wore a long blue cardigan over it. There was a *T* for *Townsend* sewn on the sweater pocket. I caught him looking at it. "You working today?"

He tilted his head. "Not directly."

"What do you mean?"

He lifted his bare foot and jacked up a pant leg to reveal a lump on his calf.

"How long have you had that?" I reached out to touch it, but he jerked back.

"Ain't nothing."

"Has a doctor looked at it?" I was already thinking the worst, like it could be a tumor.

He scowled. "Ain't no need for no doctor. Just a bad leg is all. To answer your question, Mr. Adair say he hiring a company to work the farm so I ain't got to work today."

"Are you saying he fired you?"

His face softened suddenly, as if he were switching on another part of himself. "You sure is a fox, you know that?"

I put the glass down on the floor hard and some of the water spilled. "Can I take the girls or not?"

"Hey, calm down now. I'm just messing with you."

I tried to recover. "If you need a new place to stay, I've got an idea. I was thinking I could help y'all get into public housing. Sound like you might need to move soon."

"Woman, what in the world are you talking about?"

"I'm talking about a brand-new apartment. Don't y'all get assistance? The government will pay."

He crossed one leg over the other and his foot bumped mine.

"We get all kinds of 'sistance. Every week somebody coming out here talking about assisting with something or the other."

"Then it should work for you."

I opened my purse and dug around. I still had the paperwork Mrs. Livingston had given me.

"Just sign this paper. And I'm going to need you to tell me the name of your social worker so I can make sure we go through the proper steps."

He looked down at the paper and then back at me. "That lady don't come round here no more. Act like she scared or something."

I fished for a pen. "You remember her name? All you got to do is sign here and I'll take care of the rest. I'm sorry, but . . . do you have a pen?"

"Naw, ain't got no pen."

I tried to force a smile. "Okay, well I'll bring one back when I drop the girls off later this evening. If you want to keep these papers and take a look at them while I'm gone, that'll be fine."

He didn't move.

"Mr. Williams? Here."

His lip trembled, and, for a second, my hand hung suspended in the air. I wanted to slap myself as it dawned on me. The man couldn't read, and now I was embarrassing him.

I didn't know what to do next, so I picked up my glass and finished off the water. My hands shook as I returned the papers to my purse. "Or I could just take them with me and you could sign another time."

He was quiet.

"I'm not sure yet how much you'll have to pay, but it won't be much. I'll also see about getting you a job. How long did Mr. Adair give you?" Even though I heard myself saying this, I didn't know what the hell I was talking about. I was the nurse. The giver of shots. Not the fairy godmother.

46

"Thank you for visiting, Miss Sybil." He said the "miss" in a high note, paused, then added my name in a mocking tone.

"It's *Civil*."

"Yes, ma'am."

"I'll bring the girls back around seven. Is that alright?"

"Go on and take the girls. I ain't never denied my girls a thing in they life. But you can move in your . . . apartment"—he said it so forcefully that a bead of spit tripped off his tongue—"yourself."

I stumbled on the broken porch step as I left the house. *Daddy told me to stay in the car.* I should have listened. Blew my car horn. Called them outside and given the shots right there under the clear blue sky. Then hightailed it out of there.

That old farmer didn't have to worry about me doing anything more for him. Old lizard with his dirty water and broken chair. I called out to India and Erica and slammed my car door once we were all inside. I rolled down the windows to let out the stench. I would just do what I could for these girls. Their daddy and grandmama could tend to their own selves.

EIGHT

I was shaken by the girls' daddy, but I tried not to let it show. He was just embarrassed that he couldn't read was all. I could handle that. I'd just explain the papers to him when I saw him again. I'd be patient just like my daddy was with folks who didn't understand his medical terminology. In those days, we talked a lot about that kind of thing in nursing school. Nurses had to show a genuine respect for their patients; otherwise, folks sensed condescension and clammed up. I hoped he hadn't experienced that with me, but I had a feeling he had.

"Where you taking us, Miss Civil?" asked Erica.

She turned a hopeful chin up toward me. In the rearview mirror, I noticed the same earnestness on India's face.

"I'm taking y'all to Kmart to get some clothes."

"K what?"

"Kmart. You haven't heard about it? A new store in Montgomery."

"What's wrong with these clothes?" Erica looked down at her shirt and shorts.

"Don't you need some underwear and things?" I turned onto East South Boulevard. "When is the last time you went shopping?"

She shook her head ever so slightly. I'd done it again. Embarrassed myself and probably them, too. There were clothes all over that house, but they all appeared to be hand-me-downs. And not the good kind, neither. The moth-bitten, faded, worn-out kind. And since they weren't doing laundry properly I knew anything I bought would end up on the floor with everything else.

"We're going to Kmart and then I'm taking you to my house. You can take a bath in my tub and I'll fix your hair. Feed you. How does that sound?"

Erica half smiled for the first time since I'd met her, and I could see that one of her teeth was brown. I would start by buying her a toothbrush, and once I found the social worker, I would find out if the girls had ever been to see a dentist. It was only a matter of time before their teeth decayed.

I steered the car into the parking lot and the girls leaped out. I peeked inside my purse. I'd stuck some money in the inside zipper that morning but hadn't bothered to count it.

"Is you rich, Miss Civil?" Erica peered at me through the car window. India stayed off to the side, bouncing on one foot.

"No, course not," I said, snapping my purse shut and getting out of the car. "Child, if I was rich I'd be hanging out with Billy Dee Williams."

"Who?"

"You don't know who Billy Dee Williams is?"

She shook her head as we walked into the white building. I'd decided on Kmart instead of Loveman's over in the Normandale Shopping Center because the Kmart was newer. At almost one hundred thousand square feet, it was also the largest store in the city. Inside everything was white and clean, and the aisles were so wide they never got crowded. Overhead, rows of fluorescent lights lined the ceiling from one end to the other. Furniture, beauty products, electronics, toys, clothes, shoes, even a pharmacy. All under one roof. If a fairy with wings had appeared in that store, I don't believe those girls would have been surprised.

"Alright." I pointed to the red and white sign hanging from the ceiling that indicated the kids' section. "Let's start with underwear. Y'all got bras?" I hadn't noticed either of them wearing one although Erica was well past being ready.

Instead of following me, Erica walked over to the food counter. I had eaten there once. Hot dogs. Nacho chips with cheese. India walked in the opposite direction toward a miniature horse carousel. She started vocalizing, a cross between a grunt and a cry. It was loud and startling. She slapped the metal horse's flank.

"You want to ride it?"

I knew India could hear, but I wasn't sure how much she comprehended.

"Girl, that thang too small for you," Erica said, wandering back over to us.

"Climb on." I put a quarter in the machine and India swung her leg over the horse. The lights came on, and out of the speakers came a staticky tinkle of music like an ice cream truck. The horse rose. India made a clicking noise in the back of her throat that was so loud people stopped and gaped. Some of the passersby steered clear of us and the girls' body odor. I tried not to make eye contact with the strangers. When the ride finished, I put another quarter in and watched as India threw her head back. I added another quarter. And another, until I ran out. The more she squealed, the more people stared. I went to the customer service counter and asked for a dollar's worth of quarters. Erica laughed at her sister's delight, while I hoped no one said anything to me.

"Eeeee! Yee eeeeee!!"

AFTER WE FINISHED shopping, I took them back to my house. Although the policy didn't speak on it, I knew it would be frowned upon if Mrs. Seager found out. I promised myself that I wasn't going to do this ever again. I parked Mama's car behind my Colt in the driveway and took the girls into the house through the side door.

As they walked through the kitchen, staring, I became painfully aware of every hiccup of mechanical noise. The buzzing fan of the window unit. The hum of the refrigerator. They didn't say anything, but I watched them hungrily taking it all in. Mama kept all her curtains open. She hated darkness more than anything, so our one-story house was always full of daytime light. The girls looked around, their voices hushed, as if we had sneaked into a stranger's house.

"This look like white folks' house," Erica declared when we were in my room. "You live here with your husband?"

"I don't have a husband. I didn't tell you that?"

She shook her head. I realized I hadn't shared much about myself with them, though I knew so much about their family and background. Everything was lopsided. Volunteering their personal information was part of the bargain of public assistance. Tell us everything about yourself and, in return, we'll hand you a sliver of a slice of American pie. In the meantime, we won't tell you anything, not even what we're going to do for you. Suddenly I didn't feel so bad about bringing them home with me.

"I live here with my parents. I'm an only child." I reached under my bed and took out a photo album. "Y'all sit here and take a look at this while I go draw the bathwater."

I brought in one of the dining room chairs so they could both sit at my desk. It was the same desk where I'd studied for my high school exams, and when I looked back at the two of them sitting there poring through that album, something surged within me. I cannot explain it other than to say I was filled with determination. I would get them back in school. I would get them that apartment. I would do everything I could to help them.

I sat on the side of the tub. No doubt, I was overstepping my boundaries on this case. I decided I wouldn't tell anyone, not even Alicia. I didn't want to lose my job, and Mrs. Seager would lose her mind if she found out what I was doing. When the water was ready, I brought out fresh towels from the hallway closet and hung them on the back of the door. I found the shampoo and hair grease under the bathroom sink. It was going to be a serious undertaking getting their hair untangled. The best I could do was try to comb it out. Maybe I would cornrow it. We could sit outside on the porch, and I would braid until it was too dark to see, parting their hair with a rattail comb or with the tip of my pinky nail.

"If y'all want to, you can get in the tub at the same time," I said as I cut tags off underwear and clothes. "I think you can both fit."

India jumped up first. Ever since the horse ride at Kmart, she had been warming up to me. At one point she had even grabbed my hand and held it.

It turned out that the hair was too matted to detangle. As much as I hated to do it, I had to cut the tangles out. Erica convinced India that it had to be done, but the younger sister started to cry when she saw her hair falling onto the bathroom floor. In the end, I picked it out into an Afro. I took India's hand and put it on her head so she could feel the curly softness. "I didn't cut that much," I said.

"Our grandmama going to go crazy when she see our hair."

I wanted to cuss myself. She was right. Her grandmama was going to kill me. Cutting their hair without asking permission had been tomfoolery. And not everybody was into Afros. My daddy sure wasn't. My hands shook as I put the scissors back in the drawer. All I can say is that their hair seemed a serious thing to me that evening. Life or death. If I could clean them up, I could clean their lives up, too.

In my room, India settled on the floor in front of me and I divided her hair into sections. Parting the hair, line after line, this shared geography of scalp like an ancestral road map, bound us Black girls. I scraped my nail along the pale of her scalp. The hair hung in tight coils. I ran my fingertips along the bumps at her nape.

"Does it itch back here?" I asked. She nodded, and I thought of a medicated shampoo I could buy that might clear up the fungus.

"What's that?' Erica sat on my bed and pointed to the floor beside her.

"Records. You ever played a record before?"

Erica shook her head. She and her sister were aliens and I was their guide on Earth. Here to teach our food, our music, our movie stars. I flipped through my records and picked out a new one by Gladys Knight & the Pips. The first song I played was "Neither One of Us." The music changed the mood, and Erica talked to me about her mother. Her speech was slow, but there was an intelligence to the girl.

"We used to have a radio. My mama liked to listen to music on it."

"You remember your mama?"

"We used to live in a different house. A real house. Things ain't the same after she dead. Even Daddy ain't the same."

She said the word *dead* so matter-of-factly. These girls were dulled by the world.

"Speaking of your daddy, he doesn't seem to like me too much."

"Why you say that?" Erica propped her chin up on her palm. She was stretched long across my bed in her new clothes. A yellow butterfly spread its wings across the back of her shirt. As soon as she'd seen it in the store, she'd clutched it to her as if she would not allow me to say no.

"He just . . . I don't know."

"Daddy ain't got a mean bone in his body. He just don't like government people."

When Erica turned, I saw that she was holding my baby picture in her hand. She must have found it under my bed. Before I could take it from her, she said, "This your baby?"

"No," I said and swallowed hard. "That's me."

"This you when you was a baby?"

I nodded.

"You was so cute," she said. India leaned over to see.

I needed to return that picture to Daddy's office. I didn't know why I was holding on to it. "Everybody say I'm the spitting image of my daddy," I said.

"They say India look like our mama. I look more like Grandmama. Neither one of us got her or Daddy's eyes though. I wish we had. I think I be pretty with them light eyes like they got."

"Your eyes are pretty just the way they are," I said softly.

Erica looked right at me. "Miss Civil. You staying in this job or you leaving?"

"What do you mean?"

When she didn't answer, I spoke slowly. "I'm not going nowhere no time soon, Erica. And if I do? I'll make sure you're the first to know."

This answer seemed to satisfy her. She moved over to the stack of records leaning against the wall.

Later, I took them to the kitchen, where I boiled rice and warmed up leftover pot roast. The girls sat at the kitchen table and scarfed the food down. I wished I could have fed them a better dinner, but it was all we had time for. I wasn't watching the clock, but I knew it was getting late.

"I better get y'all home."

Mama walked in the back door, a streak of yellow paint across her cheek.

"Hello," she said and walked through the kitchen into the hallway as if she hadn't even noticed there were two girls sitting at her kitchen table.

"Is that your mama?" Erica whispered, as if she had seen a ghost.

"In the flesh," I said, watching the doorway to see if she would reappear. When she didn't, I picked up the bags of the girls' old clothes. "Let's go, y'all."

India put the dishes in the sink. Then she walked over and patted me on the arm several times, hard, as if she were trying to communicate something.

"What's she saying?" I asked Erica.

"I don't know."

"Come on, India. You can come back another day, okay?" I told her. From the way she reacted, I could tell I was speaking too loudly. I still did not know how to talk to her. Newly clothed, bellies filled, the girls, smelling of cocoa butter, climbed into my mama's car.

NINE

I might have been a daddy's girl, but it was not by choice. I had always longed for a mama who read to me at night and kissed me before school in the morning. Unfortunately, that was never June Townsend. The way the story goes is that when Mama got pregnant with me, Daddy turned the shed behind our house into an art studio after declaring that the fumes in the house were not good for a baby. He placed a metal trash can in the corner for her oil-soaked rags, installed window fans so there was adequate ventilation. On one side of the room, a wooden counter ran along the wall, ending at a metal utility sink. Daddy had run the pipe himself so Mama could have a sink with running water.

As I grew older, I began to suspect Daddy might have built out that shed for a second reason. They had not taught us about postpartum depression in nursing school, but I suspect now that having a baby had only worsened her mental state. From the time I was a child, Mama would paint for hours, sometimes forgetting to feed me. I learned early on how to get out the bread and make a bologna sandwich.

Mama would put toys on the floor for me to play with while

she worked. I had my own watercolors, though I never expressed much interest in them. I preferred to cut the magnets out of the shower curtain and stick them to metal surfaces around the studio. Meanwhile, on the other side of the room, Mama would be lost in her thoughts. *Preoccupied* was an understatement. She'd have two or three things going at once. Two canvases on easels. A square of fabric hanging from a rack on the wall.

By high school, I had learned to build the frame and pull her canvases onto stretcher bars, carefully cutting the wood with a miter and saw before fitting them together. I thought doing this might bring us closer. And for a while, it did. I enjoyed the work, and Mama even asked me to sign the backs of my frames. But after I came home from college one break and discovered Mama doing it herself, cutting the wood more precisely than I ever had, I never made another one.

It was hard for me to imagine Mama without her brushes and paints and stained clothes. Sometimes Daddy would go out there and bring her back into the house. He'd literally carry her, and if I caught the silhouette of them through the window, I imagined he was rescuing her. Head cradled in his shoulder, feet dangling to one side, Mama looked like a rag doll in his arms.

The day after I brought the girls to the house I sat in the shed watching her, a brush in one hand, that signature red lipstick carelessly applied across her mouth. Mama had a habit of putting on lipstick as soon as she brushed her teeth in the morning. Even if she had slept in the studio all night without a bath, she religiously brushed her teeth, threw water on her face, and put on lipstick. The color tended to feather around the edges of her mouth and spread onto her teeth when she ate. This vanity was the one bit of fussiness to her otherwise unkempt beauty.

She wiped a thumb down the front of her shirt. Mama always

painted in the same basic clothes: a stained shirt and pair of worn overalls. Even in winter, she wore the same thing. Daddy had not installed heating, fearing a fire. Mama claimed she liked the chill, though she had cut the fingers out of a pair of old gloves to wear on colder nights.

"You alright, Civil?" She didn't look in my direction.

"You know I started my new job."

"Today?"

"Well, it's been three weeks."

"You didn't tell me that."

"You saw the girls who were here yesterday? They're my patients."

Daddy had brought home barbecue ribs for us to celebrate my first day of work, but Mama was excellent at disconnecting. I'd learned this early on, the absentmindedness a trait of her eccentricity.

"You like it?" She stepped back from the easel.

"Is it finished?"

As soon as I uttered the words, I realized the carelessness of them. The truth was that I'd always found her work indecipherable. She used a lot of negative space, but where there was color it rioted. I'd often peer into the canvas, to see what it might teach me about this mother who revealed so little.

"Not the painting. Do you like your job?"

"Well, that's what I wanted to talk to you about. Those girls who were here yesterday lost their mother a few years ago."

She used the edge of her fingernail to scrape paint off a spot on the lower right side of the canvas.

"That's sad." She said it in such a monotone that, once again, I did not know if she was referring to the motherless girls or declaring judgment of the painting in front of her. I forged ahead.

"I think so, too. They living out in this shack on a farm with their daddy and grandmother. I'm trying to get them moved to an apartment."

"Mmm."

I rattled a can of miniature wooden blocks to get her attention. She turned and looked at me.

"I wanted to ask for your help," I said.

"With what?"

"With what I'm trying to do."

"Is this job your dream, Civil?"

Mama had asked me a version of this question for as long as I could remember. When I'd struggled to choose between Tuskegee, from where Daddy had graduated, or Mama's beloved Fisk, she'd asked me, "Is it your dream to go to Tuskegee, Civil?" In the fourth grade, I'd won the spelling bee at my elementary school, and Daddy insisted on testing the city's segregation laws by registering me for the citywide bee. As we were leaving the registration area in City Hall, a white boy spit on my shoes and pretended it was an accident. The night before the bee, I threw up twice. The next morning, as I sat in the kitchen eating my cereal, Mama asked me, "Is it your dream to go to that spelling bee?" Actually, it had been my dream, but I didn't tell her that. I told her no, and she agreed to let me skip it.

"I do love nursing," I said slowly.

"That's good."

"My question is . . . how do I get them this apartment? Do you know anyone who can help me get them into public housing?"

"One of the women in the Links is on the board of the new Dixie Court development. You want me to talk to her?"

"Could you?" I moved to touch her. She seemed to sense the movement on my part because she stepped to the side and grabbed a brush.

"Remind me tomorrow. I'm so forgetful these days."

"Okay, Mama, I will."

I watched her work. I wanted to spend just a few moments longer with her. Even distracted, Mama had presence. Being around her was like standing in the glow of a candle. "I like that yellow."

She looked over at the canvas. "Yes, it did come out nice, didn't it?"

TEN

The following Sunday, I finally accepted Ty's invitation and joined the Ralseys for dinner. Alicia had been over to Ty's house twice for Sunday dinner since meeting him, and even though I had been the one to suggest it, I didn't like it. Surely he wouldn't be so low-down as to date one of my friends. I hadn't told Alicia about my history with Ty, so I couldn't blame her. As I sat across from the two of them, I quietly sorted through my feelings.

Just like me and most other folks around our age in Montgomery, Ty still lived at home. More often than not, we went to college in Alabama because it had more Black campuses than any other state in the country. Talladega. Stillman. Selma. Miles. Oakwood. Tuskegee. The list went on. If we were fortunate enough to live on campus, we moved back home after we graduated or until we got a job or, sometimes, until we married. Before Ty impulsively asked me to marry him, I didn't think he would ever settle down. He struck me as the kind of man to live with his parents for as long as he could.

Ty and his family lived in a three-bedroom bungalow filled with plants jammed into every conceivable space. The foliage turned the inside of the house into a garden, and Mr. Ralsey liked to walk around with a pair of scissors, snipping off dead leaves. In the middle of a conversation, he would reach over and poke his finger into the soil of the nearest pot. But it was Mrs. Ralsey who had the insatiable plant habit. Long after space had run out, she would come home on a Sunday with one more, searching for a shelf or table or counter where she could place it. When the time was right, Ty would take the plant out to the backyard and check to see if its roots had grown too big for the pot. He especially loved saving plants that looked like they were about to die. Ty was as tender with those plants as everyone else in his family.

Ty and I were both only children, and because we were born the same year, we had grown up together. I could remember him coming into my room once when we were around eleven years old to ask me if I knew the difference between a monocot and a dicot. I accused him of repeating words out of the encyclopedia in order to sound smart, and he got angry and called me a pickaninny. I stomped his toe and he ran off to tell his mama on me.

"Well, it's so good to finally see you, Civil. I was beginning to worry you and Ty had a falling-out or something," Mrs. Ralsey said to me after dinner.

I smiled nervously and glanced at Ty, wondering if he had told his parents we'd dated last year. Even if he hadn't, Mrs. Ralsey might have figured it out. The woman was sharp as a tack. She was the only Black woman in town who had founded her own law firm. A few years before, her husband had left his job and joined her. At one time before Ty and I were born, Montgomery had only a few Black lawyers, and the Ralseys had been two of them.

It wasn't just the plant hobby and her legal profession that made Mrs. Ralsey interesting. The woman was a cook among cooks. I am not playing with you when I say this woman could burn. She was so unlike my mother, who if anyone ever said she could burn, meant it literally.

"Let me get the dessert." I jumped out of my chair before she could say anything else. Ty followed me into the kitchen.

I set a stack of bowls on the counter while Ty took the banana pudding from the refrigerator. Ty was the type to eat his pie with a spoon and his pudding with a fork. Scrape off the meringue. Pick the pecans off his pecan pie. Watching him, I suddenly wished I had not accepted Mrs. Ralsey's dinner invitation. I gripped the edge of the counter to steady myself, but even the smooth fatness of my own hand reminded me of a baby's knuckles.

In nursing school, I took comfort in my books. For the first two years, I didn't date, and no one expressed any interest. I was not sure why no one asked me out. I knew a lot of them preferred light-skinned women, and I was on the darker side. I had my daddy's nose, and that was what you might call an acquired taste. But I had some prized attributes as well. Heavyset with a cushiony tube around my middle, I had an attractive face—straight teeth, skin smooth enough not to require makeup—and big, pretty legs.

Three close friends of mine lived in my dorm, but by our third year they all had boyfriends and no time for me. That was right around the time Ty started visiting his fraternity brothers at Tuskegee on weekends. I danced with him at a party one night, and he kissed me in the darkness. It was the most natural kiss I'd ever had. Even though our relationship had been marked by sibling-like squabbles, when we finally did turn that corner into romance, it was easy. Maybe it was because we knew each other so well. He was a part of me and always had been. By spring semester of my senior year, I was pregnant.

"What do you think about Alicia?" I said suddenly.

"Why you ask me that?"

"Just wondering."

"I see why you like her," he said. "She's got a good heart."

"Yeah, she's cool." I had been the one to break things off with

Ty, so I knew it shouldn't matter to me what he thought about Alicia.

"Civil, we need to talk."

"About what?"

He leaned against the counter. "You know about what."

"What's there to talk about?" I folded my arms across my chest.

He unhooked my hand and pulled me to him. "Have you told anybody?"

"Have you?"

"No."

"Good, cause there's nothing to tell."

"That's not true and you know it."

"I don't want to talk about this right now." I pulled away and yanked open the drawer. The silverware clattered.

"Alright, alright, suit yourself." He backed off but was still looking at me seriously. "You know you can talk to me about other stuff, too."

"Yeah, like what?"

"Like Alicia told me how shaken up you were about giving a shot to those kids."

"She told you that?" For someone agonizing over keeping her mama's secret, Alicia sure did have a big mouth.

"Yeah, those drugs y'all using, Civil, they're not safe."

"You mean the Depo-Provera?"

"Yes. We don't know enough about that drug. It could be harming all your patients, let alone those little girls."

"What do you of all people know about birth control? You never acted like you knew anything about it." Every time I looked into Ty's face I wondered if our baby would have resembled him, if it would have been a boy or a girl, if he would have made a good father.

"That's not fair and you know it. Besides, I thought you didn't want to talk about it."

64

"I don't."

"Listen, I found out that Depo hasn't been approved by the Food and Drug Administration," he said.

"That's not true," I said defensively.

"It is true."

"How do you know?"

"I looked it up and read about it."

"You don't read."

"You don't know what I do." He took the forks from me and set them down on the counter. "Civil, I'm not that little boy who used to tie your shoelaces together. I'm a man."

"I know that."

"Well, then stop talking to me like that."

Ty just didn't understand. I wanted so badly to reach for him, to hold him, but I couldn't bring myself to cross that bridge. The hurt was still too fresh.

"Alicia already told you the teenage pregnancy rate in Montgomery. We can't turn our backs on this problem and pretend it doesn't exist." I shook the spoon, the pudding landing in the bowl like a cloud. I could tell the pudding had been in the refrigerator overnight because the cookies had softened.

Ty scooted a clean bowl toward me. "Think about it, Civ. What if those drugs are doing more harm than good?"

I couldn't believe Alicia hadn't mentioned to me they were looking into this. If she and Ty had talked about Depo not being safe, then weeks had passed by without her so much as bringing it up. I tried to hide my embarrassment that I did not know it had not been approved by the government. That was news to me.

"There's nothing that says it's harmful. Some of the patients at the clinic have been getting shots for years. If there had been side effects, we would have known about it." I remembered that Erica had told me she bled every day. It was normal, according to the materials, to experience some irregular bleeding. But bleeding every day? Was it heavy? Was she cramping, too? I hadn't even asked. As her nurse, I should have asked more questions.

"You don't know the long-term effects," he said.

"It's not that complicated a drug. It just suppresses ovulation so that—"

"Since when are you a pharmaceutical expert?"

"Depo-Provera is not that complicated, Ty." I spooned extra pudding into all five bowls so we wouldn't have to come back into the kitchen for seconds. Then I followed him through the swinging door.

Mr. Ralsey's cigarette smoke filled the dining room and someone had turned on the radio. WRMA played gospel on Sundays, and somebody with a voice was singing "Just Another Day." I knew the song well, but at that moment, I could barely hear the words. I was trying to digest what Ty had just told me.

"What are you two over there whispering about?" Ty placed the pudding on the table.

"You," Alicia said, and Mrs. Ralsey laughed.

I sank into a chair.

Mrs. Ralsey spooned pudding into her mouth. "Civil, did Ty tell you he was the graduation speaker for his class?"

"No, ma'am."

"In the course of the speech, he tried to be respectful to the college president, Dr. Barnes. But he kept calling the man Dr. Bailey. At first, we didn't know who he was talking about. We figured he was talking about some professor. But then . . ." She chuckled. "Ty calls the man up to the podium. He turns around in this serious voice and say, *Dr. Bailey, I want to present this gift to you in appreciation of everything you've done for our class this year* and by this time you can hear the whispering in the crowd. Everybody was about to bust out laughing, but Dr. Barnes didn't seem to mind that the

name was wrong. You best believe he came right up to that podium and took that gold pen Ty handed him."

"Huh," I said.

"Mrs. Ralsey, this banana pudding sure is good," Alicia said.
"Tastes like my grandma pudding."

"Thank you, Alicia."

The pudding tasted bland on my tongue. I looked over at Alicia. She and I hadn't discussed the Williams girls since I first confided in her at the diner, and now she had been running around
with Ty behind my back doing some kind of investigation.

"Mrs. Ralsey?" I turned to Ty's mama. "Do you know anything about the drug Depo-Provera?"

"Depo what, baby?"

"Depo-Provera. It's the birth control drug we give to some of
the patients at the clinic. An injection that suppresses ovulation for
three months."

"No, I can't say I've ever heard of it. Why?"

"I was just telling Civil that I read up on it," Ty interjected.
"And I discussed it with one of my old professors. His brother
works in Washington, DC, for the federal government. They're
still doing trials on that drug. I don't think it's safe, but they're using it over at the clinic."

"If it weren't safe, Ty, they wouldn't be injecting people with
it." Mrs. Ralsey placed two elbows on the table.

"Unless you're poor and Black. You know how they did those
men at Tuskegee."

Mrs. Ralsey's face turned serious. All of us had been stunned by
the revelations about the experiments on men at Tuskegee. Even
though the study went on for forty years, none of us knew anything
about it before the summer of 1972. It was unthinkable to us that
they left hundreds of men untreated, letting them die long after
penicillin was available.

"Ty, what are you saying?" Mrs. Ralsey asked.

Mr. Ralsey appeared in the archway that separated the living and dining rooms, a stub of a cigarette dangling from his fingers. "What's this?"

"Ty is saying that the birth control drug they're using over at the family planning clinic is dangerous," his wife answered.

"The clinical studies suggest it causes cancer," Ty said.

"In humans?" his father asked.

"Mice. Monkeys. The studies began five years ago. And the FDA rejected its approval."

"Well it's not unheard of for unapproved drugs to be prescribed for certain uses. Civil, are your patients aware of the risks of the drug?" Mrs. Ralsey looked at me.

"I think so. I mean, I guess."

"Are they given something to read and sign about the risks and side effects?"

I tried to think of the women who had been given their first shots since I started. Yes, we had given them documents to sign, but Mrs. Seager had coached us to summarize the document. *Just standard language. Nothing alarming.* The women I'd seen had not actually read the document. They had only listened to me speak, trusted that I had correctly translated the block of letters on the page. Even the literate ones didn't read the forms before signing.

"Well, I've been thinking," Alicia said slowly, "even if the drug does cause cancer, it doesn't overtake our concerns right now. It would take a long time for cancer to show up. That's far off in the future. But a baby could happen any day now."

That was probably why Alicia hadn't mentioned it to me. She thought pregnancy was a more pressing concern and was convinced we were still doing important work.

"Alicia, that argument doesn't make sense." Ty shook his head. "You can't have a baby if you dead."

Mr. Ralsey, who had been listening quietly, spoke. "Ty's right. If it's true that these drugs carry serious risk, then you are essentially experimenting on those women the same way they experimented on those men in Macon County."

Not just women. Girls. I swallowed. I had tried to forget that I'd given India Williams a shot, hoped that it would just pass quietly through her system until it wore off. Then I'd tried to get them into an apartment to make up for my mistake. But cancer? Ty had to be wrong. Maybe they had altered the medication into a better formula since that study. The clinical studies were on animals, not humans.

Majoring in biology didn't mean Ty knew everything. Mrs. Seager had years of experience. She was strict with us nurses, but she would never intentionally harm her patients. She was there to help, just like all of us. All we had to do was talk to her and clear up this misunderstanding.

"I'll wash up the dishes, Mrs. Ralsey." I collected the plates, my mind already occupied by how I was going to gather the nerve to ask Mrs. Seager about this.

ELEVEN

Ty and Alicia had dropped a bomb on me at Sunday dinner, and I couldn't stop thinking about it. I couldn't talk to Mrs. Seager before getting more information, and I didn't like feeling like Alicia and Ty were researching this without me. So I called them that week and asked both of them to ride up to Tuskegee with me. The following weekend we all drove up to meet with Miss Pope, the university librarian. I had first encountered Miss Pope when she cornered me in the library and stuck a copy of Stokely Carmichael's book *Black Power* in my hand. *Let me know when you finish it,* she'd said, as if I did not have a choice in the matter. Later, I discussed his arguments with her over cups of Sanka in her office, both of us agreeing that Carmichael didn't acknowledge women enough in his analysis. Even though she would never have used such a term, Miss Pope was the first feminist intellectual I ever met.

She was also the one who helped me when I found out I was pregnant. When I told her I didn't plan to carry the pregnancy to term, she sat me down in her office and asked me if I had prayed on it. We talked about it for over half an hour, but when she saw I was resolute, she told me about a woman she had heard about over in the next county who was known for her safe abortions. She offered to drive me there when I was ready. On the day of the procedure, I paid one hundred dollars, and Miss Pope sat in the woman's living room with a Bible in her lap and waited while I lay on a bed in the woman's back room. Afterward, Miss Pope took me back to her house, where I stayed for the next week. She kept my secret with the grace of an angel, never asking me for details, never inquiring about the father's name.

Ty knew Miss Pope had helped me, but he promised not to say anything to her about it. On the drive up, he was unusually quiet. We entered the campus, winding around the drive. To our left, what we called "the valley" had turned a brilliant spring green, and I remembered the first time Daddy had brought me to visit, the rush of feeling I'd had for the history there, the stateliness of its brick buildings, the angled roof of the chapel. The fall advisory had been under way and I had watched young women in skirts, their hair straightened and pinned, books cradled in their arms. I could not take my eyes off them.

Ty parked in front of the library, and the three of us went through the main door. The automatic library lights turned on with a loud *click* as we passed through the stacks. The atmosphere of Tuskegee's library was serious, just like Miss Pope. You did not go in there to play around with your friends. When you asked her to help with a last-minute paper, she would do so, but not without a lecture on how the work suffered when you waited until the night before your assignment was due; and by the way, when you were finished with your paper you could shelve the books in that there pile. During my years at Tuskegee, however, I learned there was more to the woman than her tough exterior. Miss Pope lived a rich life—when she wasn't working or attending Bible study, she traveled the country by car. She had never married; she and her sister had visited thirty-two of the fifty states, no small feat for two Negro women traveling alone.

"When you called me and told me what you were looking for, I took the liberty of pulling some files you might find interesting. You didn't give me much time, calling me like I didn't have nothing to do this weekend."

"Thank you, Miss Pope, for taking time out of your day," I said. "We brought you this nice plant for your desk."

We had taken one of the houseplants from Ty's house to offer as a thank-you gift. It was not one that Ty's mother would mourn—like any good garden mother, she had her favorites. Ty had put it in a ceramic pot with bright stones set into the clay. The pot was so nice, I had a feeling Ty was also thanking her for being there for us the year before.

She took the plant and pointed a finger at some chairs that someone had moved out of place. "Young man, move those chairs back to that table over there. I don't know who's been moving my chairs around."

"Yes, ma'am." Ty stared at her for a moment before jumping into action.

Alicia covered her teeth. I tried not to look at Alicia because I didn't want to laugh. Miss Pope might not help us if she thought we were sassing her.

The librarian's eyes grazed over Alicia's dress. "You work at the same clinic as Civil?"

"Yes, ma'am."

Even though it was Saturday, we had worn our uniforms because I knew Miss Pope would like it. She was always proud to see graduates in their professional work attire. I'd once met the first Black policeman from Birmingham in Miss Pope's office. A Tuskegee graduate. She was so proud of him that she nearly tripped over his feet. As much as Miss Pope loved the work of activists like Jo Ann Robinson and Mary Fair Burks, she believed just as strongly in economic uplift. We could not effect change if we were hungry.

"After all that, they cut their bodies open?" Ty's voice rose. I placed a hand on his arm. He was leaning back in his chair as if his own body were being split open.

"How did they get the men to participate in the study in the first place?" I pressed her. There would be time for outrage later.

"Oh, they would give them free meals, free transportation; that sort of thing. You got to understand, a lot of these men never even been up on this campus before. So they come up here thinking they were getting first-class medical care. In the early days of the study, people were still using home remedies. Oil on a rash. Collard leaves around the head for a headache. Y'all young people don't know nothing about that."

"How did they find the men? They went out to the country?" I thought of my first drive up to the Adair farm to meet the Williams family.

Miss Pope fixed her eyes on me and Alicia. "We helped them."

"Who helped them?" Ty snapped back.

"You heard of Eunice Rivers? A Tuskegee graduate. A fine woman and smart, too. When I heard she knew about it all, I nearly fell out my chair."

"A Black woman?" I asked.

Miss Pope continued. "It's likely she thought she was doing good. Syphilis was a serious illness, and these white folks came down here saying they wanted to find a cure and Tuskegee could play a role in helping them find it. I believe she trusted the federal government."

"For forty years, Miss Pope?" I was incredulous.

The lights clicked off, and no one moved. The light over the main desk remained on, but we sat watching one another in the semidarkness. Ty sat stiffly in the chair, his hands spread out on the table in front of him. Alicia's face looked old.

"But penicillin was available after the war. Why didn't they start to treat them?" I asked.

"Read the papers." Miss Pope tapped a finger on the stacks. She leaned forward. "Because they were studying what would happen if the disease was left untreated."

We all sat there quietly. There was nothing any of us could say. I felt something unbearable wash over me, and a gray fog shrouded my eyes.

Miss Pope whispered, "Now, you know how some white folks feel about Black bodies. They think we can tolerate pain better than them. According to some of these documents I'm about to show you, some of them even thought syphilis couldn't kill us. It was as much an experiment about the effects of the disease as it was a crazy white man's idea of a laboratory game with Black bodies."

I wasn't sure what Alicia and Ty were thinking, but I was thinking about the families. The wives. The children. We had only just heard about this experiment the summer before, and though it had been the conversation at many Black folks' dinner tables in Montgomery, most of my community had not personally known any of the victims. I had already graduated and left Tuskegee when the story broke over the summer of 1972. So I had not had a chance to digest what it meant to our little community on campus.

Now I could not bear to think my next thought: The federal government could not possibly be doing the same thing with Depo and Black women.

"You worked here," I said. "I don't mean any disrespect, Miss Pope, but how could you not know?"

Miss Pope opened the top folder on her stack. "Baby, I keep asking myself the same question. How could it be happening right up under my feet? But once I learned about the study, I started collecting everything I could find about it. Y'all should start with this. It's an underground newsletter that was circulating around Washington, DC, a few years back. A Black statistician by the name of

Bill Jenkins found out about the study and tried to ring the alarm. You know why nobody listened?"

"Why?" I whispered.

"Because even though regular folks didn't know, the medical folks knew. In some respects, the government did this in plain sight. They were publishing articles in medical journals about it and everything. Either they didn't see what was wrong with it, or nobody cared about poor colored folks down in Alabama."

"Or they thought they were doing good," I said.

Alicia put a knuckle to her eye. Ty was still, his silhouette so dark I could not make out his face.

Miss Pope pushed the stack of materials toward us. "Stay as long as you like. I already had my dinner."

TWELVE

Jackson
2016

Of all the movement stories that haunt me to this day, Medgar Evers's murder is right up there. I have never driven through Jackson without picturing his bloody body lying in the driveway, his wife and children crouched in terror on the bathroom floor. I remember seeing him on television and thinking him courageous and charismatic. I was thirteen years old when he died, and the news marked a line into adulthood for me. If you lived in the Deep South in the 1960s, you had very few illusions about the dangers of movement work. Folks either walked right into it or stayed clear. Some just watched from the sidelines for fear of losing their jobs or worse. Even with all that we went through in Alabama, Mississippi was still its own kind of place. Nina Simone had said a mouthful when she sang "Mississippi Goddam." In that Mississippi delta with its flat swaths of farmland, Evers had marched right up to the doors of the lonely cabins sprinkled in the middle of those farms and registered voters.

I always believed the movement leaders had to be a little wild-haired. Like that fearless Fred Shuttlesworth. I swear, that man was from another world. This might surprise you, but I thought we had turned a corner by the seventies. I knew racism still existed, but I was hopeful that Black Power and education would sustain us and keep it at bay. We'd been to hell and back, so the seventies had to get better.

When I arrive in Jackson I'm not just thinking of Evers, I'm also thinking of Fannie Lou Hamer and her use of the phrase *Mississippi Appendectomy*. I didn't even learn about that phrase until I got to medical school and was under the mentorship of a Black female. As soon as I heard it, I felt a sharp pain in my body. Hamer had been sterilized without her permission in 1961, and the procedure was so common, women had labeled it. I wish I'd known about that term when I was your age, Anne. I wish they'd taught us that in nursing classes at Tuskegee. Maybe it might have changed some things.

I've been on the road since 6:30 A.M. and I need caffeine, but I'm so eager to see Alicia that I don't stop for coffee. I find her community not far from the shopping plaza, a redbrick entry sign bearing the words *Riverwood Plantation*. I wonder if the plantation fantasy bothers Alicia or if she thinks about it at all.

The houses in Riverwood Plantation are newer construction brick homes. Alicia's house is the fourth on the right. Three cars and a van are parked in the semicircular driveway. Alicia's husband owns a body repair shop. They have three grown children—all boys, all married, all college graduates. Two from Mississippi State. One from Tougaloo. Six grandchildren. Husband is on the deacon board, Alicia a missionary. The Southern American dream.

When Alicia ended her nursing career after having children, I was not surprised. A lot of Black women in the South had that dream of becoming a housewife back then. We called it "sitting down." Alicia had always been traditional, and she'd dreamed about having her own family. My upbringing was different. Mama had never worked, so I had been raised knowing that I wanted a career.

I ring the doorbell, but Alicia opens so quickly she must have been watching through the window. I'm punctual, if not a couple of minutes early. The first thing I notice is that her eyebrows are still penciled—dark and perfect. Before I can get a really good look at her, she envelops me in a red flowered housedress and citrusy scent. "Lord, it's really you," she says breathlessly. "Ooh, girl, you lost all that weight. You feel like a feather."

The hug is tight and I release into it, unprepared for her warmth. She pulls me by the hand into a great room with a vaulted ceiling. The furniture is covered in florals. The draperies, too. Above a fireplace filled with artificial flowers hangs a flat-screen television. A white toy poodle looks up from the couch.

"That's Coco. She's seventeen years old and don't get up and come to the door much anymore."

"I didn't know you had a dog," is all I can think to say. I start to tell her about my rescue dog but think it might sound forced, so I remain quiet. We sit next to each other on the couch, and from my end I can see into the kitchen. The counters are covered in clutter. I look back at Alicia. She's observing me checking out her house.

"I wonder what your house looks like, too," she says.

"A three-bedroom bungalow in midtown Memphis. It has a nice porch. A garden out back. That's all I need for me, Anne, and Mama."

"How's your mama?"

"Mama doing alright. After Daddy died, I moved her to Memphis to live with me. She and Aunt Ros can visit each other more now."

"My mama live not too far from here with that old buzzard."

From the few check-ins we'd had over the years, I know that Alicia's mama, after a twenty-year affair, had finally divorced her daddy and married the pastor. "You still haven't forgiven them?"

Alicia purses her lips. "I forgive but don't forget. Daddy is much more generous than I am. He married a retired schoolteacher. They moved to Florida."

"Good for him," I say.

"How's Anne?"

"Just graduated. Majored in anthropology. You know kids these days. Girl, they major in things for fun."

She laughs, big and genuine. "I told my boys I didn't care what they majored in as long as they came home and worked for their daddy."

"Your boys doing alright?" I say, though I'm thinking that is terrible parenting. It brings back my own indecision about the medical field, largely brought on by Daddy's pressuring. I try to focus. It was always easy to judge Alicia.

"They fine. My son supposed to be here in a minute. He bringing us some fried catfish from over at the restaurant his wife manages. I figured after driving you'd be hungry. You eat yet?"

"No, but fried catfish for breakfast, Alicia?"

"What's wrong with that? Fried fish and grits for breakfast is still a good way to start the day."

"Girl."

"Uh-oh. Here we go. May I have your attention, please? Dr. Townsend is in the building."

We laugh and the ice thaws. When her son drops off the food, he doesn't come inside, and I'm grateful we are left to ourselves. I start setting the breakfast room table.

"Girl, this fish is alright," I say, once we're seated. It is really good.

"Told you."

When we're done, Alicia leans back in her chair and pats her mouth with a napkin. Her lipstick is smudged across her chin. I don't wear makeup anymore, so I don't have to worry about such things. The only thing I'm fastidious about these days is my diet.

"I hear India came home from the hospital yesterday," she says, turning the conversation abruptly.

"What's her diagnosis?"

"Cancer."

"Cancer," I repeat softly. "How bad is it?"

"I don't know. She's getting treatment."

I press down the guilt. I have let too many years pass.

"I've been waiting to ask you, Civil: Do you think the cancer has to do with those Depo shots she got?" She speaks softly, as if it is a secret.

I shake my head. "It's not likely just from two shots. At least, I don't think so."

Alicia stands and begins to put the dishes in the sink. I open the dishwasher, and she turns on the water. She rinses, and I load. After we are done, she makes a pot of coffee. We settle in her living room on the sofa with our big mugs. Hers reads *I Am Black History*. Mine is blank. "Why did you disappear, Civil?"

"I went to med school." I know I sound a little defensive; it's instinct.

"They got telephones at Meharry?"

"Come on, Alicia. You know the commitment."

"You did the very thing you said you never was going to do."

What is she talking about? Hold on to my sanity? Try not to mess up things worse than I already had?

"Did you ever contact that green-eyed daddy of theirs? I know you had a crush on him."

Of course I had never contacted Mace. Surely she knows that. She just wants to torture me a little, and I deserve it. I cannot explain to her why I had to put distance between myself and Montgomery. I don't know how to say that without sounding selfish. I'm ashamed that I walked out on our friendship, but I also know that if I had to do it all over again I would make the same decision.

"I'm sorry I didn't do better, Alicia."

She waves my words off. "Save the apology tour." Then she leans forward. "Wait, is that what this is? An apology tour?"

"No, of course not."

"Honey, you might be making this trip to get some closure, but saying I'm sorry to everybody will not give it to you."

"I don't know what you mean."

"Yes, you do. What are your questions, Civil? What do you need answered?"

"You sound like my aunt Ros."

She doesn't say anything, her face steady and even. Suddenly, I get a sense of the older Alicia. The power between us is not the same as it used to be. I have underestimated the weight of forty years.

"I envy you. This house. This life you've made. I suppose I've spent my whole career trying to rectify that wrong."

"Why is that your responsibility, Civil?"

"You know why."

"You damn near seventy years old. There is no need for you to carry around all this baggage."

"You call what happened to those girls *baggage*?"

"Everybody has learned to live with what happened. Why can't you?"

"I just can't."

"Why not?"

"Because I keep asking myself, Did I do enough? Did we do enough? *Were we right?*"

Alicia folds her arms and leans back. "You're a doctor, Civil

Townsend. And from what I read online, you're a good one. So you ought to know good and well where those kinds of questions will lead you."

"You haven't answered my question."

She just looks at me. I want to ask her to come with me because no one understands the way she does. But I don't say anything.

THIRTEEN

Montgomery
1973

After I learned more about what had happened at Tuskegee and read through Miss Pope's materials, I became even more concerned that I might be wading in the same harmful waters Eunice Rivers had. I needed some reassurances this wasn't the same thing. Did Mrs. Seager know about the dangers of the drug, and were there other underage patients on it? Was she recording the experiences of patients on Depo? The only place I knew where I might get straight answers was in the patient files. I tried to volunteer to close up the clinic on Monday, but Mrs. Seager had already assigned the task to two other nurses. I was going to have to snoop around while the clinic was still open.

Mrs. Seager stored all of the patient files in a cabinet in her office. The nurse-receptionist, usually Lori, was in charge of retrieving the correct file from Mrs. Seager's office when a regular patient arrived. She was the only one allowed access. Searching Mrs. Seager's office while she was in the other room was nothing short of a suicide mission, but there was no getting around it.

There were a few things I already knew. For example, not all of our patients received Depo-Provera shots. A number of them used oral contraceptives, which they picked up each month. We prescribed drugs for sexually transmitted diseases, urinary tract and yeast infections. We also performed cervical exams. First, I would have to pick through the files to find the patients who were being given Depo-Provera. That was going to be difficult. The second challenge was to find Mrs. Seager's notes. Surely she had some kind of journal or book where she had written down general thoughts. My daddy kept a medical journal, so I assumed Mrs. Seager did, too.

Mrs. Seager had been head of medical records at Professional Hospital before coming to the clinic, and she had once boasted to us during training that she hadn't lost a file in over twenty years. I had never looked in her cabinet before, and I figured it would probably be locked. She was a locked-cabinet kind of woman. I was not wrong about that, but I didn't expect to find the key so easily— beneath the porcelain bell on her desk.

I could hear her speaking in the room next door. She was trying to convince a woman with six children to have a tubal ligation. Mrs. Seager had been working on this woman for months, and one of the nurses, Fiona, had remarked just this morning that every time the woman came in, Mrs. Seager spent at least thirty minutes talking to her about the benefits of getting her tubes tied. Lori thought the whole thing was sad because one day the mother had brought all six children into the clinic with her and they looked hungry, so Lori had given them her lunch to split among themselves. Of course, it was barely enough.

I could hear Mrs. Seager's every word through the thin walls.

If you have this surgery, you won't have to worry about birth control anymore. You could just spend time with the children you already have.

I hear you, but God promised me a husband. And what if I want to have a baby with my husband?

But you have six children already. Ain't that enough for any husband?

Last I checked, there were no patients out front. Among the

nurses, only Lori remained. I'd just seen her in the break room heating the water kettle. She'd be a few more minutes, at least.

The key turned easily. I stuck my fingernail between two folders, sliding one out and marking the next one out so I'd know where to return it. Mary. Age 13. Depo-Provera shots administered 01/05/72, 04/06/72. Patsy. Age 16. Depo-Provera. IUD. Yolanda. Age 14. Epileptic. Depo. I flipped through more files, searching for parental signatures and consent forms. Based on the addresses, most of the patients lived right there in the neighborhood surrounding the clinic. A few lived out in the country, maybe not too far from the Williamses, or in Clayton Alley.

At the bottom of the charts, nurses had made the kinds of notes we were trained to write down: patient complains of excessive bleeding; patient is amenorrheic; patient complains of headaches; patient experiencing abdominal cramps; patient has vaginal discharge; patient tolerates medication well—no side effects.

One of the nurses—it was the same big scrawl—punctuated her notes with exclamation points: patient late for injection! Patient does not understand reason for the shot! Patient swollen at injection site! She had not signed her initials on the chart. We were supposed to initial and date our notes.

How I'm supposed to work? Who going to watch my kids? My mama ain't able.

That's no excuse, Mrs. Seager was saying.

There were other notes that were not so clear: confused but comfortable, robust constitution with signs of fatigue, poor comprehension, poor candidate for oral contraceptives, unfit.

Unfit? Our patients were mostly young, poor, uneducated. But that just underscored the importance of our work. They needed us.

After the procedure, you can take pills that will help with the pain. Please. Just sign this form and I can get the process started.

My hand hovered over the drawer. What exactly did she mean by unfit?

Is it forever? I mean, if I get this done can I change it later?

Yes, of course you can. They can do a reversal procedure. It's easy. Just sign here.

I wasn't finding any evidence of a government conspiracy, at least not in the files. Maybe Mrs. Seager was just doing her job. Besides, Depo-Provera was being administered all over the country, not just here. This wasn't the same as Tuskegee.

There, there. Don't cry. You've made the right decision.

I pushed the file back into its proper place and closed the drawer. It creaked as I turned the key.

Sign right here. Mmm-hmm. Yes, I will come to pick you up and take you to the hospital myself. Don't worry.

Abruptly, I heard the exam room door open.

I wasn't going to make it out in time. *Think fast, Civil.* I could sit in the chair and pretend I was waiting for her. I put the key back where I'd found it, then cracked open the office door and peeked out. She was holding on to the exam room doorknob, her back to me. I slipped out of her office. Two steps left and it was as if I'd been walking down the hall. She turned to look at me, her eyes suspicious for a fleeting moment.

"Civil, I need you to run this sample over to the lab since you don't seem to have anything else to do. Can you do that for me, please?"

"Yes, ma'am."

I hoped the files I'd touched weren't sticking out. I'd moved so quickly, I couldn't remember if I'd replaced them perfectly.

I turned around. "Mrs. Seager?"

"Yes?"

"I— One of my patients, one of the girls I visited at their home. You see, I wanted to ask you about her."

"Yes?"

I spoke quickly before I lost my nerve. "She's just eleven years old, Mrs. Seager. And I discovered that she hasn't even had her first cycle yet. I didn't learn this until after I'd given her the shot. Surely the nurse before me made a mistake. I didn't see a note in the file."

She didn't say anything, and I waited. I realized I hadn't asked her a question, so I said, "I've marked her chart. I won't give it to her again."

"Keep a close eye on her, Civil. Do not let that girl slip through the cracks. She will start her cycle soon enough, and you need to be right there to protect her."

"Yes, ma'am," I squeaked.

She got close to me and spoke softly, as if concerned her patient would overhear. "Civil, you understand we have to work together to help these people. We are working for the common good. They need us. We are like . . . God's guiding hand." She inhaled sharply, then exhaled through her nose.

"Yes, ma'am."

Once I was in my car, I let out a long breath. Mrs. Seager assumed that India and Erica were sexually active or would be soon. Had I assumed that, too? I realized that I had. I started to cry, but then I quickly wiped my tears. I did not have time for tears. I had to act quickly if I was going to figure this all out.

Ty had given me a piece of paper. I took it out of my purse and unfolded it. Rhesus monkeys. Beagles. Different species, yes, but uterine cancer had shown up in both. I read the words again. I'd read them over and over the night before. Upjohn Pharmaceuticals. Dr. Harold Upjohn. The drug had first been marketed in 1960 in the United States for threatened and habitual miscarriage. And for endometriosis, a painful pelvic disorder. Upjohn was the head doctor at this pharmaceutical company. The monkeys and dogs were different species, he'd argued, so it didn't mean the same thing would happen in humans.

But they couldn't know for sure. Mrs. Seager might not even be in on it. It was entirely possible the federal government was using our patients as if they were the subjects of a live clinical trial, the same thing they'd done to those men at Tuskegee. If the drugs were dangerous, it could be years before we knew if they'd caused cancer. By then it would be too late to connect their illness to Depo. They'd be too old or maybe even dead. Could we trust the government? Hell, I worked for the government. Who was I fooling? I wanted to talk to my daddy, but I was afraid he would tell me to quit the clinic before I could investigate further. I could talk to Alicia. She'd heard it the same as I had. I needed to know if we were injecting poison into our patients.

Poverty motivated a lot of the city's crime. Despair. Racism. Lack of opportunity. We weren't just helping these families. We were doing community work. Better to step in before things got worse. By giving the patients birth control, we were saving them from more dire choices. Mrs. Seager was right to be concerned.

I thought of India and Erica, their freshly washed hair and new clothes. I thought of how much they'd enjoyed listening to my records and how they'd marveled at the needle on the vinyl and the sound it made spinning in the groove.

FOURTEEN

I was listening to Booker T. and the M.G.'s' "Behave Yourself" when Mama came into my room. I still had six more weeks before Erica was due for another shot, but each day that a woman anywhere was being injected with that drug made my head hurt. I didn't know what to do.

Mama bounced her head, and I remembered how she used to dance. Not this kind of melancholy small movement she was doing now, but arm-swinging, hip-shaking dances. Back when I was younger, Mama danced all the time. I remember waking up at night hearing her feet moving on the floor in the den and Daddy slapping the armrest as he whistled.

I noticed a piece of white paper dangling from her hand. It had been creased into a trifold, as if it were taken from an envelope.

"Some years back, your daddy and I went to see Booker T. and the M.G.'s perform at the Coliseum in Memphis. We stayed at your aunt Ros's house, but none of us slept. We partied and stayed up all night. The drummer's name was Al Jackson Jr. He hung out with us that night after the concert. Ros knew them all."

"Lord, Mama. You never told me that. Where was I?"

"You were away at vacation Bible school."

"So y'all partied while I was getting saved." I laughed.

I wanted my parents to dance again, to smoke reefer and curse and act like young people. Surely they had earned the carelessness of success. I wanted them to enjoy it.

Mama looked past me at the painting on my wall, a monochromatic green study of a woman walking into a fire. It was one of the few representational works I could remember Mama ever painting. I'd always been drawn to it, and when I'd found it in the back of her storage closet she had let me have it with a shrug. Now she was looking at it as if she were reassessing it, her small mouth puckered in concentration. I stared at her in admiration. I'd always viewed Mama's beauty as so ethereal that it was the kind you didn't pass on to children. Her face was chiseled, the skin stretched thin over sharp bones. She was wispy, ghostlike.

"What's that paper?"

"Huh? Oh, I almost forgot. It's for you."

I started, realizing what it might be. I scanned the words—*We invite your application for a subsidized three-bedroom apartment at Dixie Court. Pending approval.* I reached out to hug her. She stepped back so quickly that I almost lost my balance.

"So what does this mean?"

"I saw those girls when you brought them home. Such sadness in their faces. They lost their mama, right?"

She'd barely acknowledged them, and I had not expected her to follow through. It was never clear how much Mama took in. The girls had been so pretty that day, but I'd imagine they still looked pitiful through the eyes of someone who hadn't witnessed their state before the baths and clothes. I'd cut their hair as evenly as I could, but acne covered Erica's face and India's lips were cracked and peeling.

"How did you do this? It's been barely a month."

"This letter just means they're on the priority list. They still got to be approved. I told you my friend Delia is on the board. She merely expedited the application process."

"So I don't need to contact a social worker?"

She shook her head.

"Oh, Mama, that's fine! I've got to go tell them." I took off my sweatpants and stepped into a skirt. Between the packed hanging clothes in my closet I managed to find a barely wrinkled shirt. It was Saturday, and I had never visited the Williamses on a weekend. I needed to look respectable but also practical enough to withstand the dirt of that hill.

"Do they have furniture and dishes and such?"

"Do they have what?"

"Things to furnish the apartment in case they get it. I can't imagine whatever they've got out in that shack will be any good," she said.

I stooped to search for my penny loafers on the floor of the closet.

"Take this."

"What's that?" I straightened up.

"Go over to the Goodwill and see what they got that's nice. Don't get anything that's just as bad as what they have now. Look for some stuff that matches as best as you can. If you get a sofa, make sure to sit on it before you buy it."

She opened her palm and revealed a square of folded bills.

"Mama, you don't have to do this. I do have a job."

"I know you do."

"And I hadn't planned on buying them things. Their daddy. He—"

She tucked the money into the purse hanging from my desk chair. "I understand. They got a daddy. Just figure out a way to do it without shaming him."

"Thank you, Mama." I tucked my shirt in.

Mama touched her hair and grimaced as if there were an unreachable pain hidden in her body. "Get Ty and some of his friends to move that furniture from Goodwill."

With that, she was gone. I hesitated, then reached down to push my heel into my shoe. Ty. Always Ty. My parents thought he was untouchable. If I told them we'd been involved, they would probably blame me for the breakup. I folded the letter. I needed to get the paperwork completed. If the Williamses didn't have to sleep one more night in that awful shanty, they shouldn't. Sleeping on the floor of a new apartment was better than that sorry excuse for a house.

Mama showed her love in funny ways, and getting that apartment was the kind of gesture that reminded me of that.

FIFTEEN

When I told Mace Williams about the letter, he was not impressed. "Let's go get the application for the apartment," I said. "You don't want to lose your place on the list."

"Girl, I got to work today."

"You don't look like you're working to me."

"I got to be here in case the man come around here looking for me. I can't just go trotting off with some crazy woman."

"I'm not a crazy woman."

"Look crazy to me."

"Mace, go with her," said Mrs. Williams from her chair on the other side of the room. She was patching up the knee on a pair of her son's pants. By the way she fingered the needle, I could tell she needed eyeglasses. "This girl taking the time to come around here and see about you and your childrens. The least you can do is go with her and see what she talking about. I'll talk to Mr. Adair if he come around."

"Mama, we can't afford no apartment. How I'm supposed to work for Mr. Adair if I'm living way out in this Dixie Court place?"

"Mr. Adair done told you there ain't no work for you here no more. We got to get off this man place sooner or later and you know it," she said, eyeing him steadily.

"As I said, the apartment's free," I said. "At least, until you start working. They'll fix you up with a jobs agency."

"I done talked with them jobs people before. They ain't got nothing for me."

I did not think he had tried hard enough, but I didn't say that. Maybe he was just too stuck in farm life.

"Well, look, if you want to stay out here and drown in your own pity, that's fine," I snapped. "But the girls and their grandma got a right to go out there and live in this nice apartment, with or without you." Surely it was unbearable that he and the entire family had to share one room—dressing, eating, sleeping. What was wrong with the man?

Mrs. Williams laughed as she stretched the needle out in front of her. Somehow she had managed to thread it.

"Pssht," he hissed, and then moved to throw a twig on the dying fire. It was cold in the house, maybe colder than outside. April had not warmed up yet, and we were still dealing with blustery spring winds. A dog lying on a pile of clothes lifted his head and started barking at the sound of the wind rattling the door. "Get!" Mace yelled at the dog and it slowly rose, stretched its legs, and walked out. Mace kicked through the clothes, picking out a shirt. He sniffed it, snatched the stocking off his head, and pushed open the back door. Before it closed completely I could see him begin to pull his shirt over his head. I tried not to look. In a brief glimpse, I caught sight of the man's sinew, and just like his face, the skin was bronzed by the sun.

"I'll wait in my car," I said to his mother.

I wanted to know if India and Erica had kept their hair and clothes neat in the weeks since I'd seen them, but I didn't see them around. There really wasn't anywhere else for them to go. The

96

closest neighbors lived a couple of miles up the road. I turned the car around so that when Mace came out, we would be ready to drive down the hill. In the meantime I promised myself I wouldn't let him make me nervous. He came out wearing a clean enough blue shirt and holding a hairbrush in his hand as he limped to the car. At least he didn't look like he'd just stepped out of a barn. As we passed Mr. Adair's house, Mace gave a nod and two-finger wave to a white man sitting on the hood of a pickup truck. The man stared at us but did not acknowledge the greeting.

"Is that him?"

"One and the same."

"He treat you and the family alright?"

Mace didn't answer. He just stared out the window. I figured he didn't want to talk, so I said nothing. We did not have to be friends. The man thought I was a nuisance, but it didn't matter because I wasn't doing this for him. I was doing it for the girls. I held the steering wheel with one hand and the letter bearing the address, 3501 Dixie Court, in the other. The rental office hours were ten to six on Saturdays, so we had plenty of time. The car coasted down the highway. The static in the radio cleared, and Carla Thomas's voice floated out of the speakers.

"Hey," he said.

"What?"

"You know you low on gas?"

I looked down at the gas meter. I was less than low, more like about to run out. It hadn't even occurred to me to put gas in the car, I was so used to Daddy doing it. A 76 station appeared up ahead. As I slowed the car, a man in blue overalls sitting on a chair watched us.

"I'll fill it up for you," Mace said.

I dug in my purse for the money. Mace paid the man, then returned and flipped the lever on the pump.

I watched Mace in the mirror. He kept his eyes on the ticking numbers. I wondered about his late wife, if they had been teenage sweethearts.

"You ever been outside of Alabama?" he asked me when he was back in the car and we were on the road again.

"Of course."

"Like where?" he said in a tone as if he thought I was lying.

"Well, I . . ." I started to tell him what I usually told people when they asked me about my travels: that my daddy had taken me to New Orleans for my sixteenth birthday. That my aunt Ros lived in Memphis and we sometimes visited her at Christmas. That I'd driven with my daddy to Nashville for a conference once and visited Fisk, my mama's alma mater. But as soon as the words started to come out of my mouth, I stopped. Maybe it was the look on his face. Suspicious-like.

"I've been to Memphis," I said. "My aunt lives there."

"What's Memphis like?" he asked, as if it were some faraway country.

"It's on a river, just like Montgomery. Except the Mississippi is a whole lot wider than the Alabama River."

"One day I want to take my girls to the ocean. They need to lay eyes on it."

"That's easy. You drive?" Most men in Alabama learned to drive at an early age, whether it was a pickup truck or a tractor. What I was really asking was whether he had a car. I knew it was unusual for a family to have three cars, like mine did, but I was a little unsure of whether a man in his position would own even one car.

"Course I drive. My truck ain't working right now. Friend of mine working on it."

"Oh." I decided to switch back to the travel topic. "You were born here?"

He nodded. "Not too far from the Adair farm. Fact is, my

daddy worked the farm of a man named Philips for years. After he passed, Mama and me couldn't stay on in that house without working and I was too young to take care of things the way my daddy had. Soon as I was old enough, I got work on another farm. I met my wife and we lived alright for a while. We had a house that we paid rent on. But seem like after she died, nothing went right. Crops dead. Chickens dead. Everything turned to shit."

The death of his wife hung over the family like a shroud; I could tell by the way they all talked about her. I tried to change the subject again. "I hear the pickle factory out on Whitfield Road is hiring."

"I went for one of them jobs one time. They ain't hire me."

"You have to keep trying."

"How many jobs you done had?"

Well, this is my first, I wanted to say, but what did it matter? I did not get his grim pessimism. The man acted like the entire world was actively working against him. With him, it was hard to know where the system ended and the man began.

"Look, I think we're getting close. Look at that sign." There was a billboard for Dixie Court. On the sign, there was a picture of a Black woman and two young children in front of a one-story brick building. No father in the picture. I exited the highway and turned left on a street. Some of the buildings were still under construction, but there were no workers in sight. The street curved around in a U, and I followed it until I saw the sign for the rental office. I parked and we got out of the car. Mace looked around, his eyes skeptical.

A handwritten sign hanging from the rental door read: *Back in 5.*

"You say this is free?"

"Yes, until you get a job. Once you get a job, you will have to pay some rent. Not much."

"I hope you ain't got my mama's hopes up for nothing."

"May I help you?" a white lady called out to us from the sidewalk. She wore a belted yellow dress that screamed springtime even though it was chilly out. Anybody in a dress that bright had to be doing some good in the world, I decided.

"Yes, ma'am." I held out the letter. "We're here to apply for the apartment for the Williams family."

"Are you the social worker?" she asked as she took the paper from me. It struck me that the possibility had not occurred to her that Mace and I could be married.

I hesitated. "Well, not exactly. I'm their nurse, and this man's daughters are my patients."

The lady nodded and smiled. "Ah, I see. I hope they let you know we don't have any first-floor apartments available right now."

"Ma'am?"

"Is your patient in a wheelchair, dear?"

"A wheelchair?" Mace interrupted.

I shook my head. "No, ma'am. We won't be needing a first-floor apartment. I'm not that kind of nurse. But we do need the three-bedroom mentioned in this letter. Unless you have a four-bedroom available."

"No four-bedrooms, dear. I'll just get the key from inside and walk you over."

"Thank you."

As we waited, he stepped closer to me and whispered, "What that letter say?"

"The government will help you if you can't make the rent. Don't worry."

"That's easy for you to say. That shack on that farm may not look like much to you, but it's a roof."

"Mr. Williams, can I call you Mace?"

"Can I call you Sybil?"

"It's not Sybil. It's—"

"It's just a few minutes this way," the rental lady was saying as she locked the office door behind her. She walked ahead of us, her spring dress glowing in the sunlight. "My name's Mrs. Lacey. Anything y'all need, just holler. My husband marched with Dr. King in 1966. He got beat up real good one night. Didn't stop him. Didn't stop me, neither. Those Negro ministers made both of us want to do something better with our lives. That's why I work here now."

Many of the white protesters had come from out of town, but there had been some locals. Evidently she was one of them. We followed her until we reached a two-story building with cinder blocks out front. On the second floor, she unlocked the door to the apartment. The front room smelled of fresh latex paint. They had not finished installing the lighting fixtures, so stray wires hung from the ceiling. The vinyl on the floors was so new you could smell the glue. The windows still had the stickers on them from the manufacturer. The outlets did not have plates.

"I don't know when you planned to move in, but, as you can see, there are a few things to attend to."

Mace left us and walked through the apartment, moving more swiftly than I'd seen him move yet. I peeked in the kitchen. A narrow galley. Yellow appliances and more of the same linoleum floor. A kitchen window overlooked the courtyard. I imagined yellow curtains, something like the shade of Mrs. Lacey's dress.

"Are utilities included with the rent?" I asked.

"Oh yes, everything is included except a telephone. If they want a telephone, they'll have to pay for that themselves."

I smiled. It would be nice if they had a telephone so I could call and check on the girls.

Mace appeared in the doorway. "What we got to do?" he asked. I could tell from the rushed sound of his breath that he was already attaching to the place.

"You got to fill out the application. I brought it with me."

Mace took it from her, turned to the last page, and scrawled out a big X at the bottom. When he handed it back to her, she nodded awkwardly.

"I'll make sure they get it back to you, Mrs. Lacey," I said, taking it from her again.

When we were back outside, she turned to Mace. "If everything goes alright with the paperwork, you can stop by and pick up the keys. I'm in that office every day. Just holler if you need me, hear?"

She smiled warmly at us, turned on her heels, and started back toward the office.

Mace grabbed my hand. His touch surprised me. "Hey, Miss Sybil. You think maybe you could take me to see them jobs people on Monday?"

I had to work Monday, but I found myself nodding. "Course I can. But my name is Civil. With a *v*."

He just grinned.

SIXTEEN

The move took two weeks. Ty recruited two of his fraternity brothers to help him and Mace pick up the stuff from Goodwill. Alicia and I called ourselves being decorators, poring over blankets and sheets as if we were shopping for rich folks. I even walked through the farm shack, trying to sift through what could be salvaged. Mrs. Williams seemed eager to leave behind most of the old things. "Leave it," she said more often than not. The only thing she seemed to be especially attached to was her rocker. When we finished, the shack still had enough stuff in it for the next family. Even though Mr. Adair had fired Mace, we were all pretty sure he would eventually let the place out to some other family down on their luck. That was just the way things were in Alabama.

We did all that we could to spruce up the apartment at Dixie Court. Alicia lined the kitchen drawers with contact paper, carefully slicing the edges with a utility knife. Mace wired the lighting and hung the ceiling globes. I found a chandelier for the dining alcove that was missing just one of its crystals. A clean fabric sofa with a carved wooden frame. Glass coffee table. Mama painted red roses on two white end tables. We found decent-quality mattresses and frames for their beds. There was no money for headboards, but

I did find a solid wood chest of drawers. They would not have clothes all over the floor anymore. In the girls' room, two single beds. A dresser to share. A faded but clean green rug. Sheer white curtains covered in butterflies. After living in that shack for so many years, I wanted the family to be able to have company over.

Alicia and I could not find a full set of matching dishes at Goodwill, so Mama contributed a set we'd hardly ever used. She'd carefully covered each dish in newspaper so nothing would be broken in transport. When Mrs. Williams unwrapped the dishes, I could tell from the look on her face she didn't want to use them.

"They're made to eat off of, Mrs. Williams," I said.

"Mace so clumsy. He might drop and break them."

"You got rugs to help with that."

The idea of her not using the dishes bothered me. I wanted her to enjoy every moment of this new life. Mrs. Williams carefully unpacked the dishes and placed them on a high shelf in the kitchen, using a chair as a ladder. After we covered the old dining table with a vinyl cloth, Alicia convinced her to set the table as if guests were coming to dinner. Mrs. Williams couldn't resist. The idea delighted her. She took the dishes back out and set four places at the table. We centered a vase of plastic pink roses in the middle.

"Civil, you need anything else?" One of Ty's frat brothers was chubby with a baby face, but the man possessed a supernatural strength when it came to lifting furniture. His name was Vince and he had worn all white clothing. Crazy self. Miraculously, except for the sweat stains, he remained clean.

Vince leaned against the wall. "How you liked going to school at Tuskegee? I hear them professors strict up there."

"It was cool."

"Hey, leave Ty's woman alone and come help us," called out the other frat brother as he walked through the room.

"First off, I am not Ty's woman," I said when we'd all convened in the living room. Mace watched us from the doorway. I tried to read his thoughts. Alicia sank into Mrs. Williams's rocker. I mouthed at her to get out of the woman's chair, and she moved over to the sofa.

"Thank y'all for the help." I gave Ty and his friends five dollars each. Courtesy of June Townsend.

"Mrs. Williams, let us know if you need us again," Ty said.

"I will, son. Y'all got to come back and try some of my 7UP cake." She had wrapped cheese sandwiches in paper and placed a sandwich in each of their fists.

The three murmured *Yes, ma'am*s as they shuffled out. Ty looked back at me.

Alicia stood. "Girl, I'm beat. I'm going to ride with them. I'll catch up with you later?"

I gave her a hug, and she closed the door behind them.

"I'm a little tired, too," Mrs. Williams said. "I'm going to go lay down. You need anything, Civil?"

"No, ma'am."

Mace was standing in the doorway that led to the hall. He stepped aside as his mama moved past him. The sun had started to fade, and his shadow shifted on the walls.

"So is Ty your man?"

"No," I snapped as I straightened the pillows on the sofa. The corner between the sofa and chair was empty. I pictured a console television, something way out of my budget. I tried to shake the thought. I had no way of buying this family a television—and even if I did, I had no business doing so. Furniture from the Goodwill was one thing. A TV was out of bounds.

"How was the first week on the new job?" I asked.

He sat on the couch and patted the seat beside him, but I didn't move.

"It's not hard, if that's what you asking. Beats farm work. Pickles don't stank as bad as I thought they would. Hey, I forgot to tell you I went out to St. Jude. They say that lump on my leg wasn't nothing at all. They stuck a needle in it and now the lump gone."

"They drained it? Sounds nasty."

He laughed.

"You able to get to work on the bus alright?"

"I leave real early, but it ain't no trouble long as the bus come on time. My truck ought to be up and working next week. I can finally pay the man on it."

"That's good, Mace. I'm happy for you." He really was something sweet for the eyes. He had gotten himself together for the new job, and he cleaned up real good. "Well, it's about time we go get the girls. I can pick them up and bring them back tonight," I said. India and Erica hadn't seen the apartment yet. Mace wanted it to be a surprise.

"I'll ride with you."

"You don't have to. I'm a—"

"They my daughters."

When we were in the car, he leaned his seat back as far as it would go and closed his eyes.

"What's the use of you riding with me if you're going to just sleep the whole way?"

"I can still keep you company while I sleep," he said without opening his eyes.

"Usually when people keep the driver company, they make conversation."

He leaned up on an elbow. "Alright, Miss Civil. What you want to talk about?"

"What you think the girls will say when they see the apartment?"

"Well, Mama ain't stopped thanking God since she seen the place. I say, 'Mama, what you want to eat tonight? And she say 'I'm too full of the spirit to eat.'"

"Well, she has reason to be. Thank goodness my mama was able to get y'all past the waitlist."

He spoke his next words so quietly I almost didn't hear him over the rumble of the car's motor. "You know, we had a life before you. I appreciate all you done, but don't come around here thinking you the Messiah. All you government folk think we ought to kiss y'all feet."

"Now, why do you always do that?"

"Do what?"

"Mess up a good moment."

A truck roared by, and whatever he said in response was lost. It was fine because I didn't feel like dealing with Mace's moodiness. The man was so defensive. Everything I said was wrong, every compliment through a back door.

As the street noise died down, Mace picked back up. "You don't know how hard this is," he was saying, "accepting help for my children. I'm they daddy. I'm supposed to be the one providing for them. Before they mama passed on, I promised her that."

His voice broke. The sun started to settle in the sky and the light in the car weakened, but I could still see him clearly. He was staring straight up at the ceiling. It was hard to imagine what it must be like for him. I was just trying to do the best I could for them. But I remembered what my mama had said about not shaming him.

When we got to the house, the girls were sitting on the porch.

"Daddy," yelled Erica. "I put the fire out, but it's still warm."

"Alright." Mace walked inside the house and I asked the girls if they had anything else they wanted to bring with them.

India picked up a doll off the ground. It was a white doll with a dirty face and knotted yarn hair. She held it to her chest and pressed her face into it.

"That yours?" I asked gently. India was eleven years old and big for her age. Her attachment to the doll startled me.

"Yeah, it's hers," Erica answered for her.

"Well, I think that'll look nice in your room. You can put it on your bed.

"What about the dogs?" I asked Mace when he came out of the house.

"Them ain't our dogs."

"I hate them dogs," whispered Erica as we walked to the car.

"Why?"

She pointed under her chin and lifted her face. I could make out an old scar in the waning light.

When India saw that we weren't taking the dogs with us, she got back out of the car and walked over to one of them. She hugged it to her and pressed her face into its neck. The dog licked her cheek.

"Come on now," Mace said.

When India got back in the car, I saw that her eyes were red. She looked back at the mutt as we made our way down the hill. By the time we arrived at Dixie Court, the street was dark because there were no lamps. I slammed my door and it echoed in the street. Far off, a puppy yelped in response. India's head turned toward the noise.

"Come on, come on." Mace rushed up the stairs. All that talk about me not being Jesus and here he was acting like he had done it all.

I paused. It was time for me to go home. I wanted to stay, but Mace's accusation rang in my ears, so I didn't follow them up the stairs. Mace must have been looking for me, because he came right back down.

"Hey, lady. You better come on in here and help me with these girls. They might start crying or something. Then what I'm supposed to do."

I called to him over my shoulder as I turned around. "Be their daddy, like you said. Tell the girls I'll see them for their next appointment." It was all I could do to get those words out of my mouth. In my car, I sat for a moment looking up at the apartment window, hoping to catch a glimpse of the girls' profiles through the sheers. I wanted to see their first smiles, to know if they liked what we'd done with the place. It had pained me to decline his invitation.

But I couldn't make out anything, and I realized I was in darkness. A breeze fluttered through the open car window and the bark of the pup droned on and on.

SEVENTEEN

B efore I knew it, the time had come for me to pick up the girls for their next Depo shot. This time, I was supposed to take them into the clinic for pelvic exams. But I thought my head was about to bust wide open: I could not give either of them that shot again. Alicia had convinced me there was no way we could switch all the patients to pills. It was a supply issue. Mrs. Seager kept track of the inventory.

They'd been in their new apartment for over a month, and I hadn't seen them since the night I dropped them off. Evidence of newly arrived families littered the grounds. A deflated basketball in the grass. A fading hopscotch map on the sidewalk. A man's white drawers hanging on the clothesline between buildings. As I walked up the stairs to their apartment, I noticed that someone had swept the entry clean since I had been there last. Before I could knock, India opened the door and put her arms around my waist.

"Hey, girl." I kissed the top of her head and stepped inside. Erica emerged from the hallway, carrying a black patent leather purse, its strap tied on with a safety pin. The living room was starting to look lived in. Someone had folded a faded orange throw across the back of the couch. Baby's breath sprayed from a drinking glass on the painted end table next to the sofa.

"Come see our room."

I bet no one had told them that I'd helped decorate. Selfishly, I wanted credit for it. Mace might have been right about me after all. India held on to my hand. When I'd left there had only been a bed and a dresser. Now there was a poster of Diana Ross on the wall. The singer was wrapped in a black fur and wore a big smile on her face.

"Look at this," Erica said, straightening the covers on the bed.

"What you doing?"

"I'm making the bed." She looked pleased with herself.

"It looks real nice."

On the dresser, they had placed a brush and a jar of Royal Crown hair dressing. The only thing I was thinking they still needed was a lamp. The overhead light was dim, and I could barely see myself in the dresser mirror.

"So you took the bed by the window?"

"Yeah. India don't like the sound of the cars and the people talking. We ain't never heard so much noise at night before."

Their bedroom faced the street. I could see the rental office a few hundred yards away.

"And guess what."

I turned back around. "What?"

"India started bleeding." Erica looked over at her sister, pride written in her face.

"What? When?" I could barely think. The birth control meant something different now. It was no longer inappropriate medicine dispensed to a prepubescent minor. It was now guarding against something real. And I knew that only too well. I looked at India. Surely she didn't have an interest in boys. At least, I'd never seen a sign of any kind of interest.

Before Erica could answer, Mrs. Williams entered the room, wiping her hands on a towel tucked into the waistband of her dress. "How you doing, Miss Civil?"

"Fine, you?" I tore my eyes away from the girls.

"I can't complain."

"Here." I held out a brown paper sack to Mrs. Williams.

"What's this?"

"A gift from my mama."

She drew the white leather Bible out of the bag.

"Ooh, look at this."

"She said it's for your living room. And right here"—I pointed to the gold lettering on the front—"it says 'Williams Family.'"

The grandmother's eyes grew wet. India pulled at the book, trying to see it. I would need to bring more sanitary napkins. I'd have to show her how to use them.

"My big mama had a Bible like this. I remember some of the passages she used to read. I can recite them to you as if I read it with my own two eyes." She said it without the complicated defensiveness her son had displayed. Mrs. Williams's mother had been literate, and she was proud of it.

"My mama always said if you open a Bible and put it out, the house will be blessed," I told her.

"Amen to that." She tucked the book underneath her arm. "Every time you step foot in that front door you are going to know we doing everything we can to honor this gift you and the good Lord done brought us."

"You're so welcome." I looked at my watch. "Y'all ready?"

The girls laced up their shoes and followed me out of the house. In the vestibule, I held tightly to the handrail. The news that India had started menstruating could not have come at a worse time. If Mrs. Seager had been on shaky ground before, there would be no disputing her determination to continue giving the shot once she found out.

Since discovering the potential dangers of the drug, I had given two more Depo shots to women, mothers desperate for reliable birth control. I had been unable to convince them to switch over to pills. My head was hurting over what I was charged to do to the Williams girls.

When the clinic was in sight, I turned to Erica and said, "I want to ask you a question, Erica, and I'm asking this question as your nurse." I put the car in park and turned to her. "Has a boy ever touched you?"

"What you mean?" she asked, but from the look on her face I could tell she knew exactly what I meant. I should have asked her this question sooner.

"Do you . . . mess around with boys?"

She quickly shook her head.

I wanted to make sure she understood. "What I mean is, do you ever do anything with boys that might . . . make a baby?"

She shook her head again.

"Do you know how to make a baby?"

She paused and then said slowly, "Yeah."

"Okay, and have you ever done that before?"

She shook her head.

I didn't know what to think exactly. I still didn't understand why they had been put on Depo in the first place. "You ever kissed a boy?"

"Miss Civil, you acting strange."

"Just answer the question!"

"Miss Civil, you ever seen any boys around our farm? Other than them little white boys that be throwing rocks at us all the time?"

"You didn't stay on the farm all the time. You must have seen other kids your age. You used to go to school."

She gave me a look as if to say I was crazy or a fool or both.

"I'm sorry, baby. Let's go inside," I said.

Inside the clinic, all three exam rooms were occupied, so I asked them to sit and wait. When a room became available, I called them back. The two sisters went to the restroom together to pee in their cups. When they returned, I told them to take off their clothes and put on gowns. While they undressed, I stepped into the hallway and lined up everything on two trays. One tray held the items I needed for the exam. The speculum. Spatula. Brush. A second tray for the medicine. Alcohol. Cotton balls. Needles. Medicine. Bandages.

On the day of my abortion, the woman ordered me to undress from the waist down, and I remember thinking that I would not even remove my shirt for the most significant day of my life. I had never even had a vaginal exam before I became pregnant. My daddy had thought it unnecessary, and sex was not something Mama and I ever talked about.

I entered the exam room and carefully placed the tray on the counter. The girls stepped on the scale one at a time and I wrote down the numbers. India climbed up on the table. I wrapped a blood pressure cuff around her arm. Erica was excited by the cuff and her eyes widened as she watched it inflate on her sister's arm.

A rap at the door. Mrs. Seager opened it. "Check them for infections and sexually transmitted diseases," she said as if they were not sitting right there in front of her.

I held the chart up to hide my face. "Yes, ma'am."

After she closed the door behind her I pulled out the stirrups. Erica climbed up onto the table and leaned back. She propped up her knees. I could hear my breath raking in and out of my nose. I tried to swallow. My throat would not open, and I thought I might choke.

There had been no pain medication for me that day and I never saw the tool the woman used. Beneath my cries, I remember hearing Miss Pope call out my name in an anguished voice. After it was over, I was grateful for her, but I regretted not asking Ty to come with me. It was part of the reason he could not understand. He had not been there. The moment I got off the table was the moment I pulled away from him and our relationship. We simply could not be together after that.

"Miss Civil?"

"Sit up. Sit up." I slammed the stirrups back into the table. I could not look Erica in the face. "Roll up your sleeve."

I moistened the cotton ball with alcohol and dabbed at her shoulder.

"So why did they start y'all on the shots in the first place?" I picked up the vial and stuck the needle in. I opened up the syringe, filled it with medicine.

"This lady came around to our house one day and told my daddy she was taking us to the clinic to make sure we don't have no babies. I think she near about scared my daddy to death. He always say he don't know what to do with girls without a mama."

I squeezed a burst of air out of the needle.

"And did anybody ever ask you if you had messed with boys before?"

"No, ma'am."

"Didn't your grandmama ask y'all no questions about such?"

"Grandmama, she . . . she just kind of give up after Mama died. A lot of days, she don't even get out of bed."

Erica squeezed her eyes shut. I held the needle right next to her shoulder. When the girls were first brought to the clinic, Erica had been twelve years old and India ten. And no one had ever bothered to ask them if they were even menstruating. I believed that both girls were virgins. But here we were inserting what could be poison into them on the off chance that one of them might become sexual.

Or raped. There it was. The unthinkable word. My hand began to shake.

"Any grown men . . . ever . . . touched or messed with you or your sister?"

"You scaring me, Miss Civil."

"India can't talk," I whispered. "How can we be sure nobody never messed with her?" I held the needle close to her arm.

Erica shook her head and started to cry. "Cause I know, Miss Civil. I wouldn't let it happen."

The girl actually believed she could protect her younger sister. She believed she knew everything. But none of us knew. Not even me. Without the ability to vocalize, India was virtually defenseless. And Erica was just a child herself. Ty was right. I hadn't asked enough questions.

"Shit!" I hissed as I dropped the needle onto the tray and snapped the glove off. I could hear Mrs. Seager talking in the next room, but in my ears her voice sounded like *whack wick whack*.

India's eyes widened. Usually when the younger sister met my eye, it was pure adoration. She completely trusted me, and I often found myself fighting back a motherly feeling, which was not at all anything I had ever imagined for myself. I had never longed for children in the way that some little girls did. I did not dream of a wedding or husband. I wanted a career, a mission other than motherhood and wifehood. The choices in those days felt stark to me.

I emptied the needle's contents into the sink before filling a second syringe with the medication and emptying it into the sink, too.

"Miss Civil?"

"You can't tell nobody I didn't give y'all this shot today, hear?" I spoke quickly, hating myself for doubting their innocence and honesty, but also knowing that this decision I was making was potentially disastrous for us all.

Erica nodded.

That day was the beginning for me. I knew that the next step was for me to convince the rest of the nurses to stop giving the drug to anybody at all. Not just minors. An impossible but necessary task.

I picked up my clipboard and wrote in elegant script a chart full of lies.

EIGHTEEN

W e can't anymore," I told Alicia one afternoon, a week after the girls had visited the clinic. We were in the break room, and it was time to close the place up. I'd cornered her next to the coffeepot.

"Can't what?"

"Give the patients any more of these shots. I took the Williams sisters off birth control completely."

She paused. For a moment, I didn't know what she was going to say. Then she surprised me. "I feel the same way. I haven't been giving it, either."

"You haven't?"

"Child, I put two of my patients on the pill. I just changed it on their chart. Said they wanted to switch."

"Good idea."

"But you know it won't work. Mrs. Seager orders all the meds. Plus, the grown women can remember to take the pill; the younger ones I'm not so sure."

"Alicia, that's the thing. My girls ain't even sexual."

"Not yet."

"You sound like the white folks."

"That's not fair, and you know it."

"You're right. I'm sorry. Have you talked to Ty?"

"Yeah, I talk to him all the time," she said.

"Seem like y'all talk to each other more than you talk to me."
I wiped the coffee stains from the counter.

"Ty told me he ran into your daddy and told him about the
Depo studies."

"I heard. That boy trying to incite a riot."

"Ty's mama supposed to be looking into it, but we haven't
heard nothing from her yet. I think she know some people up in
Washington."

Val entered the room carrying the bucket of cleaning supplies.
"What are you two carrying on about over there?"

"I'm trying to convince Civil to let me borrow the extra cap in
her bag until I can get a new one. I lost mine."

I had not even noticed her bare head.

"I'm surprised Mrs. Seager didn't say anything." Val took a
rag from her bucket and wiped down the table. She was becoming more like a mother to the younger nurses, keeping us in line.
I think Mrs. Seager appreciated Val the most because she did
some of the management work, freeing Mrs. Seager from the brunt
of it.

"I been trying to avoid her, hoping she won't notice."

Mrs. Seager stopped in the doorway. "Notice what? That you
forgot your cap? If you forget it again, you will receive a demerit.
Is that clear?"

"Yes, Mrs. Seager."

When she was gone, Val pointed at me. "Your fault. If you'd
given her your cap when she first asked, she would've been wearing one just now."

"You sure are poking your nose in everybody's business to-day," I said.

"Yes, have you ever heard of an A and B conversation?" Alicia piped up.

"Please C your way out." I finished Alicia's line and we started to bust up laughing.

We quieted as Val aimed a rag at us. "Think you know everything, and don't know nothing. Now go get the broom and sweep up this floor."

Lori came in with the brooms. She passed them to Alicia and me. We divided up the rooms and began.

AFTER THE GIRLS visited the clinic, I took two packs of birth control pills from the supply closet with the intention of teaching them how to swallow them. I was scared of getting into trouble if Mrs. Seager found out I hadn't given them their shots, but I was also disturbed by the possibility of them getting pregnant. They weren't sexual, but they could be. Let me tell you something: I still believed in the mission of the clinic. Women needed access to reliable birth control and information about their reproductive health. And I did not believe in minors becoming pregnant under any circumstances. I was sure enough the deputy Mrs. Seager believed I was, and I had a duty. I was as much a bona fide member of the Talented Tenth as I was an acolyte of Booker T. Washington. Rise and lift the race. But also work like hell to pull up those bootstraps.

First task: Get them out of that shanty and into a real home. Second task: Get them into school. Erica was thirteen years old and hadn't been in school in more than three years, but I managed to get her into summer school. She wasn't the first child from out in the country to jump into school late. I had been trying hard not to judge Mace on this. After their mother died, Mace had let the girls' education fall by the wayside. It was plain old irresponsible, and I wanted to tell him so, but I held my tongue.

Third task: Keep them from becoming pregnant. The grandmother and father had given their blessing for birth control, and I was obligated to do their bidding, wasn't I? Yet I kept the pills in my purse and never handed them over. I just couldn't do it for some reason.

It was more difficult finding a school for India. The week after their appointment at the clinic, I picked up the paperwork to have her tested. I didn't fully understand the girl's abilities because she did not talk. The woman at the school had asked if she was *trainable*, and I said that I thought she was. I contacted a doctor who could administer the test the school required; he told me the testing fee would be forty-five dollars. I told him that was awful that he charged poor people that much money, and he had the nerve to say, *I'm not charging them, I'm charging you.* Old buzzard.

I called Ty to see if he would go with me to the doctor's office. I wanted to chat with him more about this Depo issue. When he got in the car, he was wearing a suit. I was glad he had dressed up. How Black men dressed mattered to white folks.

"Look at you," I said.

"My church threads," he said.

When we picked up India, she looked warily at Ty as she settled into the back seat.

"You remember Ty? He helped move your stuff out of the cabin. I've known him since I was a girl like you. He's going to ride with us to the testing place."

Every now and then she made a motion that appeared to be a nod, but it wasn't consistent. I truly believed India was trainable, but I was no expert. The girls' hygiene had improved since moving into the apartment, but India still needed to wear deodorant. An odor like onions hung over her.

"So I hear you and Alicia been talking a lot," I said.

"Yeah, we been hanging out."

"Hanging out, huh?" I had been the one to break things off with Ty, so I didn't know why I was feeling a little jealous.

"Girl, you so crazy."

From the back seat, I heard India making a noise. In the rearview mirror, I could see her pointing out the window. A spray of bees gave chase right outside the car.

"Yes, I see, baby. I see. Those are bees." I made a buzzing noise. India tried to mimic the sound. Yes, she was definitely trainable.

We rode the elevator up to the doctor's office in silence. India pressed all the elevator buttons, and since she'd only pressed the numbers above the third floor, I let her. The doors opened, and she hesitated before taking a step out, as if she thought the doors would close on her. I took her hand. "You'll be fine."

The office was at the end of the hallway. There was no placard on the door, but the suite number was the same one I'd written down on the scrap of paper in my purse. When we walked in, I was surprised by how small it was. A room with a glass window faced the waiting room. There was no receptionist, so I pressed the knob on a call bell on the end table.

A few minutes passed before Ty said, "Are we in the right place?"

The door opened, and a gray-haired man poked his head out. He didn't open the door all the way. "Yes?"

"We have an appointment with Dr. Merle. I'm a nurse, and I've brought India Williams to be tested for admission to—"

"You're late."

"Well, sir, we were on time when we first walked in and rang the—"

"Have her take a seat at the table in the testing room."

"Will we be able to sit with her?" I asked.

"Of course not. Do you have your payment? It'll be forty-five dollars."

I did not like the way he was speaking to me, and I was about to say something, but Ty reached for his wallet.

"Here you are, sir."

The doctor opened the door wider to take the money. Then he turned to India and softened his voice. "Hello, young lady. What's your name?"

India just looked at him. I had to give it to the girl. She had a certain stillness to her around strangers. It communicated to them to keep their distance.

"She doesn't speak, sir. I told you that over the telephone."

He scowled at me. "I remember that. Let me do my job, ma'am."

I took India into the room and put her in the chair. "I'm going to be right through that window while you take this test. It shouldn't take that long, hear?"

She touched my hair, and I stopped her by grabbing her hand. "This is just a test to get you into school." I repeated the same words I'd used in the elevator. "You'll be fine."

I realized I should have brought Erica with me. She could have helped to decipher some of India's responses for the doctor. He entered the room carrying an open box containing plastic toys and sheets of paper. He spoke softly to India, and she responded immediately by making eye contact with him and taking the first offered toy. I got the impression that he was a man who connected more with children than he did with adults. No excuse. He still needed to learn some manners.

123

In the other room, Ty sat down and started thumbing through *Outdoor Life* magazine. "Don't just stand there staring at her through the window. Let them work," he said, not looking up.

I sat down beside him and watched him for a moment. "You've certainly been Mr. Big Bucks lately. You didn't tell me you were going to pay."

"Since you didn't let me pay for your little Opelika visit, I figured you thought I was broke or something."

"Ty, that's not fair," I said quietly. He turned the page of the magazine, and it ripped. I touched his arm. I had underestimated this hurt between us. Ty may not have been physically in that room with me that day, but his heart had lain right alongside me. "Thank you for helping, Ty. I mean that. But I still don't know why you're doing all this. I hope it's not to impress me."

"Pshaw, girl. I couldn't win you back if I tried. Could I?"

I changed the subject. "Did Alicia tell you that we stopped giving our patients Depo shots?"

He breathed out audibly, as if resigning himself to my stubbornness. "Mama is still trying to find out more information. She's contacted some friends of hers in Washington."

"I gave shots to two patients since you first told me about the studies. What the hell is wrong with me?" I wiped at my eye.

"Come here, girl." He pulled me to him, and I placed my cheek against his chest. "Don't blame yourself, Civil. You were just trying to do your job."

"I don't know what my job is anymore."

"Maybe we're wrong. Maybe it's just overblown and the study doesn't apply to humans, after all."

"Come on, Ty. You were a biology major. You know that we have to take those nonhuman studies seriously until more clinical trials can be done. And we're talking little Black girls here. They set different rules for us." I straightened back up in my chair and peered through the window at India. The doctor was holding up cardboard signs, but I couldn't make out the images. India just stared at him, her affect blank.

Ty took my hand in his. "I know. We'll find out more soon enough, okay? I promise."

"I hope so. Let me know as soon as your mama hears back?"

"I promise, Civil. You'll be the first to know."

NINETEEN

Birmingham
2016

He is grayer around the edges and a glint of silver lines his cheeks. His chin is softer, sideburns shorter. There are lines in his forehead, but his cheeks are still smooth. Right before this trip I found his picture on the internet, but it is different seeing him in person. I feel off-kilter. When he hugs me, he pats me on the back. A friend hug. I pull him closer, and he doesn't resist. It's bold of me, but I just do what feels right in the moment.

The office is traditional—a dark wood desk, bookshelves, a round conference table in the corner covered in stacks of paper. There's a ficus in the corner and a fern on the edge of the desk. The tops of the bookshelves are lined with rhododendrons. It smells a little earthy.

"Tyrell Ralsey. President of a college. Who would have thought?"

"Funny you say that. I never had any problem picturing you as a surgeon."

"Sorry, I didn't mean—"

"No offense taken." Rather than retreat to the other side of his desk, he sits in the chair beside me.

His suite of offices sits above the main student center. So different from my days at Tuskegee. The center downstairs houses fast-food restaurants and a coffee shop. The semester has ended, so there's not the usual sea of students. This small Baptist college in Birmingham became coeducational in the early 1970s, and now its student body is nearly 70 percent women. I have read all about it online. I find myself wishing the students were here so that we could have some distraction and Ty's focus on me would not be so absolute.

His assistant brings in two cups of coffee. I'm wearing a tunic over my jeans, an attempt to appear effortlessly casual. Now I fear it makes my body look shapeless. At least my hair is done nice. Last night I braided my locks and now they are falling in soft waves around my shoulders. Ty is wearing slacks and an open-collar shirt. Gray chest hair peeks over the buttons. He crosses one leg over the other, toward me. I set my cup on his desk and pick up a picture frame.

"Good-looking children. How old are they now?"

"Ty Jr. is thirty. Dwanna is thirty-six."

"What do they do?" Mama has told me all about his children. She still talks to Mrs. Ralsey on the phone, but I want to hear the story from Ty. Being in that office, looking at his children—the young man who looks just like his namesake and the young woman who reminds me of Ty's mother—brings it all back. I put the frame down before he can notice my trembling hand.

"Ty's a physical therapist. He went to Morehouse and married a special ed teacher who graduated Spelman. Dwanna is a lawyer. Alabama State. Married another lawyer. I have twin granddaughters who look a lot like my mama."

"Oh, that's nice, Ty."

"When you get to Montgomery, you should stop by and visit my folks. They would enjoy seeing you."

"They still got all their plants?"

"You know it."

Sometimes I think of what those plants meant to the Ralseys—the life-affirming vitality of them. The connectedness of all living things in a segregated country. To the Ralseys, we were all God's creations—man, plant, animal. They cared for those plants in the same way they cared for their clients. I have also tried to have a gentle hand with my patients. That's just the way we were on Centennial Hill.

I look around for pictures of the ex-wife. I try not to be obvious about what I'm doing, but Ty knew me from a time when I could hide very little. Even so, I'm surprised he can still read me.

"Ty Jr. tells me that having pictures of his mother does not do my dating life any good."

"I-I don't know what to say." Dating life? I wonder if he's seeing someone.

"I'm sure you know plenty of divorced people. What do you usually say?"

"How long has it been?"

"Ten years. She remarried and lives with her husband, not too far from me. We all go to the same church." He chuckles to himself.

"Hmm," I say. "Is Birmingham that small?"

"No, but she's still family. We even celebrate Christmas together sometimes, all of us."

Just like Ty, I think. If things remain this good with his ex, he is probably still the same man I knew him to be. I recall mistaking that good-naturedness for silliness.

"But enough about me." He takes my hand. "It's good to see you, Civil. I couldn't believe it when you emailed me. Mama told me all about you and your daughter, Anne."

"Yes, she just graduated from college. She's trying to figure out what to do next."

"And you?"

"Nothing much more to tell."

"Performing life-saving surgeries. Publishing in all the medical journals. I'm sure you've done more than become a mother."

I let go of his hand.

"I'm sorry. Did I say the wrong thing?"

"It's alright." I look at my lap.

"I meant to say, I'm sure you've got more stories."

But I don't offer any more stories because it is disingenuous. I'm not really here to catch up on forty years of distance. Actually, I don't even know exactly why I'm here, only that it isn't to make small talk. Maybe Alicia was right. Maybe this is just one big apology tour.

He gently draws me out again, asking questions about my job. He asks about Memphis and how Mama fared once Daddy passed away.

"You didn't come to the funeral," I say.

"I couldn't," he says. "My wife and I were having problems at the time. It was a rough patch."

"I looked for you there. Your parents came."

Then he says, "Civil, I would be lying if I said I have been thinking about you for the last forty years. I loved my wife. I made an honest go at building a family. For a variety of reasons, it didn't work out. But I have to say seeing you here today is bringing back memories."

I cannot believe how quickly the conversation has turned. We are in his office, for goodness' sake. The lights are bright. There is no mood music, no wine to dull the senses and loosen the tongue. He takes my hand again, and his touch shoots a tingle through my arm. I'm healthy. Other than a little elevated blood pressure, I have very little in the way of aches and pains, thank the good Lord. But I accepted a long time ago that I lead a life of the mind. My body and its urges are secondary. It's easy to forget your own flesh when you are concentrated on other people's bodies.

"When you left, I kept thinking you would call," he continued. "I thought you would return home and we'd run into each other and finally talk. But you never even came home for breaks. I asked your daddy. He and your mama drove to Nashville whenever they wanted to see you. And when you did come home, I didn't hear about it until after you'd already left."

"You make it sound like I was in a witness protection program, Ty. It wasn't that serious."

"What wasn't serious? Us?"

"I just . . . I just . . . couldn't." Part of me wants to let go of his hand again, but I don't. He holds my fingers firmly, and I know I will be unable to squirm out of this conversation.

"Did you even think about me?" His voice is quiet.

"Yes."

"Then why not call?"

"It's been decades, Ty. You're interrogating me like it was yesterday. Why ask me all these questions now?" As I say these words, I quietly admit to myself that it is not possible to mend the hurt at this point in our lives.

"The past doesn't work that way. You can't just make it disappear. You can't pretend certain things didn't happen."

"Don't you think I know that?"

He looks right at me. "Did you ever tell anyone, Civil?"

"Tell anyone what?"

"Come on, woman. Do you think about our baby?"

How could I ever forget the day I climbed up on that woman's bed and she hurt me with those tools? The memory has haunted me at times.

"You were so closed down about it, Civil. I worried when I heard you never married."

I wonder how many women have the opportunity to complete this kind of circle, to talk to the father of a mistaken pregnancy some forty years later. "No, I never told anyone. Did you?" I whisper.

He nods. "Of course. I told my wife."

"That was between us, Ty."

"Yes, it was. But it was not a secret to be borne a lifetime. Civil, how could you have never told anyone?"

I shrug, but the tears escape anyway. In Ty's office, beneath fluorescent lights, I begin to cry openly and I feel as if I'm one of his students. He presses a tissue into my hand. "Civil. Civil."

I awkwardly dab the tissue against my face. Neither of us reaches for the other, and I'm grateful for the space. I allow myself to sit with my regret. So much regret. So much.

TWENTY

Montgomery
1973

The morning it happened, I received the letter from the doctor that India was eligible for admission to the school. Erica had already started summer school and, despite her elevated age among her peers, she was loving it. I'd gone home for lunch after dropping off one of my patients, a woman by the name of Frida who had no children and had reached out to us because she intended to keep it that way. I left her with three months' supply of pills and a box of rubbers.

"Why are you looking so happy?" Mama asked me.

It was one of those rare days Mama wasn't painting. She had dressed in a real outfit that suggested she was going out.

"India got into a school. I'm going to go deliver the news to her after I get off work today. Do you want to come with me? You could see their apartment and all the stuff your money bought."

She tied a small scarf around her neck, then untied it as if changing her mind. Montgomery was pleasant in June, but the weather was still hot.

"And the other sister?"

"She's in summer school. I was thinking about tutoring her."

"Tutoring?"

"Yeah, why not? I could do it on weekends when I'm not working."

"Baby girl, I just hope you know that no matter how much you do, God has dealt that family an awful hand."

That was the same thing Val had said. Both of them were wrong, though. Some things couldn't be changed, but this case was different. "Don't say that, Mama. Look at how much happier they are now they're in that apartment. That's because of you." I kissed her on the cheek and looped an arm around her shoulders. "You want to go over and see the apartment with me?"

"Lord, child, no. Those people got enough folk running in and out of their lives gawking at them. They are not a sideshow."

I nodded. She was right, and I was embarrassed that I had even suggested it. I really just wanted to spend time with her.

"Now, I'm going to need my car today. You got to drive your own car sometimes. I'm going to lunch with Louise and I'd never hear the end of it if I picked her up in that fire-engine-red car of yours."

"Tell her I said hello." I passed the keys to her.

The screen door slammed shut behind her, and I cleared my dishes off the table. The clock over the kitchen sink ticked loudly. Dixie Court was in the opposite direction of the clinic, but I had a little time. I considered dropping by the Williamses' apartment and telling India the news before going back to work. It was going to be too hard to keep this to myself all afternoon long. We had worked so hard, and I knew the girl was probably just hanging around the house all day with her grandma now that Erica was in school. I decided it was better to get to work, but all day I thought about them, watching the clock and waiting for it to hit five so I could head over to Dixie Court.

I will never forget; it was a glorious June afternoon. Sunny, clear skies. In the car, I hummed along with "You Are the Sunshine of My Life." The windows were down, and I drummed my hand along with the music. Things hadn't looked this good in weeks. I had a brochure to give India so she could look at the pictures. I hadn't wanted to show it to her until I was certain she'd passed the test. It was a nice place with an outdoor play yard. St. Jude Church had always welcomed Black folks; they had even founded a hospital that was the first in the region to integrate. But at the moment I was most grateful for the school that nurtured the minds and hearts of children like India. I couldn't wait to take her for a tour so I could see it myself.

As I walked up the steps to their apartment, the brochure clutched in my hand, I glanced at my watch: 5:47 P.M. I had made it through my cleaning chores and driven over from the clinic in record time. I was breathless, giddy with the news. One of my knee-highs slid down to my ankle. I knocked on the door, then stooped down to pull it back up.

"Miss Civil, what you doing here?" Mrs. Williams opened the door wearing the new eyeglasses I'd bought her. The apartment smelled salty, like there was fatback on the stove. It seemed like every time I visited the woman was cooking, especially when she'd just gotten her food stamps. On the block there was a bus stop that took her straight to the A&P.

"I'm just stopping by to tell India she got into the school. Ooh, your new eyeglasses look good on you. Can you see better now?" I tried to peek around her broad figure.

"The glasses is fine. But ain't you with the girls? They been gone since early this morning."

"The girls? Gone where?"

"Child, the nurse come and took them to the hospital. I figure you was with them."

"The hospital? For what? Are they sick?"

"No, they went for they shots."

"Shots?" My knees started to tremble. "You mean they went to the clinic?"

"No, they say they was taking them to the hospital."

"To the hospital for shots?"

"That's what they say. Least, I believe that's what the woman say. I ain't for sure."

"What woman?"

"The white lady. I know she said Professional Hospital."

"The white lady? Professional Hospital?"

"Yes, the white lady with big red hair. I believe I met her once before, but I can't remember correctly."

I rubbed my eye. Mrs. Seager had been to the apartment. And she'd taken them to Professional. That was the white hospital. It didn't make sense.

Mrs. Williams opened the door wider and I stepped inside. I closed the door behind me but held on to the knob. I touched my shoulder to the tip of my ear.

"Mrs. Williams," I said slowly, "did you sign anything?"

"I sure did. I put my mark clear as day on the paper she brung me."

I opened the door and ran down the stairs, trying to get to my car as fast as I could. There were no signed papers in the file for the Depo shots, so it was possible Mrs. Seager had just given her something to sign regarding those. It was possible. It was possible.

I gripped the steering wheel so tightly my fingers cramped. Once I arrived at Professional, I hurried through the main doors, my nurse's uniform giving me enough of an air of authority that no one looked askance. I stopped at the desk.

"I'm looking for India and Erica Williams. They came in with Mrs. Linda Seager a while ago, from the—"

"You work here?"

I shook my head. "No, ma'am, I'm from the Montgomery Family Planning Clinic."

She pointed to a thick binder on the desk. "Sign in."

I scribbled my name as she thumbed through a large book. "Here they are. They're in post-surgery on the fourth floor. The room number is—"

The elevator bell dinged and I slipped past the person waiting for it. When I got off on the fourth floor, I realized I hadn't waited long enough to hear the room number, and now I regretted it. The floor was relatively quiet, but I thought I could make out the faint sound of someone moaning. I turned down the east corridor. It sounded like India's faintly unintelligible sounds. At the last door, a chart stuck out of a clear plastic folder, and I saw the name *Williams*. I picked it up and flipped through the pages, reading quickly.

Dear God. I pushed the door open.

The two sisters were lying on beds opposite each other, India curled into a fetal position, her head between her knees, Erica holding a hand out toward her sister. When I entered, Erica turned to me, a panicked look in her eyes.

"Miss Civil!" She reached out her arms.

"Erica." I went to her and smoothed her hair back. Her forehead was cold and wet.

"Miss Civil. Oh, I hurt so bad."

"What you say?" I lifted the covers. Blood-soaked bandages were wrapped around her abdomen.

"They done something to us, Miss Civil. I thought we was coming for shots. But they done something to us. They say we can't have no babies."

Heat rose up behind my eyes, and the room fell away. I held Erica in my arms, the sound of India moaning behind me, her voice thick, a raw sound. The room smelled of blood and urine and disinfectant.

Erica started to cry. "I was doing everything you told me to do."

"Shhh, shhh." I rubbed her forehead with my hand. "Hush,

baby. Don't talk." I turned around and tried to take hold of India. She was holding on to her legs tightly, her eyes squeezed shut. "Come on, sweetheart. Let loose. Let loose."

Now, you know how some white folks feel about Black bodies. They think we can tolerate pain better than them . . . Some of them even thought syphilis couldn't kill us. I picked up a cord on the side of the bed and pressed the buzzer over and over. A few minutes later, a nurse stuck her head in the door.

"Have these patients been given something for their pain?"

She looked at my cap, which, though it didn't look that different from hers, was falling halfway off my head. Both of my knee-highs were down around my ankles.

"Excuse me, do you work here?"

"Call the goddamn doctor!" I yelled, and she escaped through the door.

India let go of her legs and went limp, her cries easing into whimpers. I did not need to look under her bandage. I knew there would be an incision running down the front of her abdomen past her navel. I had learned about laparoscopies in nursing school.

A doctor entered. He had gray hair and a neatly trimmed beard. He gave me the same look the nurse had, then said, "Do you work on this floor?"

"I'm from the Montgomery Planning Clinic, and these girls are my patients. What have you done?"

"These girls were scheduled for a tubal ligation this morning. The supervisor, Linda Seager, brought them in personally. Perhaps you should check your own records so that you can keep up with your patients better."

"A tubal ligation?"

"The surgery went well. They can go home in two days."

"A tubal ligation?"

"You say you're from the Montgomery Family Planning Clinic?"

He had a concerned look on his face, as if he were beginning to think it was possible that I was lying.

"She's eleven goddamn years old!" Now I was crying, and I could hear a commotion in the hallway. I pressed India's face into my chest, as if to shield her from him. "And they need pain medication."

"Get them some—"

"I'm going to find your daddy and let him know what happened, alright? And I'm going to make this right, do you understand me? I'm going to make this right."

I stumbled out of the room. Down in the lobby, there was a pay phone, and I used it to call Mace at work. I told the supervisor it was an emergency and they let him come to the telephone, but it took a long time. When he finally picked up, I told him what had happened and there was a long silence before he said, "What you saying?" and then the line went dead because my time was up. I dug around in my purse, but I didn't have any more change.

When I got in the car, I didn't know where I was going or what I was going to do next. I could hear a rattling in my chest, like paper crackling. I turned left out of the parking lot, hit the gas pedal. I never saw the other car, though I was told later that there was one, and as I crossed through the intersection all I remember was the impact, the whirl of the car spinning, and my body being tossed around, light as air, like a rag doll.

PART II

TWENTY-ONE

When I say to you that what happened to those girls was the greatest hurt of my life, I am speaking the God's honest truth. To understand that statement, you have to understand where I came from. When I was growing up Daddy had a good practice, and it afforded us some things. We owned our own house, took vacations. I got my hair done in a real beauty shop, not somebody's kitchen. Our little family managed to live dignified in undignified times. Daddy shined his shoes every morning. Mama wore earrings. These little acts might seem simple to you, but baby, let me tell you. They held back the storm.

In order to survive the humiliations of Jim Crow life, we sustained one another through laughter, food, music. And to that end, in the clutch of a community's embrace, Centennial Hill nourished us, and I was protected from the worst of it. It was a place where folks saved the tears for church and left their burdens on the altar.

It seemed unfathomable to me that anything like this would ever happen to someone close to me. Even with all I knew about the cruelty of humans—the beatings, the murders, the disappearances—I had still somehow underestimated people, and the girls had paid a price for that naiveté. No wonder my car got hit. It was a lesson on the laws of physics. There are consequences in life.

"Are you alright?"

A lady helped lower me to the curb. My knees hurt as if they'd been skinned. My car was still in the middle of the street, the entire passenger side dented. I touched my forehead. "Am I bleeding?"

"Well, the glass scratched you up, but you look alright to me. I don't think you need no ambulance."

I held on to her. She was wearing a white shirt, though she did not seem to care that I might get it soiled. My palms were pricked and raw.

"What happened?"

"I don't know. When I got here, I found you here on this curb. I never saw another car. I'm sure they'll find it."

"I need to go. I have somewhere to go." I started to rise, but she pushed me back down.

"Which hospital do you work at? Can I call somebody for you?"

"Hospital?" The front of my uniform was brown and mottled with something funky. I must have vomited on myself. "Can you call my daddy?"

"What's your daddy's number, baby?"

I told her, and she repeated the numbers softly.

"Okay, I'll be right back. You sit here and don't move."

The minutes dragged on. I shook my head to clear it, sniffed, wiped the back of my hand across my face, and saw that blood was running from my nose. I smoothed my hand down the side of my dress.

The lady came back with a balding man whose forehead shone red in the sun. He kneeled down and tilted my head back gently. "Your nose is bleeding." He held a tissue to my face.

"I called your daddy," the lady said. "And I called the police, too. This nice man let me into his house to use the phone."

They fussed over me though I tried to resist. I needed to call Mace. Or had I already called him? I put my hand to my forehead. A headache was beginning to stir. The man offered to pull my car over to the side of the road, and I relented. A few moments later, he brought my purse and keys to me. I was not sure how much time passed before I heard my daddy's voice. "I'm a doctor," he was saying. "Are you feeling pain anywhere, baby?" I shook my head as he insisted he would take me to the hospital himself. The woman said she would wait for the police and give a report.

"Where are you taking me?" I asked my daddy as we got in his car.

"St. Jude."

Mrs. Seager had taken the girls to Professional. At St. Jude, the care might have been better. Perhaps the nuns would have stopped them from performing the procedure. She's just a baby, they might have argued. We were eight. Eight nurses and we hadn't stopped it. A whining noise in my ear. The sound of India squealing as she rode the metal horse at Kmart. A needle scratching a record. My head was throbbing now.

Daddy took me right upstairs to a doctor he knew. Mama was already there, filling out a form, still dressed in her luncheon dress from earlier. She touched my cheek with cool, thin fingers. I sat on a steel table, and a nurse shined a light in my eyes. She told me to lay back while she pressed against my ribs. Daddy sat on the doctor's stool. I needed to tell him about the girls. I needed him to go over to Professional and see about them. I had taken them off the shots. Mrs. Williams had signed the paper. These thoughts crowded my head. I moved my lips, but nothing came out.

I tried to gather myself. My voice was hoarse, but I found it. "I'm alright, Daddy. I've got to—"

"Sometimes you can have internal bleeding and not know it. It's best to get you checked out."

Daddy had always been the calmest person in the room when it came to accidents. When I was little, he would clean my wounds with antiseptic and cover them with bandages. Bike falls. Play yard scuffles. Once, Ty got shot in the temple with a BB gun by our neighbor's kid, and Daddy calmly sterilized his tweezers and pulled the bullet out. Then he told the boy's daddy that he had better take his son out and practice on some cans with that gun before the kid hurt somebody for real.

But on the day of that car accident, I witnessed a panic in Daddy's eyes I had not seen before. Daddy's doctor friend entered the room and asked me a bunch of questions. It was hard being the patient when you were the one used to doing the examining, but I let them because I wanted that look on Daddy's face to disappear. My body ached. I asked the doctor for some Tylenol, but he made me sit down in an armchair and rest first. I closed my eyes, and when I opened them, Mama was standing there.

"They found the driver," she said. "He reported to the station. The police officer just called your daddy. Apparently, the man admitted running the red light."

So it wasn't my fault. At least that was one thing I hadn't caused. Did Mace have his truck yet? Could he get to the hospital? I needed to get back to the girls.

"Good thing you were in your car and not mine." Mama made a halfhearted attempt at a joke.

I did not look at her as I swung my legs over the side of the bed. "Has the doctor cleared me?"

"You can't leave yet."

"I need to go."

"I'll drive you home."

"I can't go home."

She helped me to my feet.

"Why can't you go home?" Mama peppered me with questions. "Were you speeding? Did you see the other car coming? Where were you going, Civil?"

"Where's my purse?"

"You don't need a purse because you're coming home with me."

The letter was in my purse. I'd never had a chance to share it with India, her acceptance to a school where she could finally receive the attention she deserved.

We found Alicia and Ty in the waiting room. I paused at the nurse's desk and signed some papers before following the three of them outside. The sun had set and it was dark. Mama held on to my arm tightly, as if she didn't plan to let go until she got an explanation. I wanted to pull away, but I had not felt my mama's strength in so long that I yearned to lean into it. The world really had turned upside down.

"I need Alicia and Ty to take me to Professional Hospital."

"Professional Hospital? Why? You had the best doctors all day here at—"

"The girls are there. They . . ." It hit me in the gut all over again. I could not say it. Here I was, lucky to be alive, while those girls were lying up in hospital beds with their motherhood destroyed. The sound of India's moaning rose in my ears, and I closed my eyes.

"They performed a tubal ligation on the Williams girls," I said finally.

"Who did?" I heard Mama's keys jingle.

"Mrs. Seager tied their tubes?" Alicia's voice was so loud, it sounded like she was screaming.

Ty looked as if he were losing a battle with his anger. He wore the same tight look as the day Miss Pope told us about the untreated men with syphilis at Tuskegee.

"She can do that?" Mama sounded incredulous.

"The clinic is doing this to patients. It's . . . allowed," I whispered. The Tylenol wasn't strong enough. "Could you just please,"

145

I said quietly, "take me back over to Professional? And Ty, can y'all go pick up Mrs. Williams and bring her to the hospital? Please?"

"They're just children."

"I know, Mama."

She placed a hand on my shoulder and said, "Jesus, we seek your mercy."

I wanted to tell her it was too late for that.

MAMA WAITED DOWNSTAIRS in the main lobby. She believed the family did not need gawkers, but she wanted to be there for me when I came back down. The elevator doors opened, and I stepped off, my shoes squeaking. Alicia had brought me a change of clothes to the hospital. We wore roughly the same size in clothes but her shoes were too small. So I was still wearing my stained white nurse's sneakers, a bloody reminder of my day, and I needed a bath.

When I saw Mace standing in front of the window at the end of the hallway, my first impression was that he looked weak, as if when he stepped away from the window he might crumple. As I approached him, I couldn't form my lips to say anything.

"You they goddamn nurse." He didn't raise his voice, but the words roared in my ears.

"I went to your apartment this afternoon to tell India that she had made it into the school. Your mama told me they'd been taken to the hospital. I came here. I was too late. They had already been to surgery. I got them some pain medicine. Then I got into a car accident. I came straight back here." My words ran together.

"Can they change it back?"

"I don't know what you mean."

"You know what I mean, goddamnit. Can they undo it? Will my girls be able to go back to the way they was?"

"No, no, I don't believe so. I think . . . I mean, the chart said

146

the tubes were cauterized, which means they were burned. No . . . I'm sorry, Mace. It's permanent."

"Why did you let them people do this to my girls, Civil? Why?" His mouth hung slightly open.

"I didn't know. I swear to God, Mace. All I did was take them off the shots and then she—"

"Wait, what you saying? They wasn't getting the shots no more? I thought that's where they was going this morning? To get shots."

"You were there this morning?"

"Where you think I was?"

"Did you sign the papers?"

I took the chart out of the holder. Sure enough, the consent papers were on the clipboard. There was his mark, and his mother's. And the signature of a witness: Valeria Brinson. Val.

"I'm sorry, Mace."

He turned his back to me.

"I'll stay here with them tonight. I'll stay with them until they come home. And after they go home, I'll help. I'll help get them well," I said.

"But that's the thing, ain't it. They ain't going never be well, is they." He pressed his forehead against the window. And it was his back that hurt the most. His back filled out his shirt like a wall.

Mace wouldn't look at me, so I entered the girls' room. They were both sleeping. I looked down at the paper on the clipboard in my hand. At least they had been given something for the pain and could rest. I opened a dresser drawer and took out clean, folded gowns. When the girls woke up, I would give them a wash-up. The room smelled sour, and I knew they had not been cleaned properly. I'd wash them up and put them in fresh gowns. Then I would feed them, by hand if I had to. After I had my abortion, Miss Pope had done it for me, and I would do the same for them. I sat down in the chair and closed my eyes. My left shoulder felt tender, and when I touched my forehead I found the unmistakable beginning of a lump.

Maybe it was for the best. India had speech problems. It would have been difficult for her to care for a baby. The family was poor, with little prospects. Bringing a baby into that life would have been a tragedy. No sooner than these thoughts formed in my mind, I hated myself for them. I hated myself then, and I hate myself now. Just remembering that day makes me hot with shame. We'd thought we were doing something useful for society, but this is where that so-called good deed had gotten us. Right smack into a nightmare.

TWENTY-TWO

The main wood-paneled room of the Ralsey office suite contained two secretary desks, a waiting area with a dark leather sofa and armchair, and rows of green filing cabinets along the wall. Spider plants hung from hooks in the ceiling. Sunlight streamed through a large window.

In Mrs. Ralsey's private office, two cacti perched on the corner of the desk. A six-foot ficus tree nearly blocked the window. Mrs. Ralsey sat at her desk taking notes—a lot of notes—but I couldn't make out her handwriting. Her husband waited beside her, arms folded across his chest. Daddy had refused the seat they offered him. He leaned against the wall next to Alicia. Ty was right beside me, his chair pulled up so close to mine I could hear him breathing.

"Did Mrs. Seager know you switched them from the shots to the birth control pills?"

"I don't know. I'm not sure."

"And after you switched them, did the girls complain about the pills to you? Were they taking them regularly?"

"Actually . . . I never gave them the pills. Why did they need to take pills?"

"But you wrote in the chart that they were taking them?"

"Yes, ma'am."

"Did you tell the Williamses what you had done?"

"No, ma'am. I wish I had."

Mrs. Ralsey scribbled again on her pad, then stopped, dangling the pen from her fingers.

"Do you believe Mrs. Seager regularly read their chart?"

"Yes, ma'am," Alicia chimed in. "She keeps all the charts in her office."

"We'll be right back." She and her husband maneuvered around us and stepped out of the room.

It didn't make sense. Did Mrs. Seager sterilize them because she didn't think the pill was an effective way to keep the girls from getting pregnant? Did she know they weren't taking the pill at all? I was still a little foggy from the car accident, so I had trouble figuring it out.

"What are you thinking, Dr. Townsend?" Ty turned around.

Daddy shook his head. He had been listening the whole time in silence. Like Ty, I was curious to hear his opinion. My insides throbbed, as if somebody had poked a fishhook into them. I eyed the wrinkled tip of the St. Jude acceptance letter sticking out of the top of my purse.

"I'm thinking," Daddy said, "that those girls might have a lawsuit if Donna is able to confirm that their grandmama and daddy didn't understand what they were signing. But it'll be tough."

They returned, and Mrs. Ralsey sat behind the desk while her husband perched on the edge. I'd always admired them, but seeing them work together was nothing short of dynamite. Both of them had been born and raised in Montgomery, had attended the same segregated high school at a time when a lot of Black teenagers in the state did not even make it to high school. Our Black professional community in Montgomery was small but mighty.

"Civil and Alicia, please don't talk about this with anyone, not even the other nurses at the clinic. We're going to start the work necessary to file this case in court. If you talk about it, you could hurt that process."

"Can I go see the girls?" I asked.

"Of course you can go see them," Daddy interrupted. "You want to make sure they don't develop any postoperative infections. Check on their incisions. And I'm here if you need me. Whatever you need."

Mrs. Ralsey continued, "Yes, you go on with your work as if nothing is happening. We don't know how long it will take, so try not to think about it too much."

"Try not to think about it? How can we work for a woman like that ever again?"

"Just tend to those girls and your other patients as best you can. They need you."

"Yes, ma'am," Alicia said.

Mr. Ralsey walked over to me and put his hand on my shoulder. "Civil, you have always been like a daughter to me. I promise you that we will do everything we can. God help me, we will make this right."

"I'm going to stay here for a few more minutes. Alicia, can you take Civil home?" Daddy said.

"Daddy, I don't need an escort."

"Of course, Dr. Townsend," she said.

When we got outside, I asked Alicia if she could drop me off at Dixie Court.

"Your daddy told me to take you home."

"I can get another ride, you know."

When we reached her car, she got in first and leaned over to pull up my door lock. She turned on the engine and we sat there for a moment as the car cooled off. "Are you going to work tomorrow?" she asked.

"Hell, no; and I can't believe you're going back there," I said. "I can't stand the sight of that woman's face right now."

"Tomorrow is payday, Civil. I got rent to pay." She folded her arms across her chest.

"So you going to shoot up those people with that drug all because of some rent money?"

"Hey, stop acting like that." She turned to me. "I'm trying to do right, just like you."

"Then don't go back there, Alicia. Please."

"I'm sorry, Civil, I can't live up to your high-and-mighty expectations. You ever stop to think about all the pressure you put on yourself? This ain't your fault."

"Are you taking me to the apartments or not?"

BY THE TIME Alicia dropped me off, the sun had slumped into the horizon, and the light in the entryway to the Williamses' apartment was not working. Although some of the apartments were still under construction, more families moved in each week. A group of kids played tag near a white cat napping in the grass. Two men sat on a bench listening to a radio playing in a parked car. Life at Dixie Court had not stopped just because the girls had been violated. I wondered how quickly word traveled among these buildings and considered, with real heaviness on my heart, how folks managed the constant barrage of bad news.

I knocked on the door. I had not seen any of them since the day I'd found out about the surgery, and I knew it was presumptuous of me to stop by unannounced. Someone yelled "Come on in!" but when I entered, the living room was empty. I walked straight to the girls' bedroom. Erica lay on the bed peeling an orange, the ripped skin scattered across a napkin.

"How you feeling?"

She nodded, and I hoped that was a "fine."

"Y'all need anything?"

Erica handed over half her orange to her sister. India sat back on the bed, pillows propped behind her back. Both girls wore pajamas.

"They had ice cream in the hospital," Erica said without looking up at me. I didn't know what to say. I couldn't tell if it was a real request for ice cream or a statement to get rid of me. I didn't have my car with me, but there was a corner market within walking distance.

I found Mrs. Williams sitting in her chair in the living room with a crochet hook in her hand. "Y'all got any ice cream?" I asked her.

"You know, I'm surprised I remember how to do this. I haven't picked up a hook in years."

"Nice color." I pointed to the ball of pink yarn unraveling on the floor around her feet.

"They give it to us over at the senior center. I picked up the yarn, made a loop, and the next thing I know, I'm making up a granny square. My mama taught me. Her name was Ella. Ella Mae. She used to make these big old blankets that we would lay across the foot of the bed. They was the most beautiful thing you ever seen, and when you slept under them they smelled like the peppermint oil she rubbed on her hands. She was talented with the needle, yes sir. Could sew anything you set your eyes on. But what she really liked was the slip of yarn between her fingers. She never said as much, but you could tell. She could do it with her eyes closed."

The veins of her hands flexed as she moved the hook over and under the yarn. I moved to the end of the couch so I could better see.

"For as long as I can remember, the women in my family have made the best life they knew how. I bet when you first come out to the house on old man Adair's place, you thought I was a nasty woman."

"No, I never thought that."

"You thought something. I saw it on your face. You looked around that house like it wasn't fit for a mule. And you know what? You was right. You ain't never lived in a one-room house with a dirt floor, nasty dogs, and the white man walking all up in there in his work boots without so much as a knock. That house wasn't never mine. Just a way station where we was stopping on our way to someplace else. Only the train never come, and so we was left sitting there on that platform waiting for near about three years."

She wrapped the loose yarn around an index finger.

"You ain't interested in the ramblings of an old woman like me. I guess I just wanted to say to you that when you got us this apartment, I felt something like hope, something I ain't felt in a long time. You know, I married Ernest T. Williams when I was eighteen years old. My husband promised me a better life. Every month, he brung home his money and put it in my hand. He would say, *Don't you ever get no ideas about me out there in them streets. You the only woman ever hug this neck.* Then he died and left me. Just out of the blue, he had the nerve to go and die on me. Just like Mace wife died on him. Second time death knocked on my door near about destroyed me. I told the Lord to just go ahead and send for me."

She stopped to wipe her nose with a tissue, then picked her needle back up. "So you come along and get us this here apartment, and the first night I slept in that bed in that back room, I dreamed my Ernest was still alive. We was living here together— me, him, Mace, the girls. Then somebody come and take it all away. Faceless people. Like ghosts but not ghosts. When I tried to stop them, they shouted words at us. Ugly words. I woke up scared. Every night since, I been expecting a knock at the door."

"Nobody's coming to take anything away from you, Mrs. Williams."

"No, that's where you wrong. They can always take it away. It ain't yours, Miss Civil. None of this." She waved a hand at the air, dropping the yarn. "Don't you know that? Ain't nobody ever taught you what they can take? They just take take take."

The room dimmed, as if somebody had turned off a lamp. It became so quiet, I could hear the wind surging. I thought vaguely of the ice cream the girls had requested. I thought of other things I could buy, things I could gift. A radio. Clothes. Shoes. A toaster for the kitchen.

She spoke her next words in a whisper. "I know you thought less of me living out there in that shack, and I didn't think so much of you neither, tell the truth."

"And now?" *Please*, I wanted to say. *Give it to me*. I hadn't known I needed her forgiveness, but my heart longed for it.

"Now I know the world exactly what I thought it was," she said and cast her eyes downward.

TWENTY-THREE

We went to church all the time when I was growing up, but by the time I reached high school we had fallen off the wagon and begun the Easter–Christmas–New Year's Eve circuit. In college I learned some words I had not comprehended before. Agnostic. Atheist. Our family was none of these. We were just irregular churchgoing Christians, though I had never been the kind of Christian to pray for intercession on behalf of my own desires. I was more of the gratitude-prayer type. *Thank you for this food. Thank you for my family. Thank you for the roof over my head.*

When I had the abortion I asked God for something—really asked, for the first time in my life. I asked for forgiveness. And though I did everything to put out of my mind that painful day of lying on a bed in a strange woman's house, I could not forget. It wasn't so much that I regretted it. I never doubted it was the right decision for me. It was that I had been raised to believe that such a thing was a sin. And that kind of upbringing was hard to shake.

The *Roe v. Wade* decision had come down on a Monday in January of 1973, and I remember the afternoon newspapers sold out as word spread. I watched my daddy sit down in his chair and silently read, shake his head and then leave the paper on the coffee table. We never discussed it, but surely he knew that there were houses out in the country where women went to have the procedure, even before the ruling. I'd gone to one in Opelika, one where Miss Pope believed I could get safe care. And it had still been a risk. Surely Daddy understood that women needed a trustworthy place. Some women traveled to New York to have the procedure, but that was too far for most of us. Make no mistake about it, that ruling was a big deal.

My belief that all women needed access to trained medical professionals, especially poor women, did not mean that I was without ambivalence. In the days after my procedure, I swung back and forth between guilt and anger. Guilt about not taking better precautions. Anger that I had to climb up on a plastic sheet–covered bed in a stranger's house. It took months to level out my emotions. After the girls' surgery, I experienced that same emotional pendulum. That's why when Mama asked me to go to church with her one Sunday morning in July, I agreed. I had some unfinished business in that place of worship.

When we entered the sanctuary, Mama walked as if she had never missed a day—right up the side aisle to her regular seat in the row behind the missionaries. The pastor asked the congregation to bow our heads. He was young, hired out of Chicago. Once Dr. King changed the course of Montgomery, the Black churches stayed on the lookout for a King twin. This one at my family's church was in his third year, and I had seen him preach only once. It struck me that he was still getting his bearings in Montgomery. Like many newcomers, he'd come out of awe for our history, but, even with his knowledge of all that our community had been through, he seemed to underestimate the will of his congregation. Black churches in Montgomery were more than buildings, more than houses of worship. They captured our collective activism, organized our frustrations. That significance of purpose, that seriousness, wore Mama out sometimes. That's why we stopped going in the first place.

The pastor ended his prayer with a flourish, and Mama leaned over to whisper, "How long has he been here now?"

"Three years, I believe."

"I'll give him another two," Mama said. She sat with her hands folded in her lap, a lace-trimmed handkerchief tucked in her palm. In church, Mama found stability, calm. Like her artistic pursuits, church was grounding for her.

The pastor's wife sat on the other end of the row, flanked by two fidgeting children. Mama nodded at her and the woman nodded back. One of the church's oldest members, Mrs. Cooper, walked to the podium next to the piano to make the announcements. "I see June Townsend and her daughter here this morning. It's so good to see you. Could y'all please stand?"

Mrs. Cooper had been old ever since I'd known her. She always sat on the row of Mothers, wearing a white cap and rocking when the spirit moved her. Once, when Ty and I were kids, we'd giggled when she acknowledged the college *gladulates*. She'd stopped midsentence and looked up into the balcony, straight at us. Her expression held the promise of a whipping in it even though she wasn't any more related to us than Adam and Eve. A look like that was always enough to quiet the restless kids.

I wondered if Ty had been to church lately, if he had struggled to make peace with these events the way I had. Inside that church, among my church family, I got the feeling that this struggle belonged to all of us. I could persevere if I stayed in that place and folded myself in the love of old church Mothers like Mrs. Cooper.

Sitting in church with Mama, I could forget that the girls were at home with their grandmother, recovering from a surgery that never should have happened in the first place. I could listen to the music and hum along with the hymn, find solace in the notion that

God knew how much burden we could bear. That first Sunday Mama and I started going back to church, I was overcome by a moment of peace. And I wanted it to last forever.

THE RALSEYS INSISTED I go back to work. Alicia and I were advised to keep up the pretense of normalcy until they filed the suit and it went public. All of the nurses knew the girls had been sterilized, but they didn't know about the pending lawsuit. We had confided in a few of them weeks earlier about our suspicions around the drug, and we hoped they were making the right decisions on their own. I worried our actions could result in more sterilizations, but I also knew it was a risk we had to take. Alicia and I tried to keep a close eye on the files before they went back in the cabinets. The Ralseys had asked us to keep quiet, so we understood the precariousness of the situation. But we also knew it was only a matter of time before Mrs. Seager sterilized someone else. When she called me into her office that Friday, I prepared myself for the worst. We were screwed six ways from Sunday.

She leaned back in her chair. "Now that you've been here a few months, do you still think this is the job for you?"

I knew how I wanted to answer that question. I wanted to yell at her and tell her she was merciless for what she had done to those girls, and hell no, this wasn't a job for me. I had not wanted to come back to work. I was only there at the urging of the Ralseys. They believed Alicia and I might be able to intervene if we saw something suspicious.

But instead of shouting at her, I took a deep breath and summoned all my strength. "Mrs. Seager, I graduated in the top 5 percent of my class at Tuskegee. I aced my exams, and I was president of our student nursing association. I spent weeks preparing for the interview with your clinic. Why would you even ask me that question?"

"Civil."

"I was raised to be humble, so this isn't something you will hear me say in the presence of the women who work in this clinic, but I strongly believe I am one of the best nurses on your staff."

"Your attitude is lousy."

"My patients seem to like me. Aren't they the only ones who matter?"

"I'm your supervisor, so the answer to that question is no." She made a noise in the back of her throat.

"The women who come into this clinic are in need of these services, and they deserve our respect. I give them that because that is the oath that I took." *I will remember that I do not treat a fever chart, a cancerous growth, but a sick human being, whose illness may affect the person's family and economic stability.* The words looped through my head.

She tapped her fingertips on the desk. I waited for the other shoe to drop. "You know by now that the Williams girls were surgically sterilized," she said.

"I do." I tried to keep my voice steady and even.

"Their legal guardians gave consent."

"Those girls have never been pregnant. They not even having sex yet."

"How do you know?"

"Because I asked them. Did you ever ask them?"

"There are boys in those apartments where they stay now. You only have yourself to blame for that when you took it upon yourself to move them clear across town."

I blinked rapidly. Somehow she had discovered that I had been involved in getting them moved to Dixie Court.

"Oh Civil, do you think I don't see things going on right under my nose?"

I sat in stunned silence. Did she also know some of us had

stopped giving the shots? Was a formal reprimand coming? "I moved them because they were living in filth."

"When they were out on the farm, at least they had to travel to get to a boy. Now they're surrounded, thanks to you. Do you think that retarded girl could take care of a baby? Besides, what about their daddy?"

I shook my head, trying to cool the rage. "She's not retarded. And what about their daddy?"

She narrowed her eyes. "I've seen his kind before."

As the meaning of what she was suggesting dawned on me, I lost my cool. "You sterilized two innocent little girls!"

"They gave consent!" She slammed the palm of her hand on the desk.

I looked around the office, at its spare, empty bookshelves. I couldn't help but compare it to the clutter of my daddy's office, his shelves crammed with medical journals, poetry collections, notebooks. In Mrs. Seager's office, there was not a book in sight. Doodads, knickknacks, a set of miniature porcelain dolls—the kinds of things one collects as a hobby. Daddy had once likened these kinds of shelves to a piano that was just a stand for photographs.

"I cannot say that I'm surprised at your insubordination. I always expected it."

"Ma'am?"

I didn't want to call her *ma'am*. I didn't want to call her anything. Mrs. Ralsey had urged us to keep up pretenses. And I had been raised right so the word flowed freely off my tongue. But if there was ever a more hostile *ma'am* uttered, I had not heard one.

She slowly slid her elbows onto the desk. "If you want to stay employed at this clinic, you had better get your act together. Because though you may think you are smart, I have two fresh resumes waiting in the drawer in front of me, and they are every bit as good as yours."

She assumed I wanted the job badly enough to accept her bullshit. She had merely brought me in to gauge my reaction to the Williamses' sterilization, whether I would cause more trouble. She expected me to comply, as many Black Alabamans did when confronted with white authority. It also occurred to me she knew even more than she was letting on.

"You knew the Williams sisters weren't on birth control, didn't you?" I said quietly as it all dawned on me. "That's why you did it. But how did you know?"

She crossed her arms and sat back. "This is my clinic, Civil Townsend. Mine."

Her bottom lip trembled. Then she turned around in her chair and faced the window. If she did not have another resume in her drawer at that moment, I knew that she would soon.

TWENTY-FOUR

The secretary led me into the small meeting room, where I found Mrs. Ralsey waiting with a young white man with brown, curly hair. He had taken his suit jacket off and his armpits were sweating. I guessed he was a police detective. Or a hospital administrator. I didn't know why Mrs. Ralsey had called me into her office. She'd only said she wanted me to meet someone.

"Please have a seat, Civil."

I sat down in a chair across from the two of them.

"Civil, this is Lou Feldman. He's going to be taking the lead now."

I looked back and forth between them. "Lead on what?"

She cleared her throat. "I've been called to go work on the Tuskegee case. A group of lawyers is assembling to take action on behalf of the men's families. There are hundreds of victims. This experiment goes all the way back to 1932, and they need all the help—"

"I've read about the experiment, Mrs. Ralsey. I know the details."

"Then you understand they're going to need a big legal team."

"What I understand right now is that a little Black girl's life in Alabama ain't worth as much as a man's."

"Civil."

"I don't mean to be rude, Mrs. Ralsey."

"Both cases are important. Lou is a civil rights lawyer. He's the right person for this case."

"And he's . . . he's—"

"I'm white," he blurted. "And I'm not what you expected. I know that. But I'm asking you to give me a shot."

He kept moving around in his chair, as if uncomfortable in his clothes. His unruly brown curls fell into his face, and he pushed them back. When he raked his hair, I could see that his nails were short and bitten to the quick. His narrow eyes peered at me through his glasses, watching me watch him. I didn't know where Mrs. Ralsey had found this young whippersnapper, but he was probably just another opportunist.

"How old are you?" I asked.

"Twenty-eight."

He was only a few years older than I was. "Have you even tried a case before?"

"Of course." He pushed his glasses up his nose.

"Did you win?"

"Civil." Mrs. Ralsey sent me a second warning signal, but I didn't care.

"I'll be honest: I've never been the lead on a case before, but I've worked for some very good lawyers. I'm ready."

"These are children. They've never won anything in their lives. Not even a cake in a church raffle. You know what I'm talking about?"

"I wouldn't recommend him if I didn't think he could handle it," said Mrs. Ralsey. "Lou comes highly recommended by people I know and trust."

I knew what she was saying. She had checked him out, and he had proven that he was on our side—not some wolf in sheep's clothing. I got the wink loud and clear. Still, I couldn't wrap my head around it. He couldn't take the lead on this. The case was too important.

Meanwhile, Lou Feldman had not taken his eyes off me. "Their names are India and Erica Williams. Erica is the older one. She is thirteen years old. She's enrolled in summer school at George Washington Carver Junior High. Her favorite ice cream is chocolate. India just got accepted to the school at St. Jude's. She loves dogs. And dolls. She's particularly attached to one doll with yarn hair. India doesn't speak, but the doctor who tested her believes she has promise. She adores her big sister, and the two are inseparable."

"So you interviewed a few folks."

"Their mother's name was Constance Williams. She died of breast cancer a few years ago. The father is Mace Williams. He worked on Frank Adair's farm until recently. Now he's working at the Whitfield pickle factory. His supervisor says he is never late and he's a good worker."

I jerked a thumb at him. "Because he got good grades, you're putting him on the case?"

"Their grandmother is Mrs. Patricia Williams. She loves to cook, and she has started a garden with the other grandmothers who live in Dixie Court."

"A garden?"

"Between Buildings 8 and 9. She speaks highly of you, by the way."

These were my people. I was supposed to know that Mrs. Williams had started a garden. I was supposed to know what the owner at the pickle factory thought about Mace. It was just like Mama said—strangers traipsing up in there like the family was a sideshow. "You're putting him on the case because you think it will be better if they have a white lawyer," I said suddenly.

"That is enough, Civil Townsend. You are out of order, and I will not tolerate it. I know your parents raised you better than that."

Lou scooted his chair closer to mine. "You're right. I'm young. I'm inexperienced. I'm white. I'm just one step out of law school. I couldn't find a match to my navy sock this morning, so I'm wearing one brown sock and one navy. My wife calls me a mama's boy, and she's probably right. But this I can tell you—I can do this case precisely because I *am* a mama's boy. My parents left Europe and came to this country fearing for their lives. And from the moment I was born, right here in Montgomery, they raised me to fight for what is right. It's in my blood, Civil. And I will follow whoever did this to hell and back to see justice for those girls."

"I still don't understand why you care. Why this case?"

"I can't give you a good answer that will satisfy you. I know you love that family. I can see it on your face. I can't promise anything other than giving everything I got."

A bead of sweat formed on his upper lip. The room was warm. We were all sitting too close in the small room, and I needed some air.

"The Williamses ain't looking for a white Jesus."

"Believe you me, I don't aim to be one."

I paused. "Will you include the Ralseys on the case?"

"I plan to include them every step of the way if they'd like. I value their opinion. I value yours, too, or else I wouldn't be sitting here right now."

Mrs. Ralsey shuffled some papers. "I have another meeting right now. Civil, do you want to come to my house this Sunday? We can talk about it some more over dinner if you'd like."

"I don't need to talk about it," I said, still angry but desperately wanting to believe in Lou Feldman. He held those girls' futures in his hands.

Lou wrote two numbers down on a piece of paper. "This is my office number and my home number. You can call anytime, day or night."

I took the paper, and they both followed me out.

"My wife wants to meet you someday soon. She's a lawyer in Selma. She said she's proud of what you've done."

I shook my head. Proud? What on earth kind of nonsensical woman was he married to? "Mr. Feldman, just win this case. That's all I want."

"Call me Lou."

Good Lord. He was still wet behind the ears and he would be the one taking the girls' case to court. The judge was going to throw the case out before Lou found that other sock. I was sure of it.

I HAD NOT spoken to Mace since that day at the hospital, and honestly I was afraid. I didn't want to talk to him at the apartment, where Mrs. Williams could hear, so I went out to the factory and waited for him to sign off for the day. When he saw me sitting in my car, he walked up to the window.

"What you doing here? The girls alright?"

"They fine. I just came by to talk to you."

"Ain't no need." He began to walk away.

"Mace." I got out of the car and followed him. "You know I would have stopped it if I had known. You know that, right?"

Some of the other men were walking toward the bus stop. They hushed their chatter as if they were listening. Mace glanced at them uneasily. He took my elbow and turned in the opposite direction.

"Come on." We turned down a dirt path that led to the railroad tracks. I didn't know the area that well, but I knew if we kept walking we'd reach the river. Trash—cans and bottles and a pair of torn pants—littered the grass. Someone had left a bucket. Mace picked it up and carried it. When we reached the railroad tracks, he placed the bucket upside down on the ground and motioned. "Sit."

I sat. I was wearing a pair of shorts and a T-shirt. I'd changed out of my uniform after work. It wasn't how he usually saw me dressed, and I felt exposed. But he wasn't looking at me. He picked up a rock and rolled it between his fingers. In this area of railroad crossover, the track split into branch lines. In one of the lanes, six abandoned cars sat rusting near an old beanery that looked as if it hadn't been functional in years. Nothing moved, but I knew the line was active. We were close enough to feel the wind should a train come roaring by. But for now, all was quiet.

"Mace, talk to me. It's driving me crazy that you won't talk to me."

"You don't understand nothing. You just a little girl."

His words stung. It sounded exactly like what I'd said to Lou. "Tell me how to make this right."

"Make it right?"

"We're filing a lawsuit to try to stop this from happening again. They got this young white lawyer."

"Yeah, I heard about him coming around asking questions."

"We're taking the clinic to court." I had not spoken to him about any of this, and I wanted to know how he felt. He had worked all day pushing pickles across the floor, as he called it. I didn't know what that meant exactly. I had never been inside a factory of any kind. The sour stench of vinegar rose from his clothes.

"You want to lose your job?" he asked.

"That clinic needs to be shut down." I stood up, and the bucket pitched over on its side. "I have done nothing but love your girls since the day I met them."

He shook his head. "You a little rich girl who think you can come over here and play around in folk lives."

"Who died and made you God and jury?"

"They done took away my girls' womanhood!"

"Having children doesn't make you a woman."

"You think you know, but you don't know." His voice was tight and strained, and I could see his eyes reddening.

I didn't know what to do. I stood there with my arms at my sides. He wiped at his dry face with the tail of his shirt.

"Mace." I stepped closer and he pulled me to him.

"You remind me of her. She was just like you. Stubborn as a mule in mud."

I started to shake my head, but he hushed me. "You got a way with the girls. And with Mama. She did, too. I think Mama grieved her passing more than anybody. But when you come around, it seem like Mama find new life again." His breath blew warm on my face.

"Your mama hates me now."

"I hated you, too. When I walked in that room and seen my two babies crying like they hadn't even cried when they mama died, I thought I might kill somebody. And you were going to be first. But when I saw you, I knew. You was just as tore up inside as I was."

The sun beat down on us, and I started to sweat. We were standing too close. He propped a foot up on the edge of the rail, and I leaned into his thigh. In the distance, I could hear the faint chug of a train whistle. I wanted to step back. He slid his arm around my waist, and something went soft inside me. For a moment I thought he would kiss me, and I closed my eyes. This rush of heat between us would make it all better. If he would just show me some tenderness, after all that had happened, both of us might survive this.

Suddenly, he let go and stepped back. He picked up a handful of rocks and threw them at a railroad car. They clanged loudly against the metal. "Let's go," he said and started walking back toward the path.

I stared at the overturned bucket. A line of ants gave chase up its side.

TWENTY-FIVE

The morning the paper announced Lou's lawsuit, I found Mama lying on the floor of her studio. Sometimes she did that when she worked late, but with her recent desire to start going to church again, I worried something was amiss. She had bundled a drop cloth as a pillow, but she was still wearing her shoes.

"Mama?"

She lifted her head. Her once-dark hair was now fine and silver. I helped her sit up, and she leaned back into the sofa.

In pictures Mama is lovely, the most stunning woman I've ever seen. She has these features that always seem to catch the light, and when you look at a picture of her, you can't stop staring. In every picture she appears caught off guard when the shutter snaps. It's always the same expression: eyebrows up, a casual look at something just away from the camera. She never relaxes into a photograph, never tries to see the person on the other side of the lens. I would say Mama is guarded in photographs, as if she has just held up a shield the moment the camera is lifted.

I used to think the same thing about her paintings. Their attraction lay in something just off-center. She often went through phases—some years everything was all bright and bold, other years the colors more muted or sheer. She would use three-inch-wide brushes to create swaths of color in the middle of a solid canvas. The works rarely left you cold. Even the smallest ones drew the eye.

Daddy said the only reason she hadn't become famous in the 1960s was that it was a time when Black artists were claiming representational art as a form of political expression. How could anybody read protest into brushstrokes and color? A lot of people could not understand the freedom in that, he would say.

Mama had exhibited a few times in the Montgomery Museum of Fine Arts. The museum director hosted her as a means of reaching out to Black folks in Montgomery, a halfhearted effort since the white patrons of the museum never came to her exhibits. But Mama's friends came. They streamed in, wearing bright outfits they considered appropriate for art, carrying cakes for the reception. Though only a few of them actually bought a painting over the years, they filled the room with love and support. Mama gave away more paintings than she sold. There was even one hanging in City Hall, though we suspected most white folks did not know it was painted by one of the city's colored residents. After the exhibit ended, Daddy and I would carefully wrap the paintings and load them in the back of someone's pickup truck to take to our house.

"Ros, what are you doing here?" Mama raised her head.

"It's me, Mama. Civil." She had mistaken me for Rosalind, her sister who lived in Memphis. Aunt Ros was a psychologist and had always complained Mama wasted her talent by staying in Montgomery. She believed Mama belonged in New York and never understood why Mama had not chosen to pursue her passion. *If you aren't going to paint, then at least get a job*, Aunt Ros would say. Daddy supported Mama's art, but he considered it a hobby. He enjoyed having an artist for a wife. It elevated the family to a sophistication that even his medical degree could not confer.

"Mama, you okay?"

We never named it. We did not urge her to go see someone. I think it was because there was stigma in that admission, so we just propped her up and helped her through. Surely we could handle her ourselves. I believe Daddy built that studio as an antidote. He bought her paints and planned her shows and cooked for us on days she could not get out of bed. And it seemed to work. Most of the time.

She blinked her eyes rapidly. "I just called you Ros, didn't I?"

"Yeah."

"Sorry about that, baby. I think I was dreaming."

"What were you dreaming about?"

"I don't remember."

"Let me help you wash your brushes," I suggested.

I led her over to the worktable. Together we squeezed solvent onto our rags, then fingered the bristles, gently working out the paint. I kept an eye on her, as I had for most of my life. My and Daddy's job was to keep Mama from sinking too deep. And we knew the answer—painting. It was her medicine.

"What day is today?"

"Monday," I said.

"No, I mean the date."

"August 6."

"Good morning."

I had not heard Daddy open the door. Mama dropped two brushes into a cup beside the sink.

"I got fresh coffee in the kitchen," he said.

The faint crow of a rooster rose from a nearby backyard. I knew that bird. He was always late. The sun had already risen.

"Mama was sleeping on the floor, Daddy. Why didn't you come get her last night?"

"I like sleeping out here," she said.

"What are you working on?" He walked over to a canvas.

"A series."

"I didn't know that, Mama. How many do you have so far?" I peeked beneath a cloth covering a painting that rested against the wall.

"Just one," she said. "I got a long way to go."

Inside the house, Daddy made me and Mama sit at the kitchen table. I watched his hands, elegant and soft, lift the coffeepot and pour. They could have been surgeon's hands. When I was younger, he had been one of those unusual daddies who liked to do my hair, carefully making the parts with the pointed end of a rattail comb and greasing my scalp with just the right amount of pressure. Once, I'd told my teacher that my daddy did my hair every morning and she'd whispered to me, "The devil love a lie."

He poured cream until the coffee turned beige. Two spoonfuls of sugar in each. Ever since mama had let me try coffee at fifteen years old, I liked my coffee exactly the same as hers: sweet and milky.

"You see the paper?" Daddy touched a finger to the newspaper sitting on the counter.

"No," I said. "But I know they're filing the lawsuit today."

"I see you're not dressed for work."

"I can't."

Mama put her hand over mine. "That's alright, baby. What about the girls? You think Erica will hear? Maybe not. Summer school classes are usually small. There's a chance she might be able to escape the brunt of it."

"I'm picking the girls up today. Getting them out of town."

"Where y'all going?"

"I'm taking the whole family out to Rockford near Talladega. They got some cousins out there they haven't seen in a while."

"Who's driving? You need to be careful, Civil." Daddy folded his arms.

"My car is running good again. It'll be fine, Daddy."

"What happened to Williams's truck? Didn't you say he had a truck?"

"Daddy, stop."

"He's got two girls to raise, a mama to take care of, and he can't even piece together a truck?"

"Daddy." The truck was fixed now, but I didn't say that. We couldn't all fit inside, but I didn't say that, either.

He sipped his coffee and studied me.

"I'll see y'all later tonight." I kissed Mama on the cheek. Her skin was soft and smelled faintly of turpentine.

BANKS OF OAK trees broke open to reveal wide patches of land. We drove through a few lazy towns—Wetumpka, Titus, and even a little place that called itself Equality. I kept an easy speed. The girls' faces opened up once we were on the road. I'd forgotten they were country people at heart. In the apartment on Dixie Court or wearing the Whitfield uniform, Mace shrank. Out here, his chin jutted and the ruddy tone of his skin came to light. In the rearview mirror, I could see Mrs. Williams had finally let go of her purse. "You see that there?" Mace said, pointing. "That right there is a crepe myrtle. Ooh, prettiest tree you ever did see. My daddy loved crepe myrtles. And you see those red mulberry trees? We used to eat the berries right off the tree when I was little."

The road curved and I turned off the highway. When we got to the T-stop, Mace hollered out for me to hook a left. Suddenly he seemed to know exactly where he was going. When I said as much, he responded, "Girl, I know this here part of Alabama well as I know the hair on my head."

"Is the land disappearing, too?" I joked. There was no sign of thinning hair on his head, but he touched a hand to the top as if I'd spotted something.

"Quit playing, girl."

"Mace, you reckon we done brought enough food? Nellie so sweet and liable to cook a feast. I don't want to seem like no beggar."

"Mama, you bringing cobbler, collards, and macaroni. That's practically a whole dinner."

I shouted over the wind. "Is that too much air on you, Mrs. Williams?"

"No, it's fine by me, Civil. Too hot to let these windows up."

A truck in front of us was going too slow, but I was afraid to pass it. Daddy was right to be concerned. The car accident had made me a nervous driver. I slowed down and turned up the radio. Aretha Franklin's voice belted out of the speakers, and Erica started singing. The child was off-key, but she knew all the words.

"Right here!" Mace shouted and I hit the brakes. We had almost missed our turn. The next road was narrow and unpaved, just wide enough for one car. But it was well tended, and someone had filled in the pitted holes with rocks so my car had no trouble making its way. The road ended at three houses that sat haphazardly across from one another.

"There go Nellie right there!" shouted Mrs. Williams. "Nellie!"

We all piled out of the car. I stood back as the family hugged. Nellie was a tall, thin woman with a narrow face. When she opened her mouth, a glint of gold shone in the midday sun. Behind her, a man waited for the talkative ones to finish. He stepped forward and patted Mace on the back and waited for Mrs. Williams to kiss his cheek.

They introduced me. I extended a hand, but Miss Nellie pulled me to her. "Out here we don't fool with none of that hand-shaking business. Come on over here and let me squeeze you."

The woman's hug was strong but brief. It left me wanting more. I could not remember the last time my mama had hugged me. Daddy, either. We were not a hugging family. "Y'all come on inside. I hope you brought an appetite. I ain't know if y'all had a proper breakfast, so I got some biscuits and jelly on the table."

"She make the jelly herself," said her husband. "Make you lick the jar."

We followed her up the steps into the house. The wooden plank floors creaked with every step. I looked around. Miss Nellie had a thing for lace. Lace curtains. A long dining table covered in a brown vinyl tablecloth with a lace runner down the middle. A lace doily on the sideboard. The house was cozy, as if no room went unloved. It smelled of baking bread, and a cross breeze sailed through the windows. Nellie's big voice boomed in the house.

"There's three beds upstairs, and I've set up the couch out back. Maybe Miss Civil can take that one. It's nice at night. Now, y'all go on and wash up and then come on in here and get some of these biscuits. I got some more coming out the oven in a minute. Mace, you sit over there next to Leotis. Your cousin Ricky and his family will be here later on. Your cousins Patsy and Doe, ooh, you wouldn't even recognize them; they so tall I say they need to play basketball. Erica and India, y'all look good and healthy like you can eat good. I made two different kinds of jelly, what kind you like? Leotis, go out there and get that food out the car that Pat brung with her so I can put it in the icebox. Ooh, I'm so happy y'all here."

I took India and Erica to the bathroom to wash up. Upstairs, it was just as neat as downstairs. I peeked through the wide-open doors of the bedrooms. It didn't immediately appear that anyone lived with Nellie and Leotis. Such a large house for just the two of them. I'd had no idea the girls had cousins like this. If Nellie had known how they were living, surely she would have invited the girls sooner? I wondered if she was a first or second cousin. All Mrs. Williams had told me was that she was a cousin.

In the bathroom, the girls washed their hands in the sink. I showed them how to cup their palms and splash water onto their faces. Erica did it once and dried her hands on a pink towel. India did it over and over again, smiling at herself in the mirror. I stepped back, trying to stop myself from treating them too tenderly.

"Y'all been out here before?"

"I remember coming when Mama was alive. India probably don't remember."

"She's your mama's cousin?"

"Yeah. In Mama family, we got a lot of cousins."

"Oh, okay."

In the dining room, Mace had already started buttering and spooning jelly onto his biscuit. Leotis sat next to Mace at the table, sipping on a glass of iced lemonade.

The girls scooted into chairs and I moved the plate of biscuits closer to us. When I bit into one, it crumbled and melted on my tongue. I paused for a moment, then washed it down with lemonade.

When Miss Nellie came back in the dining room with a plate of butter, I couldn't help but praise her. "Miss Nellie, these biscuits are out of sight."

"Thank you, Civil. Eat as much as you want. I got some more cooling on the pan now. And take some more of this lemonade. This here ain't made from no powder. Fresh from the lemons."

The girls poked each other and giggled. I had not seen them act like this since before the surgery.

Everybody sat at the table, and I reached for another biscuit as Nellie talked on and on. The sound of her voice soothed like a rush of air, and none of us interrupted. I ate until my belly was full. Then I slipped my shoes off under the table.

"I'm so glad you made greens, Pat, because I didn't have time," Nellie was saying, "and I'm just hoping that pie holds up until after dinner, because them Joneses love to stick they fork into the dessert before dinner over."

TWENTY-SIX

I had not fellowshipped with a family like this in a long time. All of my grandparents were dead by the time I turned thirteen years old. Daddy was an only child, and Mama just had one sister with no children. I didn't have the dozens of cousins that so many Alabamans had, so being in that house fed my soul. We ate, rested and talked, and then ate again. We must have sat at that table for hours. They were talkative people, and it took the pressure off. I just listened and nodded.

After dinner, we sat around the table drinking coffee. There was Ricky, an auto mechanic from Lowndesboro who had married a much younger woman, Dina. They had three boys all under eight years old, who ran around the house chasing one another with toy guns. Dina kept an eye on the boys, punctuating their squeals with "Stop that running now!" Ricky just smiled and picked at his teeth with a toothpick. During dinner, the youngest boy sat in his daddy's lap and ate from his plate.

"His first wife passed away. They never could have children," Mrs. Williams whispered when we cleared the tables and moved into the kitchen to stack plates. "He love them boys more than a dog love a bone."

Just as Nellie had said, Patsy and Doe were tall for women. They were sisters and had once babysat India and Erica. Both of them were magazine-cover pretty with identical puffed Afros and hoop earrings. Patsy sat beside India at dinner and kept refilling her lemonade and offering her more food. I caught Doe just staring at Erica, as if weighing what life would be like now for the girl, as if trying to determine if this barrenness was something you could see with your eyes.

Although we had not spoken about it at dinner, I was all but certain everyone had heard about the surgery. When Nellie introduced me, they observed me for a second longer than normal. At one point, a latecomer showed up—Tim, Mace's brother-in-law. It was Tim who broke open the dam while we were sipping our coffee.

"Y'all see the news today?"

In the back of the house, the high-pitched voices of the children drowned out the din of a TV set. Only the adults were still seated at the table. I leaned back in my chair, focusing my eyes on the dusty light fixture overhead.

"Which channel?" asked Nellie. "We don't get all the channels out here."

"All of 'em," Tim said.

Mace touched a finger to his temple. I took another swallow of coffee, and the movement drew Tim's eye. He looked at me as he removed a section of the paper from his back pocket, unfolded it, and spread it out on the table. I wiped at some crumbs on the table where my plate had been and sneaked a peek at the paper headline.

Lawsuit Filed in Federal Court Against Montgomery Family Planning Clinic. Everyone looked down at it. Nobody had to read to know what it was about. There was a picture of the girls someone had taken of them outside their apartment.

"Y'all going get some money?" Tim asked.

"We going get justice for my granddaughters. That's what we after. The man say—"

"Justice?" Tim's voice rose. "My sister is rolling over in her grave, and you talk about justice? Justice was this thing never happening in the first place."

"Don't you speak about my wife," Mace said.

"She was my sister before she was your wife. And what you done, huh? Messing up the only thing she ever loved more than herself."

"And where was you?" Mrs. Williams interjected. "Where was you when we was living in that doghouse out on old man Adair's farm and the rain was coming through the roof? Did you ever come see about your nieces?"

Nellie stood. "Let's not talk about this, y'all. Ruin a good dinner. I'm going to go get the rest of the pie."

I wanted to read the article so I could see if it mentioned Mrs. Seager. I also wanted to know what Lou's complaint alleged. I had brought the Williamses out here to see their family, but the devil's mess had followed.

It had been almost two months since the surgery, and it had been hard to gauge how much word of it had spread beyond Montgomery. Now that the lawsuit was filed, it would be beauty-shop gossip, church basement tittle-tattle. The clinic wasn't well known, but it would be now.

"Stop playing!" I heard Erica yell. I wanted to go see what they were doing. I hoped the boys weren't terrorizing India, but I knew Erica would defend her sister.

"What you got to say, Mace? Huh? How this happen, man?"

Tim wasn't trying to stir trouble. The man was hurting over it. Everyone at that table had to be hurting over it. It occurred to me that I didn't belong here. This was a private family moment, but I couldn't figure out how to get up from the table and excuse myself.

Mace's voice sounded strained and high. "I don't know. I can't explain it myself. Them white folks come to the place near about every day. Always asking questions, leaving me papers I can't understand. We wasn't starving, but getting that bit of assistance helped, man. I work hard as a mule, but it ain't never enough. Mr. Adair give me just enough to scrape by."

"That's how they do it," Patsy said. "I was on food stamps and they made me tell them everything but the color of my panties to get them."

"My boys get free lunch. They sit all the free lunch kids on one side of the room together like a bunch of rejects. Ain't right," said Dina.

"I ain't been to the doctor in I don't know how long. Poking and asking me private questions. They don't care nothing about me." Nellie stabbed the pie with a knife.

"They tried to take this house. Told me something wrong with the deed. I got my shotgun and they ain't been back since," said her husband.

Take take take.

The ends of my fingers itched, and I did not trust myself to open my mouth. Who knew what might come tumbling out. The children must have settled down to something, because I could no longer hear their voices or the complaints of the floor.

"But I hear you got a new job now out at the pickle factory," Tim whispered.

"Yeah, this one here helped with that." Mace tilted his head in my direction without looking at me. "She got Erica back in school. We finally start to see some sunshine and then this happen. What I do, God?"

"Don't bring God into this," said Mrs. Williams. "This ain't got nothing to do with Him."

"Sure ain't." Nellie pushed the plate of pie down the center of the table. "Them white folks give you that assistance and then act like they own you."

Everyone got quiet again.

"Can I see it?" I said quietly. Tim slid the paper over to me, and I began to read. Lou Feldman had done it. Not only did the suit name Mrs. Seager and the clinic, but it also named the doctor who performed the surgery. The article outlined the details in Feldman's statement: how the girls were taken from their home, how the father and grandmother, due to their illiteracy, were not fully capable of understanding what they were consenting to.

The article named me as their nurse. *Good Lord*, I said under my breath. Folks might think I had something to do with this, that I was the one instead of Val.

"So is there money or what?" Tim asked again. He was staring straight at me. So was everyone else.

"I don't know," I answered, my voice shaking. "I think right now they're just trying to make sure it doesn't happen again."

"What good is that when it's already happened to my nieces? Somebody need to pay!"

"Tim, that's enough." Nellie's husband Leotis was the only person in the family who didn't talk constantly. When he spoke, it had a settling effect on the room. "That lawsuit ain't got nothing to do with us. That's just more of the white folks' meddling."

I shook my head, but everyone ignored me.

"What we got to do," Leotis said, "is step up as a family. Them girls been through enough. Pat, I want you to send them out here whenever you feel the need. It's just me and Nellie now. All we got is this roof and our social security. Lord knows we too old to raise 'em. But we can feed 'em. And we can love on 'em. We should have done it long ago after Constance passed. But we here now."

"Leotis, don't be so hard on yourself. None of us could have seen this coming," his wife said.

"I'm the one what signed the papers," Mrs. Williams said.

"I signed them, too, Mama."

"I'm the nurse," I said quietly.

"Maybe . . . maybe," Doe began.

"Maybe we just got to wait this out and see what happens." Patsy finished her sentence.

I thought of Lou and his youthful face and innocent enthusiasm. He could not possibly understand that he held the hopes of not just this family but our entire people in his hands. I truly hoped he was not just another meddler, as the family put it. If he didn't win this case, then I was putting them through all of this for nothing. And even if he did win it, it might be for nothing anyway. They might never get money. It was possible nothing would ever change for them.

We got on the road early the next morning because Mace had to get to work. The girls and their grandmother slept in the back seat, their heads resting on each other's shoulders. Mace stared straight ahead out the window. I did not know what to say, so I kept my mouth shut. He was quiet for so long that I figured he had nodded off. I concentrated on driving. When he spoke, the soft sound of his voice startled me.

"Maybe if my girls could read good, they could do better than me."

I had never heard him mention their schooling before. I'd always assumed he believed school was misplaced energy, something with limited use for poor folks in Alabama.

"You know, it's not your fault, Mace. You doing everything you can for your family."

"That right?" He turned his head toward me, but I kept my eyes on the road. I couldn't look at him.

"Yes."

"Well sometimes everything you can ain't good enough, is it." He paused and we turned to each other at the same time. The passing headlights of a truck illuminated his face. "Is it, Miss Civil?"

TWENTY-SEVEN

Our appointment was at 8 A.M., but India was dressed long before we needed to leave. After lounging at home for two months, she was ready to get out. I was also excited about taking her to visit her new school. When we arrived, the nun met us in the front lobby and introduced herself as Sister LaTarsha. I could not believe my eyes. The sister was a *sister*. Her hair was hidden beneath her habit, but her clothes were unfussy—elastic-waisted jeans and a simple pink top, clean skin covered in a veneer of sweat.

"Don't look so happy to see me, Miss Townsend."

"I'm sorry. I just thought—"

"You aren't the first. Black nuns do exist. Come on. I'll show you around."

The school was located in the basement of St. Jude hospital. Four classrooms and offices for the staff. There was no gym, though they did have an outdoor play yard. She explained there was no cafeteria. The children ate in their classrooms.

"There are fifty-five students here with various needs," Sister LaTarsha told me and India as we stepped inside one of the classrooms. The students had not arrived yet. I noticed there were no individual desks—only tables. A round rug featured an image of a rainbow. A wall with low bookshelves contained baskets of toys. A reading area with cardboard books.

"We don't separate our students in the same way as standard schools. We separate them according to a range of factors—temperament, ability, developmental goals. Our aim," she said, "is to train them well enough to be functional adults."

"What does that mean exactly?"

"Well, it means different things for different children. Some need help with fine motor skills. Others need speech therapy. It might even be something straightforward like learning how to share a toy or brush their teeth or hold a fork."

"You say they have different needs?"

"Some of our students have significant physical disabilities in addition to cognitive concerns. One of our jobs is to figure out where we can help them. Most schools write these kids off as soon as they see them. Others just sit with them all day, not teaching them anything. Even some of the teenagers come here with very few skills. But you'd be surprised, Miss Townsend. We have discovered that some of our kids are smarter than the kids without challenges."

"That's really something." I was liking her already. She appeared older than I was but younger than my mother. Her face was placid, and she smiled with her eyes.

Sister LaTarsha turned to India and said in a soft tone, "We are excited you're here, India." She pointed to the chairs around a table. "Please have a seat." She picked up a wooden puzzle. It contained three round pegs in different colors. She asked India to place the pegs in the correctly colored holes. India placed the pegs in the holes, but the colors were all wrong. Sister LaTarsha praised her for inserting the pegs without any trouble. India clapped her hands. Then Sister LaTarsha explained that each peg needed to match the space on the board. She did it for India, matching red with red, blue with blue, and yellow with yellow. India watched intently. The second time, she still mismatched the pegs.

"Let's try again," said the sister.

They must have gone through the exercise six or seven times. Finally, India got it.

"Excellent, India!" I was unable to contain myself.

Sister LaTarsha put the puzzle away. She took India's hand and walked her over to an area where large foam building blocks lay scattered on the floor. The sister stacked them. "See? You build whatever you want with these blocks."

India balanced the blocks as high as she could and knocked them over. She lined them up and tried to walk on them, losing her balance. It crossed my mind that she had never had good toys like these to play with.

"You're so patient," I said as Sister LaTarsha came back and sat across from me.

"She wants to please you."

"Me? How can you tell?"

"I've been doing this for fourteen years," she said. "I see how she looks at you. I hope I can gain her trust the way you have."

I tried to suppress my emotions and looked away. The girls had trusted me, and that haunted me. "How long do the students stay at this school?"

"Why do you ask? Are you thinking this is a temporary solution for India?"

"No, the opposite. I want stability in her life." I had read that the mission received a mix of funds. I couldn't help but worry that those beneficent individuals controlled the school. What if they read about the case and knew India was enrolled? People could be weird about their good deeds and the conditions placed upon them. I couldn't bear the thought of India's disappointment again.

"It really depends on the child." She opened India's folder. "I see that her test had a pretty good result."

"Sometimes I say things and she knows exactly what I'm saying. I'm sure of it." I wanted to see where Sister LaTarsha stood when it came to India. I was ready to knock folks down in the same way India was over there handling those foam blocks.

She closed the folder and pushed it aside. "One issue we've had with students in the past is truancy. If she doesn't come regularly, she will lose her spot in the school. I know that you are not her legal guardian, so her family will have to come into the school to sign the documents in person."

She had not said anything about the scandal, but everybody in town had heard about it. At least, I figured as much. I didn't know enough about the St. Jude nuns to know how much they concerned themselves with current events. "It's just their daddy and grandmother. And the two of them aren't literate. So if you don't mind, I'll be here to read and explain those documents to them." India would need to ride the bus alone sometimes. I worried a little about that.

Sister LaTarsha looked straight at me. "This school has been here for twenty-six years, Miss Townsend. I've been here fourteen. We've seen it all. You should know that."

I tried to relax. My chest was so tight. New worries surfaced. How would India do around the other kids? She had not been to school in years. The only real playmate she'd had was her sister.

"She will be fine, Miss Townsend."

She had such a gentle manner. I wanted to speak honestly with her about everything; I just didn't know how to begin. My experience with Catholics was limited to this hospital, so I didn't even know if I was addressing her correctly.

"Tell me. How's the case going?" she asked softly.

So she did know. Still, it was an awkward question to answer. "To be honest, I don't understand all the technicalities of it. I just know their lawyer, Lou Feldman, is committed. I can tell you that."

"A lot of folks in this town are outraged over this," she said.

"Outraged over the lawsuit or the surgery?"

"Good question."

"A lot of folks wish it would go away, I think."

"Civil, may I offer one piece of advice?"

"Course you can."

"Be careful."

"Careful?"

"Sometimes love can kill you, just like hate. You love too hard and you can lose yourself in other folks' sorrow. You hate too hard and you know the rest of that story. Take care of yourself. You can't help others if you're down and out. I have to remind myself of that all the time."

"I never thought a nun would tell me I could love too hard."

"Only Jesus's love is infinite, Miss Townsend." She suddenly looked older than she had when I'd first walked into the school.

India yelled out in triumph. We turned. She had built a pyramid, which teetered for a few seconds, then tumbled over.

LOU'S OFFICE SAT above a restaurant and the scent of grease wafted up from below, weighing down the air. Foam takeout containers overflowed from his trash can. I'm fairly certain that restaurant kept him from starving to death. The office was a one-room operation with just a front reception area sectioned off by a folding screen. Behind the screen, two desks overflowed with papers. I plopped down in the chair across from him.

"She fired me."

"Who did?"

"Mrs. Seager. And she didn't even have the nerve to do it to my face. She had a letter delivered to my house Monday morning."

"I'm sorry, Civil. I suppose that was inevitable."

"You got somebody to help you on this case?"

"Sure. I've got a dozen lawyers working for me."

"You do?"

He grunted, and I realized that was the sound of his laughter. He was just messing with me. I watched as he riffled through a stack of papers.

"What are you looking for?" I asked him.

"Some notes I took."

"Can I help? It's not like I have a job to go to anymore."

He looked up. "I'm sorry you got fired, Civil. We should have prepared for that."

"It's not your fault. Will you hire me?"

"I appreciate the offer, but you're a nurse, Civil. You should be over there applying to work at the hospital."

"I used to help my daddy organize his office when I was in high school. I'm good at filing."

"You want to be my paralegal now?"

The *rat-tat-tat* of a typewriter started up. His secretary was a fast typist. The regularity of the keys clicking was punctuated ever so often by the return bell. I had never learned to type at all.

"Here it is." He pulled a piece of yellow legal paper out of a stack and seemed to momentarily forget I was there. His eyebrows lowered as he wrote something down. After a while, he looked up at me again. I was embarrassed to still be sitting there, but I couldn't bring myself to leave. Not yet.

"Do you want to read the complaint? Here. Read it." He handed me a slim, stapled stack.

The statement described how Mrs. Seager and another nurse

went to the girls' house after determining they were candidates for sterilization. Mace had signed an X on the permission document. So had Mrs. Williams. Val signed as the witness. It crossed my mind to ask Alicia if she knew about Val's betrayal. I had not seen Alicia in a few days. She had not put her finger in the telephone to call me since I'd been fired. Not one word. Not hello, how you doing. Not nothing. Mrs. Seager had somehow discovered that I'd moved the family to Dixie Court and taken the girls off birth control. Alicia had to have been the one who told her.

Val had played a role, too. I knew Mace's mother had trusted Mrs. Seager because Val was there. Mrs. Seager was wily to bring one of her nurses, understanding that a Black face would help her accomplish the mission. The nurse had worn the same uniform I wore.

"What do you think?"

"It hurts to read."

He lit a cigarette. "I'm sorry, Civil. I didn't mean to—"

"Lou, you never really told me why you're doing this, why you took this case?'

"Not all white people in Montgomery hate Black people, Civil."

"I never said that."

"I know tensions in this city have always been high. Hell, tensions in this state."

"Tensions," I repeated.

"How would you put it?"

I paused. And then I told him a story. I asked him if he remembered what Montgomery was like in 1963. I was thirteen years old, I said. It was the year George Wallace was elected governor and declared segregation would define the South forever. The year students were hosed down in a Birmingham park. The year hundreds of thousands of people marched on Washington demanding their civil rights. The year President Kennedy promised a civil rights bill but was later gunned down in front of his wife. But it was also the year somebody knocked on our front door. Hard. The kind of knock that made Daddy wake the family. Three of Daddy's friends carried the white woman into our living room and lay her on the couch. She was bleeding, and her face was swollen. The men argued in panicked tones. *Who was she? Are you trying to get us killed? They'll blame one of us. Okay, I'll look at her, but she cannot stay here.* And then Daddy had brought out his medical bag and stitched up the woman's scalp, put ice to her face, squeezed ointment in her eye. An arm was likely broken, but it would require a hospital visit and an X-ray, he told the men. He had done all he could do.

Lou was staring at me intently. One thing was for sure: He was a good listener. No wonder he'd been able to rattle off those facts about the Williams family the first day I met him.

"They had found that woman on the side of the street, likely beat up by a husband or boyfriend. And they had tried to help her, though they'd known they were putting their own lives in danger. It's not that I think you hate us. It's that this risk you're taking is real. It has consequences, Lou. Montgomery has come a long way, but race relations in this city still ain't no county fair."

His chair was black vinyl with silver metal armrests, the kind of chair that spun around and had wheels for feet. The way he leaned, I thought it might tip over and deposit him on the floor.

"You're not even getting paid," I added.

"Now you're sounding like my mama."

"Lou, how far are you willing to take this thing? I mean, what if it starts to blow up in your face? Will you stick by those girls?"

He sat up. "If you're wondering whether you can trust me, I'm telling you now, Civil, that you can."

I squinted at him. This white man still believed in the goodness of the world. I was younger than he was, but I had lost my faith the day I walked into that hospital room and found those two little girls wailing like babies. I longed to believe again. Maybe this optimism was a powerful thing to have in the girls' corner—somebody crazy enough to stay in the ring even when his head was about to get bashed.

TWENTY-EIGHT

Montgomery
2016

I know what you're thinking: This is just another white savior story. The white person drops in from the sky, saves all the Black folks, and by doing so, redeems themselves. We're the channel through which they save their own souls, but we cannot save our own. I grew up reading *To Kill a Mockingbird*. I know the story. And I can't say I blame your skepticism. Right now, I'm just trying to tell you the truth. If this story shakes out into something all too familiar, I apologize.

What I can say to you is this: We are at the center of our own destiny. Always have been. Yes, there have been times this country has tried to destroy us. But we have not been doormats. No, ma'am. We have fought and used every resource. Lou Feldman was a resource. And I grew to love him. But this story was and always will be about those sisters. I'm talking to you right now because of them. And the idea that Lou or I or any of us were redeemed by this whole thing ignores all the contradictions, the baggage we came in with, and the baggage we left carrying.

When I arrive in Montgomery it is late, and I'm bone tired. I have just enough energy to check into my hotel. I've never stayed at a hotel in Montgomery before. When the woman at the registration desk asks me if I'm traveling for business or pleasure, I respond by saying "Neither" and leave it at that.

The next day, I phone his office and they put me through to his wife. She asks how I am doing and gives me his cell phone number. I text him and he responds by saying he will be out of court by noon. He agrees to meet me on the south side of the courthouse. I know a lot of years have passed, but when I see him I'm surprised at how different he looks. In fact, I don't think I would have recognized him if I had run into him on the street. All the youthful boyish looks that once caused me to distrust him are gone. And so is his hair. What is left of it is combed thinly over his forehead. It is the first thing he jokes about.

"I know, I know. I had a lot more hair when you saw me last."

I laugh. "How you doing, Lou?"

"I'm good. Come on. There's a little vegetarian place near here."

"Vegetarian?"

He pats his stomach. "My wife is trying to keep me around for a few more years. But it's got the best hash browns in town."

When Lou and I sit across from each other at a table near the window, he studies the menu as if he has never been here before. But I know he is a regular because the server shows up with a cup of coffee, one sugar, and a single package of creamer, and he asks about her husband by name. Lou's eyeglasses are rimless, unlike the thick black frames he used to wear. The current pair sits on his nose, and you can clearly see the lines on his face. After we order, he laces his hands and rests his chin on top of them. He launches right into his cases, and I know he is still just as driven as he always was. He tells me he now has a team of lawyers working for him, but he still loves the thrill of the courtroom. He recently worked on a trial to get a man off death row and won.

I ask him about his family. Both of his children became lawyers, though he laughingly says they went for the money. One is in-house counsel at a tech company in Silicon Valley, and the other practices tax law in Montgomery. He asks about my medical practice, and I tell him about life as an obstetrician-gynecologist, the study I have been working on about reducing the high rate of maternal morbidity among Black women.

He nods. "But right now you're back in Montgomery. You said over the phone you're going to see about India."

"Yes," I say. "She's sick. Have you heard anything?"

"I haven't heard anything about that family in decades. I just got too busy, I guess."

"Me, too."

We both nod, two professionals who can always rely on our work as an excuse.

"I hear about the family through Alicia. She keeps up," I say.

"Alicia?"

"She was the nurse I worked with." He doesn't remember her. It surprises me; but then again, it has been over forty years. "She tells me India has cancer."

"Oh no. That's terrible news."

"Do you remember them, Lou? The Williams family?"

"Of course I do, Civil. I remember Senator Kennedy, his graciousness with them. I remember their grandmother's hot-water corn bread. I remember their daddy. The hurt in that man's eyes kept me up at night."

I'm surprised to hear him say that, and Mace's face rises behind my eyes. "The sisters. What do you remember about them?"

"To be honest, I regret that I did not get to know the girls better. I tried to keep a respectful distance because they were just children. I was sensitive about that. I suppose I left that part up to you."

"I understand."

"I remember you," he whispers. "Your determination. Your toughness. You were nobody to mess with, even back then."

"You thought I was tough, huh? I thought you were crazy."

He laughs. "Back then I thought justice was a moral right."

"And now?"

"I still believe in right and wrong or else I wouldn't be practicing law after all these years. It's just that now I know justice is as complicated as everything else in life."

His eyes grow distant. I can see that his memories of that time are different than mine. "Listen, Civil. I've tried a lot of cases over the years. But I've never forgotten that one. Never. You hear me? We did something back then. It may not have all worked out the way we thought it would, but we did something. You hear me?"

My eyes sting. The grain of the table is etched with scratches. I can see the waitress approaching with our food, but I want the moment to linger a little longer before we return to our bodies and the mundane act of nourishment. Lou and I are not so dissimilar. I have done some important surgeries, saved some lives I thought were lost. He has also had ups and downs. But I could not save those girls, and that has left its indelible mark. I just wish I could pull snatches of memories like him. But I remember everything. Every single little thing.

TWENTY-NINE

Montgomery
1973

Ty, Alicia, and I were sitting in the den with all the lights on. We had picked up some food from Church's Chicken, and the room smelled like gravy. I knew my parents wouldn't like us eating back there, but I wanted to use Daddy's eight-track player. I never tired of listening to Otis Redding.

"My mama told me Lou's trying to see how many other victims there were." Ty wiped his hands on a napkin.

"Have other patients from the Montgomery clinic come forward?" Alicia asked.

"Not yet," I said. "Actually, I was thinking the nurses could help."

"Help? You mean like talk to our patients? Ain't that against the rules?"

"The rules said Mrs. Seager could sterilize those girls."

"You don't work there no more, Civil. And I don't want to lose my job. I can't just go home and live with my mama."

"Speaking of your job, there's something I've been meaning to ask you. How did Mrs. Seager find out I'd moved the girls to the apartment? And that I'd taken them off birth control? You told her, didn't you."

Alicia just stared at me.

"I knew it!" I threw my box on the table. "This is all your fault!"

Alicia's face crumpled. Ty walked over to the stereo and turned the volume down, then turned back to us and said, "Civil, that's not fair. This ain't nobody's fault."

"Why did you tell her, Alicia?"

"She asked me," Alicia said in a weak voice, "and I couldn't lie. She had already found out on her own about them being moved to Dixie Court—the agency sent her notice of their new address. She started asking me a bunch of questions, and I didn't know what else to say. I swear I never thought she would do what she did."

"Why didn't you tell me? And I haven't even heard from you since I got fired." I handed her a tissue, trying not to cry myself. It was a horrible situation for all of us, and I knew that.

"I'm sorry, Civil. I should have told you, but I didn't know how."

Ty sat beside me on the sofa and put an arm around my shoulders. "What's done is done, y'all. Now we've got to figure out what to do next."

"She still has the legal authority to do this to the patients," I said. "Maybe she's stopped doing it to minors, but what if she's doing it to twenty-year-olds? Having them sign forms they don't understand? I've overheard her pressuring women to tie their tubes." I moved to pick up the boxes and trash. I had lost my appetite.

"She wouldn't do that now. Not with the lawsuit," Alicia said.

"Alicia, you know who was with Mrs. Seager that day, right?" I asked after I had put everything in the trash can. "Val was there. Have you said anything to her now that the lawsuit is public? How can you work with her?"

"I told you, I need this job."

"Y'all need to cut it out," Ty said. "How many nurses are there, anyway?"

"Eight. Well, seven now that Civil's gone."

"Civil's right, Alicia," he said. "The nurses can help."

"Help how?"

"Think about it, Alicia," I said. "If you're one of our patients and you've had a tubal ligation, you probably don't come to the clinic anymore unless you got an STD or an infection. Surely there are other women in Alabama who've been sterilized against their wishes."

"Or maybe they didn't understand the procedure was permanent," Alicia whispered.

"Some women can't read those forms that well, and others sign without reading. The system is built on trust."

"How do we find those women?" Alicia said.

"The nurses can help us reach out to folks all over the state."

"That's a long shot, Civil. It'll never work."

The telephone rang. The clock above the console ticked loudly between rings. It was probably Daddy calling to say he was on his way home.

"Be right back," I muttered as I ran to pick up the telephone, which was in the hallway. "Hello?"

"Civil, it's Lou Feldman."

He had never called me at home. My mind went to the worst-case scenario. I sat down on the stool we kept beneath the phone.

"It appears that Senator Ted Kennedy has caught wind of our case down here."

"Senator Ted Kennedy? As in . . . John F. Kennedy's brother?"

"The very same one. He's established a subcommittee to investigate federal oversight of health care–related abuses. A few months ago they interviewed a survivor of the syphilis experiment. Now they want to question the Williamses."

"You kidding me."

"No, I'm not."

"Question? Like testify?"

"He wants them to tell their story to the committee."

"The committee? How is that? They coming to Alabama?"

He made that strange grunting laugh again. "No, we're going to Washington, DC. This is big. It means the case will get national press coverage."

"I thought we were already getting national press coverage. Besides, it's out of the question. India already started her new school. I just met with her new teacher. Did you know they got Black nuns—?"

"Civil, we have no choice but to go. The case needs this coverage."

"And what about the girls?" I was trying to wrap my head around what Lou was saying. The girls had just started to adjust to their new normal. The last thing they needed was a media circus.

"I was hoping you could help with them. We'll all go up."

"*We?*"

"Yes. Civil, we can't do this without you."

The girls would need me. If they were going, I was going. "How will we get there?"

"We'll walk. It ain't that far."

"That's not funny, Lou. Mace could get fired from his job if he takes too many days off."

"I'm sorry; you're right. I didn't mean to sound insensitive. We'll fly. The government will pay for our travel. I can put in a call to the Whitfields to get Mace a few off days."

"You're putting the Williamses on an airplane?" I thought of our conversation in the car that first time, when Mace had asked me where I'd traveled. "Have you told the family yet?"

"No. You were the first person I called."

"When do we leave?"

"We'll fly up Monday."

"This Monday?" I ran my finger over the calendar hanging on the wall beside our telephone. That was just four days away. I mumbled a good-bye and placed the telephone back in its cradle.

"Senator Kennedy wants y'all to come to Washington?" Ty stood at the entrance to the hallway. "Y'all going to Washington?"

They would travel to Washington, DC, for the fancy politicians to stare and make a spectacle of country Alabamans. Mama had been right all along. I nodded, overcome with emotion.

THE DAY BEFORE our trip I stopped by the Williamses' apartment to bring the suitcase Mama had loaned them and help them get packed. In the bathroom, I slicked the girls' hair into three or four smooth ponytails with plastic barrettes and crossed my fingers the hairstyle would hold up. Mrs. Williams had been surprisingly calm after I'd cut their hair that first time. She said she would have done it herself if she'd had a pair of sharp shears. Since then I could tell she had been keeping up with their hair, because it was starting to grow.

I finished up and opened the suitcase. It was blue with a gold buckle. The girls and Mrs. Williams would share it. While I folded their dresses, Erica chatted about her new friends. She was the tallest girl in the class because she was two years older, but she had still managed to make friends.

"What do you like most about school?" I asked her.

"The morning prayer."

"Oh, really?"

"Yes. Miss Civil, every morning I pray to God to give me a baby one day. You know he can, Miss Civil. He can do anything."

I didn't respond. If the prayer was giving her comfort, I didn't want to mess with that. My hands shook as I struggled to latch the suitcase.

"Let me help with that." Mrs. Williams entered the room and waved me aside. I wondered if she'd heard what Erica had just said.

India sat on the bed, watching us. She had now been in school for a week. When I talked, I noticed her watching my lips. On Friday, when I'd picked her up, Sister LaTarsha had explained to me that it was entirely possible that India understood more than she let on, but she was really shy, which people could misread sometimes as incomprehension given her limited verbal ability.

"Y'all going look pretty in your dresses," said the grandmother.

"Do it snow up there, Miss Civil?"

"I think so. But not this time of year."

"They sell Funyuns?"

"We can take some Funyuns with us just in case."

"I'm scared to get on an airplane. What if it fall from the sky?"

"It won't."

"How you know?"

"Planes are built to fly. It's what they do."

"Anything can fall from the sky, Miss Civil."

Mrs. Williams turned the suitcase straight up and set it by the door. "Y'all put your toothbrush in there tomorrow morning before we leave out the door. What time Mr. Feldman picking us up?"

"He say around eight o'clock."

"Okay, that'll give us time to have a good breakfast."

"You got something to put on their hair when they take their bath tonight?" I asked.

"Yes, I'll wrap it up. Don't worry. We are going to be ready to meet Mr. Kennedy. Yessirree. Ooh, child, I wonder if he knew Dr. King. I'll have to tell him about that time I met the man himself."

I walked over and kissed India on the forehead. Her skin was dry and cool. The bedroom window was open, and a breeze kicked up the curtain. In less than twenty-four hours we would board an airplane. Erica peered at her reflection in the mirror over the dresser. The family was excited about this trip, and I prayed it would be a good experience for them.

THIRTY

On the way to meet the senator, I walked between the aide and the girls. The entire way, I worried we would all be soaked in sweat by the time we arrived. The humidity in the air seemed to oppress more than it did in Alabama, its stickiness quickly reaching underneath my clothes. I had never seen a city like Washington. The streets were wide with freshly painted white lines, but the traffic came from all directions, and I wondered how the cars did not collide in the middle of the intersections. Men in suits rushed past us. A group of white children wearing uniforms gathered on the sidewalk. A policeman blew a whistle, and the traffic slowed as the group crossed. A woman chased after a bus that was already rumbling down the hill, until it stopped, letting forth a steaming sigh as the doors opened. I held on tightly to India and Erica as we entered the Senate office building.

The aide couldn't stop talking. She pointed out the names of senators on the doors. Howard Baker. Barry Goldwater. Strom Thurmond. Adlai Stevenson III. When we passed the door of Senator John Sparkman, Alabama's senator, she asked me if we wanted to take a picture. Many people like to take a picture next to their senator's nameplate, she explained. My eyes widened in amazement. Could she really be that clueless? For years Black Alabamans had understood the limits of placing our hopes in politicians. Sparkman had been in office since before I was born, and it had come as no surprise to Black Alabamans when he'd joined the effort to stall the Civil Rights Act of 1964. As hard as we'd fought for our voting rights right there in Alabama, the blunt force of political exclusion remained. I held back from asking about Shirley Chisholm's congressional office even though I knew Miss Pope would have wanted me to be so bold.

"No, thank you," I said curtly, trying not to sound rude. Bless her heart.

The aide's heels clicked on the wide hallway's tiled floor. Mrs. Williams walked right behind me, and Mace trailed all of us, his gait slow and easy. He had lost his confidence in this environment, but none of his suspicion. I worried that people might mistake his silent ambling for hostility. All morning I had tried to keep my distance from him, but there was no denying I was drawn to the man. I wondered if he watched me.

We got off the elevator on the third floor. The senator's office turned out to be a suite, framed by a reception area with a fireplace and a blue couch. The room was long, with a large, square window at one end. I walked to the reception area window, which overlooked the street. There were two open doors revealing small offices and a closed door on the other side that led to the senator's private office.

"Mr. Feldman is already in there," the woman at the desk told the aide. "They're expecting you."

She gave a quick rap on the door, and we trickled in. The senator and Lou stood. The senator was shorter than I'd expected. A high forehead shaped his wide face and a thick lock of curl fell over one eyebrow.

"Senator, let me introduce everyone. This is Civil Townsend, the girls' nurse. She is the brave lady who brought this case to me in the first place, as I've been telling you," said Lou.

I blushed. I hadn't expected any kind of credit for anything. I hadn't even expected to be introduced to the senator. I was just a chaperone.

"This is Mrs. Patricia Williams, the girls' grandmother. She has been helping to raise these girls since their mother passed. And this is Mr. Mace Williams, their father."

The senator extended a hand, and when Mace didn't immediately step forward to accept it, the senator came out from behind his desk. "Mr. Williams, welcome to Washington. I'm so pleased you could come. Mrs. Williams, it is my pleasure."

"The pleasure all mines, Senator," she said a little too loudly. "Ain't every day you get to meet a Kennedy."

The senator smiled shyly, and the rest of us tittered. "Mr. Williams, I appreciate you traveling all this way. I know how difficult this time must be for you and your family, and I want you to know that I wouldn't have asked you to come if I didn't think some good would come out of it. I want people to hear the story of what your family has been through. You have the power to make a difference in your country tomorrow, and I want you to know that I stand with you."

"Thank you, sir. I mean, Your Honor."

The senator laughed, a deep belly laugh. "Call me Ted," he bellowed.

"And Senator, here are two very special young ladies," Lou continued. "India and Erica Williams."

"India and Erica. You do me the honor of being here today."

Erica offered the senator four limp fingers. India held on to my blouse, a section of it balled in her fist. Erica stood so close I could feel the heat coming off her body. She was still sweating after our walk in the sun.

"Please, everyone, sit down. India and Erica, you can sit here." He gave them the seats closest to his desk.

The senator spoke quietly to Erica for a few moments, asking about her school and what grade she was in. The more he talked, the more Erica loosened up. India held on to her yarn-haired doll, and I saw the senator glance at the doll more than once. Lou had obviously informed Senator Kennedy that India wasn't verbal, because he did not ask her anything directly. He spoke to both of them but directed his questions at Erica.

A young woman brought in a small tray with several glasses and a pitcher of iced tea.

"We drink tea up here, too."

The tea was a nice gesture, but it tasted bland, despite the pretty glasses and fresh slices of lemon. We sipped politely as he told us how the proceedings would go the next day. As he spoke, I took in the office. There was a fireplace and a model of a sailboat on the mantel. Two people stood quietly in the back, taking notes. The office warmed with all of us in it.

"Tell me, Mr. Williams." He turned to Mace, lacing his hands together. "What did the nurse say to you the morning she came to your house?"

"She tell me and my mama to sign some papers. We ask her what was the paper for and she just say . . . federal government."

"That's all she said?"

"She say she taking the girls to the clinic for some more shots."

I wanted to interject, tell the senator that the family didn't speak out of turn to the government workers. They depended on us too much. They did what we told them or they didn't get their benefits that month. They let the girls go with Mrs. Seager because they were told to. They signed those papers because they were told to. He probably did not understand all of that. He seemed like a nice man, but he was undeniably part of that system.

"Then what happened?"

"I ask her where was Miss Civil."

I moved around in my seat. I was having a hard time keeping my mouth shut, but I reminded myself that the senator had not asked to interview me.

"What did she say?"

"She say *Miss Civil ain't working today*." Mace imitated Mrs. Seager's voice.

The senator turned to the girls. "Do you know what happened to you?" he asked, and before I could interrupt, Erica answered.

"They do surgery on me. It hurt real bad."

"Yes, I understand you were in a lot of pain when Miss Townsend came to your room."

Looking into the senator's intelligent face, I understood the charisma of a good politician, the ability to respond with empathy.

"Do you know what kind of surgery it was?"

"Me and my sister can't have no babies."

"How do you feel about that?"

"I want babies. My friend Dinesha got a baby. I want one just like her. I pray every day God change what happened to me and my sister."

She had told me about this new friend Dinesha, but I had no idea the girl was already a mother. I placed my glass down. There wasn't a coaster, and I worried it might leave a ring on his wooden desk. I uncrossed my legs, crossed them. There was a run in my pantyhose.

"Mr. Senator," Mace began. "Ever since my wife died I been trying to make a way for these girls. I do the best I can."

I could see from the look on Mace's face that he was ashamed of what the girls were saying. He had signed those papers, and he would never live that down.

India picked up a tiny sailboat from the desk in front of her.

"India," I whispered.

"It's okay," the senator answered. "She can have that one. If you like it, it's yours."

India made a noise and tucked the boat under her fingers.

"Mr. Williams, are you ready to testify under oath tomorrow?"

"Under what?"

"With your hand on the Bible."

"Yes, sir."

"And you, Mrs. Williams?"

"That's why I got on that steel bird and come up here, ain't it."

The senator explained how the hearing would go, how many people would be in the room. "Nurse Townsend, you've done an excellent job with these girls," he added in a raised voice. "I'm going to try to do the right thing by them tomorrow."

"Thank you, Senator. I believe you will," I said and I meant it. There was an earnestness to him. I studied the pictures on the wall as we walked out, hoping to catch a glimpse of John F. Kennedy. I paused before a framed handwritten letter. I didn't have time to read it, but I saw that it was signed *Jack* in curly script.

"His brother was the president," I told the girls as we walked down the hall.

"He not president no more?"

"No, he was killed."

Erica whispered, "By who?"

"A crazy person."

Erica looked stricken, and I instantly regretted telling her that.

When we got back to the hotel, the girls watched television on the bed in my room, their eyes fixed on the screen. I sat beside them, thinking I'd let them hang out until dinnertime. I wanted to give Mrs. Williams some time to be alone and enjoy the trip.

India pointed at the television and laughed. They sat very close to each other, their arms touching. *At least they have each other*, I thought. *Thank God for that.*

THIRTY-ONE

H e'd warned us there would be a lot of media, but photographers rushed us when we arrived at the Capitol, and as much as Lou tried, they were hard to hold back. The senator had sent two more aides, but the young men didn't look like they could protect a lampshade. Mace did a better job holding his hand out in front of the girls so we could make it through the crowd. I wrapped an arm around India, shielding her. Erica wore a blank face, even when the flashbulbs went off in her eyes, but once we were inside the building she started to cry. Mrs. Williams called out to her granddaughter. "Come here, baby."

The aides led us through a rotunda with soaring ceilings. We could barely see where we were walking because we were so busy looking up. Finally, we reached a room that resembled an amphitheater. Paneling scored the walls, and the ceiling dovetailed in period molding. There were a lot of white people in that room. It felt strange to be the lone brown faces in the place. They seated Mrs. Williams and Mace next to Lou at a long table. The girls and I sat together, six rows behind them. In the back of the room, bright lights shone from hooded tripods. Everyone was talking at the same time. Men in suits mingled, walking in and out of the room. I couldn't tell who was a senator and who wasn't. Finally, Senator Kennedy saw us. He gave a nod to the girls before calling the room to order.

"Today's hearing is on the issue of sterilizations occurring in federal clinics across the country. This is an important issue because some of these sterilizations are of minor children, and this subcommittee hopes to get to the bottom of the process and procedure by which these surgeries are occurring."

He began by calling government officials from the Department of Health, Education, and Welfare, who were all seated at various points at a second long table. The secretary. The assistant secretary. And so on. Finally, it was Lou's turn.

"Now we will hear from Mr. Louis Feldman, an attorney representing the family of India and Erica Williams in Montgomery, Alabama. His testimony before this subcommittee will help to shed light on the kinds of things happening at the local level in regards to our federal clinics. Mr. Feldman?"

Lou leaned into the microphone and it squeaked. "My name is . . ."

I quietly hoped the Williamses weren't thinking the same thing I was thinking—Lou looked terrified.

"My name is Louis Feldman. I am a lawyer for Feldman Law Firm in Montgomery, Alabama. I am here today with Mr. Mace Williams and Mrs. Patricia Williams. I represent India and Erica Williams. On June—"

"Excuse me for interrupting," said the Senator. "Could you please tell us the ages of the children?"

"The children are eleven and thirteen years old, Senator."

"Thank you. You may proceed."

"On June 16, 1973, two nurses from the Montgomery Family Planning Clinic visited the home of India and Erica Williams. The nurses informed Mrs. Patricia Williams, their grandmother and legal guardian, and Mr. Mace Williams, their father, that the girls were being taken for shots. The Williamses were under the impression that the children would be given Depo-Provera, the same shot they had been given for months. Mrs. Williams and her son, Mr. Williams, do not read or write. They each put their mark on a document that they later learned was an authorization for tubal ligation. The nurses transported the Williams girls to the hospital, where the children were surgically sterilized. The children were sent home two days later."

"When did the family find out that India and Erica had been sterilized?" asked the senator.

"Later that afternoon, another nurse from the clinic, Civil Townsend, made a visit to the girls at their home and learned they had been taken to the hospital. When she arrived at the hospital, she was informed the surgery had already taken place that morning."

There was silence in the room as the senator and his colleagues scribbled on notepads. I could not see Lou's face, but I watched his profile carefully from where I was seated.

"Mr. Feldman, did the clinic agents ever reveal why they authorized surgery for the girls?"

"The director of the clinic has given a statement that the reason for the operations was that the girls were sexually active and that the surgery was performed to prevent their pregnancy. They had been taken off Depo-Provera for reasons related to concerns around the safety of the drug, and she felt the only way to ensure against pregnancy was sterilization."

Lou was defending my actions, though he failed to mention that I had not been authorized to cease the drug. But Mrs. Seager knew why I had taken them off. Still, she had chosen to move forward with the sterilization.

"Mr. Feldman, why do you believe that the system failed these girls?"

"Senator, let me give some context to the system under which the Williams family lives. The family receives $147 per month from the Alabama Department of Pensions and Security, as well as food stamps. In order to receive this aid, they are visited each week by a government representative. They are surrounded by a welfare state upon which they depend for their very existence. So it is understandable they can be easily coerced into doing what is recommended to them. It is a very sophisticated, though perhaps unintentional, form of coercion, but it is coercion nonetheless."

Lou's voice gained volume. He was rolling, and suddenly he didn't seem so young anymore.

"Would this medical complex have permitted a middle-class white or Black parent to so easily sign away his child's ability to procreate? Would the middle-class parent, absent the kinds of dependency programs exerted on a welfare family, have even considered surgical sterilization for his children? I believe this committee will find that the daughters of middle-class families would not have been sterilized. It is the free clinic patient who is fair game for this most final of birth control methods."

I dared not move. Even Senator Kennedy didn't look like he was blinking. The room was quiet and still.

"Sterilization is not birth control, especially when applied to minors. It is not the same as a birth control pill. It fundamentally and forever halts the ability to conceive. Frankly, it is mayhem. And this, Senator, frightens me."

Senator Kennedy breathed audibly. I could hear it through his microphone. Lou's hair was slick at the nape, where he was sweating at the collar. Someone coughed, and it echoed.

"Mr. Feldman, what do you propose?"

"I propose that strict guidelines for sterilization be established and distributed to all agencies, hospitals, or individuals who, in any way, participate in federal- or state-funded sterilization programs. I have every reason to believe that what happened to the Williamses is not uncommon, that for some time now, OEO-funded and HEW-funded family planning projects have been securing sterilization operations for the minor children of poverty-stricken families, particularly poor Black families."

The room broke out in murmurs. Senator Kennedy tapped his gavel. "Mr. Feldman," said the senator slowly, "that is a very serious charge. Can you tell us what you base that statement on?"

I wished we'd had time to track down other women before this hearing. I was pretty sure that Lou didn't have as many depositions as he needed at that moment. But Lou answered the senator with math.

"Five hundred planning units participated in this program in 1971, just two years ago. I have read interoffice memos that indicate about 80 percent of those units desired to perform sterilization operations. Senator, that is a lot of units. I also have a report from a man in charge of operations for OEO. He estimates that there are forty to sixty units around the country performing sterilizations. I believe there are many more than that."

"And your point is that there are no guidelines at the present time in relationship to these sterilizations?"

"There are no guidelines established by OEO, and apparently not by HEW. The Family Planning Clinic in Montgomery receives a certain amount of money each year for sterilizations, but they do not, as far as I am aware, have any formal procedures to guide the physicians and members of the units as to how the sterilizations are to be decided on and conducted. Senator, I implore you and the members of your committee to give this matter your closest attention."

"Thank you, Mr. Feldman."

Lou had hit them right between the eyes. I could see the side of his face, but I still could not make out his expression.

"Welcome, Mr. Williams, to the committee. We had a nice visit over in my office yesterday with your mother and daughters."

"Yes, sir," Mace said. He pulled at his shirt collar.

"We want to tell you how much we appreciate the fact that you are here this morning." The senator was turning on his charm again, and Mace appeared to relax.

"I sure appreciate it, sir."

"As you know, Mr. Williams, we are trying to consider legislation so that the kind of thing that happened to your children will not happen to other children. That is why we have asked you to help us with this, and we want to thank you very much for being here today. We know it is not easy to share with us the kind of concern and sadness you must feel, but I would appreciate it if you could just tell us what happened to your daughters, in your own words."

Mace stared down at the microphone.

"Please take your time, Mr. Williams."

"Well, see," Mace began. "I was on my way to work that morning. I work over at the Whitfield Pickle Factory." He cleared his throat. "And the nurse come from the clinic. Two nurses. They say they need to take the girls. They wasn't our, not Miss Civil. Civil Townsend, that's they regular nurse. I ask where was she at and they say she wasn't working that morning. So I say alright then. They say you just need to sign this here paper and we be on our way."

"Where did you believe they were taking your daughters?"

"For shots, sir. That's what she say and I believe."

"Birth control shots?"

"Yes, sir."

"So you signed the paper?"

"I put my mark on it; yes, sir."

"Then what happened?"

217

Mace shifted in his chair and ran a hand over the top of his head. "That afternoon I get a call at work saying they done had an operation. Miss Civil, they nurse, called and told me. And this here news got all over me."

"I'm sorry, could you speak into the microphone, Mr. Williams?"

"I say this got all over me, sir. Like a fester."

"You are saying you were upset, Mr. Williams?"

"After the surgery, they said to me . . . 'Daddy, we ain't never gone have no babies?' And it break my heart to have to answer that. They just children. They don't even know no boys. It ain't right."

A lone camera bulb popped. I saw that Erica was closely watching her father. India fingered the sailboat in her hand, turning it over and examining its parts. I wished they didn't have to be here for this. I should have kept them in the hotel room watching television, but perhaps if they remembered this day it would help them somehow. Somebody had cared about two little Black girls from Alabama. Somebody important.

Mace's eyes roamed the room behind him. I lifted my hand, but he didn't see me. It was too crowded in there.

"So you were upset about it?"

"Yes, sir," Mace said, holding his chin down and looking across at the row of senators. "Wouldn't you be?"

The senator wisely pivoted to Mace's mother. "Mrs. Williams, could you tell us about what happened, in your own words? Talk right into the mic so we can all hear you."

Mrs. Williams told a similar story about that morning, how the nurses had come into the house saying they had to take the girls immediately.

"Did they tell you that they were giving the girls shots?"

"Yes, sir, I believe they did. They said they was going to get shots."

"And when you talked to your granddaughters for the first time after the surgery, what did they tell you?"

"They say, 'Grandmama, they done surgery on me. They say I can't have no babies.' Mr. Senator, so many people come to my door. Government this and government that. I can't keep 'em straight sometimes. But this was the first time I done ever felt so betrayed."

"Would you have permitted it if you had known about it?"

"No, I would not have allowed them to do that. Not to my grandbabies. They just babies theyselves."

"Forgive me, Mrs. Williams, if my questions seem simple. I just want to get all this down for the record. Would you go back to that clinic?"

Mrs. Williams put her mouth right on the microphone. "Sir, I wouldn't send a cockroach to that clinic."

People chuckled, then quieted, as if not sure whether to laugh in so serious a moment.

"Thank you, Mrs. Williams. Mr. Williams. As I mentioned earlier, what we are trying to do in this committee is make sure that this never happens again. You have two wonderful daughters. You are a lovely family. We all owe you a very deep sense of gratitude for coming here all the way from Alabama and sharing your personal experience today. Do either of you have anything else you would like to say? Mrs. Williams? Mr. Williams?"

Mace shook his head. "No, sir."

"Thank you. Thank you again," said the senator as he turned to whisper in someone's ear.

THIRTY-TWO

We returned to Montgomery on a high, but a few days later the evening news reported that Lou Feldman had dropped the case against the Montgomery Family Planning Clinic.

"What's that all about?" Mama walked into the room, drying her hands on a towel.

"I don't know."

I called Lou's office from the hallway. The telephone just rang and rang.

"Mama, I'll be back!" I called out as I left the house. When I got to Lou's office, I knew he was there because the upstairs light was on. A cook from the restaurant stood outside smoking a cigarette.

When Lou opened the door, I could tell that he had not slept. His clothes were wrinkled, face unshaven.

"You didn't answer your telephone," I said and followed him inside.

He sat down in a chair and pushed his fingers through his dark hair. "Too much work to do."

"What work? I just heard on the news that you dropped the

case." I was too wound up to sit, so I gripped the back of the chair in front of me.

"We didn't drop the case exactly."

"What do you mean by 'exactly'?"

"Civil, this thing is bigger than the Montgomery clinic."

"Of course it is," I said. "The federal government funds it."

Lou sat up straighter. We hadn't talked since returning from Washington. I was afraid of what he was about to say, thinking we might have made a mistake by going there.

"There's a doctor out in California who called me to say there are thousands of Hispanic women getting sterilized out there without their knowledge. There are incidents in North Carolina involving women going in for a Caesarian section and the doctor removing their uterus. Some have even been told by the doctor that if they don't consent, the doctor won't sign the forms authorizing their Medicaid. One doctor is doing it as soon as a woman delivers her third child. No consent whatsoever."

"So it's happening all over the country?"

"Poor Mexican women. Black women. One doctor in Georgia told a woman while she was in labor that he wouldn't deliver the baby unless she signed the form!"

I rubbed my head. It was unfathomable. After learning about the Tuskegee experiment, I knew people were capable of all kinds of harm. But hearing this was like learning that evil people were everywhere. I put a hand to my chest.

"Sit down," I heard him say, and I sank into the chair.

"They trying to kill us off, Lou?"

"Well, not exactly."

"It's like the Holocaust, what they did to your people in Europe, isn't it? What you say your parents fled."

"Not exactly. But it's bad."

Those words sat between us for a few moments. I had learned about the Holocaust at Tuskegee. I remember thinking that I could not believe they hadn't taught us about it in high school. How could they leave something like that out? When we got to that unit in my college world history class, I'd sat in the library just staring into space. The horror of the events was overwhelming. I had not known white people had gone through something so tragic, and I remember walking around that weekend wondering if every white face I met was a Jewish face, a descendant of a survivor, or even a survivor themselves.

"Listen, we are still naming Erica and India in the lawsuit. But this time we're going after the big fish—the federal government. The Secretary of Health, Education, and Welfare. The Office of Economic Opportunity. We're taking this case to the very top. When this is all over, the girls can sue for monetary damages. But first we've got to stop the government in its tracks."

"You're suing the federal government? Lou, you're twenty-eight years old. What if presidential cabinet members are involved?"

"That's the only way we're going to stop this, Civil. We've got to go after the agency that oversaw the units."

There had been two men sitting in a car outside Lou's office building when I'd walked in a few moments earlier. It was after nine o'clock at night. I recognized the vehicle; those same two men had interviewed nearly every resident in Dixie Court. Now I was thinking it was possible that they weren't reporters at all but government agents. I feared the agency might find some bogus reason to evict the family.

"What about Mrs. Seager? What about my girls . . ." Young people had been killed before. Those four little girls in that Birmingham church. Students registering people to vote. This case had the potential to bring out the ugly.

"If I get the injunctive relief I'm seeking, it will affect women and girls all over this country. Girls like India and Erica. The poor. The innocent. The exploited. We'll protect them. This has turned out to be bigger than any of us expected."

So I was going to have to communicate with the Williamses and help them understand what Lou was asking. He was right—this was big. But it would happen on the backs of my girls. On the backs of Mace and his mother. And I just didn't know how much more the Williamses would be willing to sacrifice in the name of the common good. Mace wasn't concerned about women in North Carolina or California. He was just trying to keep his job at the factory so his family could eat without depending on the federal government. The man had never even voted.

Lou picked up a pencil. I knew it was the signal for me to leave, but I wasn't ready.

"What can I do?"

"Right now, just concentrate on keeping those girls away from reporters."

He sounded irritated, and that, in turn, irritated me. I walked to the door. He had made this decision without me, and that left me feeling helpless. But who was I? I didn't even have a job anymore.

"By the way, I heard Mrs. Seager resigned. Or was fired. I'm not sure."

"You kidding me," I said, stunned.

"There are a lot of people in this community who need those services. They could use your passion. And I'm sure you could use the job. Go back to the clinic, Civil."

"I will never go back. I hate it there." Mace had not been the only one duped by Mrs. Seager. I had believed in that woman, in the mission of the clinic. I had overheard her pressuring women to tie their tubes, and I had not intervened, believing at the time that it was the right thing to do. Babies born into poverty did not have as good a chance as babies born into families with more money.

223

That's what I believed. What a hypocrite I'd been. I'd had all the resources in the world, and I had still terminated my own pregnancy. Meanwhile, I'd thought I knew what was best for other women.

Lou began to write hastily, as if trying to capture a thought before it escaped him. When I walked out the door, he didn't even say good-bye, and neither did I.

Outside, the night was clear and warm. I could make out the darkened silhouettes of the two men sitting inside the sedan across the street. I didn't want to go home. I didn't want to go to Dixie Court. I thought about going inside the restaurant, sitting at the counter, and ordering some fried food. Across the street, I watched a light flicker in an office and then darken. The city had shut down for the night. Reluctant as I was, it was probably time for me to do the same.

THE FOLLOWING WEEK Ty asked me to meet him at the diner. I arrived before he did, thankful my friend Irene was working, because I did not want to talk to anyone I didn't know. She seated me in my favorite booth in the back and brought me a Coca-Cola. The bells above the door jingled. Ty came straight to me, a bag slung over his shoulder.

"Hey. How was Washington?"

"Crazy. The Williamses were like celebrities or something. I didn't know so many people knew who they were. And Lou showed out. He had the whole room fixed. Now he says he's suing the federal government."

"Does that mean the clinic gets off scot-free?"

I shrugged. "The clinic is no longer named as defendants. Now it's the bigwig secretary of HEW, the director of OEO, and so forth. Lou says the sterilizations are happening to women all over the country."

Ty opened his bag and took out a bunch of folded-up newspapers. "Miss Pope called the librarian over at Alabama State library and saved these for us. They all came out yesterday. I told her I'd bring them back after I showed them to you."

He spread the newspapers out on the table and I scanned the headlines.

"The *New York Times*. The *Chicago Tribune*. The *Washington Post*. The *Chicago Defender*. Even *Time* magazine ran a story. Everyone is talking about the Williams sisters."

There were pictures of the girls walking into the Capitol building. A picture of Dixie Court. The clinic, on Jefferson Davis Highway. There was even a picture of them standing next to me in front of the hotel. My face was fuzzy, but you could see the girls clearly.

"So they're the face of a national scandal?"

"Yup. This case is on fire."

"I heard Mrs. Seager quit," he said.

"Lou told me that. How'd you hear?"

"Alicia."

"That ain't surprising. She stay running her mouth."

"She's just trying to do the right thing, Civil. Same as you. Hey, you and I still need to talk. You keep avoiding the conversation about the baby, and I need to talk about it with somebody."

"Baby?"

"There was a baby, Civil. Our baby."

"Don't use that word." I lowered my voice. "I was barely even pregnant."

"Ain't no such thing as barely pregnant."

"What is there to talk about, Ty? We made a mistake. We avoided disaster. It's over."

"You call our baby a disaster?"

"Yes, me being pregnant would have been a disaster."

He grabbed my hand. "What about us? Would that have been a disaster, too?"

"You're being ridiculous." I tried to pull my hand away, but he held on. I did feel sorry for Ty, but I didn't want to talk about it. I was too wrapped up in my hurt to even articulate my feelings to myself, let alone to him.

THIRTY-THREE

In a town of Black and white, the Singhs moved into a house on the Black side of town. Their only daughter married a Black army officer. I was in high school when the family bought the Regent Cafe, which became one of the first truly integrated diners in the city, a place where Black folks felt safe sitting in a booth on the opposite side of white folks. But we also came for the food. You would have thought it was your own family back there cooking. Mr. Singh understood Southern food. He had worked in the kitchen under the previous owners, and he had surpassed them with his skills. The family's involvement with civil rights was to simply serve good food to anybody who came in the door.

The old man usually stayed in the kitchen. Mrs. Singh moved back and forth but preferred the office, where she kept the books. A white retired schoolteacher ran the front side of things and called everyone *hon*. Sometimes Mrs. Singh might come out near closing time wearing her sari, a long braid running simply down her back. She might refill your coffee, ask about your mother, or how things were going since you started your new job. Her daughter now lived out on the base, and Mrs. Singh was known to grouse that she would be too old to enjoy grandchildren if they didn't come soon.

A few days earlier, Ty had asked if he could step into the kitchen to have a word with Mr. Singh, but it was the wife who came out of the office to talk to Jim Ralsey's son. The Singhs had known the Ralsey family for years. It was the Ralseys who had helped them establish their business insurance. After the conversation, Ty reported that Mrs. Singh had approved the meeting at the diner for after hours as long as we closed the blinds.

That Wednesday evening, all of the nurses from the clinic showed up; Alicia had somehow convinced them. I wasn't sure if she did it out of guilt or loyalty, but I appreciated her help that night. We pushed the tables together and arranged the chairs. As a show of solidarity, I asked the old turncoat, Val, to sit next to me at the head of the table. I was still angry with her, but I knew I couldn't get anything done without her.

"Thanks for coming. I realize y'all got dinners to cook, kids to get in bed."

The kitchen door flapped open, and Mr. Singh appeared. For a moment, he stood there, motionless, as if he had no idea who all these people were and what they were doing in the diner. Three lines lay determinedly across the center of his forehead. Then he announced, "I've made tea. Tyrell, can you help bring it out?"

"Yes, sir."

After he left, I took a deep breath and began to address the women. "As y'all know, there is currently a lawsuit filed in Alabama's federal court against the US government. The attorney, Lou Feldman, has filed a class-action suit on behalf of all the women targeted for coerced sterilizations by federally funded clinics."

I paused for a moment and studied them. Fiona, Lori, Margaret. Fresh out of nursing school like me, their faces a mix of fear and nerves. Fiona kept glancing at the closed vinyl blinds. Lori could not drive, so she never did home visits. She stayed at the clinic all day and was the primary nurse for walk-ins. She had a double chin and blinked a lot. Margaret chewed gum all the time, a habit Mrs. Seager had hated. She had been written up twice for it. She was chewing ferociously right now, popping the gum between her back teeth.

Then there were Liz and Gina. Younger than Val but older than the rest of us. They had been employed at the clinic the longest. Although it had been Val who accompanied Mrs. Seager on the day the Williams girls were sterilized, I was pretty sure Liz and Gina had known about it. You didn't work for Mrs. Seager for as long as they had without participating in your share of surgeries.

Ty returned and set a tray of cups stacked inside one another on the table. Cinnamon-scented steam rose from a porcelain teapot. Alicia passed the cups around. There was a lot of tension around the table while we waited for Ty to pour.

I continued. "I understand Mrs. Seager is no longer at the clinic. Did they hire a replacement yet?"

"Why should we tell you? You was fired," Gina said. "I'm only here because Alicia asked me."

"Yeah, they hired somebody," said Liz. "A Black lady. She just started this week."

"What's her name?" I asked.

Nobody said anything. They didn't trust me. In their eyes, I was the traitor.

"Her name is Mrs. Parr," said Liz. "Why you asking? We ain't bringing her in this, are we? She had nothing to do with it."

I shook my head. "I want to start by saying that I'm not going to ask y'all to do anything that will jeopardize your jobs."

"Jeopardize our jobs?" interrupted Val. "I thought we was here to talk about how we can help them girls. How we can make this right."

"We are," I said. "If we help with Lou's case, we can help them."

229

"Case? We ain't no lawyers."

"I thought you just wanted us to send the girls some clothes or something."

"Why are we here?"

"See, that's your problem right there. You don't mind your own business."

"I told y'all we shouldn't come."

"Ladies, ladies," I said, spreading my hands out in front of me. "Just hear me out."

Val pushed her tea away. "Now look, Civil. I feel terrible about what happened to them girls. If I could turn back the clock, I would tell Mrs. Seager to kiss my behind. They was too young. I know that, and that's why I agreed to this meeting. Ain't a day go by that I don't pray to God to forgive me for what I did that morning. I don't know what I was thinking." She began to cry. Her tears startled me. She didn't seem like the crying type.

Alicia moved her chair closer to Val and put an arm around her. Someone else sniffled. We were all sharing in this burden. We had all been taken by the authority of the clinic. We had followed orders.

"I went with her once," Liz said. "Sixteen-year-old girl with four children. I thought we were doing the right thing."

"I've been there for five surgeries," said Gina.

Five? I needed to stop this rush of confessions before everybody fell apart. Before I fell apart. "Lou is making an argument about coercion. How poor women can't make an informed decision when the government is all up in their business. We were coerced, too. By an authority figure who had the US federal government behind her. We got to forgive ourselves and get to work."

"Not you," said Margaret, snapping her gum and sipping tea at the same time. "You tried to help that family, Civil. I heard you even got them a new apartment."

"No, Margaret. I am part of the problem. I was in their lives making decisions that weren't mine to make. Sure, I had good intentions, but so did Mrs. Seager. We all did." I had not thought this part through. The words rushed out of my mouth.

"That woman is evil," Gina said.

"Sure is," Margaret said.

"Hey." I accidentally bumped the table and the teacups tinkled. The noise got their attention. "Y'all want to make this right? Help me help Lou."

Val's face grew hard and composed again. She had pulled herself together. "What can we do?" she asked.

"Let's get Lou some evidence of sterilizations of minors in Alabama. There are other federally funded clinics around the state."

"Around the state?" Lori whispered. "How we supposed to find out what's going on around the state?"

"I got three kids at home and a husband that work two jobs. My mama had to come over to watch the kids tonight for me to even be here," said Liz.

"You know I can't drive," Lori added.

I shushed them. "There's eight of us. Between us, we got telephones and good handwriting. We got family and friends all over this state, from Huntsville to Mobile. Call your cousins, aunts, uncles. Reach out to white folks you think got a warm ear and ask for help. Ask around. Get your church involved. This case is national news, and everybody knows you work at the clinic where it all went down. There's no need to sneak."

"Why can't that white lawyer do all this? Why us?" said Gina.

"He's working on it, too. And yes, we could leave it all to him. But don't y'all want a chance for redemption? Don't you want a hand in turning this ship right-side-up?"

I was hoping they wouldn't ask me if Lou knew about my plan, because he didn't. I waited while everyone sipped their cooling tea.

My hand shook as I lifted my cup. Ty hadn't uttered a single word. Before the meeting, we had agreed that I would lead things off.

Alicia directed her questions to me, but she watched Val as she spoke. "How do we do it, Civil? Where do we start?"

Ty handed me a manila folder. I passed around the Xerox copies. "I've made a list of the places in the state that get money from the federal government and have the authority to sterilize. I've also listed all the hospitals where the surgeries could possibly take place—telephone numbers, addresses, even hospital director names."

"Where'd you get all this?" Val asked, running a finger down the list.

"The telephone book. The library."

"When we call, what do we say?" Val asked.

She had said it. I heard it loud and clear. *When we call.* "You tell the truth. Tell them who you are. Your name. Your association with the clinic. Tell them you are just trying to gather information, and leave it at that. The key is to find a sympathizer, a fellow medical professional who has heard about the case and wants to help."

Liz asked for a pen, and Ty rolled blue Bics across the table. As she picked up the pen she said, "I got an ex-boyfriend who works in medical records at Regional Med in Anniston. He cheated on me, so I do believe he owes me. Y'all can cross that one off the list."

"My old boss is a doctor at the big hospital in Birmingham. He heads up one of the departments there. He'll help."

"My cousin a janitor at Providence down in Mobile. He a talker and know everybody and everything. Leave that one to me."

They rattled off their connections.

"Remember," I said, "don't do nothing illegal or immoral. We are nurses, not liars. And we don't want to justify one bad deed with another. You don't need names, just verifiable numbers of cases."

I thought of Daddy and the time he'd shared with me some of the burdens of being a family doctor, how he carried his patients' secrets, the diagnoses kept from their loved ones—cancer, high blood pressure, diabetes. A family practitioner in communities like ours knew a lot.

"Civil," Val said.

"Hmm?"

"I'd like to lead a prayer if you don't mind."

"Alright, then."

When we'd first begun this journey I'd always been respectful of Val. Somewhere along the way that respect had diminished. But as we all joined hands and closed our eyes, I was moved by the power of the older woman's prayer, the conviction of it. If someone had been able to see through the blinds that night, they would have seen eight grieving nurses joined together in a fight that we believed was just.

THIRTY-FOUR

The trial had not even begun, but the media arrived in droves. Daddy made note that Montgomery hadn't had so many journalists since the Selma march eight years prior. Two vans camped on the street running through Dixie Court. It was a good thing the Williams family didn't have a phone, because the newspaper people seemed to have everybody's telephone number. Daddy left ours off the hook at night when he got home. He told anyone who needed to reach him to call Glenda. One night, I walked out of the beauty shop and a flashbulb popped off in my face.

At church, the pastor preached on "Unnecessary Trouble." It may have been my imagination, but I could have sworn he was looking at me throughout the entire sermon. He talked about allowing God to fight our battles, waiting on the Lord. After service, one of the members asked Mama if I would get any money out of the case. Before she could answer, a woman dressed in red from head to toe walked by, saying, "That white lawyer probably taking all the money." The exchange upset Mama, and on the way home she asked me if it was true.

"Lou is trying to change the law, Mama. Later, the girls can sue for damages."

"What's motivating him?" She slipped off a white lace glove.

"I think he's doing it out of conviction."

She spoke softly. "Well, I suppose that's not impossible."

"Mama, I'm surprised you letting these gossips get to you."

"I'm just asking. Don't be so defensive. By the way, you need to look for another job. Or go work with your daddy in the office."

"I'm looking for a job, Mama."

"You apply to anything?"

"Well, no, not yet. I can't just walk in a place and fill out an application."

"Why not?"

"Because my name is all over the papers. Besides, they don't just advertise in the paper for nursing jobs."

"Actually, they do. Look, if you can't get nothing over there at St. Jude, then see if the schools are hiring. Maybe you could be a school nurse since you seem to be taking this sudden interest in children."

"What's that supposed to mean?"

She didn't answer, and I didn't push it. I supposed I could apply at a hospital. The moment I'd seen those girls lying in that bed without enough pain meds, I'd wondered if there was a place for me at the hospital, giving patients the extra care that the doctors didn't bother to give.

Mama pulled into the driveway. "Looks like somebody was following us."

The man parked his blue Ford under a tree in the shade, and it shuddered to a stop. I could just make out the outline of a hat.

"Got their nerve. On a Sunday."

"You alright?" Mama asked as we walked into the house.

"I'm going to change. Then I'm going to meet up with Ty. Make sure you lock up when you go out to the shed."

Ty had told me he would meet me outside Lou's office that afternoon. He wanted to be with me when I told Lou how the nurses planned to help. I watched my rearview mirror the whole drive over. Daddy had warned me to drive slowly so that the police wouldn't have a reason to harass me. By the time I arrived at Lou's office, my nerves were frazzled.

"What's wrong with you? You alright?" Ty was standing beside his daddy's car. It was late August, and the humidity was suffocating. He wore a collared shirt, open at the neck, and the sun glinted off his sunglasses. I tried not to remember the warmth of his arms around me, the scent of him. I was glad for the sunglasses. They kept me from having to look in his eyes.

"Some man followed me and Mama home from church this morning," I said.

He held on to my arm. "Come on."

We walked up the stairs to Lou's office. The door was unlocked. A 7-Eleven Slurpee cup sat on the edge of Lou's desk.

"Somebody followed Civil home from church today. She's all spooked."

Lou arranged the chairs. "You alright?"

I nodded. "Journalists, right?"

"Who else would they be? I gave a few interviews yesterday. They're going to write the story anyhow, so I may as well tell our side. But, Civil, you don't have to talk to them. And you can always walk over to the car and tell them you have no comment so they're wasting their time."

I nodded. Lou didn't understand that I was afraid they weren't really journalists at all.

"So what's happening with the case?"

"I'm sure y'all heard of Judge Frank Johnson."

We all knew Judge Frank Johnson. He was the head of the federal court in the middle district of Alabama, the judge who had ended the Montgomery Bus Boycott. He was also the judge who had ruled on our side for voting rights after the Selma march. He was already something of a living legend in Alabama.

"Is he the judge on this case?" I asked.

"Unfortunately, no." Lou let out a breath. "It's another one. Judge Eric Blount."

"I don't know him."

"Yeah, well, he ain't no Frank Johnson. We've got an uphill battle. Last year, Blount made a ruling barring Negro jurors from a case he was presiding over."

"On what basis?"

"Well, as you know, the jury has to spend a lot of time together during the course of a trial. He barred the Negro jurors on the basis that white jurors weren't used to eating with Negroes and so they wouldn't be comfortable having lunch together to discuss the case."

"So he's a bigot," Ty said.

"A segregationist, at the least," I added.

"That's generous."

"Let's just say," Lou said, "he's not the friendliest judge to have on this case."

"Bullshit, Lou. Just say it. He's going to rule against the girls," I said.

"We don't know that. Besides, we may not have a choice, Civil. I don't really have grounds to protest."

"How about protesting that he's a racist?"

I walked over to the window and pressed my forehead to the glass. I didn't see the blue sedan. A couple wearing their Sunday clothes was walking by. The man stopped to wipe his brow with a handkerchief and looked up at me through the window. For all we knew, that couple was spying on Lou's office, keeping up with his activities. Maybe they weren't churchgoers at all. Now that the case was federal and Lou was suing the government, it was possible we had attracted the attention of the FBI.

Ty pushed Lou to continue. "So why did you bring up Johnson?"

"*Wyatt v. Alderholt.*"

"Which one is that?"

"It was a case decided last year by Judge Johnson that invalidated an old eugenics law from the 1930s."

Eugenics? Why hadn't I thought of that word? I'd learned about it in an ethics class once.

"Eugenics," repeated Ty. "Like gene selection."

"In 1919," Lou continued, "thirty-three states enacted sterilization statutes. But in Alabama, state legislators never were taken by the idea. Here, we didn't go as far as some of the other states."

"Why is that?" Ty asked.

Lou shrugged. "I don't know. I hesitate to say it was for moral reasons, but it could have been. Eugenicists never gathered enough support here to make anything of it."

"So the idea was what . . . to stop us from having children because we were inferior?" I whispered.

"Well, the ideas were often aimed at specific populations that included Black people, yes. But also the poor, the mentally retarded, the disabled, the insane."

"So that's why Mrs. Seager went after India." I was all cried out, but this dawning realization opened my wound fresh again. Why had I not thought of that before? Mrs. Seager probably put the girls in three of these misguided categories: poor, Black, and mentally unfit. Had I done the same? I had initially deemed the girls unfit to be mothers, too. Because they were poor and Black. Because they were young. Because they were illiterate. My head spun with shame.

"Did they target poor white folks, too?" Ty asked.

Lou nodded. "Back in 1927, the US Supreme Court ruled that compulsory sterilization of people deemed unfit was constitutional. People in asylums all over this country were sterilized."

"I never knew that," Ty said.

"Neither did I, before I started researching."

"So what did Judge Johnson rule exactly?" Ty asked.

"He rejected the *Wyatt v. Alderholt* statute. In Alabama, state legislators had passed a bill that mandated sterilization for every person in an insane asylum."

Lou rearranged a stack of papers. It appeared he was still working through everything in his mind, fitting the pieces together himself in the same way that we were trying to.

"Lou, listen," I whispered. "We've got to help you."

"A local law firm across town has agreed to give me some staff support. There's no need."

"You could have asked my mother," Ty said.

"Your mother has helped. She's the one I call when I get stuck on something, and she helps talk me through it. And that won't change."

"Everybody keeps thinking you're getting rich off this case," I said. "Little do they know."

Ty and Lou laughed, but I wasn't in the mood.

"I can type," I lied.

"I'm sure you can."

"Let us help."

"Civil."

I had a hand in breaking all of this. I had to have a hand in fixing it.

"So will the Williams girls get anything in their damages case?" Ty asked. "Everybody keep asking me."

"First, we need to win this one. That'll give them vindication and justice. It will also generate positive attention. When it's over, they can focus on compensation. Yes, I'm hoping those girls will never have to worry about money again in life."

Lou was talented and mature, so it was easy to forget sometimes that he was, in certain ways, just as naive as the rest of us.

THIRTY-FIVE

They'd finally put some equipment on the Dixie Court play yard. Mace and I sat on the edge of the spinning wheel. Whoever had installed it had forgotten to oil the main crank in the center, and it was creaky when it spun. Mace braced his feet on the ground. Every now and then, he used his toe to move it back and forth so that it whined faintly. The two of us sat watching the sun sink in the sky.

"What I'm supposed to say to them newspaper people? Half the time I can't even understand what they be saying."

"Say good morning and keep walking," I told him. "Say *no comment*."

"'No comment'? What's that supposed to mean?"

"That means you have nothing to say to them."

He breathed out slowly. Although they had installed brand-new equipment, the single lamp in the park didn't work, so the kids usually cleared out at dusk. We were alone, lit faintly by the light in apartment windows, though Mace's face was completely in shadow.

"Do you ever wish we'd never filed the lawsuit?" I asked him.

"What you mean?"

"Do you wish I'd left it alone and never stirred up all this trouble?"

I had come over to see the girls, but they were eating dinner, and Mace asked me to go for a walk with him. The wheel was as far as we got. We had not talked much since we'd come back from DC, and I hadn't even had much of a chance to ask him what he'd thought about testifying before Congress.

"The onliest thing I wish," he said, "is that they had never butchered my girls. I ask God all the time why that happened. What I done wrong. Maybe I should have took another wife. Maybe if they had a mama it might not have happened."

I flinched when he said that. I had tried to be a mother to them. I had tried to do what his wife would have done.

"I'm sorry," he said.

"Why are you apologizing?"

"Because that hurt you, didn't it?" He put his hand on the back of my neck. I wanted to relax into his touch, but I couldn't. He was thinking of Constance, not me. There was grief in that touch, I realized.

"You tried, Civil. I know you tried . . ."

I gently removed his hand from my neck. "You won't get any money out of this lawsuit. You going through all this and you won't see a dime. At least not now."

"Do the girls got to tell they story to the judge?"

"No. Lou has a sworn statement from them. That's all he needs."

"Well, they all I care about. I just want them to go to school and be regular kids."

I nodded. "I saw a picture of your wife once. In your room. I know I shouldn't have been in there." I had been leaving the girls' bedroom and noticed Mace's bedroom door standing open. I was surprised by how tidy Mrs. Williams kept the place, especially given the disarray of their shack out on the farm. Mace's bedroom, on the other hand, was proof that some of that mess was due to him. Stuff everywhere. Clothes. A pile of shoes. Dirty underwear in the corner. I kicked a rolled-up sock as I stepped inside. He had only a bed and a bureau. No dresser. No mirror. Even in the apartment, he was still a man of simple grooming habits. Tie up a do-rag at night. Quick brush in the morning. Shave. Brush his teeth.

I'd begun to straighten, making the bed and picking up items strewn about, when I noticed something on top of the bureau. A small picture in a silver frame. The frame was peeling and black beneath the outer silver coating. I picked it up. It had to be the girls' mother, Constance. I had never seen her before. Dimples. A wide face with eyes ringed by dark sockets. A gentle face, one my mama would have called homely, but which I called naturally pretty. I could see why the family was in disarray when I found them. The woman practically looked like an angel.

He kicked, and the wheel spun noisily.

"I'm sorry. It's just I wanted to say . . . she was pretty."

"You didn't have a right."

"I said I was sorry."

"You can't just walk all through somebody life. You can't do that." He hit the ground with his toe and we came to a stop.

"You want me to leave?"

"I want you to stay." He touched my hair again. I had sweated out whatever hairstyle I had left, but the man made me feel like I had on a face full of makeup. He was just so . . . admiring.

"I see you looking at my girls and I know you fight for them like a wildcat if somebody mess with them. You nice to my mama. And she change since you come around. She keep the house straight. She even iron her clothes. We ain't never even had no iron out on that farm!"

We quieted. He began to make a whistling sound through his teeth.

"What tune is that?"

"They say my daddy used to sing while he worked," he said. "Say the birds would stop to listen."

"You remember him?"

"Not really, naw."

"You got that tune from somewhere."

"For sure."

"You don't remember nothing about him?"

He placed a finger to his lips. "Shh. There you go walking all up in it again. Stop asking so many questions. I ain't your case."

"That's what you believe I think of you?"

"I don't know what you think of me. Woman, you mess me all up inside."

I stood up. "I got to go."

In his easy way, Mace leaned back on his elbows. It was too much to even look at him. His shirt was open at the neck, and my eyes were drawn to his smooth collarbones.

"It's a lot pent-up in you, ain't it," he said so softly that I almost didn't hear him.

I didn't look back as I crossed the yard. I was glad the lamp was out, because I knew he was watching.

ALICIA CALLED AND left an urgent message with Glenda because our phone was off the hook. I was to meet the nurses early on Friday morning before the clinic opened. When I arrived, they were congregated on the porch. I parked my car right in front, and, as I walked up to them, I could hear them murmuring. I stopped in the middle of the path.

"Please tell me this ain't more bad news," I said.

Alicia turned to me. The others looked right at me, and I could tell something was off. Some of them wore uniforms, others didn't. Gina and Lori sat on the porch steps. The rest stood.

"Come closer, Civil," Val said.

My feet were bricks. I couldn't take hearing that another child had been sterilized. Surely Mrs. Parr had not allowed it. Mrs. Seager was gone. Everything was supposed to be better now.

Alicia extended her hand. I took a breath and approached the porch. Alicia looked at the others before she began speaking. "Civil, the nurses have found out a few things since we last talked."

"Okay. That was quick." It had only been about two weeks. I placed a hand on the rail to steady myself. "So what is it? Anything Lou can use?"

"Civil." Val's voice was a whisper. "Civil."

"What is it?"

"There were eleven."

"Eleven what?"

"Eleven girls in the past three years."

"What do you mean? Eleven girls sterilized? In Alabama?"

"No," Alicia's voice rose. "Eleven at this clinic!"

A few women started to cry. I heard one of them gasp for breath, but I could not tell who it was. "What are you saying? Why didn't y'all tell me this before?"

"I'm sorry. I was only there for the Williams girls. I promise to God," Val said.

"I ain't never been present at nothing like that," said another.

"That number can't be right." Tears stung my eyes.

"I was there." Gina stepped forward. "I was there for two of them."

"Oh dear God." I could barely stand.

Alicia moved toward me. "Come, sit down," she said. I sank onto the steps.

I could hear the sobs of the nurses and tried to block it out of my ears. I needed to stay strong. I couldn't collapse under the weight of this news. "This is just clear proof that we need more information. If this happened at our little clinic, imagine the rest of the state. Are there girls being sterilized in other parts of Alabama? If so, how many? Where exactly is it happening? Who is authorizing all this?"

Alicia pulled my head to her chest and I relented, but I was still talking. "Do y'all hear me? We got work to do. We don't have time for no grief. We've got to save them. We've got to save them all."

THIRTY-SIX

Montgomery
2016

At the end of our lunch, Lou tells me he once saw an obituary
in the *Montgomery Advertiser* some years earlier for Linda Seager. He can't remember the year. I stop at the public library and
easily find her name while searching the digital archives.

> Mrs. Linda Seager, 85, died peacefully at home surrounded
> by family. She leaves four daughters, two sons-in-law, eleven
> grandchildren, and four great-grandchildren.

Surrounded by family. I wonder if her children and grandchildren know anything about her past, if they know about her role in
the Williams scandal. I do another online search and find her
daughters. One works as a physical therapist at the University of
Alabama in Tuscaloosa. The other lives in town. She's a nurse. Eugenia Wooten. When I get back to my car, I call the hospital and
they put me through to the nurse's station on the oncology floor.
I'm sorry, Mrs. Wooten is on her lunch break. I hang up and sit there for
a few minutes, shaking. I know the hospital is only a few minutes'
drive from the library, but I don't immediately turn on the igni-

tion. I try to think of what I will say to her. It was never in my plan to visit Mrs. Seager or any of her relatives. But when Lou brought her up, I knew I had to see one of them.

When I arrive at the hospital, I still don't know what I plan to say. An old resentment rises in me, and I realize I'm still incensed by the idea that the woman just walked away from it all after Lou dropped the charges against the clinic. Yes, she lost her job, but I'm certain she got another one. I imagine her going home each night, fixing dinner for her family, watching television, putting rollers in her hair before going to bed.

Eugenia Wooten is at the desk when I approach. I immediately know it's her even before I read the name tag. She looks just like her mother, the same bright red hair. But the face is softer, rounder. The woman smiles brightly at me.

"May I help you?"

I place my hands on the counter. There's no one at the station with her. The hospital smells as they all do—slightly bitter, antiseptic. I have been on the oncology floor many times. It's different from the other floors: the voices more hushed, the families more tense. The work is dismal, and the mood reflects it. Mrs. Wooten's disposition seems at odds with that seriousness. I'm put off by her. She isn't what I expected.

"My name is Civil Townsend."

"Do you have a loved one on this floor, Mrs. Townsend?"

She looks at me quizzically. I gather my nerve, galvanized by the familiar hospital environment. "I worked at the Montgomery Family Planning Clinic," I say. "In 1973. With your mother. I was the nurse for the Williams sisters."

Her face drops. The smile disappears, and my first question is answered. She knows everything. Her hand moves slowly to her mouth, and I see the fingernails are polish-free. Blunt and short and clean, just the way her mother had required of us. She squeezes her eyes shut so tightly the lids wrinkle. Then she opens them and slowly comes out from behind the desk, unhooking the half door.

I face her and cross my arms over my chest. She steps closer to me and places a hand on my forearm. "I get off at seven. It's a twelve-hour shift today. Will you meet me after work? I really want to talk to you."

I relax and drop my arms. "You'll be ready to go home. I don't want to—"

"I have wanted to find you so many times over the years, Mrs. Townsend. Please. Meet me in the cafeteria downstairs?"

"Alright," I say. "Around seven?"

"Yes, perfect. I'll see you there."

We eye each other warily, but for the moment, I'm relieved.

BY THE TIME she arrives in the cafeteria, I have already drunk three cups of weak coffee. I claimed a table near the window, close enough to the entrance so she can see me. There's a garden outside with two stone benches, and ashtrays throughout. The cafeteria is too warm and smells sweet like ketchup. Dinner is still in full swing, but I'm not hungry and couldn't eat even if I were.

Eugenia Wooten enters, carrying a large purse on her shoulder. She has changed out of her scrubs into street clothes—a pair of jeans and a simple scoop-necked gray top. When she spies me, her face breaks into another wide smile. She sits down and apologizes for taking longer than she'd expected. I dismiss the apology and study her. Her eyebrows are natural and unruly. There are pinch marks from her eyeglasses on each side of her nose. Her shoulders are covered in light freckles.

"Do you still live in Montgomery?" she asks me as she hangs her purse on the back of the chair.

"Not anymore. I've lived in Memphis for years now."

She nods. "You still a nurse?"

"A doctor."

"Oh? What kind?"

"OB-GYN."

"That makes sense."

"Really? Why?" She pauses, and I regret my confrontational tone. I offer a weak change of subject. "You hungry?"

"I'm too knotted up to eat," she says.

"Me, too," I say. I have nothing to do with my hands. My coffee cup is empty. I pick it up and take a sip of nothing.

"How is that family? The Williamses. Are they alright?"

I don't know how to answer that question. It seems so complicated, the way she phrases it. It could be read as a question of whether they are dead or alive. Or it could be asking whether they survived the trauma. Either way, the question feels fraught.

"India has cancer. She lives in Rockford. I'm headed down that way."

"Oh God." She blinks rapidly. "You know, Mama never wanted to talk about it. I knew, of course. So did my siblings. But we never told our children. Then one of my sister's grandchildren found the story online. She wasn't but thirteen years old and was sure enough mad at us for not telling it to her. Little Miss Nosy." She shakes her head, as if to say, *kids*.

Thirteen. Same age as Erica when her tubes were tied. "Then you told all of the children?"

"No; I mean, not all of them. Dr. Townsend, it was just so awful."

"Yes, it was."

"I mean, Mama was trying to do the right thing, right? That's what I always wanted to believe. It's why I always wanted to reach out to you. I wanted to ask. Were you ever able to forgive her?"

"Forgive who? Your mother?"

"Yes."

I stutter. "N-no. To be honest, no."

"Mama wasn't a Klan member or nothing like that. She wasn't a Confederate or a slaver. She was just a nurse trying to do the right thing at a difficult time. I mean, it was the year of *Roe v. Wade*, for goodness' sake."

"It was."

"She wasn't a monster, right? She was a nice lady to Blacks? I mean, she did work at the clinic."

"She did."

"She wasn't no racist, right? Please tell me, Dr. Townsend, what you thought of her. Was my mama a racist?" The woman's eyes are desperate, pleading.

I twirl the empty coffee cup between my fingers. I want to give this kind woman the relief she craves. I have carried this burden for so long that I understand her anguish. We are bound together by this tragedy. As much guilt as I have carried over the years, I know, with the discernment of a woman my age, that my pain does not rival what Linda Seager inflicted upon her own family.

THIRTY-SEVEN

Montgomery
1973

India and Erica walked timidly into the water.

"Come on. I'm not going to let you fall."

The white sand stuck to my feet, and a shell pricked my toe. I was thinking of our last trip to the beach, when Mama had laughed and laughed. This beach had always meant something to my family, but it was usually where Mama lit up the most. As soon as Mace had said he wanted to take the girls to see the ocean, I had known exactly where I would take them.

Mace was still wearing his tube socks and shoes. I had not invited him, but when I arrived to pick up the girls he had followed us out of the house with his fishing pole in his hand. I must have suspected he would want to come, because I had taken extra care choosing from the three swimsuits in my closet. All of them made me self-conscious, and on my drive over to their house, I worried how much weight I had gained that summer.

India laughed, an audible hawing sound, and her smile lit up her face. With one moist palm in mine, she used the other to bend down and scoop up water. We stopped walking once we made it in up to our shins. A foaming wave hit our legs, and India squealed. The water was cold.

"Can we get our hair wet?" Erica asked.

"If you want to."

"Grandmama will kill us if we get our hair wet. We just got pressed."

"Don't worry about it."

When I'd started coming to this beach as a child, it had been free. Now we had to pay a park ranger. He had given us a piece of paper to put on the dashboard of our car. It was an early Sunday morning, right in the middle of the church hour, so we'd been able to choose a quiet stretch without anyone around. I'd brought three chairs, and Mace sat in one of them, squinting. His fishing pole lay untouched at his side.

I took off my shorts, but I was still wearing my T-shirt. My swimsuit was dark blue with an orange floral print. It was impossible for a woman built like me not to show cleavage, but this swimsuit gave me decent support. Even so, I was shy about taking off the shirt.

The girls didn't have bathing suits, but it didn't stop them. Their splashing had already dampened the bottoms of their shorts.

"Where's your bra, Erica?"

"I hate that thang. It ain't comfortable."

"You won't have a choice soon."

India wobbled, panicking. "You're fine. Hold your arms out to get your balance."

Both of them put their arms out like windmills. A seagull swept the water in front of us, rising again with a fish tail dangling from its beak. I watched as India followed the bird with her eyes.

"That's a seagull," I said. "It's pretty, ain't it?"

India shaded her eyes with the side of her hand.

"Come on, let's sit down."

We walked to the edge of the water and sat, hugging our knees to our chests. The water lapped at my feet, the cold seeping between my toes. India dug up shells. I dragged a stick in the sand and wrote out Erica's name. E-R-I-C-A.

"You know, my mama taught me how to write my name. She spelled it with a *k*."

"Spelled what with a *k*?"

"My name."

"Has everyone been misspelling your name?" I thought of all the times she had been mentioned in the newspapers, the registration papers for school.

She shrugged.

"How is it on your birth certificate?"

"I don't mind spelling it with a *c*. I feel like that other way was just between me and my mama. Not for strangers."

"But that doesn't make sense. We should spell it the proper way."

"I said I don't want to." She threw aside the stick I had been using to write.

"Alright, alright." Mace was right. I needed to accept that they were not a case for me to fix. I had never known that good intentions could be just as destructive as bad ones. Surely this was a family capable of making its own decisions.

Erica's brown eyes glinted in the sunlight. I had never noticed that her eyes were brown. I just registered they weren't the same hazel as her father's.

A wave hit us, and India startled. Erica scooted her pile of shells over to her sister. India took them and began sorting them by size and color. Sister LaTarsha's influence, no doubt. It was difficult to be around the girls and not want to share in their bond. Their closeness changed the air around them.

"I'm going to go check on your daddy."

Erica drew letters in the sand with a finger. I-N-D-I-A. "See? That's your name, India," she said to her sister.

Mace had settled on a towel farther back from the shoreline. As I approached him, I could see that his eyes were closed.

"You not going to fish?"

"Might."

I sat in the chair next to him. Daddy had taught me how to swim in this ocean. He wanted me to be comfortable in the waves. He would carry me out until the water came up to his chest. Then as the waves came in, he would jump into them. His comfort in the water taught me there was nothing to be afraid of. Once, he grabbed a fistful of seaweed and held it to my nose. Then he said, *You smell that right there? That's the scent of the Maker. And the Maker loves you and your beautiful brown self.* I wiped my wet brow. My daddy's footprints were all over this sand.

"When I first started coming here as a child, this was a colored beach. It was named after a soldier killed in the Korean War. Rosamond Johnson."

"A colored beach?" Mace said.

"Umm, you do realize that Negroes are from Africa, where it can get hot enough to fry an egg on the sidewalk?"

Mace's scratchy laugh sounded like sand was lodged in his throat.

"Speaking of frying, I remember there used to be a fish shack where a man fried fish in a pan over a fire. And a place called the Sunset Riding Club."

His eyes scanned the beach. Of course, there was no longer any sign of a shack or club.

"The white folks closed it all down. No sign of it now. Now the beach belongs to the government, I guess."

"I ain't surprised."

I wanted to continue with the story, to share with him that my granddaddy had also been a doctor and that he had been friends with the dentist who owned the Sunset Riding Club. When we were young, Daddy would buy me a Popsicle and it would melt and run down my wrist. I wanted to share all of that with Mace, but I could not bring the words up. I worried how it would make him feel. He might not even believe me. Coming from a family of doctors was as far away from his world as humanly possible.

"A colored beach . . ." he whispered again.

Erica turned to us and waved. Mace held up a peace sign with his fingers.

"I got something to ask you," he said to me. I sat up in my chair and brushed the sand from my feet.

"Shoot."

He squinted at me. "You think it's too late for me to learn to read?"

"Read?" I had heard him, but it was the last thing I expected him to say.

He kept his eyes focused on the girls, and I could tell he was studiously avoiding my eyes. He did not repeat himself.

"No, it's never too late. They got free classes at the library, I think."

He shook his head. "I ain't going to no library."

"Alright," I said slowly. "You want me to find somebody to teach you?" I thought of the nun who ran India's school. Sister LaTarsha might know someone. Then there was our church. Surely they had an outreach ministry for this kind of thing.

"I already found somebody," he said.

"Sure enough? Who?"

"You."

"I don't know how, Mace. I've never taught anybody to read before. I wouldn't even know where to start. I can't even remember learning myself."

"Forget it."

"No, Mace, I—"

"I said forget it."

He rose and brushed the sand from his shorts. Slowly, he took off his shirt and walked down to be with the girls. I had not seen him shirtless since that day at the cabin, and I looked away and then back at him and then away again.

Stop it, Civil. You are at the beach. That's what men do at the beach. They remove their shirts. You're the one sitting around with clothes over top of your swimsuit.

Mace expertly skipped a rock over the water. He tossed a second one and it bounced twice before sinking. I tried to think clearly. Mace was the one too proud to go down to the library and stumble through words with the other grown-ups who would be there. That was his problem, not mine. It wasn't my responsibility to teach him to read. I had done enough for him and his family.

He walked out into the water with India. I could tell from the way he stepped that he was frightened. He did not know how to swim, and even the shallow tide of the ocean could make you unsteady on your feet. India pulled his hand, as if she were the one leading a child, the way I had led her and Erica out there. She was so busy pulling that she fell down and he caught her. "Girl!" I heard him shout. She hugged his legs and he leaned down to kiss her temple. India smiled up at him.

There was no lifeguard. If one of them got into trouble in the water, I would have to be the one to try and save them. And that would be nearly impossible. I had tried so many times to save them. A gargantuan task. The knowledge of that futility did not stop me, however. It could not.

I reached in my bag and took out the Coca-Cola I had brought with me. I used the opener on Mace's key ring to remove the cap and took a long swallow.

India held her daddy's hand and pointed. Some kind of sea animal had leaped up. It might have been a dolphin, but I couldn't make it out from where I was sitting. I loved this family, plain and simple. I fought the urge to go join them. They were not my family. They would always belong to Constance. Still, I loved them.

I would teach him to read. I would help Lou with the case. I would get another job and move on. And that would be the end of it. It had to be.

At least, that's what I told myself.

PART III

THIRTY-EIGHT

Montgomery
1973

The trial began in early October in the Montgomery federal courthouse that oversaw Alabama's Middle District. It was scheduled to take place in the same courtroom where Judge Frank Johnson ruled to integrate two of the city's prominent all-white high schools, where he ruled to end the bus boycott by integrating city buses, where he ruled that the Selma to Montgomery march could proceed. The building occupied a city block, its stately Renaissance Revival–style architecture anchoring one end of the city. There was no mistaking that the Williams case had become a national story.

As he delivered his opening statement, Lou Feldman did not appear intimidated by the moment. Standing before the judge, he grew taller. His voice deepened, brow wrinkled. It was the same transformation he had undergone in DC and, once more, I was transfixed.

While I admired his demeanor, it was still difficult for me to listen to Lou declare that Mace and his mother had been outsmarted by Mrs. Seager. Yes, it was true, neither of them could read, but his portrayal of them as simple country people whose priority was day-to-day survival fell short. These people were smarter than that. Mrs. Williams could put a piece of sweet potato pie in her mouth and know exactly how much nutmeg was used. Mace could stick his finger in the soil and tell you what would and would not grow in it, could recall the names of trees I had never even known existed. They were more than illiterate farmers, more than victims who'd been duped by the federal government. They were a family who, given other opportunities, could have accomplished much more.

On the other side of the room, Caspar Weinberger, the secretary of HEW, propped his elbows on the table. He had flown in for the trial the day before, and word had it that he was staying at the Holiday Inn. Two of the government's lawyers flanked him on either side, but I had already gotten a good look at Weinberger out in the corridor. Dark hair curled away from a long face; eyebrows arched up; eyes sank deep into the hollows of his sockets. According to Lou, the man was deeply concerned about the case and wanted to know exactly how many children had been affected. At the other end of the table, the other defendant, Alvin Arnett, the director of the Office of Economic Opportunity, stared intently at the judge. I was struck by the deep chasm that existed between these Washington politicians and my beloved Williamses. We breathed a different air, walked a different road.

The courtroom audience was sparse. I recognized two of the men in the third row as journalists. They scribbled notes onto slim rectangular pads. A couple of young men in the back row carried packs resembling something students might use. Two women in floral-printed dresses sat together, whispering. Three or four others appeared to be nosy onlookers. I was the only colored person among them.

Listening to the drone of trial technicalities, I did not understand half of it, but it was better than sitting at home. During the recess, Lou refused my offer to take him to lunch. In the days that followed, I think he was both irritated by my presence and buoyed by it. I always sat in the same seat, and on more than one occasion I caught him looking for me when he entered the courtroom. I wore loafers and skirts and tucked my hair back so as not to stand out. During court breaks I went to the bathroom and splashed cold water on my face.

One day, after I handed Lou a sack containing a peanut butter sandwich and a banana, I heard him mutter something under his breath.

"What's wrong?"

"The American Civil Liberties Union just sent me documents revealing that hundreds of Black women in North Carolina and South Carolina were sterilized. But the defense is objecting to me introducing them, because they weren't in pretrial discovery."

"Can you ask the judge for an exception?"

"I can, but he might not allow it."

"Eat your banana." I peeled back the skin. He took a bite, resting his other hand on the railing. The mezzanine had emptied. Two students smoked cigarettes over an ashtray in the lobby down below.

"What's happening here is unfolding every day, Lou. Surely the judge reads the newspaper."

Lou paused his chewing. "He's not supposed to read stories that might affect his judgment."

"You have indigestion, don't you?" I watched him closely.

"How do you know?"

"You just rubbed your belly."

"Do you mind going to buy me some Tums?"

"Sure. How long do we have?"

"An hour. I'll meet you back here." He took off, swinging his briefcase at his side.

After the recess, Lou sat at the table, rolling the unopened

Tums package between his fingers. The judge entered, and everyone stood.

"Please be seated."

"Your Honor," Lou said. "Counsel would like to approach the bench."

The defense lawyers followed Lou to the judge's podium. They conferred with the judge and returned to their places.

"Your Honor, you have in front of you Exhibit A. The Food and Drug Administration's Code of Federal Regulations, updated April 1 of this year."

"Thank you."

"You also have Exhibit B, the FDA's guide on the protection of human subjects. This guide references the Kefauver-Harris Amendment to the act in 1962, which increased the FDA's regulatory authority over the clinical testing of new drugs."

Either the judge's face was naturally set in a permanent scowl or he did not like Lou. Whenever he peered at the young lawyer over his spectacles, it appeared to be a look of disdain. I could see why Lou was wary of him.

Lou continued, "As you will see, Article 130.37 stipulates that any use of investigational new drugs on humans must be based on the condition that investigators have obtained consent. In the eighth section of that article, it defines consent as"—he looked down to read—"'the person involved has legal capacity to give consent, is so situated as to be able to exercise free power of choice, and is provided with a fair explanation of pertinent information concerning the investigational drug.'"

"I can read, Mr. Feldman."

"Of course, Your Honor."

The defense lawyer stood. "Your Honor, the use of Depo-Provera was hardly used for investigative purposes. It was authorized for use as a contraceptive."

"It was not authorized by the Food and Drug Administration," Lou countered.

"This was not an investigational study. The federal government would never do that, particularly in the case of minors."

"Gentlemen, please be seated. You will have your opportunity to present your case. Mr. Feldman, are you alleging that the plaintiffs were injured by Depo-Provera?"

"Your Honor, this is a new drug. The long-term effects on human subjects are yet unknown. We do know that it has caused cancer in laboratory animals."

"Mr. Feldman, the threshold question is whether the plaintiff alleges that the drug has caused an injury in fact."

"No, Your Honor, we cannot yet make that claim."

"Thank you, Mr. Feldman."

I thought of the time I'd injected the needle into India's arm. The girl could not speak. She could not protest. She had merely trusted. I had given her the shot only once, but the memory of that moment haunted me. I had not known about the drug, but it had been my duty to know. I was the medical professional, the one with the knowledge that was out of reach for a family like the Williamses. I might as well have landed from outer space and told them I was going to feed them a miracle food that would save their lives. And they'd partaken. Because even though I was a Martian, I looked like them. Sitting in that courtroom, I understood for the thousandth time the enormity of my mistake. The utter failure of it. I should have questioned Mrs. Seager about this new drug I knew virtually nothing about before I shot it into the arm of an eleven-year-old girl. Ignorance was not an excuse. I should have known. I had been trained to know and to ask.

"Your Honor, I submit Exhibit C, the Food and Drug Administration's policies on oral contraceptives. The plaintiffs were never given written material outlining the side effects of the drug."

The defense lawyer stood again. "Your Honor, the plaintiffs signed consent forms containing the obligatory warnings and notices."

"Your Honor, three directors at clinics across Alabama have signed affidavits claiming that it was not standard procedure to give written notices to the patients to review. The prosecution contends that this administration of experimental drugs is particularly egregious when the recipients are poor."

I sat up straighter. The nurses had helped with those affidavits. That was our contribution to the case so far. But we would need more. Three were hardly enough. We had worked in the Montgomery clinic, and we knew firsthand that the warnings about Depo-Provera were given orally, if they were given at all.

The defense lawyer scoffed. "Your Honor, the federal government treats all people the same. These allegations of bias against the poor are unprovable and histrionic. And it doesn't change the fact that the written notices were always available upon request."

"Histrionic never, and I disagree that it's unprovable."

"Now cut it out before I hold both y'all in contempt of court. I won't give another warning."

Available upon request? The man lived in a fantasy world. And he had the nerve to say the federal government treated all people the same. He obviously was in denial about what happened up at Tuskegee.

Lou's plan became clearer to me. He would first argue that the federal clinics were administering Depo-Provera without informed consent. Then he would move that argument to the issue of sterilization to prove an entire system of abuse.

I liked the strategy. But he had to prove it in this court of law. And I was seeing firsthand that it wasn't going to be easy.

THE SCHOOL YEAR had started, and so had football season. I'd always loved Centennial Hill this time of year. When the leaves were changing and peaches were stewing on the stove and the camellia was blooming out back, the city became one of the most beautiful places I'd ever seen. People sat on their porches and waved at cars. Men in hats walked to the corner store to buy a bottle of Coca-Cola. The Popsicle truck sang out a tune from its bullhorn. Children played stickball in the street. The mailman knew you were waiting to hear from your sick cousin and knocked on the door to make sure he put the letter in your hand. To the world, Montgomery was the Cradle of Dixie. To me, she was home.

Of course, Montgomery had its other side, too. Meeting the Williamses had reminded me of that. On my side, we were protected by our education and jobs and ability to make noise, while poor Black folks went hungry or were humiliated by their employers who exploited the precariousness of their very existence. A lot of Negroes still lived in shotgun houses without indoor plumbing. There were none of us on the city council, and the idea of the city electing a Negro mayor anytime soon was laughable.

It was especially bad in the country. Out there, folks lived in ramshackle houses, eking out a living. Children ran barefoot because their shoes were too small, a lot of them hungry even as their parents cleared crops of perfectly edible food. Erica had told me that last Christmas her daddy had given her and India a bag of clementines. They ate those sweet little fruits until their stomachs hurt, she said.

In fall 1973, folks like the Williamses were never far from my mind. Every time I shopped at the market, I thought of them. Every time I checked a book out of the library, I thought of them. When I put gas in my new car, I thought of them. I tried to hold myself together because the trial was in full swing, and I didn't want to disappoint anyone by getting in the way, but I was troubled and uneasy in those days.

Lou worked tirelessly. I believe the man slept in his clothes some nights, if he slept at all. He had a wife who worked in Selma, but no one had ever met her. I feared a divorce might slip up on him if he didn't tend to his personal life, but when I noticed the determined look in his eyes, I dared not get in his business.

On Sundays after church, I went to Mace's house to teach him to read. We sat in the living room while the girls played outside and Mrs. Williams prepared her Sunday dinner. Mace's reading was improving. The local librarian helped me find more books. I couldn't find very many books with Black characters, so I found ones that featured animals, books such as *Swimmy* by Leo Lionni. Although Mace had not wanted to stumble over words in front of people in a literacy class, he seemed to have no trouble with me correcting him. He would say "Come on now, girl," to encourage me to teach even faster. He'd sit so close to me that I could feel the warmth of his breath as he sounded out the letters.

One day I heard his mother drop something in grease and the sizzle of the fry start up. Suddenly Mace turned and kissed me. It surprised me, but I was ready for it. After months of something rising up between us, we gave in to our attraction. The man tasted like I had imagined he would, like the outdoors. And kissing him was different than kissing Ty. Mace kissed hard, pressing himself to me, holding me tight like it was the last moment we would ever have together. He was a little rough and, frankly, I found that exciting. Ty had been all soft and inquisitive, more concerned with my comfort.

It wasn't just that Mace was ten years my senior. He was different than any man I'd ever known. When the whir of the mixer blade started, we moved closer. When his mama opened the window to yell out to a neighbor, he put an arm around me. I kept telling myself *Control yourself, Civil*. And somehow, I did manage to convince myself that I had everything under control.

Eventually, as her dinner was finishing up, Mrs. Williams came in and sat in her chair to crochet. I continued with the lesson, as if nothing had happened, and I could tell she was concentrating on my words. Out of nervousness, I offered to teach her to read, but she declined, preferring instead to listen in.

THIRTY-NINE

For a long time, Daddy didn't question my refusal to look for a job, nor did he mention my obsession. Each day I woke up and dressed for court as if I were going to work. I rotated three dark skirts and sweaters. Court-appropriate, as they called it. Sometimes I would pick up the girls in the afternoon, asking Erica if there were any school supplies she needed and what was the latest with the two friends she had made. The sole evidence of India's love for her school was the big smile on her face when she got in my car. Somebody anonymously dropped money off at Lou's office for Mace, and with that payment he bought a new carburetor for his unreliable truck and was able to get the two of them to school every morning.

The middle of October arrived, and so did my twenty-third birthday. I didn't think it was right for me to celebrate until the trial was over, but Ty and his family invited me and Alicia to the Magic City Classic up in Birmingham. We were just going for the day and then driving back later that night, so I relented. I woke up early to dress and pack a cooler of drinks. Daddy appeared in the doorway.

"Ooh, Daddy, you scared me. What you doing up so early?"

"I saw you the other day at the store."

"Which store?"

"You were with that man Williams. Shopping. You using the money I give you to support that family?"

"Daddy, he get food stamps. He don't need your money." The bottles clinked as I nestled them against one another in the bag. Daddy thumped the side of his hand against the table. My words sounded hollow even in my own ears.

"You used to study in high school all the time right here at this kitchen table, you remember? Valedictorian. Most likely to succeed. It's not too late, Civil."

I had not expected Daddy to rise so early. I wanted to find a way to slip past him and avoid this conversation, but I had to wait for Ty and his parents to pick me up.

"Too late for what?"

"You can still make an impact as a doctor."

"Daddy, please, not today."

"You could have gone to school anywhere in the country. Spelman. Fisk. Howard. But you go right up the road. The Tuskegee Tigers. Did you think that would make me happy? Going to my alma mater?"

Oh, good Lord. He wanted to have a deep talk and I had just wiped the sleep out of my eyes. "Probably," I answered truthfully. "But once I got there, I liked it."

"It did make me happy, Civil. Everything you've ever done has made me happy."

"Except go to the store with an illiterate country farmer." I was sassing him, and I knew it. I didn't know how else to react. He had caught me off guard. "Daddy, you remember what you used to tell me when I was little? Why you named me *Civil*?"

"Because we wanted you to be free," he said. "The Thirteenth and Fourteenth Amendments were supposed to guarantee civil rights. But the year you were born, it was still just a hope."

"Then let me be free."

"I know you feel bad about what happened with those girls, baby, but what's done is done. That man is—"

"Mace. That man's name is Mace Williams."

"Civil, you need to live your own life. Move on. Those people are not your family."

"Why do you talk about the Williamses as if they're aliens from another planet?"

"What do you see in that man, Civil? What kind of life could you have?"

Goodness gracious, Daddy thought Mace and I were courting. It had just been a kiss, nothing more. But I couldn't open my mouth to convince him otherwise because the alternative might sound like I was being loose.

"And what about Ty?"

"Daddy."

"He's a good young man. Got his college degree."

"Ty's mama still does his laundry."

"Ty's mama is one of the most outstanding lawyers in this town."

"I know, Daddy. I'm just saying—"

"Williams is a grown man. You ready for that?"

"Yes, I am." I said it before I could stop myself, but even as the words formed I knew I had not meant to sound that way. I couldn't look at him. The tiles on our kitchen floor were blue with streaks of yellow. Mama had bought them while in Mexico for a painting retreat. They'd been transported back to Alabama by truck. The Williamses' kitchen floor was covered in vinyl. Why did every beautiful thing in our house have to be a reminder of their lack?

A soft knock thumped at the side door, and Ty waved at me through the glass.

Daddy spared me by remaining quiet as he got up to pour his

coffee. I slung the cooler strap over my shoulder, grabbed my jacket, and mumbled good-bye.

IT WAS EARLY in the morning, but traffic up Interstate 65 had already started to thicken. Blacks in Alabama had been traveling to the Magic City Classic for as long as I could remember. When white Alabamans talked football rivalry, they talked Alabama Tide versus Auburn Tigers. Their game, known as the Iron Bowl, was held at Legion Field in Birmingham, just like ours, but it was typically in November. When Black folks talked football, we talked Alabama A&M versus Alabama State. Our football culture had grown up alongside theirs, like sisters who didn't speak much but wore similar hairstyles. These parallel football universes shaped our lives in more ways than you could imagine.

Daddy was a Tuskegee man, but he had met my mother while he was at Meharry Medical College and she was a student at Fisk in Nashville. None of us Townsends had the connections to the bowl that a lot of folks had. Even so, my family had made the trek up to Birmingham for the game several times over the years.

The rivalry between the Alabama State Hornets and the Alabama A&M Bulldogs was more than just a football game. A lot of fans showed up just to watch the famous Battle of the Bands. The high-stepping majorettes, the military-sharp drum line, the hornet dancing across the field. It was an annual excitement that few events in Alabama could eclipse. The Ralseys were serious about it and never missed a year. Everyone in the family was an Alabama State alum, and when I got in the car the three of them were wearing various combinations of black and gold, the school's colors. Mrs. Ralsey wore a sweater with a gold collar.

With all the traffic, the drive to Birmingham took over two hours. When the Ralseys went to the Classic, they left work behind, so I knew better than to bring up the Williams case. In the car we sang along to Natalie Cole, Gladys Knight, and the Jackson 5. Ty did a perfect Richard Pryor impression. Alicia made us play some dumb word game where you had to come up with a word associated with the word before it. Then Mrs. Ralsey started up with "name that tune." Ty's daddy was tone-deaf and nobody could guess his songs. Ty passed around Coca-Colas, and we drank until we had to stop and use the restroom. Mr. Ralsey kept driving for a while, careful about where he pulled over. A lot of the gas stations required a key, and if you were Black and asked for it, they claimed the toilet was broken. When they did give you the key, you walked around back to find the toilet a funky mess.

When we arrived in Birmingham the Ralseys went to find their friends while Ty, Alicia, and I asked around about the start time of the parade. Ty wanted to find his fraternity brothers, but he refused to split up, taking both of our hands. "Come on, y'all."

My spirit opened up when I heard the echo of drums, sniffed the salty scent of pork sausage. The tin of a radio blasted the air. People walked around in full-on color. Black. Gold. Blue. White. Red. Pink. Green. I smoothed my hand down the front of my sweater, feeling chunky in my blue denim bell-bottoms. They were too long for me and grazed the ground. Afros. Halter tops. Beret-wearing revolutionaries. The crowd was a medley. Old and young. Families and couples. With fourteen historically Black colleges across the state, the bowl was a mecca.

We watched the parade for a while, cheering as the bands marched by, but I was too short to see. I ran into two nursing students from Tuskegee who briefly mentioned the Williamses and gave us a Black Power fist pump. Alicia said she was hungry, and Ty relented. He unfolded three chairs and brought us plates of chicken wings and potato salad. The wings were drowned in hot sauce, the potato salad soupy with mayonnaise. Alicia slurped lemonade. Ty finished his beer and said he'd be right back. Alicia opened up her tote bag.

"I have a new case." She showed me a folder. "A young lady out in the country."

"Damnit, Alicia. Why you bring that?" I could not take my eyes off the file.

"Fourteen years old. Two babies. Refuses birth control for religious reasons."

"You can't change them folks' mind."

"But I got her to try the pills. Finally convinced her. And guess what. After all that, they made her sick."

I grew still, then reached for the folder. "Have you tried changing it?"

"Yup. Tried a couple of different pills."

I read through the notes. The teenager was already caring for three younger sisters by the time her babies were born. Now she had dropped out of school. *Don't read any more*, I told myself. *Don't read any more.* But if someone didn't intervene, this girl's destiny was fixed.

"What's Mrs. Parr saying about it?"

"She wants me to keep talking to the girl. We got limited options here, so I'm just working within that."

I closed the file. "Why are you showing this to me, Alicia? What's the point?"

"I just wanted to get your opinion."

"My opinion? I don't work there anymore. And I don't exactly have a great track record with opinions."

"That's not true, Civil. You got a gift."

"Gifts? Did I hear gifts?" Ty clapped his hands as he approached. His eyes glistened, as if he had downed a couple more beers.

"Now, don't get too excited, Civ. My part-time job at the university only pays $1.60 an hour," he said. Ty had recently started working as a resident adviser in the freshman dorm. He seemed unsure of what to do next in his career. Daddy had questioned a future with Mace, who had likely never had the luxury of time to "think things through." Daddy judged the man, but it did not seem fair to question Mace's future when the word *future* held a different meaning for him.

Alicia opened the tote at her feet and took out two wrapped gifts.

"For me?"

"Isn't your birthday tomorrow, crazy girl?" Ty said.

"Looks like you wrapped it yourself."

His gift for me was the size of a men's shirt box. Images of Christmas trees covered the red paper. Typical Ty. Once, when we were thirteen years old, he'd wrapped two Mounds bars in newspaper and put them on my desk at school. The newspaper ink had been damp and smudged onto my fingertips. The chocolate bars were melted, but I still ate them. I held the box out in front of me, recalling all the times Ty had given me goofy little gifts.

"Open mine first," Alicia said.

I could tell from the shape and weight of her box that it was a book. She kept looking at it in that nervous way givers had when they were worried what you would think of it.

I tore off the paper. "I didn't expect this."

"It's not meant to be pressure. Just a little inspiration," Alicia said quickly.

"Naw, I'd say that's definitely pressure," Ty said.

I turned the book over. *MCAT: A Study Guide.* It was the kind of gift my daddy might give. I didn't know how to respond.

"Well, say something."

"I don't know what you mean by this."

"Would you believe I stumbled on it in the used bookstore? And it's still like new. Some poor soul only owned it long enough to change her mind about medical school. So I thought, the book is still looking for its destiny. I'd better buy it, gift it, and see if it's another person's opportunity to change her mind."

I frowned at her. "Maybe you're the one who is really thinking about medical school?"

"Naw, girl, if anything I'll marry me a doctor. But you? You different."

"Different?"

She touched my hand. "I know you feel rotten about what happened to those sisters. But whether you see it or not, you are gifted, Civil Townsend. Special. You would make an excellent doctor."

Somebody was blasting Marvin Gaye, and the people in front of us started to move as if there were a dance floor beneath their feet.

"Ooh, if Civil's daddy could hear you now. Alicia, you might get the good Dr. Townsend to church after all!" Ty said.

"Let's just enjoy ourselves for now, alright?" Alicia took the book out of my hands and stuck it back in her bag.

"I'm sorry I sound ungrateful," I told her. "It's just that I like being a nurse. I think we're the real caregivers. Alicia, you know doctors couldn't do their work without nurses. Who is the one who notices when a patient is constantly rubbing her chest? Who is the one who writes down they sweating even though the room is cold? Who do they complain to that the medicine is making them sick to their stomachs?"

Neither of them responded.

"Medical school is for people that want a title. I don't need a title. I don't need somebody's respect."

Someone cranked up the music. I started to shout to be heard. "Do you get what I'm saying?"

Ty held up a hand. "Civil. It's just a book. Put it in your closet and don't even think about it. Now open mine."

277

"Y'all really didn't need to get me anything. I wasn't expecting this," I said as I tore off the Christmas paper. It was definitely a recycled box, wrinkled at the edges. He'd Scotch-taped the sides. I ran a fingernail under the edge and pulled off the lid, rummaging through tissue paper.

It was a photograph of me, Erica, and India outside our hotel in Washington, DC. I remembered one of the photographers calling out to us as we descended the steps. I had drawn the girls to me, an arm around their shoulders. I had been taking them for a walk to see the National Mall. My face had creased with irritation, but both of the girls had smiled. It was the only picture I had of the three of us.

"Ty, how in the world did you get this?"

"It was published in the *Tri-State Defender* in Memphis. They printed the photographer's name. Man by the name of Ernest Withers. I found his phone number and called him. Turns out he's a Black man who traveled up to Washington to cover the hearing."

"But . . ." I rubbed my eye.

"Girl, come here," he said. He wrapped his arms around my neck and almost knocked my chair over, our clumsiness reminding me of just how young and clueless we all were. We were just stumbling our way through a situation that was the biggest event of our entire lives. But there was no denying that my love for those girls was genuine, inadequate and flawed as it may have been.

I pressed the picture to my chest. My girls. My little girls.

FORTY

On Wednesday of that week, Lou delivered a bombshell in court. "Your Honor, you have before you the pamphlet containing sterilization guidelines."

A copy of the pamphlet lay open across my lap. Lou had given it to me the night before. Today was the first day he would be able to frame an argument around it. The government lawyers had theirs in binders. All originals. There were enough to go around.

"Your Honor, there were twenty-five thousand copies of this pamphlet printed. Twenty. Five. Thousand," he repeated slowly. "Yet they remained in a warehouse, and, as a result, federally funded clinics across the country never received them."

The judge peered at Lou over his glasses. "Were the guidelines replicated in any other material sent from HEW to the clinic?"

"Not to my knowledge, Your Honor. After the national media attention of India and Erica Williams, the twenty-five thousand copies of the printed guidelines were discovered in a federal warehouse on Third Street in Washington, DC."

Lou emphasized *Third Street* with a dramatic flourish and waved a hand at the defense table as he said it. There was no doubt about it, at least in my mind: Distributing these guidelines could have prevented some of the sterilizations, though surely trained nurses and doctors did not need written instructions to tell them not to sterilize a minor.

I listened to the scratch of pencils on paper as I watched the judge's face. The existence of the guidelines proved that the federal government was at least aware of the potential for abuse and understood the clinics' need for a set of standard practices on the issue. The fact that the clinics never received those pamphlets meant that the government had doled out money and then negligently failed to provide guidance on how the money was to be utilized.

Sometimes it was hard to hear in the courtroom, but other times you could hear someone's stomach growling. The Washington lawyers likely believed they were at a disadvantage, coming down here to unfamiliar territory where the judge had the same accent as the opposing lawyer.

Then again, if anyone was at a disadvantage in this whole mess, it was my girls. The system was not designed for poor people to win. To his credit, the judge ran a careful trial. He listened intently, never asking anyone to repeat themselves. He made a lot of notes and at the end of each day thanked everyone politely. I looked over at the court reporter, a sallow-faced woman. Every day she wore a different floral dress, and today she was wearing one with daisies. The keys of her machine thumped softly. The bailiff's face was reddened from the sun and sweat stained the armpits of his shirt despite the draftiness of the courtroom. The radiators ticked softly when they fired up.

"Mr. Feldman. Is your witness ready?"

"Yes, Your Honor. I would like to call Dr. Lance Paasch."

A man rose from the pew and passed through the aisle. After being sworn in, he sat in the seat to the judge's left.

"Please state your name and position for the record."

"My name is Lance Paasch. I am the former branch chief of the Family Planning Division of the Office of Economic Opportunity."

"Thank you."

Lou walked out from behind his table. "Mr. Paasch, is it correct that you are the author of these . . . sterilization guidelines?" Lou held up the pamphlet.

"Yes, sir."

"And you wrote these guidelines in your official capacity as branch chief?"

"Yes, sir."

"Were you instructed to write them?"

"Yes, sir."

"Who ordered you to carry out this task?"

"The deputy director of the Department of Health, Education, and Welfare, or HEW as we call it."

"What is his name?"

"Anthony Marcus, sir."

"And do you know why you were asked to write these guidelines?"

"Objection, Your Honor. Counsel is asking the witness to speculate on another person's motivations."

"I am simply asking about Department policy, Your Honor."

"Overruled. Please answer the question," said the judge.

"We created a new policy in 1971 that allowed us to fund voluntary sterilization services. We needed guidelines to implement the new policy, and my division was tasked with developing the guidelines."

"How long did it take you to complete the guidelines?"

"It took a few months. We began in summer 1971 and they were written by Christmas. I remember because I visited my mother for the holidays." He turned to the judge and smiled.

"Once the guidelines were finished, did you send them to the appropriate agencies?"

"Well, we sent a letter to all the community action agencies, asking them to withhold funding for sterilization services until the guidelines could be approved and issued."

"And did the agencies wait?"

"I don't know. The guidelines were approved by Deputy Director Marcus on . . ." He held up a piece of paper to read. "January 10, 1972. It took another month to print them up and get them ready for distribution. But then my division got a note that they needed to be approved by the White House."

"By the White House? You mean by the president?"

I leaned forward in my seat. I had suspected that these government projects could be traced all the way to the top. I had told Lou as much, too.

"Well, I have no way of knowing whether or not the president himself was personally involved in the matter, sir."

"Did you have communication with the White House during this period?"

"Yes, I reached out to the White House staff several times over the course of about four months. Finally, I got ahold of the White House legal counsel's office to find out what the holdup was, but instead of information I received a reprimand. So I resigned."

"A reprimand?" Lou said, acting surprised.

"Yes, sir."

"Why did you resign?"

Mr. Paasch hesitated. He glanced over at the government lawyers, then back at Lou. "I resigned because I was concerned that this delay was creating a dangerous and urgent situation."

"What do you mean? Didn't you write the agencies and ask them to hold off on sterilizations until you could distribute the information?"

"Yes, we did, but I was still concerned the surgeries were happening and that they would be undertaken without patients being given adequate counseling."

"You were concerned that they would not be able to give informed consent?"

"Objection, Your Honor. Leading the witness."

"Sustained. Please rephrase your question, Mr. Feldman."

Lou spoke slowly. "Why were you concerned enough about this issue to resign, Mr. Paasch?"

"I was concerned about a lot of things. Sterilization was becoming a political issue in the administration. It was an election year."

"Objection, Your Honor. This testimony is irrelevant speculation."

We were all aware of the growing controversy over President Nixon and his administration. The vice president had just resigned after pleading no contest to tax evasion. A Senate committee was leading an investigation into the circumstances surrounding a burglary at the Democratic National Committee headquarters. The special prosecutor had been fired. By bringing up the president, Paasch lit a fireball inside the courtroom.

"I have no more questions, Your Honor," Lou said before the judge could respond to the objection.

When Lou walked back to his chair, he made eye contact with me. I could tell from his triumphant expression that he knew he had just had his best day in court so far.

I HAD NOT seen the girls in over a week, so I decided to take them some groceries and check on them. Daddy had guessed right. I had been buying them food, but I'd also told the truth about their food stamps. The stamps were barely enough to feed a family of four, so I helped out when I could. Mrs. Williams didn't cook more than they could eat, but she certainly wanted to put two hot meals on the table every day. And there was nothing she liked better than frying up some drumsticks or putting a roast in the oven. Because they had not had a kitchen out in the shanty on Adair's farm, she delighted in her new one. The woman could work magic with very little. When she was in a creative mood, she might cut up an apple and throw it inside the tinfoil with the ham, or she might roll the chicken in cornflakes before frying it.

Mrs. Williams took the sacks from my hands.

"Where the girls?"

"They outside somewhere. Come on in here and help me wash these greens. I'm making chicken and dumplings tonight. You had some lately?"

"No, ma'am. Fact is, I can't remember the last time I had chicken and dumplings."

"Me, neither. That's why I'm making them. Now wash up."

There were two seashell soaps in the bathroom dish. There was even a hand towel. I had never seen a hand towel in their bathroom. With every visit, I witnessed one more step in the Williamses' journey. They had lived the way they had because that was how that shack had made them feel. It was hard to keep things tidy with a dirt floor, hard to maintain dignity in a urine-soaked hovel. On the Adair farm they had shed the best parts of themselves. In this new apartment, with its actual kitchen and indoor bathroom, the family was on the mend.

I looked at myself in the mirror. I didn't know why Alicia had given me that test book. I couldn't even picture myself as a doctor. To have people place their trust in me and then disappoint them would be devastating. I thought about the parade of health professionals testifying in the trial. How did they live with the gravity of their mistakes?

In the kitchen, Mrs. Williams was running the faucet.

"You can use this sink of water to soak while you pick. I don't like no tough stems in my greens."

"Yes, ma'am."

The sour scent of boiling chicken rose from a pot. She shook some flour into a bowl.

"These greens from the neighborhood garden?"

"Sure enough." She didn't look up. "We planted greens, turnips, tomatoes, and cabbage. About the onliest thing I miss from being on the back of that land."

I snapped off the end of the stem.

"How the trial going?"

She surprised me with the question, because she rarely asked about it. "It's going fine. Lou is still presenting our side."

"That is some white fellow, I tell you. God don't make many like him."

"Yeah, he's something."

"I used to hear of young whites coming down here for the protests. Some of them even gave they lives for the cause. Do you remember that young white woman who came down here to march for voting rights? I heard about her, though I never caught her name. That woman disappeared and was never to be found. And she had four children! I imagine her family must still be making sense of why she came in the first place."

"Mmm."

"Course I never did go march. India and Erica was young. I was helping they mama with them. She used to go clean houses and I watch the kids while she work."

"Mmm."

"When she die, that white family she worked for didn't send us no flowers, didn't say sorry for your loss, didn't say kiss my foot, nothing. She worked for them people for seven years, and I heard they hired a new maid before her body was even cold in the ground."

"You jiving me." I wiped my forehead with the back of my hand.

"Anyway, I been thinking about them because I'm thinking now that the girls in school and I'm near the bus line, I can start working again. Maybe they hire me."

I dropped a handful of leaves into the sink and swished them in the water. "You would go work for that family after what they did?"

She shrugged. "It's work."

"Maybe one of the schools is hiring. I can talk to—"

"Now, there you go again."

"There I go again what?"

"You done enough, Civil."

"I'm just saying that if—"

"Civil."

"You sound like Mace."

"Hand me that pot. It's a hock in the icebox."

"Yes, ma'am."

As I squatted to get the pot, I heard the front door open. The girls came straight to the kitchen, and when they saw me both of them wrapped their arms around my neck.

"Where y'all been?" I kissed India's forehead.

"Look what I got." Erica held up a tube of lipstick.

"Where you get that?"

"I found it. It's been used a lot, but my friend say I can just wipe it off with a tissue and it be like new again."

"Oh." The lipstick was dirty and flattened all the way down to the tip. It was just on the edge of my tongue to offer to buy her a new tube from the drugstore, but I stayed quiet. I knew Mrs. Williams was watching me.

That woman could say all she wanted to about me trying to fix things. These girls were my girls, too, and I was going to do for them what I wanted. Tomorrow I would pick up some new lipstick for Erica.

FORTY-ONE

Lou dangled a pen from his fingers.

"Lou, I was thinking about something, how the government is saying that these sterilization policies didn't intentionally target poor women. About how you got to prove it."

"Yes?"

We were sitting in an office the courthouse designated for lawyers during trials. Two desks and two chairs faced each other. A small window overlooked the street. The room was cold and drafty and the walls were bare.

"This ain't that different than what happened at Tuskegee."

"What we are talking about here is a little different. Eighty-two people have been sterilized in the state of Alabama in the past year, forty of them white. The defense will claim that percentage proves their point. Far as I know weren't any white men infected in the Tuskegee study." Lou didn't talk down to me when we discussed the trial. In fact, I'd say he took me seriously. He used me as a sounding board to think things through.

"But half the people in Alabama aren't Black. That's not a proportionate number," I said.

"True, but their point still sticks."

"What about the locations of family planning clinics? Ours is right in the middle of a Black neighborhood. Isn't that typical? That seems like something easy to find out. We can look up the addresses, and make the case that the clinics target our communities just by the location."

He nodded. "Good idea."

"So if Tuskegee doesn't work, what if we linked it to abortion rights?"

"What do you mean?"

"Abortion and forced sterilization seem to me two sides of the same coin. On the one hand, they restrict our access to abortion. On the other hand, they tie our tubes. They got women caught between two rocks, Lou. Even with the Supreme Court decision, an abortion is still hard for poor women to get."

"This is Alabama, Civil. I'm not sure we want to wade into the abortion waters."

I tried to swallow, but my mouth was dry. "But it's relevant. If we somehow draw a connection between the killing of unborn babies and unconceived babies, we might get the judge's attention."

"Too risky."

"Look, a woman ought to have the right to end a pregnancy if she wants to. The issue in our case has to do with whether the women wanted to."

"Civil."

I carried on, ignoring him. "Seriously, what do you think?"

"Get me the addresses of those clinics. That's a good place to start."

"Fine." I crossed my arms.

"You know, Civil, I had a law professor at Auburn. His name was Maddox. I clerked for his daddy for two years after law school. The old man taught me a very valuable lesson about trial law that I've never forgotten."

"What's that?"

"Don't get ahead of yourself. Take things one step at a time, and eventually your argument in court will reflect that precision. Passion is good. But only when it's focused."

"Sounds like he needed to loosen up," I said, but I remembered it was similar to the advice Ty's mom had given.

He unwrapped a Tums and put it between his teeth. "You don't quit, do you."

He had a point. My own spunk in recent months had surprised me. I'd always believed I was a cross product of my parents. Daddy, the cautious and conservative one. Mama, the impulsive artist. Maybe I was more than the sum of my parents.

The medical school admission book Alicia had given me was still up under my bed. I'd stuffed it under there as far as it could go. Alicia had said she became a nurse to prove that God was real. Well, I had gone to nursing school to make a difference.

I could not be cautious like Daddy, nor could I live in the clouds like Mama. I had to act.

THE NEXT DAY, Lou called three doctors to the witness stand. The first was a petite white man wearing a tweed jacket and small, round glasses, dressed more like a professor than a medical doctor. I scooted forward in my seat so I could hear him better, because he spoke softly.

"I am Dr. Walter Rosenstein, licensed to practice in the District of Columbia, and a specialist in internal medicine. I am director of the Health Research Group, a nonprofit public interest organization that conducts research and publishes articles related to health care."

"Thank you, Doctor. I'm holding here a report—Exhibit F, Your Honor—authored and published by your organization, titled

'Health Research Group Study on Surgical Sterilization—Present Abuses and Proposed Regulation.' My goodness, that's a mouthful. Did I get those words correct, Doctor?"

"Yes, sir."

Lou walked back to the table as if to consult his notes. I never knew how much of his walking back and forth to read documents was courtroom theatrics. "For the court record, can you state the publication date of this report?"

"May of this year, sir. Approximately six months ago."

"And could you explain to the court the contents of this report?"

The doctor pushed his glasses up his nose. "In our research, we gathered information from Baltimore City Hospital, Los Angeles County Hospital, and Boston City Hospital. In our findings, we documented numerous sterilization abuses in all of these hospitals."

"Could you please describe what you mean by *abuses*?"

"Well, women—many of them Medicaid patients—were asked to consent to sterilization during childbirth, especially women who already had three or more children."

"During childbirth?"

"Yes, sir. Most of the women reported that they had never discussed sterilization with the doctor prior to the delivery room. We also found that the forms they signed at Baltimore City Hospital consisted of only seven lines. The lines stated that the patient was voluntarily consenting to the sterilization and would in all probability never bear children again. There was no information provided on the form about the benefits, risks, or alternatives to sterilization."

"Your Honor, we have a copy of the Baltimore City Hospital sterilization form."

Lou waited while the judge reviewed it. Sunlight streamed through the window. It was one of those chilly fall mornings when the sun shone so brightly that you could not help but want to be outside. I knew with this kind of sunlight Mama would be in her studio all day. Daddy would try to wrap up his day as early as possible so he could get home to cook dinner. I had never been one for the outdoors, but I had awakened early that morning and sat in a chair on our back porch, looking out at the yard, watching as the leaves rose and fell with the wind.

"Dr. Rosenstein, did you find that the women were legally capable of consent?"

"Yes, they were legally capable in most instances."

"But they were given limited information?"

"Yes, sir. We even found that many believed the procedure was entirely reversible, despite the form's language."

"So they believed sterilization was a temporary form of birth control?"

"Exactly, sir."

"And many of them were poor women who received Medicaid?"

"Yes, sir."

"I have no more questions, Your Honor."

"Mr. Peters. Would you like to cross-examine?"

The government lawyer did not stand. "No, Your Honor."

Weinberger was not in court today. On the defense side, it was just the three government lawyers. Two unidentified men sat in the pew directly behind the lawyers. Later, I would learn one was the Assistant Secretary, the other an Alabama congressman. Had I known who they were, I might have had a better guess as to how important the case was becoming. Lou didn't appear concerned. He was like a soldier, looking neither right nor left. The government lawyer appeared relaxed as he asked his questions from the comfort of his swivel chair. Lou never stayed seated when he was examining a witness.

As Dr. Rosenstein left the witness stand, I noticed the smartness of his attire. I could not help but think that even with all his information and knowledge, he was powerless to stop the surgeries.

I wished I could see Lou's face. His back was to me. He was trying to get the laws changed, and his case might be thrown out if the judge determined that the laws had already changed and there was no longer any need for injunctive relief.

Lou called a second doctor. "Your Honor, I call Dr. Barbara Robard."

A woman who had been sitting in the back row stood. I had assumed she was a local, an onlooker like me. I waited impatiently for her to be sworn in. I had been around enough of my dad's Meharry friends to have met Black women doctors, but even I had to admit there had not been many.

"Dr. Robard, please state your position and title."

"I am director of research at the Health Policy Advisory Center in Washington, DC."

A PhD or a medical doctor? Or both? I wished Lou would clarify. The woman intrigued me.

"What has your research revealed about the rates of sterilization in this country?"

"Mr. Feldman, we have found that sterilization is the rule, not the exception. It is widely endemic in this country. It is a form of reproductive control."

Lou was nailing it now. This was exactly what he wanted the judge to hear.

"Objection, Your Honor."

"On what grounds, counsel?"

"Hyperbole."

"Sustained."

I shook my head. The defense lawyer hadn't even offered a real objection, and the judge had let him have it. The woman on the stand did not appear perturbed and neither did Lou.

"Dr. Robard, could you give us some statistics from your research?"

"Last year we did a survey and found that although two-thirds of federally funded clinics' patients are white and only one third are Black, 43 percent of those sterilized are Black. A report from the US government"—she pointed at the government lawyers—"found that between the summer of 1972 and the summer of 1973, twenty-five thousand adults were sterilized in federally funded clinics. Of these, 153 were under the age of eighteen—"

"Objection, Your Honor."

"In North Carolina between 1960 and 1968, of the 1,620 sterilizations that occurred, 63 percent were performed on Black women—"

"Objection, Your Honor."

"And 55 percent of those were teens!" Dr. Robard shouted.

"Objection!"

The judge slammed down his gavel. "Order. Everyone needs to settle down. This is my courtroom, not some circus."

The numbers! Robard had the numbers.

"Your Honor, the witness is merely answering my question about statistics," Lou said.

"Those statistics are broader than the scope of this case," protested the defense.

"Counsel, I will overrule a portion of your objection. Though the numbers from the 1960s are irrelevant to the current legislation, any statistics concerning the previous year or two are directly relevant and will be allowed. In addition, Miss Robard, you will answer only to the question asked. This is not a zoo. Have I made myself clear to everyone?"

I did not like the judge's reference to a zoo. And he had addressed the doctor as Miss Robard. I supposed we could count ourselves lucky that he had not called her by her first name, as many white folks did with Black women. I wondered if this was the bias Lou had been concerned about. Maybe the judge's professionalism was all a ruse to pretend impartiality. We were setting ourselves up for heartbreak by believing in his fairness.

"Proceed, Counsel."

Lou spoke softly. "How large are the recent numbers, Dr. Robard?"

"Our findings show that HEW's numbers are grossly underestimated. Our research reveals that over the past few years, nearly one hundred fifty thousand low-income women from all over the nation have been sterilized under federally funded programs."

I put my hand over my mouth. All of this had happened under the government's watch. I didn't want to even try to guess the total number of underage sterilization victims. She'd mentioned 55 percent were teens in North Carolina, but now everything melted together in my head and all the numbers merged into one outraged thought: *How dare they?* Our bodies belonged to us. Poor, disabled, it didn't matter. These were our bodies, and we had the right to decide what to do with them. It was as if they were just taking our bodies from us, as if we didn't even belong to ourselves.

I needed some air. I had to get out of there, but I didn't want to disturb the proceedings. Not desiring motherhood had once made me wonder if something was wrong with me. I'd tried to make peace with that after my abortion, believing with all my heart that there was a scientific basis that could explain every facet of human nature. But I had exercised a choice, something that was being denied these women.

"No further questions, Doctor."

As the doctor walked past me, my insides gurgled as if a volcano might erupt right into her path. I waited for the judge to dismiss court for the day, but when I went to find Dr. Robard in the lobby she was already gone.

FORTY-TWO

Lou rested his case at the end of October, and court temporarily adjourned. He had worked hard, but no one could be certain it was enough. After I left the courthouse, I just wanted to eat a sandwich and go home to bed. The lunch I'd packed that morning was still in the sack on the back seat of my car.

When I arrived home, all the lights were on, the living room and dining room all lit up. I figured Mama was on one of her cleaning binges. Every now and then she would get a bucket and start cleaning the whole house, throwing out stuff and rearranging furniture. Sometimes the cleaning surge ended in her painting the walls. Other times she quit halfway through and Daddy and I had to put everything back. Yet when I stopped to think about it, she hadn't done that in a long time. In fact, I couldn't remember the last time she'd cleaned the house.

In the kitchen, I could smell the scent of gardenias. Company. "Daddy?" I called out.

"Back here, baby."

I took an apple from my lunch sack and walked back to the den. My aunt Ros was sitting in Daddy's chair. He leaned against the bar.

"Aunt Ros, when did you get here?"

Wrapped in endless layers of fabric, Aunt Ros was the queen of draped clothing. She had once bragged she did not own a belt, and I believed her. She shared Mama's high cheekbones, thin frame, and long neck, but the likenesses stopped there. Unlike Mama and her trademark red lipstick, Aunt Ros never wore makeup or high heels. And she picked her hair out into one of the biggest Afros I had ever seen.

"Your daddy has been ignoring me for weeks, so I decided to come down here and see what was going on for myself."

"I didn't see your car in the driveway."

"I took the bus."

I perched on the edge of the barstool next to Daddy. Mama sat on the floor, her legs crossed, picking pink polish off her finger-nails. It did not appear she had washed up before coming into the house.

"Civil, you're a nurse. I'm a psychologist. We both take care of people. You see what's going on in this house. You know it and I know it."

"What's going on?"

"You mother stays out there in that studio all the time. She's even sleeping out there."

It was true. Mama was sleeping out there more and more, but it didn't happen every night. At least, I didn't think so.

"How do you know?" I asked softly.

"Your next-door neighbor Mabel Turner called me. She was concerned. Said when she tried to talk to your daddy about it, he claimed everything was fine."

"Mama's just painting a lot, that's all. She's working on a series."

"I know my sister well as anybody in this room, and I can tell this ain't about no series. Why didn't y'all get her some help? They got counselors over at the hospital."

"Counselors?" I asked. "Why would she need counselors?"

Aunt Ros sat up in the rocker and it tipped forward. "Henry, you stay at that office all the time. You even working on Saturdays now. And June, you fooled yourself into thinking that you out there trying to finish a doggone series. But really all y'all doing is sinking in a pit of mud."

I shook my head. Aunt Ros had bust up in here like she had a magic telescope that could see inside us all the way from Memphis. Aunt Ros had always been like that, thinking she could fit everybody into a psychology textbook.

"Mama, tell her you're fine," I said.

Aunt Ros did not stop. "June. You are coming to Memphis with me for a couple of weeks, and I won't take no for an answer."

"Ros, I can't do that. I can't just up and leave." Mama's voice sounded weak.

"You getting on that bus with me, Junebug."

Daddy did not protest. Maybe he was grateful for the interference. Maybe they both were. I tried to read his face, but his eyes would not meet mine.

"And Henry, you are going to—"

"Aunt Ros. You can't just come down here and uproot the family. You don't know everything. Mama and I go to church on Sundays now. She's fine. And Daddy doesn't work any more than he always has. It's just his practice is growing."

She turned to me. "Civil Townsend, why ain't you working? You ain't worked since summer. Mabel say you at that trial every day. Those are not your children. You trucking down to that courthouse every day like you they damn mama."

"Ros."

"I'm sorry, Henry, but you know it's true."

"It's hard for me to get a job in Montgomery right now, Aunt Ros. Everybody blames me."

"Nobody blames you, baby," Aunt Ros said.

"They talk about me behind my back. They call me a trouble-maker. Blame me for what happened to those girls. Even the folks at church look at me funny."

Aunt Ros did not move to comfort me. "Who talks about you?"

"Everybody."

"Baby, there's always been people who don't understand the sacrifice of justice. You trying to make a bad situation better. If you know that in your heart, that's all that matters."

The sacrifice of justice? How little Aunt Ros knew. She had been away from Montgomery too long. Whether it was the Birmingham church bombing or Ruby Bridges, there wasn't any justice for little Black girls, and never had been.

INSTEAD OF US going to church that Sunday, Daddy took Mama and Aunt Ros to the bus station to see them off. I couldn't go. It just hurt too bad to see Mama looking all pitiful and vulnerable like that. Ros had held up a mirror to the family, and Mama had finally given in to her exhaustion. Her eyes seemed to have sunken and her cheeks drooped, showing her age in a way I had not seen before. When I walked into her room the morning of their departure Aunt Ros had been dressing her, Mama just sitting there, cata-tonic.

I said my good-byes at the house. Aunt Ros declared that by the time Mama returned home she would be so transformed she would be cooking. Daddy just laughed because on their wedding day, Mama had made it clear that she could not cook and never would.

A few days after they left, Daddy launched a hiring search for a junior doctor who could help in his practice. He joined a men's poetry circle that met Saturday mornings. I lounged around in bed all morning, and watched TV in the afternoons. It seemed like the family had left me behind.

One day, Ty knocked on the side door, but I didn't answer. He left a note.

Alabama State got an opening for a registered nurse. If you work here, I'll bring you coffee.

Attached to the note was a flyer with pinholes at the top. Instead of writing down the information, Ty had taken the entire paper. I folded it and put it in my desk drawer.

I was still wallowing in self-pity when Lou called me later that afternoon and told me the defense had rested its case.

"Already? What does that mean?"

"They submitted their documents, then motioned to have the case dismissed. Said the plaintiffs filed prematurely. Then they presented evidence that HEW is currently revising its sterilization guidelines. Said my case didn't have legs to stand on anymore."

"What did the judge say?"

"He said," and Lou imitated the judge's gravelly drawl, "*I will take this into consideration.*"

"You sound just like him."

"Yeah, well, I've listened to that voice so much I hear it in my sleep."

"So now what?"

"We wait."

"How long?"

"Not long. He'll go through the court notes, write up his judgment."

"How long is not long?"

"I don't know. Hey, what are you doing at home in the middle of the day? Want to go get something to eat? I'm about to go down to the Ben Moore Hotel."

"No, I've got something else I need to do today."

"Okay, well, I'll give you a call if I hear anything."

"Thanks, Lou. I'm serious. Thanks for everything."

"Don't thank me yet."

It was afternoon, but I was still in my pajamas. I put on slippers and walked out to our backyard. The white plastic chair creaked as I sat in it. That crazy rooster started to crow and I called right back to him. He stopped short, as if confused by my response. I slid my fingers through my shirt between the buttons and felt the round softness of my belly, trying to imagine what it would feel like to swell with the rising firmness of a growing fetus.

The wind rushed my ears. I had so many questions, but I knew most of them were questions for God. Was Mama really sick? What was I doing with Mace? Should I go back to the clinic and work? Was it my fault those girls had been sterilized?

There was a time when we'd talked about things. I'd talked to Daddy. Daddy had talked to Mama. We carried no secrets, thoughts circulating through our family with the neatness of a simple triangle, intimacy working its natural path until the answer was reached.

I had never really understood my mama, so the notion of dealing with her depression any differently than usual mystified me. The paintings seemed to hold a key, how they meant different things to different people. I could comprehend that interpretive freedom was an important creed of civil rights for her. Black art, she'd always said, did not have to be representational or realistic to be political. The power of art to speak to you sometimes lay in its unwillingness to be penned into one thing. It was the kind of argument that had always made me look at Mama and think: She cannot be penned into one thing, either. As for me, I craved order and rationality. I needed to understand. Not understanding was knocking me clear off my feet.

My belly warmed beneath my fingers. I breathed in and out; it rose and fell. How on earth would I make sense of it all if that verdict came back against the girls, if the judge did absolutely nothing to change things?

The rooster started to make another sound, something that didn't sound birdlike at all.

FORTY-THREE

On November 3, the judge sent word that he was ready to deliver his verdict. On the way to the courthouse, I explained the possible outcomes to Mace and Mrs. Williams. "Today the judge is going to make a ruling that could end all sterilizations at federally funded clinics. He might order this temporarily until the clinics prove they are compliant with regulations regarding informed consent. Or he could dismiss the case altogether. We just don't know."

"Dismiss?" Mrs. Williams said from the back seat.

"Well, you know what we're really trying to do, Mrs. Williams. We talked about it. We got to make sure that what happened to Erica and India never happens to anybody else. Nobody should be pressured to get their tubes tied. Nobody."

"Ain't that the God's honest truth."

"Hopefully, the judge will tell the government that what happened was illegal and that they need to fix the problem."

Mace had been quiet the entire ride. A terrible kind of quiet. "How many has it happened to?" he finally asked.

"In the past few years, thousands of poor women have been sterilized around the country."

"The devil is busy," Mrs. Williams murmured.

"Well, nothing that judge say today can change what happened," Mace said.

"No, it can't," I said carefully. "But it can give what they went through some purpose. If the judge rules in our favor, it will be because of your bravery, your testimony before Congress, your willingness to let the girls stand for what was right."

"Mace, son, that's why we went to Washington. Remember we talked about it? And that nice Kennedy man listened to us. He wrote it down. He told the other white men what they needed to hear."

Mace didn't say anything. I was glad we had decided not to bring the girls. They were at school, and the three of us had agreed this was the right decision. If the verdict turned out bad, we did not want them to see that.

We arrived to a sea of television cameras. Police cordoned off the area around the courthouse. Lou had sent an escort to meet us, but as we made our way through the crowd a journalist recognized the Williamses.

"What do you hope is the outcome today, Mrs. Williams?"

"The out what?"

"What do you hope the judge will say?"

"Naturally, we just hoping he do what's right. What happened to my grandbabies was a sin against God and the whole world know it."

"Come on." I ushered them inside.

Mrs. Williams followed the escort up the stairs, ahead of me and Mace. "Y'all walking too slow," she called back to us.

Mace took my elbow. I dreaded going into that courtroom. I did not know if I could look the girls in the face again if things didn't go our way. When we shared with them the verdict was coming, India had just stared and Erica had asked, "Do everybody know it's today?"

The escort handed us off to a woman in a brown and white suit at the courtroom door. "Civil Townsend? Mr. and Mrs. Williams?"

"Yes, ma'am."

"I'll take your coats and show you to your seats."

Court was set to begin at 9:30 A.M., but the room was already full. I noticed the nurses first. All of them in uniform. A tall Black woman in a baby blue version of their uniforms and identical cap sat at the end of the row. It was my first time seeing the new director, Mrs. Parr. When she saw me, she waved. Looking at her warm, open face, I regretted never going in to meet with her. Alicia waved, too, and some of the others nodded. I hadn't expected to see them all there, and it felt odd not sitting with them. We had started this journey together, and although I had only worked at the clinic for a few months, I was one of them.

The Williamses and I sat in a reserved row right behind Lou's table. Mace took my hand, and I saw Mrs. Williams glance down out of the corner of her eye.

"Hey," he whispered. "After this over with, no matter what happen, I want you to know you done good."

Mace flashed the same playful grin he had shown me the first time I met him. The kind that made you think for a second that he was just fooling with you. Daddy was right: Mace was real. A grown man, a father, a son. I had no right to play around in his life. I pulled my hand away gently, carelessly, as if by accident.

The door at the back of the courtroom opened, and we all turned to watch the lawyers enter. Lou was wearing a stiff new suit, and it swallowed him in a sea of pinstripes. His face was freshly shaven, hair clipped short; he was the picture of a church deacon. He walked straight to his table and set his briefcase on it. I'd heard his closing argument the night before. It was good. But neither of us was sure if it was good enough.

The bailiff closed the doors to the courtroom. I scanned the room. I spied the Ralseys, but there was no sign of Ty.

The bailiff announced, "All rise for the Honorable Eric Blount."

The judge entered briskly.

"You may be seated."

"This is the Middle District Court of the State of Alabama, in the case of Civil Action Number twenty-three dash two five six one. The case of Erica and India Williams, et al., plaintiffs versus Caspar Weinberger et al."

I wiped at the moisture on the back of my neck.

Mr. Weinberger sat next to his lawyers. Then there was Mr. Arnett. Behind them, a group of what could only be Washington government types, strangers I didn't recognize. The bigwigs in Montgomery had turned out for this verdict, too. George Wallace leaned forward in his wheelchair near the back of the room, Mayor Robinson in the seat beside him. From our community, I spotted Johnnie Carr. Rufus Lewis. Fred Gray. I even spotted Sister LaTarsha sitting next to two other sisters.

The judge began to read without much introductory pomp and circumstance. "I hereby order that the plaintiffs India and Erica Williams may prosecute their claims as a class representative under Rule 23 B-2 of the Federal Rules of Civil Procedure on behalf of all poor persons subject to involuntary sterilization under programs that receive funds administered by the Public Health Service or the Social and Rehabilitation Service of the United States Department of Health, Education, and Welfare."

Mrs. Williams turned nervously to me. I nodded to indicate this was good.

"The family planning sections of the Public Service Act and of the Social Security Act do not authorize the provisions of federal funds for the sterilization of any person who has been judicially declared mentally incompetent or is in fact legally incompetent under the applicable state laws to give informed and binding consent to the performance of such an operation due to age or mental capacity."

He cleared his throat.

"I order that the defendants, their successors, subordinates, agents, and employees are permanently enjoined from providing funds under the aforesaid family planning sections for the sterilization of any person who has been judicially declared mentally incompetent or is in fact legally incompetent under the applicable state laws. The Sterilization Restrictions issued by the United States Department of Health, Education, and Welfare are arbitrary and unreasonable in that they authorize the provision of federal funds without requiring that the person be advised at the outset that the consent to such an operation have no bearing upon other benefits provided to the person by the federal government, and without further requiring that such advice appear prominently at the top of the consent document mentioned in those regulations."

"Praise God!" someone shouted.

The judge did not respond to the outburst.

"It is ordered that the defendants shall promptly amend these Sterilization Restriction regulations to bring them into conformity with this order. It is further ordered that the plaintiffs' motion for summary judgment is granted in the above respects, and the defendants' motion to dismiss is denied."

I did not move. I could not think, not even when the judge finished and began the business of adjourning court. No one else seemed to respond either. Perhaps people had not understood. The order had been as technical as a medical diagnosis. Had two little Black girls from Alabama just won in federal court? Slowly someone began to clap.

"Civil, Civil."

"Yes?"

"We won, right?" she whispered.

I nodded. "Yes, yes, Mrs. Williams. We won."

The room came back into focus. The nurses surrounded me, Alicia's arms around me first, her voice in my ear. *You did it, Civil. Girl, you did it.* Mace and Mrs. Williams dropped back to allow the nurses some room. I started to cry, then gulped it back.

I watched Lou walk over to shake hands with the defense lawyers. I could hardly believe what I'd just heard. I wanted to see the girls, tell them they could stand proud. They were heroines now. Strangers spoke to me as they passed out of the courtroom.

"Congratulations, Miss Townsend."

"Good job."

"Give my regards to the girls."

"You done alright."

"God bless you, young lady."

"We're going to ask the press to wait outside the building for interviews so we can clear the courtroom and hallways," the bailiff announced.

All of us nurses gathered into a knot. Val wiped my cheek. "I will spend the rest of my life repenting for what I done. But I thank God for you today, Miss Civil Townsend. And for your big old heart."

Val, Liz, Fiona, Gina, Margaret, Lori, Alicia, and me. Eight of us had been in this together, bound by an oath to help people. Good intentions, we now knew, did not excuse the wounding. Working in the name of the good did not negate the hurt. As long as these injustices continued, all of us were culpable. I wanted to tell Val that, make a speech of gratitude to the women, but I thought if I opened my mouth, all my pent-up emotions would come tumbling out.

Mace and his mother walked toward the door. I heard Mrs.

Parr tell the nurses it was time to get back to the clinic, and one of them offered her a ride.

"Mace, I can drop you off at your truck so you can get to work." My voice rasped. I wanted to shout for joy, but I also wanted to cry. Maybe Aunt Ros was right. I had some things going on in my body that needed working through, because let me tell you something: That verdict left me all tied up.

"I'm too riled up to work, but I best get on over there," he said.

"Well, I ain't got to work. Mace, go get our coats. Civil, how about me and you go to that diner you like? I got a few dollars. I buy you some breakfast, treat you for a change."

"Alright, Mrs. Williams. Sounds good to me. Soon as we drop Mace off."

We followed the last of the crowd down the wide stairwell, our shoes clicking on the stone floor. I knew the press would want to interview Mace and Mrs. Williams, but I did not believe I was in a state to answer any how-does-it-feel questions. Anything I uttered would be gibberish. I needed more time to let this news sink in. My girls had finally won something. Right here in Montgomery, Alabama, justice had prevailed. It baffled me how hatred and goodness could coexist. The world was an enigma. My country was an enigma. Still, she was mine. And I loved every square inch of her.

When Mrs. Williams and I got to the bottom of the stairs, Ty was waiting.

"Ty, where were you? You missed the whole thing."

He put his hand on my shoulder and leaned in to speak into my ear. "Civil, one of the girls is missing."

"What do you mean *missing*?" I said loudly.

"The school called the police about an hour ago. One of Mama's friends in the police department called the house, and I answered right before I was about to head over here. It's Erica."

"What's this about Erica missing? That can't be right. She got on the bus this morning," Mrs. Williams said. "I saw her with my own eyes."

"Yes, ma'am," he said. "They say she came to school, but she disappeared right after the bus let them off. They noticed she was gone a little while ago."

"Maybe she's somewhere near the school. There's no need to panic," I said.

Mace came down the stairs carrying our coats. Mrs. Williams walked over to meet him, but I didn't hear what she said.

"Take me to get my truck, Civil," Mace said, already walking toward the door.

"But you got to get to work," I called out stupidly.

"You got a car, young man?" Mrs. Williams fixed her eyes on Ty.

"Yes, ma'am."

"Let's go pick up India. Then take me over to Dixie Court. Erica is probably making her way home. I want to be there waiting."

"Yes, ma'am."

The escort led us through the crowd so we could get to our cars. Once the horde of journalists understood we were not stopping to comment, they turned and moved back toward the building. I caught a glimpse of Lou coming out of the big double doors with his briefcase. I could hear the crowd quiet, and I caught his first few words.

"Ladies and gentlemen, two little girls received justice in Montgomery, Alabama, today. And so did poor women all over this country."

FORTY-FOUR

Rockford
2016

The neighborhood is run-down, but it is a community. I detect the smoke of charcoal as I turn the corner. An elderly lady waves at me from her front porch, and I wave in return. Two boys stand aside as I drive by, then resume kicking their ball after I pass. The house is one story with stone steps and a balding yard. There is a dead car parked in the driveway. Grass grows through the concrete and loops through the flattened tires.

I slow my car in front of the house. The second number is missing from the address on the mailbox, but this must be it. There is a sturdy-looking iron door on the front, bars on the windows. It is a real house, not the shanty the family once inhabited on the Adair farm. An air-conditioning unit hangs from the front window. I notice a chimney and imagine a warm fire in winter.

Before I go on any further, I have to say there are some things I've forgotten to tell you about India and Erica. They were tall for their age. This was probably part of the reason Mrs. Seager had misjudged them. When I met them they were my height, but by fall, Erica was at least an inch taller. Though they weren't the healthiest girls, neither of them was skinny. Mrs. Williams had always been a cook, able to turn most anything into a meal. She kept meat on their bones.

Their hair and skin were a mess. The combination of puberty and poor hygiene had wrecked those girls' faces. In the first few weeks, I spent a lot of time grooming. After I cut off the dead ends, their hair grew into long enough Afros for me to part and make cornrows. I bought them Ivory soap and Vaseline.

In the Dixie Court apartment, the girls took regular baths and kept their bathroom stocked with feminine products. They used deodorant, and though I had never shaved my armpits and didn't teach them to do it, Erica picked up the habit somewhere. After their baths at night, they would go in their room, close the door, and lotion down. I used to joke they kept Jergens in business.

By the time of the verdict, they looked like the other kids in their schools, having lost the telltale signs of kids in deep poverty. Erica had dark freckles on her forehead and sneezed a lot in spring-time. She loved to wear lip gloss and dance to soul music. Whenever she visited my house, she went straight for the records. I was a Stax girl—Carla and Rufus Thomas, mainly—with some occasional James Carr thrown in, but Erica gravitated toward the smoother Motown sounds. She was captivated by the lyrics of Stevie Wonder and had listened to *Music of My Mind* so much that I told her she was wearing a hole in the record.

The fungus on India's neck finally cleared. She had a mole in the crook of her nose, and her favorite food was peanut butter. She ate it straight from the jar. And the girl had never met a dog she didn't like. She would feed the strays wandering around Dixie Court pieces of stale sandwich bread, a day-old biscuit, crackers. I remember this white German shepherd that followed her every-where. When India mounted the swing, the dog would sit nearby and watch her, as if to make sure she didn't fall. India didn't have the language to give the dog a name, but she could whistle. It wasn't a loud whistle, but the dog could somehow hear it and would come crawling out from underneath one of the buildings. It took me a while to realize that those mangy dogs on the farm had been tolerated by the family because they soothed India. After moving to Dixie Court, Mrs. Williams swore never to allow a dog in the house again, but India cared for this shepherd outside, drawing comfort when the dog lay at her feet as she scratched its back with her fingernails. Her other passion was dolls. She owned six of them and propped them against the pillow on her bed.

Erica: left-handed. Stubborn. Polite. Made her bed every day. Slept in her socks. Lover of chocolate ice cream, Motown music, and her little sister.

India: right-handed. Tender. Dog lover. Mother of dolls. Peanut butter addict. Climber of fences. Rider of carousels.

Their names always had the ring of twins to me. Erica and India. India and Erica. Though very different, there was no mistaking it: The sisters were soulfully connected.

The Williams sisters. Two of the greatest loves of my life. And two of my greatest heartbreaks. They are both the reason I never had biological children and the reason I found it in my heart to love and mother you. I never had confidence in my ability to mother, but my love for them has endured over the years.

FORTY-FIVE

Montgomery
1973

Erica had been missing three days. She knew my home phone number, but with Mama in Memphis and Daddy working, she wouldn't be able to reach us even if she did have access to a phone. We didn't have an answering machine back then, and I couldn't just stay at home and wait for her call. The family didn't have a phone, so Mrs. Williams held twenty-four-hour watch at the apartment. People in Dixie Court brought her groceries because they knew cooking soothed her nerves. But she did not cook, and one of those days I found India eating slices of bread and government cheese when I stopped by.

Mace's boss gave him time off to help with the search without fear of losing his job. He didn't get paid for those days, so my church set up a fund to help his family. I worked the telephone, calling everyone in my parents' telephone book to inform them about the meeting places and times of the search parties. Ty led the morning searches. Mace went all day, stopping only to eat and catch an hour of sleep here and there.

India was inconsolable. Recently, she had started to communicate more—pointing, grunting, tilting her head—but when Erica went missing, she became silent again. No facial expressions. No sounds. Nothing. Thinking it would help take her mind off things, Mrs. Williams allowed India to come sleep at my house. I didn't plan to take her to school, but Sister LaTarsha called me and said she thought it would do India some good to get back into her routine. When I asked India, she didn't nod or make any response whatsoever. She just sat on the edge of my bed, staring at the floor.

I moved her into the den, where I planted her in front of the television. That seemed to ignite a flicker of light in her eyes. I let her watch *Sanford and Son* while she munched on Funyuns.

I sat beside her on the sofa, thinking about Erica and trying not to imagine the worst. But the worst still crept into my thoughts. Kidnapping. Murder. Rape. *Please, Lord*, I prayed, *have mercy*. The school wasn't within walking distance to anywhere. It had been built on the outskirts of the county, a desegregation decision that didn't make sense because that meant everyone in town had to take a bus or a car to get there. Erica didn't have any money, so she had to be eating somebody else's food. If she was stealing, I prayed she wouldn't get caught. If she had found food, I prayed it was enough.

I thought about all the things I could have done differently, but everything that went through my mind toppled into some other unforeseen mistake I had never considered. I could have applied to medical school instead of coming back to Montgomery to work in the clinic. I could have notified someone as soon as I found out about the Depo. I could have gone to the girls' house that morning instead of waiting until the afternoon. I could have left the case alone.

Maybe the verdict hadn't changed anything at all.

On the third morning, the only thing that made me get out of bed was India. I needed to take her to school, but when I woke her, she seemed to be just as unrested as I was. I got her into the bathroom to brush her teeth, only to return and find her standing in front of the mirror with the dry toothbrush in her hand. I thought she might be ill, so I asked Daddy to check her. He said he did not believe it was a medical problem, said the school understood her disability better. He urged me to take her to Sister LaTarsha. Some ailments are not meant for a medical degree, he told me.

I helped snap her bra and wrestled a shirt over her head. "I'm sure Erica will be back soon. Now, I made some toast and boiled us some eggs. There's marmalade, too. Let's get something in our bellies."

In the kitchen, it was dark. I turned on the light and opened the curtains. I had been preparing meals since I was younger than India. I would have to make food when Mama slept late. Before school it was toast, jelly, and a boiled egg. In winter, oatmeal. After school, I emptied beans from the can and spread them on toast, placed a slice of cheese on top, and put it in the oven until the cheese melted. I wasn't a cook like Mrs. Williams, but I understood how to make food that kids liked. India's appetite was still good. That relieved me.

"You want some more toast?"

She didn't respond. When Erica was around, she answered for India. This forced separation probably had India feeling like half of herself was missing.

After I dropped India at school, I drove to their apartment. A police detective was there taking another statement from Mrs. Williams, and from the look on her face I thought the grandmother might curse someone if she had to answer one more question. She wasn't a cursing woman, but I had never seen her look so tired.

"I think she's done for the day," I said.

I tried to think of any other friends Erica had mentioned. There were only two names that came to mind—Dinesha and Tonya—and they'd already been questioned. Erica's picture was in the paper. Some of the kids gathered outside the school each morning asking one another if anyone had heard from her. Everyone was doing everything they could.

The detective wore a badge tucked into his front shirt pocket.

The notebook rested untouched in his lap, and he sat with his hands folded over his paunch.

"I have three girls myself, Mrs. Williams."

She rubbed her hands together, as if she were washing them under water.

"Is there anything you have forgotten to tell us? Is there a . . . boyfriend?"

I drew back. He had probably been waiting to ask that question the entire time. I wanted to cry because secretly, I had started to entertain such a possibility. Erica was getting older. Surely she was starting to have crushes. I thought of the lipstick she had started to wear. I had even bought her a new tube after throwing away the dirty one she had found.

"I said that's enough."

"It's alright, Civil. No boyfriend," Mrs. Williams said. Her voice sounded listless and faraway.

"Alright." He tightened his hands over his belly. "Have you taken any special trips?"

"Special trips?" she asked.

"Yes," I said, suddenly remembering. "I took them to the beach."

"Which beach?"

"Down in the Panhandle."

It was too far, but maybe she had hitched a ride? She might not have realized how far it was. I thought back to a night when I'd gone over her math homework with her. Her reading skills were still behind, but she'd been revealing a talent with numbers. She already knew her times tables, learning them so quickly that the teacher had moved her on to simple division. She was such an intelligent girl. I hoped that intelligence was helping her survive whatever she was going through.

The detective didn't write anything down, just studied my face for a few long seconds. I got the impression he was wondering about my role in this. I was their nurse, not family.

After he left, I helped Mrs. Williams straighten the room. If I kept my hands busy, I could endure the slow ticking of the clock. Mrs. Williams told me to leave. I knew she wanted to be alone, but I didn't want to be alone. I could go talk to Lou about the verdict, but what did it even mean if something had happened to Erica? I was hungry again, the toast barely making a dent in my stomach. I could go talk to Irene at the diner. It had been so long since she and I had been friends. Alicia was at work. Ty was out searching. I wanted to hug Mrs. Williams, share in this burden with her. Who else loved those girls the way she, Mace, and I did? It was something rare to share such devotion over another human being. I perched on the arm of the sofa; it was a rude way to sit, but I wasn't thinking about that.

"Civil."

"Yes, ma'am?"

"How's your mother?"

I didn't say anything. I had spoken to her twice in the weeks she'd been gone. I had not really missed her before then, but I sure needed her now. I needed her to come home and help me through this.

"She's fine."

"Is she? You ought to check on her."

"Check on her?"

"Baby, I know about them blues. I been meaning to tell you. I seen her at the hospital that day waiting on you in the lobby. I seen something in her eyes. I know it cause I been there. I was there for a long time after Constance died."

I shouldn't have been sitting on the arm of her sofa, but I did not move and she did not correct me. We sat there silently, each lost on our own islands of sadness.

FORTY-SIX

I called Mama that night, and she arrived in Montgomery the next morning. Aunt Ros drove this time. They entered the house in a sheath of perfume. Mama was wearing Aunt Ros's clothes, a black dress with blue flowers and large hoop earrings. The first thing I noticed was that she was not wearing her usual red lipstick. And she did not go immediately out to her studio to check on her canvases. She and Aunt Ros fluttered around the house talking loudly and teasing each other. They connected a long telephone cord and set up a call bank in the den, spending half the evening making phone calls to the same people I had already called. I sat on the sofa in my pajamas, worried they were tying up the phone line when Ty might be trying to call me. He and Mace had gone out again to walk the woods on Hunter Road.

Daddy came in with a plate of hot dogs. "I made the slaw myself."

"I don't know how y'all get any nutrition around here. This got to be the worst house of cooks in all of Alabama," Aunt Ros said.

"Don't knock my coleslaw until you tried it."

Mama laughed and both Daddy and I turned sharply. We had not heard her laugh like that in a long time.

"Y'all so jittery. We are going to find her," Mama said, mistaking our surprise for nerves.

"Mama, what you and Aunt Ros been doing in Memphis?"

"Girl, your auntie crazy. She hold meetings in her house where the women talk about the bad stuff in their lives. Then they write it down and drop it in her fireplace."

Daddy set up four TV trays for the food.

"Then she start this meditation where she give them a piece of paper with a chant on it. You know they don't bit more know what the hell she got them reading on that paper."

"They trust me, June. I'm licensed."

"You licensed, alright. Certified crazy."

The two of them laughed again, and I could see how easily Mama had fallen into her sister's embrace. She had gotten something in Memphis that her art studio could not give her, something that Daddy and I could not give her. Perhaps Aunt Ros had given her some kind of medicine. The legal kind, though I wouldn't put the illegal kind past her. Daddy had never approved of pharmaceutics for this kind of trouble, but my aunt was defiant like that. I was still studying the two of them when the telephone rang.

I pushed aside my tray.

"I got it, baby. Hello?" Mama listened for a moment, then passed the handset to me. "It's Ty."

I grabbed the phone. "Ty?"

"Hey. I just got word from the police. They found Erica."

"Is she hurt?" I rubbed my chest and could feel my heart beating.

"They say she fine."

"Where they find her?"

"They say she went back to the old house where they used to live."

"I thought y'all checked there. Nobody checked there?"

"Course we checked there. Two, three times. She must have hid from us when she heard us coming up the drive."

"Where is she now?"

"They took her down to the station."

"The station? She's not a criminal." I tried to calm myself. "Do you know which station they took her to?"

Mama wrapped her arms around my chest from behind and I wanted to lean into that unexpected hug. I needed the arms of my mama so badly. I put my hand over the receiver. "They found her. She's fine."

I had to put on some clothes, so by the time I got to the precinct, Erica was gone. Mace had just left with her. According to the lady at the desk, Mace had gotten fed up with the questioning and asked if she was required to stay. When they said no, he took her by the hand and walked out.

I drove to Dixie Court so fast, I prayed I wouldn't get in another car accident. Cars filled the street, and I struggled to find a parking space. Inside the apartment, the living room was crowded. I'd never thought of it as particularly large, but with all of those people in there, the room appeared small and dark. It was mostly neighbors—men who had searched with Mace, women who had brought food to the searchers, the policewoman who had found her. They sat in the dining chairs. They stood, hands in pockets. Lou and Ty sat next to each other on the couch, and it was an odd sight, because I had never seen Lou inside the Williamses' apartment. Mace sat on the sofa with an arm wound tightly around a visibly exhausted Mrs. Williams. When I walked into the room, they all looked at me, but I could only focus on Erica. I rushed toward her, and my nostrils filled with the scent of her. I took her face in my hands, scratching away with my thumbnail the crust at the edge of her lip.

"Thank God. Thank God you alright," I said. She looked at me with an unreadable expression, her eyelids puffy with exhaustion.

"Sir. Officer—" I read the police officer's badge. "Officer Hatch, this young lady has obviously been through an ordeal. If you don't mind, I'd like to get her cleaned up."

"And who are you exactly?"

"I'm her nurse."

I said it as if I'd uttered the word *doctor*. And I must have sounded authoritative, because they began to stir. I suspected I'd given them the perfect excuse to wrap it up. Mace walked to the door. The men shook hands. Mrs. Williams promised everyone pies as soon as she could get back in the kitchen, her voice tired but sincere. The detective handed Mace a piece of paper with a phone number on it. He lingered the longest, asking if there was anything else he could do. I understood the man. It was difficult to accept that everything was over, that you'd done the job you set out to do.

I led Erica to the bathroom. "I'll run you some water, alright?"

I sat on the side of the tub. Erica closed the toilet lid and sat down.

"Somebody bring me a clean towel!"

Erica pointed to the one hanging on the back of the door. I thought it might be the dirty one she had used before she disappeared. It occurred to me that she might not realize how many days she had been gone. *Four days, baby*, I wanted to tell her, but I remained silent.

While the water ran I went to go see about India. She was at the dining table eating a bowl of cereal, Mace next to her, one hand resting absently on the carton of milk.

"So she was just at the old house all this time?"

"That's what she say."

"How did y'all miss her?"

"That was one of the first places we looked. But she hated that place. I never thought she would go back there."

"Did they examine her? She's not hurt at all?"

"No, she said she was by herself the whole time. I think she was just scared and cold."

"She made a fire and nobody saw it?"

He shrugged and propped his elbow on the table. "She stole from Mr. Adair house. Once he find out, I reckon I'll owe him. That's the kind of man he is."

At one time, I might have judged her theft. Poverty did not warrant disobedience to God, our pastor had warned on more than one occasion. But I was glad she had done what she had to survive.

I went to check the bath. Erica had already gotten in the tub and was lying back with her eyes closed. I turned off the water and took the pitcher from the shelf. I dipped it and poured water over Erica's hair, raking my fingers through it.

"Why, Erica?"

I knew I should wait until she had a chance to rest up, but I couldn't stop myself. I needed to know. There was nothing else to say until I had the answer to that question. "Was it because of the court case?" I hated myself for asking this question, but it was honest. I had known all along that if something happened to this girl, it would all be on me.

"I just don't want to live in Montgomery no more."

"Where do you want to live?"

"I don't know. But I done told my grandmama I don't want to live here and she just say, *Girl, you crazy.*" She closed her eyes. I couldn't tell if it was to avoid getting water in them or just because she didn't want to look at me. I pushed her chin to tilt her head back.

"We won the case. Did they tell you?"

"I want to go back to that beach."

"You heard me? We won."

"The only place I know how to get to was the Adair place. When I took a look and seen the house was empty, just the way we left it, even one of the old dogs what used to come around for scraps still hobbling around, I took up there."

The bar of soap had dried and stuck to the porcelain holder. She pried it off and dropped it in the water, turning it over and over in her hand until the water clouded.

"Erica, you scared us all. The whole city was searching for you. It was even in the news—"

"The news." She splashed the water as she sat up. "I'm sick and tired of them news people. I'm sick and tired of kids talking about me and my family like we got some kind of disease."

I touched her shoulder, but she was slippery and I couldn't make solid contact with her.

"I'm sick and tired. I'm sick and tired." Her words came out in a rush. "No husband. No life. No babies. I ain't never going to be happy."

"Let's just finish up your bath so you can get some rest."

She rubbed the bar of soap over her face and blinked rapidly.

"Erica, are you alright? Were you hurt?"

I took the towel off the hook behind the door and handed her the corner of it. She wiped her eyes.

"Come on. Let's get out."

I helped dry her as if she were a baby, and pulled a gown over her head. India was already in the bed. I kissed both of them on their cheeks before turning off the ceiling light.

"You sure you not hurting anywhere?"

"No, ma'am."

"Alright, y'all get some sleep. It's been a long day."

"Do I got to go to school tomorrow?" Erica asked.

I paused. "I reckon not. Let's talk in the morning. I think my daddy might stop by and examine you. That alright with you?"

"Yes, ma'am."

In the living room, Mace had spread a blanket over the sofa. His face was haggard and lined. He did not look at me when he said, "I'll get you a pillow."

I sat on the sofa, waiting for the pillow. Then I closed my eyes and did not remember opening them again until morning.

FORTY-SEVEN

Rockford
2016

The face of the house is flat and unremarkable, and I comprehend with a sudden and intense pain that they are still poor.
There was never a large monetary settlement, never a large payout
from the government to right the wrong inflicted upon those girls
and that family. Mace has been dead some twenty years, Mrs. Williams gone ten. Their deaths don't sit right with me, most likely
because I was never able to make my peace. At least, it feels that way.

The morning after my meeting with Mrs. Seager's daughter,
I'd driven out to Dixie Court. Alicia had said the apartments were
scheduled for demolition and I wanted to get a last look at them. At
first they appeared abandoned. Windows boarded, grass knee-
high. But as I drove through I realized there were still some families inhabiting the complex. It was grim to know families were
living next door to empty units, critters taking up residence alongside children. The Williamses' apartment was one of the boarded-up
ones. Someone had spray-painted something illegible in red across
the boards. The stairs were dark, but I could see India bounding
down them, the memory fresh.

Now, in front of their new home, I understand a little better
this stretch of time that has passed. I tentatively touch the doorbell,

understanding with full certainty that this is more than a door. It is a portal. I hear a faint chime and the yap of a dog. And there is Erica, unmistakably Erica. She smiles at me through the iron door as she unlocks it with a key. It all happens so fast I am barely able to think. I bite the inside of my cheek.

"Dr. Civil is here, India. Dr. Civil!" she calls out over her shoulder.

I touch my sweaty neck. Erica, on the other hand, looks cool and comfortable. The same broad forehead dotted with dark freckles. The generous nose and quick smile. It hits me in the stomach that she looks like Mrs. Williams, her grandmother.

She ushers me into the house and I awkwardly step inside. The air-conditioning unit whirs softly. A brown Chihuahua sniffs my feet and runs in circles, though its yapping has ceased. The curtains are pulled. The room is lit by a large television. A sweet scent hangs in the air.

"Something sure smells good," I say.

"I can't cook like my grandmama, but I can bake a cake. It just come out the oven, too."

"You didn't have to go through the trouble."

"Honey, it's so good to see you. We been waiting for you. Traffic was alright?" She places her hands on my waist, and I quietly stand there, momentarily unable to square the child with this middle-aged lady holding me.

"Sit down, sit down," she says.

I choose the sofa. There are two recliners, and I assume they belong to the sisters. A crocheted throw hangs over the back of one of the chairs, and I wonder if it is the handwork of Mrs. Williams. I'm filled with ache. I should have come years earlier. I should have called and kept in touch.

"India!"

She tells the dog to sit down as she hurries to go get her sister.

The room is small but cozy, the floor covered in wall-to-wall pink carpet. Beside the front door hangs a picture of Barack Obama. It looks like it was cut out of a magazine and framed. Below him there is a picture of Martin Luther King Jr. Above the front door, a cross-stitched sign quotes John F. Kennedy: "Every accomplishment starts with the decision to try."

A console table behind the sofa is covered in framed pictures. I stoop to look and a window into the lives of the Williamses opens up. There is Mace, standing beside his pickup truck. He wears tight jeans that flare at the bottoms and his hair hangs in a shag to his shoulders. He is not smiling in the picture, but the sun has caught the glow of his eyes and he's relaxed. I look for other pictures of him, but there are none. I know that Mace passed away of heart disease. While I know that he never remarried, I want to know if he found love, healing. But I'm too embarrassed to ask.

Another picture captures Mrs. Williams in her Sunday best. She's wearing a white suit and hat, as if it is Missionary Day at the church. Swollen fingers clutch a white beaded purse in her lap, and she's sitting in a wheelchair. I glance toward the hallway and wonder if Erica was also tasked with taking care of her grandmother in her last days. From what I understand, Mrs. Williams married again, but the husband passed away a few years before she did. They pose in one of those Sears studio photographs with a fake forest background. He stands behind her, his hands wrapped around her waist. He has salt-and-pepper hair and thick sideburns. His round face reminds me of Dennis Edwards from the Temptations. Mrs. Williams looks settled, satisfied. One of her teeth glints gold.

Just as I pick up a picture of the sisters, they enter the room. I put it back in its place. Erica leads India slowly by the elbow. India is wearing a housedress and looks much older than her sister even though she's the younger of the two. It may be because the pin-curled wig she wears is styled for an older woman. She smiles at me.

"India," I whisper as I go to her. "India."

She's a couple of inches taller than I am now, so when she places her head on my shoulder she has to lean down. I hug her to me.

"India? Do you remember me?"

The younger sister smiles at me but does not answer.

FORTY-EIGHT

Montgomery
1973

M ama baked a cake for the Williamses to celebrate the verdict and Erica's safe return. Like most things creative, she was a magician when it came to piping frosting. And she sang while she was doing it. I remember because I hadn't heard her sing in a long time. Mama had not been to her studio since she'd returned from Memphis. Daddy and I made faces at each other as we tried to wrap our heads around this change. Every day, Mama and Aunt Ros sat down on the floor, held hands, and did some kind of meditation chant. They made tea and listened to Tantric music. Ros told us not to worry, that Mama was still a Christian. That made Daddy laugh.

Aunt Ros decided to stay through Thanksgiving. Daddy wanted to entertain, and we all agreed. He got Mr. Singh to cook the entire meal, even though Mabel Turner insisted on bringing crackling corn bread, one of India's favorites. Aunt Ros and I decorated the house with fake pinecones and paper turkeys. Every now and then she would go out back and smoke a cigarette. While I waited, I noticed how quiet it was just for those few minutes. Aunt Ros's presence lit up the house, and I knew when she left it would change the air.

On Thanksgiving night, Lou showed up with his wife, Jenna, and she was not at all what I expected. Given his habit of nonstop work, I thought she might be soft-spoken. I was wrong. By the way she shook my hand, I could tell she was no wallflower, and I liked her instantly. Her eyes were intensely intelligent, and I had a feeling she knew as much about the case as I did.

She was also pregnant. Very pregnant. She placed a hand on the back of one of the barstools in the den.

"You need to sit down?" I asked her.

"No, I'm fine," she said.

"Lou, I ain't believing this," I said to him. "When is the baby due?"

"You know Civil was my co-counsel," he said to his wife.

"That's what I hear," said Jenna.

"Baby's due next month," he said.

"And y'all don't live in the same city?" Mama asked, also visibly reacting to Jenna's belly.

"Girl, young people do it different nowadays." Aunt Ros dropped her cigarette pack in her purse and walked behind the bar. "I can dig it."

"She's been driving back and forth, but now she's about to settle here until the baby's born," Lou said.

"Driving back and forth to Selma? In that condition?" Mama said.

Aunt Ros placed two stem glasses on the counter. "Anybody want some wine?"

I pulled Lou aside and whispered. "Lou, you already knew your wife was pregnant when you took the case, didn't you?"

He nodded.

"And it bothered you to hear of the girls being sterilized, what with you becoming a new daddy."

"Civil, you know me better than that by now. You know I would have taken this case regardless."

"I guess I'm just piecing it together is all."

"Once you do, make sure to enlighten me," he said.

The Ralseys showed up next and brought Alicia with them. I hugged Alicia when I saw her, and she held on to me for a long time. Mrs. Ralsey asked Ty to bring in the pot of greens they'd forgotten in the car. She went straight to Mama, and I could hear her apologizing for being too busy to check up on her. Mama waved her apologies off and asked about the Tuskegee case. That launched a whole new conversation.

In the kitchen, Alicia helped me arrange the food on the table so everyone could serve themselves. "Can you believe Lou didn't tell us his wife was pregnant? All that time he spent in the office?"

"I thought the same thing," I said. "You know she works at a law firm in Selma."

Alicia shook her head. "It's a different world now, isn't it?"

I unwrapped the bowl of macaroni and set it down next to the corn bread. "She told me she followed the case closely. I want to ask what she thinks about the family's chance to win a civil suit."

"The Williamses are here." Ty poked his head in the doorway, then disappeared.

I wiped the table though I had just wiped it minutes before. It was the first time Mace had been to my house, and I knew my daddy still suspected there was something between us. There wasn't and never would be. Ever since Erica had gone missing, he had pulled away from me. And I had done the same. A kiss on a living room couch did not mean anything.

Alicia touched me on the arm. "Civil, he's in love with you, you know."

"Who is?"

Before she could answer, Erica and her sister came into the kitchen. India grabbed me by my waist. I pushed a strand of hair behind her ears and used the edge of my fingernail to smooth her eyebrow. Out of the corner of my eye, I watched Erica over India's shoulder. Daddy had examined her after her return and found nothing amiss. Mostly, he said, she was exhausted and needed rest. But she still seemed wary, distant.

"I got a couple of new records," I said, hoping that might interest her. I had bought them after she went missing, promising myself that if she returned I would bring her over to listen. I had to do everything in my power to resist just giving her my record player. She would have enjoyed it more than I did. But I couldn't do that any longer. I could not try to buy their salvation. "Come on."

The two of them followed me back to my room. Daddy had started playing some music, so I told them if they closed the bedroom door they could hear better. As I left I heard Erica explaining to India how to start a record without scratching it.

In the den, Mrs. Williams sat stiffly in the barrel chair in the corner. Aunt Ros sat in the chair next to her and was asking the woman if she had made contact with her inner spiritual animal. Mrs. Williams said "uh-huh" in an amused voice. It did not deter Ros, and within a few minutes Mrs. Williams was smiling and playing along. It was impossible to resist Aunt Ros.

Daddy squatted next to his stack of 8-tracks. Somebody had opened another bottle of wine. Mace had a glass in his hand, but it did not look like he was drinking. He and Ty were talking football. Lou's wife was halfway between sitting and leaning on the edge of a barstool. The Ralseys sat in two folding chairs Daddy had brought inside from the storage room. Ty excused himself, and I took his place next to Mace.

"You alright?" I asked him.

"Yeah," Mace said. "You?"

"So-so. Still can't believe it's all over."

"Me, neither."

I leaned forward. "You been avoiding me?"

Ty walked back into the room with a corn-bread muffin wrapped in a napkin.

"It's rude to eat before dinner is served," I told him.

"Who died and made you the queen?"

Mace giggled as if he and Ty were buddies now. I frowned. When it was time for dinner, we connected two tables in the dining room and covered them with a tablecloth. There was barely enough room to walk around the tables, but we managed it. I sat between Alicia and Ty, with Mace across from us. Aunt Ros chatted about her therapy practice, how her new methods incorporated alternative spiritual paths. She lamented that more Black people needed counseling and how she wanted to serve our communities in Memphis.

"I've got women that's been sexually abused, or who were homeless from a young age and don't trust anyone. There is some real damage, but the possibility of healing is there. I have seen so many women go on to live healthy, happy lives."

"Ros, we could use that down here in Montgomery. St. Jude has some of those services, but it sounds like you really getting to know your patients," Mrs. Ralsey said.

I didn't say anything. I had learned the hard way that no good deed went unpunished.

There was a lull in the conversation, and my father raised his glass. "We haven't had a chance to properly celebrate Lou's victory. I want to raise a glass to Lou, to thank him for his belief and commitment."

"Yes, Lord," Mrs. Williams added. "Bless you, young man."

"Thank you." Lou put his face in his wineglass and took a long sip.

333

Erica asked for more sweet potatoes, and I passed them to her. I was nervous all this talk of the case brought her anxiety. I had not had enough time with her lately.

"Well, I got something to say, too." Mrs. Williams set down her glass. "I want to thank all y'all for everything you done for my family. When my son, Mace, here lost his wife, the mother to these girls, I thought life couldn't get no darker. But this year taught me that only God knows how much we can bear."

I heard a sniffle. India chewed a mouthful of corn bread. Erica was staring at her grandmother. It appeared the sniffle had come from Mace. Was he really going to cry in front of everybody? If he did, I wouldn't be able to take it.

"No, sir. We wasn't never promised this here road would be easy. But I kept my faith. And knowing folks like you, Mr. Lou, and you, Miss Civil, make me see good in the world again."

She cleared her throat. "I want to thank you. Each of y'all. I ain't got much to give. I brought them pies in the kitchen. Made them with my own two hands. Put my heart into them. But I know I could never pay you enough. And I can't express how I feel. I just ain't got the words."

"Yes, ma'am, of course," Lou said. "No words needed."

Mrs. Williams acted like she hadn't heard him. The woman had more to say. "After they found Erica, I talked to her. I talked to my son. And I decided it's time for us to quit Montgomery."

"Quit?" I repeated.

"We going to live with our cousin Nellie. The one you met. She got a big house, enough room for all of us. Her husband can help Mace find work."

"What about the girls' schooling? India just found that school, and it's going to be hard to replace it in that little town."

"Civil. You done enough. You have become like a daughter to

me. But I'm sitting at this table in this here beautiful house, and I see you got your own family. And they lucky to have you."

I shook my head. This wasn't the first time Mrs. Williams had told me to butt out, but to do it in front of everybody was too much. "Don't the girls have some say in this?"

"They the ones want to go. Erica needs it. You and I both know that."

Erica had mentioned moving, but that was emotional talk. She was just a child.

"Mace?" I looked over at Mace, but he was staring down at his plate. "Mace?"

He said nothing, and Erica still would not make eye contact with me.

I passed the rest of the dinner without hearing or seeing anything. I couldn't taste my food and moved it around aimlessly on my plate. After dessert, everyone got their coats and started for the door. The girls put their arms around me, and I squeezed them to me. *I love y'all*, I wanted to say. *I love y'all. I love y'all.*

"Walk them to their car," Daddy told me. He must have seen how torn-up I was feeling. Outside, I watched the girls climb into Mace's truck. Mrs. Williams stayed beside me in the middle of the driveway.

"Civil," she began. "I know it was hard for you to hear that tonight. And I probably should have told you before announcing it in front of everybody. I'm sorry."

I didn't say anything.

"I want you to know I appreciate everything you done for us. But I can handle my family from here on out."

Her words cut me, and I couldn't hide it. "How? How will you manage? You couldn't handle that house on the farm."

Her eyes narrowed. When she spoke, her voice was tight but

patient. "Mace will stay here and work. When he ready and can find some steady work down there, he'll come, too."

"You're going to just give up the apartment? Don't you know how hard it was for me to get it in the first place? And does Nellie know about this plan?"

"Now, you know I wouldn't be saying this if she didn't. She welcome the company."

I opened my mouth to speak, then shut it knowing how foolish I sounded.

"You worried about the girls' schooling, but the social worker say somebody can come to the house for India."

"You got a new social worker? She can never do what Sister LaTarsha and the nuns can do. They're trained. They have toys and puzzles and everything India needs to learn."

"Civil, the girls will be fine."

Mace started the engine and the headlights lit up the street. Mrs. Williams lingered in the driveway, illuminated by the flood of light. "I meant what I said. You like a daughter to me. I'm always going to think of you, and I want you to know you always welcome to visit the girls. You don't even have to ask. But I want you to move on with your life."

"Move on?"

I didn't understand her words. How did one move on from family? Didn't she understand that family was so much more than blood? It was shared experience and history and pain. Those girls were as much my family now as they were hers.

"You want me to move on from Mace, don't you?" I said quietly.

I could not see her face clearly, but I could tell that she was not surprised by the question. She had surely had her suspicions, and Mace taking my hand at the courthouse had probably confirmed them.

"You and Mace are grown, Civil. I ain't got nothing to do with that. Here is what I do know. You done touched us in a way that no one ever did. And for that, I'm grateful. But you got some things in your heart to work out. I see that. I know that. Take it to the Lord, Civil. He will answer."

And with that, she walked to the truck, climbed up into the cab with the girls, and they took off. The only one who turned and waved at me was India, the white of her palm against the window.

FORTY-NINE

Rockford
2016

In the years after the family's departure, I wore the cloak of their absence. Records Erica might like. A doll that might catch India's eye. An ice cream they both loved. The gap opened wider and wider until ten years turned into twenty, thirty, forty. And now I find myself in their living room, holding on to India as I have not held her in years.

"Let's sit down," I say and lead India over to her chair. The woman moves slowly, and my medical training kicks in. "How are you feeling?"

Erica arranges India's housedress around her so that she can sit comfortably. Then she settles into her own chair. "She on her second round of treatments. With the grace of God, she'll be done in a few months."

The mention of her poor health jars me. My memories live in my bones, and I cannot fathom the idea of losing her. I struggle not to wear my doctor's coat. There will be time enough for that, if they desire it. But I decided before coming on this trip that I was not coming here to save them. I have made that mistake once before, and I don't plan to make it again. Still, I cannot help but softly ask, "Is the medicine making her sick at all?"

"The first round did. They hoping this one will be better."

"She eating alright?"

"She love brown rice. You ever eat brown rice?"

"Yes, I love it."

"So do India. She tried it in the hospital, and now she can't get enough of it. She like it with a little butter on top."

"That's nice, Erica. I'm glad you're taking care of her."

"How about you, Dr. Civil? Alicia say you a fancy doctor now. Tell me about your husband and family."

I lean back into the sofa cushions. Marriage is not a conversation I relish, but there is no avoiding the catch-up. I tell her I have taken care of my mother and raised a daughter on my own. I don't mention that, for many years, I was the one who all the doctors with families relied upon for relief work. I was the one they assumed did not have plans on a Friday night. And for many years they were right. When my period began to slow and my own personal doctor told me I was perimenopausal, I began psychotherapy for the first time in my life. I had thought it would be liberating to be freed of this monthly inconvenience, especially since I had never desired it or the egg it nurtured, but all I could think about were those girls. As the lid of my childbearing coffin began to close, I did not mourn the loss of all those years of soiled sanitary napkins, the telltale pink stain on a square of tissue. I did not wish I had physically birthed children. I thought only of the sisters and their periods, disappointing them month after month, year after year, for decades. And after a year of speaking with my therapist, I realized that I had changed. I no longer viewed motherhood as a trap or punishment. I no longer owed it to those girls never to have children. I was not my mother, whose mothering was affected by her illness.

Rather than mention any of my tortured past, I just tell Erica how, at forty-eight years old, I experienced a change of heart and began the process of adopting a child out of the foster care system.

I pass Erica my phone so she can see a picture of you. She shows it to India.

"She's precious. How old you say she is?"

"Twenty-three."

It is not lost upon me that I'm talking to two motherless women, deprived of this opportunity by circumstance rather than choice. I have exercised a choice and that has been a powerful thing. Even as a single mother, the system favors me because of my status as a doctor. For Erica and India, the adoption process would have been more difficult. The judge scrutinizes you more closely if you're poor. Disabled. Unmarried. I am still just as aware as ever that there is work to be done in this world.

After she gives me back the phone, Erica looks at me again with that grown face, which I find unnerving. It is as if I am now the child and she is the adult in the room.

"Let me get the cake." She returns with two saucers. "I used to waitress. Did you know that?"

I shake my head. It's a sponge cake covered in strawberries. Strawberries are India's favorite, she explains. The taste and texture are perfect, light and airy, something a professional baker would have been hard-pressed to beat. She asks me if I want coffee and I gratefully accept. As I eat, I remember that first day I met the family, the time Mrs. Williams fed me the stew cooked over a hole in the ground. I had never seen anybody cook like that. The Williamses had always fed my soul, even when I did not know I was hungry. It occurs to me that I have received more from them than I ever could have given.

We talk ourselves breathless. We recall the time their grandmother had walked around the house with flour on the tip of her nose and no one had told her, and that one day we went to Kmart and I spent a small fortune in quarters letting India ride that horse, and how once India brought the white German shepherd into the apartment and Mrs. Williams ran him out with a broom, and how funny it looked when Mace walked into the ocean in his socks. They remember.

I put the empty saucer on the coffee table, and thank her again.

"Don't thank me no more, alright? Now, Dr. Civil. Tell me something. I'm glad to see you and all. Your visit means the world to us. But why are you here after all these years? I'm not trying to be rude or nothing. But when I heard you was coming, I wondered if everything is okay with you? You not bringing us no bad news, is you?"

I shake my head and sip my coffee. The woman thinks I'm here on a last-rites trip. Still, I don't quite know how to answer. The question is the same one I faced with Alicia, and it is time for me to come clean. I have tried carefully to consider my intentions. It is not easy to sort everything out. Apologizing to the women after all these years seems demeaning somehow. It works on the assumption that I have been the center of their lives. I also do not want to imply they are people to be pitied. They have passed through this hardship and lived full lives, finding meaning in sisterhood and family, making this beautiful home. And they have won a court case against the US government. They are so much more than little girls wronged by the system.

I speak softly, and, despite my better intentions, it is an apology that comes out. "I wanted to tell you that I'm so sorry. I'm so sorry, Erica. I wish, I wish—"

"Miss Civil, there ain't no need for all that. You hear me? No need."

Before I can respond, India begins to make a noise. Erica takes her sister's empty plate.

"Let me get her some more cake. And when I come back in here, we got to watch my talk show because it'll be on in a minute. You take off your shoes and make yourself comfortable, hear?"

As she smiles at me before leaving the room, I lean back in my chair. I have not seen them in decades, but these women are my family and I am theirs. I was struggling with how I would make up for lost time, but now I know the time was not lost at all. It is just passed. Thankfully, there is more of it. Not as much as I would have liked. But more.

FIFTY

Montgomery
1973

The week after Thanksgiving, Aunt Ros left, and Mama returned to her studio, but only in the mornings. She went out
for lunch in the afternoons. She advertised to teach a watercolor
class and got three people to sign up the first day. She unwrapped
dinner and placed it in porcelain serving dishes, setting the table as
if the food had been cooked by her own hands. The three of us sat
down to dinner each evening as we had not done in a while.

At night after my parents went to their room, I sat lonely in my
bed. Winter had picked up, and it grew cold outside. Lou's wife
had recently given birth and I dared not call him. But as the year
neared its end, I couldn't help myself. I drove downtown around
midday and circled the block where his office was located. On the
third round, Pamela, his secretary, spied me as she walked down
the steps. I leaned over and rolled down the passenger-side window.

"How you doing, Civil?" She waved.

"Just fine. How about you?"

"Busy."

"Lou around?"

"Yeah, he's up there."

"Alright. I'll stop in and say hello."

"You do that. Take care, now!"

When Lou opened up, I said, "When y'all start locking the door?"

"Somebody vandalized my car. Might have been random, but you can never be too careful." He locked the door behind me. I followed him up the stairs.

"When?"

"Right after the trial ended. I didn't tell you because we were all too busy looking for Erica."

The papers were gone. The desks were clear. Four file boxes lined the wall. He opened a bag of Lay's chips and held it out to me.

"No, thanks. Don't tell me you still eating junk for lunch."

He stuffed his mouth. "Pamela went to go get me something. But these chips keep me going."

"You got a new case? I thought you'd be home with the baby."

"Oh, I'm kissing that baby every chance I get. Besides, my wife is pushing me to take this one. Two women applied to be Alabama State Troopers. Both were denied."

"And you've accepted the case?"

"You think I should?"

"I think you're crazy."

He laughed. I missed hearing his strange laugh. Right before my eyes Lou had acquired a way of knowing in the world, what the folks used to call an old spirit. At Thanksgiving, Aunt Ros had said, *That Lou Feldman been here before.* She was right. It was hard not to feel the light of his presence. I wanted nothing more than to roll up my sleeves, take the notepad from him, and begin making some notes about this state trooper case. It wasn't so much that I wanted to be a lawyer, more that I was energized by Lou's moral compass.

"What about you, Civil?" He spoke softly. I didn't like his tone. Everyone had such high expectations of me. I wished they would leave me alone.

"I don't know what I want." I could go work for my daddy, but I was unsure.

"You'll figure it out."

"Can I see that pad?"

"No, you may not."

"Are the women who want to be state troopers Black?"

"None of your business."

"You ain't right, Louis Feldman."

I had not sat down. My purse hung from my shoulder. I knew it was time to leave, but I also knew that walking out that door would have a finality that it had not had before. I didn't want to do it. If he had tried to push me out the door, I would have resisted. But he didn't. He just sat there munching on his chips.

"I'll be seeing you," I said at last.

"You take care, now, Civil Townsend."

I walked out of his office wondering if I was the only one of us who'd been feeling this emptiness since the trial ended. I was so lost in my thoughts that I did not see Mrs. Seager pass right in front of me. By the time I recognized her big red hair, she was halfway down the block. I lingered at my car, the wind biting my neck, as I watched her and listened to the click of heels on the pavement. I wanted to call out to her, to see if she would turn around and speak or if she still held a grudge against me. I needed to talk to her, to tell her I understood how a person could get so caught up in doing good that they forgot that the people they served had lives of their own.

FIFTY-ONE

I went to work for Daddy at the start of 1974. It was the week after the holiday and Daddy's waiting room was full. And as I walked through the room, a room filled with people I'd known since childhood, I began to think of the connectedness of us all. Mother Cooper from church. Mr. Jones from the post office. Dena from the hardware store. They were all waiting to see my father, a man they trusted with their pain. It had not been what I wanted, but it made sense. He needed help in the office, and it gave me something to do. Besides, I enjoyed the work. I got along fine with his new junior doctor, and, contrary to my expectation that the patients would treat me differently because I was his daughter, it seemed as if they trusted me more. Sometimes, while I was taking someone's blood pressure, they would just start talking to me. I would listen, write it down on the chart, and discuss with Daddy afterward. He would nod and say, "He told you that?" Even he was impressed with how readily they opened up to me. There was joy in this caretaking. A simplicity coupled with a stretching of my mental powers.

"Daddy, I put Mr. Jones in Room 1."

"He's going to need blood drawn today," Daddy said. "Can you set up the cart?"

Daddy had an uncanny ability to remember details about his patients. He got there early and read the charts of everyone coming in that day. Patients wanted to know that you remembered them. They responded better when you asked, "Are you still experiencing those chest pains?" I had worked for him only a few weeks, but I had already learned a lot.

Later that afternoon, I helped straighten the office and chatted with Glenda while she turned off the lights. My mama had dropped off a new painting earlier that day and we had nowhere to put it. It was not one of her best, but it was a soft blue color and not too complicated. Perfect for an office.

"It's too blue. People be staring into it thinking they about to fall into the sky."

"Glenda, now I'm going to tell Mama you said that."

"Tell her. I don't care."

We giggled.

"I'll go lock up." I unhooked the key from above her desk just as Ty walked through the front door.

"Hey."

"Child, what brings you here? You sick?" Glenda peered at him through the window over her desk.

"Do I look sick?"

"He always look sick," I said.

"No, that's just my natural handsome face. Civil, have you talked to the Williamses lately?"

"No. Why do you ask?"

"I stopped by to tell you Mace is moving tomorrow."

I knew Mrs. Williams and the girls had already moved down to Rockford, but I had not heard anything about Mace. I had been trying to give the family their space, but I missed the girls already and was sad I hadn't had another chance to say good-bye.

"You been in touch with him?" I asked, trying not to feel hurt that the two of them were talking behind my back.

Ty nodded. "He finally found a job down there, so he quit the pickle factory. He turns in the keys tomorrow. I figured you'd want to say good-bye."

"I don't know why you think that."

He tilted his head, and I hated him for knowing me so well. I touched the edge of Mama's picture frame, which was propped against the wall. Glenda was right: I did feel like I was going to fall through the sky.

TY DROVE ME to Dixie Court the next morning and waited for me in the car.

"I won't be long," I told him as he rubbed his hands together to keep warm.

The door stood wide open. Inside, the apartment was empty and I could not stand it. I tried not to remember all the furniture we'd so carefully picked out, the place where Mrs. Williams had sat in her chair, the sofa with the throw blanket. The living room smelled faintly of sweat and the air was chilly. They had already turned off the heat.

Mace came out of the back, a small box in his hands. He looked at me, then carefully set it down on the floor. He walked up to me and wrapped his arms around my waist. I shivered, but I was not sure if it was because I was cold or nervous. He put his lips to my ear. "Ty brought you here?"

I nodded.

"That boy loved you all your life. You know that, don't you?"

I could not answer. He brushed his fingers up and down my

cheek. "Civil Townsend. You done gave me my family back. Did I give you something?"

How could he ask me that? I had been the one to bring about all this damage. For years, I would wish I had answered that question, had given him a confirmation of how much our time together had meant to me. But my emotions were tied up in knots that day. I just had no way of knowing it was the last time I would ever see him, but I think I sensed it.

"Why y'all leaving?" was all I could say.

After Mace's death, Alicia made the drive to hear the preacher give a eulogy at the gravesite, because they could not afford a church service. They had just enough to put him in the ground in a pine coffin, though Alicia told me he was buried on a beautiful fall day, and the preacher joked about how Mace loved to read and drove everybody crazy quoting newspaper articles. Erica and India sat next to each other, two straight-backed young women, one of them quiet, the other in the settled look of caregiver as she straightened her younger sister's hat. Mrs. Williams got winded as she climbed the hill to reach her seat, but she strode on the arm of a new husband, a retired widower who offered her a simple life in a small but neat house, the house the sisters would inhabit after the couple passed on, the house I visited years later, where I ate sponge cake with strawberries.

But on that final day in Dixie Court, the day his hand brushed my cheek, Mace was very much alive. "You free, Civil. Use your freedom to change as many lives as you can."

I had been entrusted with the key return, and I watched from the window as Mace's truck spewed exhaust. It grunted and then moved off slowly, the truck bed filled with household items. I waited to see if he would turn around. He never did.

I bolted the door behind me and walked down the stairs. Across the street, Ty waited inside his car. I could not see his face through the glare of the window. As I walked toward the rental office, I thought of that first day, when Mace and I had followed the rental manager to see the apartment. The Williamses had not stayed even a year, but with the demand so high for these Dixie Court apartments, they probably had another family ready to move in.

All around me, families made their homes, gratefully accepting this government help, their kids running through the play yard, shouting.

FIFTY-TWO

Montgomery
2016

The morning after my visit with the sisters, I put on the nicest outfit I brought with me and check out of the hotel. When I look in the rearview mirror, something doesn't seem right. I stop at a drugstore. Inside, beneath the harsh lights, I scan the shelves in the cosmetics aisle, unsure of what to choose. Will blush make me look cheap? Do my eyelashes need mascara? Are there chin hairs to pluck? Finally, I settle on a plum-colored lipstick. At the register, I grab a pair of silver earrings on display.

I call Ty from the car. I know that, once again, I have not ended things right with him. This business between him and me is unsettled and refuses to disappear. He answers right away.

"I'm on my way to Birmingham." My voice shakes a little.

"How long will it take you to get here?" he responds, as if it is the most natural thing in the world for me to call him at eight o'clock in the morning and say I am on my way. He seems to immediately understand that I am coming to see him.

I look up into the sky, and I can see young Ty: watering his mama's plants, driving me to Tuskegee, holding out a gift for me, teasing me. Ty—the kid with the long legs and ashy knees who stole my pencils in third grade, the kid who grew up into a gorgeous young man full of heart. Though I could not see it at the time, he had cared about those girls as much as I had.

And there I am, too. Twenty-three years old. Eager to prove my daddy wrong. Anxious about my mother's illness. Longing for love. Hoping to make a mark on the world. Young Civil, smiling shakily and unsurely but with all the awareness of a future that remains to be lived.

Now I know why I came on this trip. I needed to make my peace. Ain't nothing like peace of mind, Anne. Nothing.

As I drive north along this stretch of I-65, the sky over Alabama is cloudless and clear, as luminous as one of Mama's paintings. I feel protected, the whole of me, in all my broken pieces under that blue. It is a wonder to behold this land, this God-filled country. My daddy hovers in it, whispering to me that it will all be fine, his thick fingers on my brow. He has always been with me, and he is with me now.

On the horizon behind me is my community—Montgomery, Centennial Hill, my friends and loved ones—all here in this place that birthed me. This is your lineage, my dear daughter, your history. More powerful than blood. The story of those sisters and what happened in Montgomery in 1973 is a history you share with people you have never even met. They are your family as much as I am your family.

You are now the age that I was then, and I hope you will benefit from the wisdom of our mistakes. This knowledge, this triumph, can, if we let it, make all of us stronger.

If we let it.

AUTHOR'S NOTE

This novel is a work of fiction loosely inspired by the real-life case of *Relf v. Weinberger*. In June 1973, Minnie Lee and Mary Alice Relf, sisters aged twelve and fourteen, were sterilized without their consent in Montgomery, Alabama, by a federally funded agency. Outraged by this terrible violation, their social worker, Jessie Bly, reported it to a local attorney. Eventually, the case went to federal court in Washington, DC. The lead lawyer for the plaintiffs was Joseph Levin Jr. of the Southern Poverty Law Center. This case is considered a pivotal moment in the history of reproductive injustice, as it brought to light the thousands of poor women of color across the country who had been sterilized under federally funded programs.

What was particularly shocking to me, when I first learned of this case, was that it had happened just one year after the Associated Press had revealed the story of how the federal government left hundreds of Black men in rural Alabama untreated for syphilis in a study at Tuskegee that lasted four decades. Both cases prompted national discussions about medical ethics and racism, but how could these events have been allowed to happen in plain sight? I began to ask questions about culpability and silence that contemporaneous documents in the archive could not answer.

My inability to shake these questions resulted in three years of research and, ultimately, this novel. Eager to seek more answers, I traveled to Montgomery to speak with Joseph Levin and Jessie Bly, who were so generous with their time. I am always led by my curiosity, and I found myself wondering about the nurses who worked at the Montgomery Family Planning Clinic. How did they make sense of what happened on their watch? I was never able to find firsthand accounts of nurses who worked there, so I decided to imagine what it must have been like to work there at the time. Thus, I created the characters of Civil Townsend and the other nurses at the clinic.

It is important to note that *Take My Hand* is not a retelling of these events; instead, I have used the historical record as inspiration to imagine the emotional impact of this moment and others like it. The Montgomery Family Planning Clinic is a real place, but all people associated with it are imagined.

The moral and ethical questions I explore in *Take My Hand* remain salient today. In 2013, the Center for Investigative Reporting revealed that between 2006 and 2010, nearly 150 women in California state prisons had been sterilized without official approval. A year later, the Associated Press reported on multiple instances of prosecutors in Nashville, Tennessee, submitting permanent birth control as part of plea deals. In 2020, a whistleblower alleged that immigrant women detained by Immigration and Customs Enforcement (ICE) were being forcibly sterilized without their consent in US detainment facilities. In fact, compulsory sterilization of "unfit" inmates of public institutions is still federally protected by a 1927 US Supreme Court ruling, *Buck v. Bell*.

Reproductive justice, a phrase coined by Black feminists at a conference in 1994, remains elusive for African American women who struggle to access affordable health care due to social and economic inequalities. The abortion rate for Black women is nearly five times that for white women. African American women are three to four times more likely to die in childbirth than white women. Furthermore, health conditions that disproportionately affect Black women, such as uterine fibroids, receive very little government research funding. My hope is that this novel will provoke discussions about culpability in a society that still deems poor, Black, and disabled as categories unfit for motherhood. In a world inundated by information about these tragedies and more, I still passionately believe in the power of the novel (and its readers!) to raise the alarm, influence hearts, and impact lives.

ACKNOWLEDGMENTS

First, I want to thank you—my readers—for waiting so patiently for my books. I have heard from so many of you since my first novel, *Wench*, was published. Your words of encouragement have kept me going more times than you know. Your passion for history inspires me. Your thirst for another book club pick motivates me. I am so indebted to you, and I want you to know that you are always foremost in my mind and heart.

Not everyone is lucky enough to work with the same literary agent for fifteen years. I have been one of those fortunate authors who has found not only an agent, but a lifelong friend, sister, and creative muse in Stephanie Cabot of Susanna Lea Associates.

This book would not have been written without the kind generosity of Joseph Levin Jr. and Jessie Bly. The two of you shared with me all that you remembered, and I am grateful. I have taken liberties with the story, of course, as any good novelist would do, but your answers to my questions opened my eyes to the seriousness of this moment. You are two of the most special people I have ever met.

Thank you to the Southern Poverty Law Center for taking on this case, and so many others over the years that were instrumental in righting the injustices of our nation.

With utmost respect, I want to acknowledge the entire Relf family, especially Minnie Lee and Mary Alice Relf. May God continue to bless you.

I asked endless legal questions of lawyer friends, though I deserve the blame for any mistakes: Kathy Smith, Milton Brown, Rashida LaLande, Tasha Hutchins, Tracy Colden, Jessica Waters, David Valdez. Thanks to Nyoka Beede for the constant support over the years. Thanks to Sharony Green for sharing some of the history of Alabama and always teaching my books. Thanks to Regina Freer for being my intellectual sounding board. Terry McMillan's generous spirit is as wide and deep as an ocean. The first readers of my earliest rough drafts were Sarah Braunstein and Sarah Trembath. It does not seem coincidental to me that two brilliant Sarahs were instrumental in helping me figure out what story I was trying to tell. This finished book probably looks very different from the manuscripts you saw, and that is largely because you helped me figure out my vision. I have turned repeatedly to these writers for inspiration and sustenance over the past few years: Tina McElroy Ansa, Naomi Jackson, Lauren Francis-Sharma, Marita Golden, Lalita Tademy.

Special shout-out to the late Randall Kenan, who, years ago, urged me to write about Black class dynamics in the South. I miss you, Randall.

Dorothy E. Roberts, author of *Killing the Black Body*, has been a pivotal voice in the history of scholarship on reproductive justice. I am indebted to her work and that of so many others.

I am truly grateful for my friends, allies, colleagues, and students in the Department of Literature at American University, who are the most collegial and supportive community I have ever experienced in academia. Thank you to the Rowland Writers Retreat— and Pleasant Rowland—for providing a cozy bed, a spectacular view, and unlimited tea while I worked on this manuscript.

I do not exaggerate when I say Berkley Books is a dream team: Ivan Held, Claire Zion, Craig Burke, Jessica Plummer, Lauren Bernstein, Sareer Khader, Jeanne-Marie Hudson, Jin Yu, Dache' Rogers, and Elisha Katz. And, of course, I have to give a very special thanks to my editor, Amanda Bergeron, for believing in me and this book and this story. I love working with you, Amanda.

This book will be my first published in the UK, and for that I am so grateful to Francesca Main, my editor, and the entire team at Phoenix and Orion. I have been so inspired by the team's hard work and enthusiasm. Thank you!

Finally, I want to thank my family: my mom, Barbara, who was my first fan and supporter; my beloved late daddy, who encouraged my life of the mind; my brother, Harry, who always has my back; my brother-in-law, Roscoe, who is steady and loyal. And to my sweet sister, Jeanna: You are my forever angel, my forever love, my forever best friend, and I miss you. A whole host of Jones family members—nieces, nephews, aunts, uncles, cousins—keep me grounded in rich Memphis soil. My Aparicio family in Los Angeles feeds my soul. Words cannot express my gratitude to my husband and partner for life, David, who patiently listens to every frustration, every story idea, every roadblock, every triumph. You are my rock. Samanta, Monica, Ana, and Paty: Thank you for watching over my girls. Speaking of my girls, Elena and Emilia, I hope you will carry this story in your hearts. This is your lineage, too.